THE WITCH OF
VERSAILLES

JESSICA MASON

MURMURATION BOOKS

For Tam, who reminds me to believe in magic.

Author's Note

THE WITCH OF VERSAILLES is a historical novel of witchcraft, midwifery, herbalism, and sexual exploration. It contains adult themes as well as content that may be triggering, including: sexual assault, pregnancy, childbirth, child loss, abortion, infidelity, poisoning, drug use, and explicit sexual content. For more information, please visit my website at www.jessicamasonautho r.com.

The herbal remedies and properties in this book are in no way intended as medical advice. No herbal or plant-based medical treatment should be undertaken without proper research and safety measures.

This is a work of historical fiction based on real people, places, and events. While I have endeavoured to be as accurate as possible to history, this remains a work of fiction. Sources and further reading on the practices, people, and events that inspired this tale are listed in the acknowledgement section.

CHAPTER 1

THE FOOL

LE MAT.

Paris, 1660

FINDING A WITCH IN Paris was harder than anticipated, even for a lost soul like me. I had been searching for magic all my life. Now, here in the King's city, I could barely find a street I knew, much less a sorceress. Despite my failure, I was determined. I had always been good at finding secrets.

I'd heard for years that Paris was a playground for the devil, where his minions dealt in potions and souls. Everyone had some story of a city was full of secret covens and dark rituals. But those were rumors. I wanted something real.

Discovering where to actually find an enchantress was more than a matter of asking the right questions; you had to ask in the right places and be careful who you believed. A mistaken word meant death, and not a swift one. I scrambled past the ancient turrets of the *Hôtel de Ville*, shivering at the thought.

There would be torture first, then fire. And yet, I risked it. *Claude the Curious*, my father had called me, and meant it as a warning. He was dead now, and I did not intend to follow quite yet. I had learned to temper my curiosity with care and disappear when the wrong eyes found me, and I hoped the skills I had would help me on my quest for some sort of magic. Or whatever I could find close to it. I was desperate, after all.

I avoided notice by soldiers and priests as I stumbled through the sweltering city, making my way east, parallel to the river. More than once, I caught the eyes of a beacon of holiness, like a pair of nuns walking dutifully among the poor, and I rushed away before they could see the need for sin on my face. I had been told years ago that my dark eyes and hair were evil's mark upon me. He had said I was meant for sin, and my curves were sent to incite it, as if I had no choice in the matter. Condemned, he'd said I was. Relegated to the gutter and to take what was on offer.

It was because of those warnings I hid myself in modest, dark clothing, even on a summer day like this. Maybe if my lot in life changed, I would not be so shy. I would wear the fashionable styles with wide sleeves and low necklines that exposed the shoulders and décolletage like ladies I saw in palace courtyards and fine boxes at the theater. So much could change for me.

I just needed a witch to do it.

The idea had come to me in a dream; my father, still gray from the grave, had told me it wasn't hoping that would fix my future: it was doing. He'd pulled out his cards, the ones we had used to play games and tell fortunes when I was small. They had come all the way from Marseilles, the magic deck with pictures of queens and beasts and staves and cups printed in yellow, red, and blue.

I couldn't make the cards out in the dream, but they had turned into leaves in his hands. They'd grown vines, then thorns. The hands bound by the plants had become Arnault's and they'd choked him. I'd woken in my dingy pallet on the floor before dawn, confident of what to do.

The dream could have been sent by the devil. My mother would have said so, but I would never have told her of it. It hadn't been the devil that had put magic on my mind; it had been two pretty girls. Granted, the way pretty girls had affected me all my life did seem to be the devil's work, so that wasn't entirely wrong. They had been talking backstage three nights ago, about love charms. One had a few strawberries gathered from the edge of a churchyard and swore that smearing the juice on their lips like rouge would bring them true love. It had worked for at least one of them: I'd caught Yvette with a stagehand rutting into her later that night. If their strawberries could bring love, something else could do the opposite.

That was if I could find anything growing. The streets of Paris barely supported weeds, and on dry, dusty days like today, it felt impossible to find a bit of real green in the crooked streets. Yes, there were men and women in clothes dyed the color of pine or jade, leaves of cabbage in the slop thrown out from kitchens. There were lemon peels and bits of hay all over. But real, growing green – the kind that I had loved in my years in the country? That was hard to find. That's why those churchyard strawberries had been so powerful, I reckon.

If I could find my witch, she would know where to find her ingredients and charms. The cards said I would. I'd pulled out the old deck from where I had kept them hidden. I'd drawn the Eight of Coins, the Star, and the High Priestess. A beacon would lead me to a magic garden. Or that's what I assumed, but now, feet aching in my soiled, thin shoes as I trudged past another church and then another shop full of silks and lace I could never afford, I was doubtful. The city was new to me still, and more than intimidating. I wasn't really lost, I just didn't yet know where I was going.

Paris was a great honeycomb of streets and neighborhoods, full of secret places and grand palaces alike. Centuries-old, twisted like a snail, and dirty as the river seeping through her center, she was not an easy place to conquer, as my aching legs had begun to learn. From the old castles and cathedrals in the Île de la Cité and the new palaces around the Tuileries to the poor districts like the Marais (so-called for its status as a marsh until recently) to the northeast, the capital of France was ancient and new all at once.

It was the greatest city in the world according to half the people who lived there, and the worst place imaginable according to the other. In the months since our company of actors had taken over the Théâtre de la Paix, ending our years of wandering in the country, I had learned a few of the streets and stories. I loved the buildings built of daub and timber mixed with the houses of white limestone quarried from the mines outside the city walls that had fed the beast of Paris with stone since the time of Rome. Maimed soldiers who had been on the wrong side of the Fronde walked the streets, looking to the city walls they had defended against the forces of the King, never far from the sight of their treachery.

What I had marveled at most were the palaces, like the one in whose shadow I found myself now: the Palais des Tuileries, one of so many residences for Louis, the fourteenth monarch to bear that hallowed name, and his court of nobles and heroes. Across from it was the great edifice of the Louvre. Nearby was the Palais-Royal. I'd found my way to them by accident, drawn like a moth to the light of our king, away from the darkness I sought.

The walls on which I leaned as carriages rolled by and merchants screamed for sales were empty. No flags flew above the high walls and no soul was visible in the gardens. The king was in the country preparing for his wedding, his court along with him, while Paris baked in the July sun. The refuse of hundreds of horses and thousands of people dried in the gutters and flies filled the air, buzzing.

I'd never find my witch here. I needed to turn my lost feet to a quieter, less grand part of town, if I could find it. I walked north, away from the river Seine, through more markets, past more shops, and I kept my eyes open and sharp. An apothecary might know about herbs and such, but every store I found was manned by a glowering man that I would sooner stab than trust with my questions. The same was true of the barbers who served as surgeons. They competed with the midwives and wise women I was looking for and didn't share knowledge or names.

I needed help, I finally admitted to myself. I would not ask any of the men in their long coats and broad hats, nor any of the young women in their silks and cinched bodices. Pleasing sights though they might be, they would not think the same of me in my threadbare skirt and jacket. A washer woman, perhaps? Or maybe one of the flower sellers? What would I even say?

At last, I found the sort of woman I needed. She was bent and frail, shoulders lost beneath rags. She stood where three roads met, with a basket at her feet of little bouquets tied with reeds, holding one up high like a torch.

"Fancy a posy, sweet girl?" The crone asked me as I approached, and I could see her eyes were milky with cataracts as she squinted toward where I stood in the sun. "Just a penny."

I pressed two into her palm and took the small bundle of flowers from her gnarled hand. They didn't smell sweet, these yellow flowers with clusters of small blossoms bunched together to make a larger head. The scent was more like the wet earth itself, or the field from whence they had come; somewhere outside these city walls, where cool streams flowed. Like magic.

"Would you know, Madame, of any place I might find a dealer in herbs or other flowers like these? Or perhaps a wise lady to tell my fortune?" I could tell my own fortune, meager though it was, but oracles tended to know more about what I needed.

"A fresh fool you must be, if you don't know," she cackled back, and shame rose in my gut.

"Pray tell me. I'm lost."

"If you seek your future, the Court of Miracles is where you go. Everyone knows that. But be careful with those coins in your pocket, and don't walk there alone at night." She raised a crooked finger and pointed down the street. "Go that way for a quarter mile, then left and follow the Rue du Temple."

I did not bid her any goodbye before I took off. I had my heading at last, and what was more, it was to a place I had thought was a myth: The Court of Miracles. The very name evoked magic in my ears. When I had set out on this quest hours before (and it had felt more feasible), I had considered looking for the famed hub of criminals, and now, I knew where to go.

I would surely find someone among the thieves and cutthroats who knew some magic or mystery. I found the Rue du Temple soon enough. My heart sped up as I walked down it, the houses more dilapidated with each step, their plastered walls crumbling and the beams and roofs sagging. Strange enough, the smell was better here. Maybe all the shit drained downhill to the west and into the river. I was almost in the Marais.

The streets were narrower here than in the core of the city, newer because the poorer a place was, the more often fire cleansed it. The theater my company now occupied was built on the site of the five theaters that had burned down before it. To my annoyance, it wasn't very far away from where I now found myself.

The sagging houses would be ash in the next great fire or wash away in the next storm, yet they were worn from all the life they had seen and endured. In shades of brown and gray and dirty white plaster, they all huddled together, like thieves themselves, leaning in to count their stolen coin.

I came, at last, to a square where several streets met and what had to be the fabled 'court.' Crowded and raucous, it was a rough plaza that looked as if it had been hollowed out of the buildings by some giant, clumsy hand. The smoke of open cooking fires and chimneys obscured the summer sun above, making this court a shadowed, secret place.

I did as was my habit and looked closely. I was good at that – watching and seeing things that escaped others. There was a lot one could learn from a quiet hiding place when people didn't know you were looking. When I looked, I saw a bustling Paris square like any other.

This supposed haven of degenerates was not much worse than the rest of Paris, if I was to be honest. The faces here were unfortunate and sickly, but they were people, sharing food and waiting in doorways and going about life, with nothing to indicate who among them knew any dark arts or secrets.

Vendors called out, friends met, quarrels were had. A woman with a red face slapped another, younger, and I flinched, my own cheek burning with old pain. I touched the flowers I had bought from the old woman where I had hidden them in my bodice to bring me luck as I began a circuit of the square, keeping my head low. I was a woman alone, still young at twenty-three, and I only wanted to be noticed by the type of person I needed.

"Butter and cream!" someone cried.

"I buy gold – don't care where it come from!" another bellowed.

"Need a new dress, dear?"

"Pretty face you've got, I know some would pay good coin to give it a kiss!"

"Fresh bread!"

"Fancy your fortune told?"

I turned at the words in elation, then caught my breath. The woman who had asked the question was as beautiful as a rose, so much so that she was out of place in such a dirty, decrepit part of town. She had red hair that was barely contained by her cap, and green eyes that reminded me of the hills of the country.

"You're a fortune teller?" I asked in awe. I had expected something closer to the old woman at the crossroads, not a young woman like me.

"I'm many things," the redhead shrugged. "But you look like you need guidance. Come along."

"I didn't say yes," I protested as the woman turned and walked into a dingy shop where the summer sun feared to penetrate. I wanted this flower to know I was smart enough to read my own fortune, that I knew a few mystic secrets too.

"You didn't need to."

I did follow her into the musty shop – a tailor, maybe, judging by the modest bolts of cloth and leather stacked haphazardly around. The air was thick with the scent of old wool and dust, making my fortune teller stand out all the more, like the first green shoot from the cold ground in spring. She sat at a small table by the window and I joined her. "Give me your hands."

"I'm sorry they're dirty," I muttered, obeying instantly. There was always grime under my nails and stains on my hands, marks of the hard work I had to do at home and in the theater. I resented the reminders whenever I saw them.

"I can see well enough," said the woman. Her hands were soft and gentle as she took mine, and I shivered as her fingertips traced over my palms. "Your hands aren't meant for whatever has made them so dirty. You want finer things."

"We all want finer things," I muttered, unimpressed by the guesswork, but still flustered by her attention. When she smirked, it reminded me of Thérèse, which should have brought me back to myself.

"True. But you dream of them like a flower bud dreams of the sun. You have a destiny before you. And oh –" She gave me a crooked, playful smile. "Quite a few lovers, each grander than the next."

I laughed at that – an ungracious, braying noise that made her raise an eyebrow. "I came here looking for someone to drive a suitor away. Can't you see that?"

The woman looked at me suspiciously. "Drive away?"

"There's love charms a-plenty in the world; I want the opposite. If I can find someone to sell me one."

"What's your name?" she demanded, and my stomach fell. Was she going to tell some authority?

"Why do you need to know?"

"Because you are asking something very dangerous, and if I point you down the right path, I become responsible for you. I want to know whose fate I'm changing," she said, and there was kindness and perhaps even pity in her tone as she looked back at my hand. "Or maybe it's already been changed."

"Claude de Vin." I found myself holding my breath as she considered me. "And yours?"

"Veronique Pelletier," she muttered, distracted. "Did you come here looking for someone to cast a spell for you or help with one of your own?"

"Either." The word slipped out before I could stop it, helpless and hopeful. Maybe she did have gifts, this Veronique, to see the desire within me that I dared not even confess to myself until that moment.

"Hm," was all she said in reply. "Is this suitor you wish to drive off yours? I see a powerful man in your future, but none now." That question made me blanch, and whatever guilty face I made caused Veronique to give a warm chuckle. "So you have a friend being courted?"

"She's being harassed! Nightly!" I snapped back, my ire rising at the thought of how Arnault slavered after Thérèse. "He's unworthy of her."

"Does she think so?"

"That's why she sent me," I lied. I think Veronique could tell, but she shrugged. "I have money, if that's what you need. I'll give you an *écu* if you help me."

I pulled the gold coin from my pocket and could practically hear her belly rumble at the sight. It would buy bread for three days. I knew that because I had gone without the same number of days to be able to offer it. With a sigh, she took the money from my hand.

"I'm only a student of these things," she admitted. "I know one charm. But it needs pennyroyal and rue and a walnut shell—"

"Where am I supposed to find those?" I thought of the barren roads I'd followed to get here. There was the new public garden on the other side of the Seine, but that would take all day to visit…

"And you'll need some of his hair," Veronique added, like a challenge. I straightened.

"That I can get. The rest…"

She gave me another pitying look.

"Think on if this is really something you want to do. Come here tomorrow, then follow the Rue Saint Lazare from the north corner. There's a house with plants growing in front and a red door. She's better at this than me. Maybe she can talk you out of it."

"I will decide my own future," I snapped back. That didn't dim her smile. "I'll see you tomorrow. I have places to be now."

Indeed, the July sun was beginning to sink, and I had a performance to prepare for that should have hastened my feet on the journey back to the streets I knew. Somehow, I found myself by the gates of the Louvre instead.

It was the heart of Paris, this great palace with walls of limestone and engraved arcades. The center of a vortex that had drawn me in since the first day I had entered the city. I did now as I had done then, and peered through the iron bars of the royal gates. They were crowned with gold, high at the top, dozens of fleurs-de-lys, the emblem of France, transformed into the points of spears to keep anyone out who was foolish enough to try to climb over. But even poor girls like me could see glimpses of what was inside.

The Court of the King. In these gardens and halls, nobles and princes walked and laughed, free of the sort of cares and burdens that weighed on me now like a hundred stones. They paraded among manicured gardens, arranged perfectly like green embroidery upon the earth. They feasted and danced and were free. They revelled in the light of our King, Louis, who had been given to France by God.

I watched as servants skittered through the gardens, and a few ladies in blue dresses walked among the trees with their lacy fans. I'd sought out a witch today for a trivial concern, hoping it would matter. I prayed that saving Thérèse would help me. Was there any magic in Paris or beyond that could grant me what I wished?

To walk in the gardens beyond my reach and feel the light of the sun?

CHAPTER 2

THE STAR

I ARRIVED DIRTY AND breathless at the theater, exhausted from navigating my way back through the stinking streets. While the lengthening shadows outside had broken the heat's grip, inside the theater was sweltering and the air was thick with odors of sweat and greasepaint. It felt like home, crowded and cacophonous, with a dozen actors all wound up in their preparations, completely oblivious to anyone else around them. The badly plastered walls were the same color as the half-dressed bodies in the smoky lamplight. The company yelled for costumes, help with make-up, or some food before we went on.

"Jesus, Claude, you look like you groomed a horse with your face," Édouard (one of our leading men) said as I stumbled past him. "And you're late."

"Well, you look like the horse's ass," I muttered under my breath, and Édouard scowled.

"Thérèse is waiting for you to help her dress," he snorted back. "And your mother's been looking for you too. Do these bitches realize you only play a maid?"

"Tell my mother I'm not here yet," I shot back before rushing to what passed for a dressing room in the furthest corner of the theater, separated from the rest of the chaos by a large sheet hung on a fraying rope, supplemented with laundry.

"There you are!" the woman I was looking for cried when I entered, her beautiful face lighting up when she turned to see me. Thérèse Du Parc, our resident ingénue, was barely dressed, her bodice half-laced and her blonde curls cascading freely over her bare shoulders. I grinned at the sight of her. "You're late! My hair is a disaster!"

"I'm sorry, I had an errand," I said as I rushed to start on Thérèse's coiffure.

"Well, get on with it! They say Monsieur Molière will be here tonight!"

"Why would he come to see our company? Doesn't he have his own?" A much better, richer company, where the man's comedies were the talk of the city. "He's come to see you, I'm sure. You'll dazzle him."

"If I can do something interesting with this mop," Thérèse grumbled. I had no doubt she would impress the esteemed guest. Thérèse made any room brighter by being there. Like a star that had fallen from heaven into this dirty corner of the world, sparkling with life and laughter.

From the first day I had met her, months ago, I had been enchanted. I'd spent most of my life around actors, my mother chief among them, but no one sparkled like her. No one else made me feel like I mattered when she looked at me. Thérèse made everyone feel like they were special and wondrous, but only I had succeeded in entering her good graces. As soon as she learned I'd do anything for her – from styling her hair to laundering her costumes and fetching her food – she'd welcomed me. My mother had done nothing but resent that I'd found someone else to serve. A distraction and a fancy, she called it.

"You'll be wonderful," I assured Thérèse as she began making up her face in the cloudy mirror. I twisted her hair into the latest fashion I had seen on the ladies going to and from the palaces; parted in the center with curls piled on the sides.

"Your mother was looking for you. As usual. Says there was no bread for supper," Thérèse said as she daubed her fingertip in a red paste and began to color her lips.

"She knows how to buy her own food," I grumbled with a few pins in my mouth, the metallic tang reminding me of my empty stomach.

"Does she?" Thérèse sniggered. "Since Étienne kicked her out of his bed, she's been more hopeless than usual. Today, she was flirting like mad with that old poet, Scarron. Trying to convince him she'd be a better nursemaid for that club foot of his than his young wife."

"And she'd have me do the nursing," I scoffed. Monsieur Scarron was a regular at the theater and a fixture of the class of men who fancied themselves intellectuals and artists. He walked with a cane, thanks to an injured foot, but he was smart and kind and had married a poor, overly-pious girl twenty-five years his junior to keep her from poverty. He was too good a man for my mother. "She has to know that's a dead end."

"That's my point. She's running out of men to seduce and she's getting desperate." Thérèse laughed as she said it, her blue eyes sparkling. "You should have heard her in her cups the other night, talking about how she missed her husband. Ow!"

Thérèse spun to look at me as I scrambled back, the pin I'd nearly driven into her skull falling from my hands. "What about her husband?" I demanded in terror.

"She said she'd never take him back," Thérèse reassured me, and my racing heart slowed. Even so, I feared that Thérèse might ask about why I had reacted in such a way. "I pity women like her. We know better. Don't we?" she said, grabbing my hand and squeezing it. The solidness of her grip stopped my panic from taking me completely.

"We only need each other," I agreed unsteadily.

"Help me get into this, won't you?" Thérèse asked with a smile and handed me her costume. I averted my eyes from the way her bodice pressed her breasts up into two perfect half globes above her neckline, trying not to blush as I helped her slip into her skirt and overdress. She would dazzle Molière and anyone else who came to see, looking so lovely in the frock of dark pink. I had but a moment to appreciate her before another actress burst through the sheet.

"There you are!" my mother cried, and I winced. "Christ, you look like a chimney sweep. Clean off your face, get those rags off, and go talk to Henri for me before you get into costume."

"You want me to talk to him half-dressed?" I asked, somehow not surprised. My mother, the great Alix Faviot, (or La Faviot, as she liked to be called) was not much taller than Thérèse, but she was older, louder, and darker in coloring, like me, and to me especially, she took up the whole room. I felt so small when she glared at me.

"He owes you seven écus and we need that money! Don't argue. He agreed he'd pay you for all the extra work you do around here. Go and demand it!"

"Why can't I do it like this?" I asked back, my stomach churning at the thought of crawling to the theater's owner in any state to beg for money for my mother to lose at a gaming table.

"She thinks because Henri can't talk to me without getting addled by my tits, he'll give in to you if you're half dressed," Thérèse hissed, then looked my mother up and down. "No doubt she needs money for the gambling tables. Again."

"Shut your mouth, you foolish whore," my mother snapped. But Thérèse was right – the only thing my mother loved more than the sound of applause was the thrill of winning and losing at whatever game of chance she could find a way into. And since she had come to Paris, her luck had turned for the worse. That was why I had to hide money from her: so we would not starve, but it was better than relying on a man to support us…

"I won't do that," I protested. "You know I don't like—"

"Are the cats fighting again?" I shrank further back as the makeshift curtain opened again and the person in the theater I detested the most entered.

Arnault was the lead actor and fancied himself a poet. He was tall and handsome, with a perfectly maintained little beard and sharp, flint-colored eyes. It was he who relentlessly courted Thérèse, demanding her time and attention at all hours. She complained about it to me alone – about how she hated the smell of his rotten breath when he whispered in her ear and how she did not know how much longer she could keep leading him on before he would take her as a lover by force or coercion.

Arnault leered over Thérèse before turning to my mother with a scoff. "What's it you want Claude to do for you now?"

"I want her to tell Henri she should be paid for acting as a maid, stagehand, *and* actress," my mother shot back. Someone who didn't know her would assume she was defending me.

"Oh! Here." Arnault smiled and pulled several coins from his purse. He offered them to me and I kept my hands at my side in defiance. Or it would have been defiance, if my mother had not grabbed the money with a relieved sigh. "You keep our beautiful Thérèse happy and should be compensated." Arnault leaned over and pressed a quick kiss on Thérèse's cheek. I saw her try not to shudder.

"Say 'thank you,' Claude," my mother whispered. "Don't let Arnault think I didn't teach you manners."

"Thank you, Monsieur," I said through gritted teeth as I braced myself for a plunge. Without any more hesitation, I forced myself to embrace Arnault, as a grateful friend might. He was so surprised, he did not even notice my hand in his hair. I caught several strands in my fingers before my mother pulled me back in shock.

"I did not mean for you to be so unseemly," my mother hissed. "Go get yourself washed and ready. I'm sorry for her boldness,

Arnault, she's never learned to control herself, despite how hard
I've tried. If you knew what I've had to endure…"

I shut out the rest of her words, carefully tucking the hairs into
my bodice. It made me feel unclean to have a piece of that man
so near, and so I washed my hands and face harder in the cloudy
water from the jug. I felt as if I disappeared when I changed into a
black overdress that sufficed as my costume. Nothing too showy,
like my small part. The idiot maid didn't need to draw attention
away from the great ladies on the stage.

My mother had encouraged me to join her on the stage after
fate had forced us onto the road, telling me it was what I was
meant for. I had taken it as a compliment years ago, but now I
understood that 'what I was meant for' was to support her and do
as I was told.

As I stumbled through my role, listening to the audience laugh
and clap, I wondered what my mother would think of the treasure
hidden against my skin and what I meant to do with it. She was
not a pious woman, my mother, but she was as suspicious as other
theater folk. She feared witches and spells and malign charms.
She'd slap me if she knew where I'd been today. She'd do worse
if she knew where I meant to go tomorrow.

T HIS TIME, I FOUND the Court of Miracles easily. My steps
were quicker too, as I fled the moldy straw of my bed and
the dreams of spiders and stars and monstrous crones that had
kept me from rest all night. Arnault's hair was still tucked in my

bodice and his money was in my pocket. My mother would be disappointed it was gone, but I'd make it up to her some way. I'm sure she'd see to that.

The little square at the heart of the slum was busy still, but there were Musketeers there today, glowering and threatening as they strode, three abreast, through the crowd, their blue and silver tunics standing out like jewels in the dusty mob. They weren't there to make arrests, just to make sure the King's power was known and ensure that no one would make trouble for the great wedding that fast approached. Ten years ago, men in squares like these had tried to rise against Louis; now, they would be kept in their place as he wed the Infanta of Spain.

I slipped away before they could see me. I was, if you went by the letter of it, either breaking the law or on my way to break it. Witches were not hunted in Paris the way they could be in the country, but it was still a crime against God and a violation of the law to seek enchantments and to bewitch others... But so was stealing the apple that had broken my fast this morning, and that didn't weigh on my soul.

The summer heat was heavy and humid today, and my skin was sticky and uncomfortable. The Rue Saint Lazare smelled the same as the rest of the city, with scents wholesome and rank warring for attention in my nose: fresh bread and fresh refuse, dust and flowers, piss and perfume. The wet stench of the Seine was far off here, in the northeast of the city, but there was still the odor of straw and fresh plaster as I passed an old house under repair, the smoke from a hundred chimneys mixing with the enticing vapors rising from pots of stew that were kept ever boiling in little alcoves and taverns. The houses were all varying colors of beige and cream and dirty white, with roofs of brown wood and slate. It was still early in the day, only the sounds of dogs and babes crying in the distance mixed with the tap of my steps on the stone.

Amidst the stench and dust of the city, the house on the Rue Saint Lazare stood out all the more. A house with a garden and a red door. 'Garden' was perhaps too kind a word for the collection of pots and planters affixed to the windows, but it was a small oasis of green in an otherwise barren street, with ivy growing up the side of the house as well. There was something inviting about seeing even a few flowers and leaves thriving at the end of a dry, hot summer. I knew a few of the varieties, I was almost sure, and I knelt on instinct to caress flowers that looked like purple stars...

"There you are."

I looked up at the voice that came from the now-open red door to see a woman. Her face was lined and darkened from decades in the sun – perhaps in her garden. I could tell immediately it was hers – she had the same character to her as the flowers and leaves, warm and welcoming, but out of season and out of place. She looked at least sixty and her hair was silver under her cap. Her eyes were a clear blue-gray, and while she was small and wiry, she looked strong and alert.

"I've been waiting for you," she said with a smile.

"Did Veronique say I was coming?" I asked, flattered and worried to be discussed. "Is she here?"

"No, alas. She wanted to wait, but one of our charges began her labors, so Veronique was sent for."

"She's a midwife? I thought she was a fortune teller," I muttered.

"Women like my apprentice and I must be many things to survive in this world," she shrugged.

"And are you also a—"

The woman stopped me with a gentle glare. "Come inside to speak of such things, Claude."

I followed the woman, who, of course, knew my name, into the front room of her house. It was simple and welcoming; low embers in the hearth and clean plaster on the walls. But it was also an echo of the garden outside, with plants of every type hanging from the rafters to dry and others in jars. This was her shop.

"You're an herbalist too," I sighed, breathing in the earthy, green scent of the woman's workplace.

"I am merely Madame Lapère, and I am a woman who helps other women in need," the elder said cannily. I felt at ease with her, as if I had known her for years.

"I am happy to make your acquaintance, Madame," I began, straightening and making myself as tall as I could, the urge to impress her coming from somewhere deep within. "I already paid Veronique – how much will I owe you for your services?"

"Did you bring the hair of the suitor you wish to discourage?" Lapère asked instead, and I nodded. "It will be an écu for the spell – if you let me look at your hands first."

"Why do you need to see my hands? Veronique already looked." Not that she had told me much that I trusted. Her talk of lovers and powerful men in my life had left me more annoyed than intrigued.

"Because I dreamed of you last night," Lapère said plainly, and it made the air in the room go still. "What did you dream of, Claude?"

"A spider in a web of stars," I replied, as if the words were being pulled out of me by some invisible string I could not resist. Even so, I shivered at the recollection of what had woken me. "And a woman with three faces."

Lapère smiled again; impressed or amused, I couldn't tell. "Come along out to the garden – our spell will make some smoke." She raised her hand before I could ask why we were going back out into the street. "Those posies are merely for ornament and cooking," Lapère said as she led me through the house and out the back. "The things I grow in the back are too precious and dangerous to have out by the road."

She opened the rear door. It was like a portal into a dream. The walled garden presented to my aghast eyes made the little conclave of pots in front of her door look like a scrap compared to the paradise of green that waited here. There were vines growing up the walls and stone planters full of rich soil and green herbs. Halved barrels and terracotta pots housed plant after plant, with flowers of magenta, indigo, sunshine yellow, and white. Some of the plants were taller than me, with great torches of yellow flowers reaching up towards the sun, and others grew in tight low clumps, clinging to the ground. It was so beautiful, I wanted to weep.

"This is wonderful," I sighed, taking in the riot of life hidden here in the city's slums. The air itself was fresh and cool, as if the occupants of the garden had made it pleasant just for us.

"I'm glad you like it," Lapère said warmly. "I've tended it for years. My friends and students all say I should move somewhere finer and do better business. But it is a rare and blessed thing to plant a garden and live to see it grow and thrive."

I turned to her to see peace and sadness in her face. She wore a faded dress that might have been black years ago, like a nun's habit. It brought back memories to see a color like that among such green. "This reminds me of places I used to know."

"Does it?" Lapère asked, taking a seat on a wooden bench next to a trestle table set off from the center of the oasis. I joined her on the bench. "You're new to Paris. You're used to greener conditions."

"I traveled the country with a theater troupe for a few years."

She looked me over and smiled again. "You were born among the flowers."

"Yes. In Provence," I answered without hesitation. Perhaps it was because no one had asked me in years, or perhaps I already trusted this strange woman who was able to see beyond what I could. "My first memory is the lavender fields. Miles of purple as far as I could see."

"A magical sight," she sighed. "Give me your hands."

I obeyed without hesitation. The older woman's fingers were bony but undeniably strong when she gripped me with hands of cool, papery skin that had seen many years of work. She pulled me close and peered at my palms, tracing the crooked line on my left hand with the dull tip of one finger.

"You were happy there, where you were born. Then, someone left you." It wasn't a question.

"My father. He died when I was eleven," I answered, pushing away the memories of blood and bile and decay.

"But you found some peace after that. Somewhere safe, under the protection of Our Lady." Again, not a question, but the specificity made me shiver.

"We had some money for me from a relation, so Mother left me at a convent to be educated while she went to Lyon and Poitiers to act." It had been peace, though it had been short-lived.

"You found a great deal there to love," Lapère went on thoughtfully, and I told myself not to blush. Who knew what she meant or saw.

"They had a garden there, like this one, for medicines and food. It was my favorite place in the world."

Lapère met my eyes in a challenge, amused and intrigued. "Do you remember anything you learned in that garden?"

I turned my eyes to the array of herbs and flowers around us and tried to focus on their details and individual features, calling back the memory of Sister Constance's instruction. I had been distracted in those days, carried away with the petty politics and shifting alliances among the girls I was educated alongside, as well as the intoxication of first love.

My eye fell on a halved barrel, overflowing with many stalks of the same plant. Her leaves were a mottled, dusty sort of green, her stalk spiny and threatening, with minuscule barbs that I remembered pricking my unsuspecting fingers like glass. She bore indigo flowers in the shape of five-pointed stars. "That's borage. It likes to spread."

"It's good for cough and fever. The flowers can bring courage," Lapère added. "An interesting choice for you. It can help melancholy too, they say."

"You think I need it?" I asked, trying to put on a defiant smile.

Lapère looked back down at my hand. "Yes. You don't like to think of it, but you feel trapped in a dark, rotten place, like a spider

in a rafter with no way out." I shivered as she traced another line
on my hand.

"I…"

"You were taken from that garden, from the place you loved,"
Lapère went on, and her eyes darkened. "To that dark place.
Stolen away. Hands laid upon you—"

"No!" I snatched my hands back, shuddering as a buzzing,
murky void opened up in the pit of my stomach, waves of terror
radiating from the blackness. I couldn't look. I wouldn't *think*
about what lurked in that pit. There were memories there, and if
I touched them, I would drown. "Please – please don't make me!"

I couldn't breathe, and all I could see for a second was that
darkness, pierced by one single flame as I…

"Claude, come back. It's over and done." I blinked. Lapère was
there again, her gnarled hand against my clammy cheek. "Take
some breaths. I'm sorry I brought that up. What happened to you
was terrible. But I needed to see it to know where you go next."

"I just need to drive off a man who won't leave my friend alone!
I don't want him to—" My breath shuddered as the black pit roiled
in my gut again… Then stopped. I looked down at my left hand,
covered by Lapère's. There was something pressed against my
palm. Lapère let go and I saw it was a borage flower, small and
starry. Blooming in this dusty place. Brave. "I can't let him do to
her what was done to me."

"Give me the hair and the money, Claude," Lapère said calmly.

I did as she asked, then watched her gather fresh leaves from
two plants, then fetch a walnut shell from a shelf at the back of
the garden. She placed the herbs and Arnault's hair in the shell

and set it on the table before me. Finally, she pulled flint and a knife out of her pocket and handed them to me.

"Think of what you want to protect your friend from; let that fear and ugliness be in your mind, but do not let it touch you," Lapère said as my hands tightened around the stone and steel. I tried not to shake as I imagined Arnault violating my poor, good Thérèse. "Now, strike a spark, and burn that harm away."

I struck the knife against the flint, and sparks flew, landing in the walnut shell and setting the hair and herbs aflame. They burned quick and bright for an instant before they were gone, reduced to ash as I imagined Arnault's lust would be. Something thrummed through me for an instant, hot and wild as the flame – something that could only be magic.

"Very good. If you can, sprinkle these ashes on his shoes," Lapère said as I sat there in awe. She wrapped the shell in a rag and handed it to me in exchange for the flint and knife.

"Will it work? Can you see in my hands if he'll go away?" I asked shakily. Lapère gave me an indulgent look.

"It's hard to be that specific, but I do think we should look at what's before you. You stand at a crossroads." I presented her my left hand again, eager now to know what she meant. "No. The left hand is the past, the right is the future." She took my other hand and another pulse of something skittered through me at the touch.

"You said I was trapped," I murmured as Lapère examined the lines of my palm. "I want to get out. I think Thérèse can help me, but I don't know for sure. Can I? Can I get out?"

"Yes, of course. But—" Lapère squinted, and as she did, the garden seemed to grow quieter, and cold. Perhaps a cloud had covered the sun. "There are always paths out, but you are afraid to take a road when you don't know where it leads. Where you are now – you can turn away in fear or take your power."

"I won't turn away," I said breathlessly. I thought of my straw bed on the floor and nights filled with terror, of years of rootless wandering and dusty streets and sweaty theaters. I thought of audiences who never noticed me and men who noticed me too much. I thought of my mother's orders and disappointment and her need for me and how she stood between me and the world. I thought of iron bars and palace walls and gardens I could never enter. I hated it all. "Tell me where I can go. Tell me *how*," I begged.

The air around us stilled and the shadows thickened, the wind whispered through the walls, and the flowers and plants turned all their attention to my hand as Lapère's milky blue eyes focused on something past my palm and the marks there. When she spoke, her voice was low and distant, as if echoing from far away.

"You will journey halls of gold and gardens of silver, to beds of silk and grassy green. In wisdom and pleasure's service, bathed and burned in the light of the sun. You must serve, to become a mistress of yourself. You must be an adept of secrets to change the course of many lives. The world awaits you, Claude de Vin." I shook at the words, and then Lapère's eyes darkened with a distant shadow.

"Power will be yours, but the toll is blood. Blood will be paid. It must be."

I snatched back my hands and scrambled away from the woman. "What devilry is this?" I demanded, the place where her fingers had touched my hand smarting and viciously cold. "I don't want blood! I just want…"

Lapère blinked at me, looking as shocked by her words as I was – as if she had not been the one speaking them. The fear in her eyes was the final straw. This woman was not only speaking of prices paid in blood, but she was a vessel for something powerful and dangerous. Something I could feel reaching for me out of the shadows.

I ran. Through the witch's parlor, past her unnatural garden, and into the streets of the Court of Miracles. I had done what I needed to do; I had banished Arnault and now, it was finished. I would go back to my life and to Thérèse and whatever meager dreams my mother would allow me to enjoy.

I would stay in my small, dark corner of the world and claw my way out on my own, no blood or magic needed.

CHAPTER 3

THE CHARIOT

I T TERRIFIED ME HOW quickly the spell worked. The first time
Arnault walked by Thérèse as if he hadn't even seen her,
shivers went down my spine and I spent the night dreaming of
costs paid in blood. The next night, Arnault did not even speak to
Thérèse at all. She was giddy about it as I helped her undress after
the performance five nights later and her joy made her radiant.
And that radiance helped me to relax and revel in her attention.

"Molière was here again tonight! Did you see?" Thérèse asked
me as I laced up the overdress of her regular street clothes. Even
out of her costume, she was lovely enough to rival the finest
of ladies, as far as I was concerned. I had started studying their
fine hairstyles and fashions, watching them in the streets as they
walked to the palace, and anywhere else I could find them.

"I didn't. I was too focused on the finest actress in Paris," I replied, putting on a smile.

"You're as terrible as Arnault," Thérèse giggled. "Though I do like you better."

"Me?" It made my head spin to be included in such a thought, just as it made me dizzy when Thérèse looked at me with mischievous, seductive eyes.

"Why, of course," she said. "Did you not know that Monsieur Racine invited me to supper with him? Oh, I forgot, your mother dragged you off last night."

I frowned at the reminder. My mother had demanded I leave the theater with her and not wait for Thérèse because she claimed she was suddenly afraid to walk home alone. There were too many thieves in the city ahead of the King's wedding, she said, and any ruffian might set upon a good lady like her. I had not argued.

I seldom *really* argued with my mother at all. I doubt she would have listened if I'd tried. She was a force to be reckoned with; charming and vibrant, so as to enthrall any crowd or man. She never failed to remind me how little I resembled her and how much I favored my father. Where she was bold, I was careful. Where she was a brazen flirt, I would rather hide than let a man think I wanted anything to do with him. And where I was willing to work for what I needed, she wanted support. I was the only one who gave it to her, but at twenty-three, it felt like a burden more than an honor. She was happy to have me, I knew that, but I wondered if she never encouraged me to marry or seek a match because she could not contemplate being alone.

"Perhaps tonight she'll be occupied," I muttered as Thérèse and I made our way out from behind the sheets to the stage, where actors and audience were still milling about. The theater was where people came to revel and enjoy themselves, even on hot, summer nights. Men of all stations discussed great ideas in the audience, while the few women with them gave one another bored looks.

One such bored woman was indeed my mother, draped over the arm of a man I did not know, but who looked rich enough for her tastes. He was in deep conversation with two men I did recognize – Messieurs Molière and Scarron, who both smiled as Thérèse approached. Scarron was a kindly older man with a limp and a cane, and we all knew him for his generosity. And there was not an actor in Paris who did not know Molière – with his caramel hair and blue eyes as sharp as his wit. The man my mother was with, who had long brown hair and a face the shape of an egg, looked suspicious of the famous poet. I was too.

"A beautiful performance, Mademoiselle Du Parc," my mother's companion said, casting my mother aside with utter rudeness to take Thérèse's hand and kiss it. I scowled at that, then schooled my face when I saw my mother had caught my disgust.

"Indeed, we were transported to the halls of kings," Scarron said, before turning to a rather plain woman who was hidden behind him. "Don't you think so, Françoise?"

"I think none of us know much of the halls of kings to make a comparison," the woman – who had to be Scarron's wife – said. She was barely older than me and married to a man over sixty. But that was what a woman with no family had to do to survive. "Except, perhaps, our esteemed Monsieur Molière, who has played for Louis and his family many times."

"Not enough," Molière replied with a wink.

"And only with comedies – never with anything of deep substance," the man who had jilted my mother said. "You, Mademoiselle Du Parc, deserve to be in dramas, not these farces."

"And when, pray tell, Monsieur Racine, will you be gifting Paris with such an elevated work?" Françoise Scarron asked wryly, and her husband smiled in pride. I decided I did not dislike this woman.

"Soon enough," Racine replied. "With the right actress as a muse," he added with a smile to Thérèse that turned my stomach. I didn't like the way she smiled back either, and seemingly, neither did Molière, for he began to step between the two.

"Well, we shall all know Louis's glory in a few days' time," Scarron offered before the men could argue further. "Our balcony at my theater overlooks the route of the procession. You will all have to join us."

"We would be delighted," my mother said before I could refuse. She gave me a look that told me I had no choice but to do as commanded.

"As would I," Racine said. "I am composing an ode for the occasion I hope to present at court."

"If you're ever welcomed there," Molière sniped. Thérèse laughed and I followed suit, though quieter, so I could still hear the silvery sound.

My mother was in an ill mood as we traveled home. The August heat had barely loosened its grasp on the city, but the half-moon above lit our way, along with the golden lights from open doors and a few lamps. Even with the sky clear above, it felt like a storm was brewing and that danger lurked in all the shadows. I was taller than my mother, but I felt small and helpless near the roiling anger that it was my duty to diffuse.

"You can do better than that Racine fellow," I tried, and received a scoff in return.

"I pray that he or Molière has mercy on us when the theater closes and takes me into their company," she replied with a growl.

"Why would our theater close?" I asked in horror. We didn't always fill the house, but Arnault and Henri had not said anything about the money running dry. Then again, I had not heard a word from him in a week. And he had been bewitched...

"How can you be so blind, you idiot girl!" my mother cried. "Your precious Thérèse is ready to fly off with whatever poet gives her the best price, and without her, no one will attend. Not even I can compete, not without the support I need."

"No! Thérèse would have told me!" I tried to think back on all we had spoken of in the last week, but everything had been inane talk of fashion and new plays and other actresses.

"Why? Because you're important? You idiot. Don't even think about trying to follow her wherever she goes. She won't take you. You don't matter to her, Claude."

"You don't know that!"

"You're nothing more than a maid she doesn't have to pay. Your fortunes are tied to mine, not hers. She is not your blood – I am. I'm the one who really needs you." In another woman, those words would have come out as sad or desperate. But from my mother, they came out calm and unquestionable. "Maybe if you'd tried to make something of yourself, I'd be begging you for help. But I failed somewhere along the way. At least we aren't alone."

I said nothing else as we continued home, nor as we prepared for bed. My mother was plotting silently, considering what her options would be in Paris or elsewhere if the theater closed or turned us out. I watched as she settled into a bed meant for two that she slept in alone, and prayed her mind had not turned to others. She wouldn't call on him. She had said she was done with *him*. She had to be.

Maybe what she thought of Thérèse and the future was wrong, but the doubt and anxiety gnawed at me all night as I tossed and turned on my pallet on the floor. The endless cycle of thought tortured me: I had no control over my life and the one ray of light I'd found in Thérèse would be snuffed out. When I finally slept, I dreamt I was a spider caught under a glass or a fox trapped in a snare. Panicked and doomed. And worse: powerless to escape.

*T*HE WORLD AWAITS YOU, *Claude de Vin.*

That world seemed even more distant in the days leading up to the wedding of the King. We were busy at the theater, entertaining the throngs that had come to the city, and I had no chance to speak to Thérèse. Or rather, she had not given me one. She had much to say about everyone in the theaters of Paris and deftly compared the works of Molière to what she had read from Racine. But she laughed whenever I asked if she fancied them, and I longed sadly for the days when only Arnault used to pursue her.

His attentions had not disappeared, they had turned, and of course, it was my mother who had turned them, using every wile she could conjure to get his attention in the hopes he would make her the lead when Thérèse left, even though she was a decade and a half the other woman's senior. She never even considered pushing for me to take other parts, which I partly resented. I was not a great actress, but I knew all the lines and could pull faces and deceive a crowd if I needed to.

What I truly wanted was Thérèse to take me with her wherever she went. She laughed when I mentioned her taking any poet as a lover. She said she didn't need their flattery when she had me. I cherished those words; tucked them close to my heart like a magic charm, even as the world around me grew more crowded and chaotic. I considered turning to my father's old cards for insight more than once, or slinking back to Madame Lapère to learn my fortune, but in truth, I was afraid they would tell me how I was doomed. She had said the world awaited me, but what did I need with the world if I could keep Thérèse? She could be the one to free me from my mother's service, once and for all. Somehow. Some way. Without a price to be paid in blood…

The day of the King's wedding came, and we found ourselves at the door of Scarron's old theater early in the day, and even then, the crowds had begun to gather on the street below to catch a glimpse of the King and his new Spanish bride. We heard the bells of the churches tolling throughout Paris, celebrating the union of our beloved King in matrimony with his cousin. I thought it odd that his wife's father was the Dowager Queen's brother, and more so that the new Queen's mother was sister to Louis's long-dead father; but the ways of royalty and marriages such as these were a mystery to folk like me. All I knew was that it was a happy day for our King and our country, one we needed after so many years of discontent and war.

This theater was far finer than ours. It was a *real* theater, where nobles and the rich came for entertainment and to mingle. There were gold ornaments – or at least gold paint – and fresh plaster on the walls. There were even cushions on some of the seats, and it looked like it would take at least an hour to burn down, unlike the mere seconds it would take flame to destroy ours. Even this was nothing compared to the grander houses and royal theaters, or so my mother told me before abandoning me to the swelling crowd.

What we had thought was an exclusive invitation had been extended to every person of theatrical mind in the city, and half the actors and playwrights in Paris were there to watch from the balcony it seemed.

I spotted Madeleine and Armande Béjart, sisters who happily shared the spotlight, and sometimes lovers, it was said, including Molière. They reminded me more of my mother and I in disposition than any sisters I had ever met, and it was their glares towards the entrance of the theater that let me know Thérèse had arrived. I rushed to her through the milling crowd of performers, cutting in front of Racine himself to take her hand and lead her to the balcony.

"We must secure the best spot," I stammered as Thérèse laughed in confusion at being so abducted. Already, the crowd below the balcony was growing restless in anticipation of the royal procession.

"Always taking care of me," Thérèse grinned. "My sweet Claude." She pressed a quick kiss to my cheek and I wanted to sing.

"You look lovely," I said breathlessly. "Dressed for the occasion." She was in a new frock of pale violet, which looked very comely with the ribbons in her golden hair.

"So do you," Thérèse replied, and I blushed deeply. I had on my best bodice and skirt, I'd combed out my dark hair, and the kerchief tucked at the top of my chemise was new. Well, new to me. I'd made it from scraps of an old costume, and Arnault had not noticed. He wasn't even here to see, I realized with a smile.

"No Arnault," I commented, and Thérèse sighed happily.

"His father died in the Fronde, so he has no loyalty to Louis."

I felt a pang of something. It wasn't pity, because why would I pity a man whose father had risen with the discontent nobles against the King? No, it was something more akin to satisfaction. I had known not to trust the man. It was good, then, that he was not there to share in the King's celebration.

All conversation stopped as a cry went up from far down the street and more bells rang, announcing the happy union of our sovereign.

"May God bless and keep our King and Queen and show them his mercy and wisdom." The sincere prayer came from behind me from Françoise Scarron. She was as plain and conservatively dressed as I had seen her before, but there was a blush to her cheeks now, and a brightness in her eyes that I only saw in those of true faith.

"Amen," I said. I hoped she would not ask when I had last been to Mass or what my thoughts were on the condition of anyone's soul. I hated such conversations. "How long do you think it will be before the procession arrives here?"

"Soon," was all Françoise said, and I turned my attention to the street.

Sure enough, in a few minutes, the first trumpeters appeared in the distance, with a regiment of soldiers behind them, halberds polished so that the summer sun glinted off them like they were mirrors. There were Musketeers after that, in their plumed hats and blue tunics. And then came the carriages, pulled by teams of beautiful horses with bejeweled bridles.

"What kind of wealth is it to dress a horse in more finery than any of us could ever afford," I muttered aloud, but no one could hear me over the cheers of the crowd and echoes of the trumpets.

In the months since I had come to Paris, I had lingered so often by the gates of the palaces or in the public gardens and squares hoping to see someone of consequence. I had watched nobles in silks and satins and jewels come and go, their faces bright with health and laughter, and I had wondered who they were. Of course, there were the names we all knew, but now I watched the parade before me, hoping to see a face I had observed before. If I had even shared but a breath of air with anyone so elevated, it would make me closer to the spectacle below.

A beautiful older woman with jewels on her brow and a man the same age in cardinal's robes rumbled down the street in an open carriage, and the crowd called out and cheered as they waved. That had to be the Dowager Queen Anne, and the chief minister, Cardinal Mazarin. This was the woman who had held

France together through the Fronde on behalf of a son who had been made king at five. Next to her was the man whom Richelieu himself had picked out as his successor, who ruled the country and had amassed wealth that some said outstripped even the King's. Following them were others, and my eye was drawn to a handsome man in a coat lined with lace and gold – surely, he had to be the King's brother, Philippe, Duc d'Orléans.

And here I was, curious Claude from Provence, the most forgotten actress in Paris, little more than a servant, looking at them, sharing the light of the same sun. It made me so fiercely proud of how far I had come. I could stand next to someone like Thérèse and see such wonders...

My thoughts stopped as the cheers from below tripled in volume as a chariot, grander than anything I had seen in my life, came into view around the bend. It was drawn by six white horses, built to look as if it was made from golden leaves, the spokes of the wheels like the rays of the sun, and the occupants flanked by sphinxes lacquered in vibrant paint. The people began to throw flowers, filling the air with petals that fell like snow as Louis himself came into view.

I had known Louis's name since I was a child. Since I had been old enough to understand that I was ruled by a king, Louis had been that king. He had been as distant to me then as Saint Joan, Apollo, or any other legend. When a sect of his nobles – the frondeurs – had gone to war to take his power, I had heard the terrible tale of how he had been forced to flee the very city where I now found myself. Years later, he had made his triumphant return, taking on his rule and showing that he was strong. He was the heart of our nation, its spirit in flesh – or so the priests would say when we were bid to pray for his health and success and glory. It is one thing to think of a king all your life, to know he is there, as constant as the stars that sleep unseen in the day.

It was another thing entirely to *see* him. I had never felt any sort of thrill looking at a man, but this – this was no mere man. He was divinity on earth, gracing us all with his light.

"He's even more handsome than I've heard," Thérèse gasped from beside me, seizing my hand. She was entirely correct. Louis was clad in blue and gold, his long, dark hair cascading over his shoulders, a crown upon his head that glittered with diamonds. His smile was radiant, his brow noble. Even his hands as he waved were graceful and perfect.

I barely noticed the pale Habsburg Queen beside him, with her big eyes and pointed chin. Her gown was splendid too, but it swallowed her in its grandeur. Louis, however, shone like Helios in the chariot, blinding and beautiful. I found myself cheering, calling out blessings to him and the Queen, along with everyone around me. My heart jumped when Louis looked up to our crowded balcony and gave a wave. He had seen us! The King had seen *me* and suddenly, the world did seem to await. A world of gold and light and glory, at which he was the center.

We all cheered until the carriage was far out of sight, and when I finally looked away, Françoise Scarron was flushed and smiling as broadly as Thérèse and me. "The Queen must be the happiest of women," Françoise sighed.

"Indeed, I hear Louis is the most skilled of lovers," Thérèse grinned, and Françoise looked scandalized.

"It is unseemly to speak so of our monarch," Madame Scarron muttered and rushed away.

"Well, that settles it – the girl is still a virgin. That old man married her to protect her, not deflower her, and that's why she's never borne him a child." Thérèse sighed. "Lucky girl. The Queen is luckier though, she's right."

"I wonder what she feels like right now – our new Queen," I murmured as I stared down the street that was littered with flowers. It was still sunny, but now that the procession had moved past us, it felt like the light had dimmed. "I wonder what all of them feel like to be at court with him…"

"I'll know soon enough, when I'm performing with his favorite troupe," Thérèse giggled, and my heart stopped. She couldn't mean what I thought. I had to be mistaken.

"What?"

"Molière has the Duc d'Orléans as his patron," she said lightly. "You know that."

"But he is not our patron," I argued, desperate. "Arnault says we may impress the prince of Conti at a performance soon, if he can convince him to come."

"Arnault has been making claims about securing that traitorous *frondeur* for months," Thérèse scoffed. "I said I wouldn't take him to my bed until he had a real patron, and I think that's why he finally gave up on me."

"No, he didn't—" I stopped myself. "That's not what we were talking about. What do you mean about Molière?"

"He's offered me a place in his company, sharing some roles with Armande Béjart," Thérèse said easily, as if my world wasn't growing smaller and darker with each word. "I think the poor girl is pregnant by him. Idiot."

"I know someone who might help with that," I said in panic, thinking of the herbs in Madame Lapère's house. She was a midwife who dealt in magic, and that meant she helped women who needed to be rid of children. Or I hoped, until Thérèse looked at me in pure shock.

"Claude de Vin, don't even think of such a thing!" Thérèse hissed. "That's a mortal sin that would damn your soul, and I *want* little Armande out of the way! It's a great opportunity for me!"

"What about me?"

Thérèse looked at me – and it was like she was doing it for the first time. She surveyed me from head to toe, unimpressed by what she saw before her. "What about you? You have a place with your mother."

"But I want to be with you," I said from my heart, and her laughter in reply was like a stab through it.

"You're not really my maid, Claude," Thérèse said. "If you want to change your circumstances, you'll need to do it for yourself."

I wanted to ask her how I was expected to do such a thing when no one in the world would see me, let alone help me. I wasn't like her or my mother, flirtatious and fearless, but I was smart and skilled and true to her. Or I would be, if she'd have me…

"Thérèse, if you go, our company won't survive. My mother and I will be out on the street!"

"You'll have to find a way to survive," she replied. "Now, I must go see if I can find Monsieur Molière."

I stood there unmoving as she left me, darting off into the milling crowd of actors without another look. Other people pushed past me or around me, but no one looked at me to see why

I was frozen still. Not until my mother walked up and sighed at me.

"Whatever's upset you, forget it for now. I'd like you to go speak to Scarron. Maybe he'll have us or put in a good word with someone. His wife was talking to you - say you're friends." Another command to grovel and scrape on my mother's behalf.

I walked away without replying. My feet carried me down from the balcony and out of the gaudy theater and to the street, where more strangers who did not care to see me rushed around me like a stream around a stone.

I stared down the street where the King's procession had gone, wishing I could follow and see him again. In his light, I had not been myself; not this pathetic creature of no consequence to anyone, barely more useful than a dog and just as powerless. When he had looked up at me, I had been part of his orbit for a second, and that moment of perception had elevated me beyond my lot.

On the ground before me lay the flowers that had been thrown to celebrate the King, a whole garden's worth of blooms scattered and trampled. They had been offered in sacrifice for the moment of glory as he passed, then squashed by the wheels of his chariot and the feet of his guards. But they had still been close to him.

I picked up the most intact bloom I could find, a lily, and hid it in my pocket next to the dried flowers I still kept there from the woman at the crossroads and the borage blossom.

I clutched all three in the dark watches of the night when I finally came home to be berated by my mother while she bemoaned our hopeless fate. I refused to be hopeless. I prayed to those blooms for protection tomorrow, when I would seek out witches again – and the power they promised, despite the price.

CHAPTER 4
THE HIEROPHANT

It was easy to find Lapère's house once again. Her red door and little garden stood out like a beacon in the plain, poor streets around the Court of Miracles. The setting sun made the stone walls burn orange and gold, and there was a sweetness to the evening air that only nights in the waning of summer could hold. It felt like magic already. Somehow, I was not surprised at all when the door opened before I could knock.

"There you are, just in time," Lapère said with a broad smile. Her teeth were crooked and discolored, and the skin around her eyes was creased with wrinkles. But she was not ugly. Not at all. There was an aura about her of beauty and warmth that made me smile back.

"I hope I did not offend you by leaving so suddenly before," I said contritely. "I have reconsidered. I want—"

My words failed me. I knew in my heart what I wanted – to share in that secret power that radiated from her. The wisdom and sight. But how could I ask that? I was a poor actress, fresh out of the country, who dreamed of greater things, but what right had I to seek them?

"You want to know more about your future?" Lapère asked, gently suspicious. I thought of the flower I still kept in my bodice that had been close to the king. My magic charm. I shook my head.

"I want to *change* my future. I want to decide what it can be," I replied.

Lapère nodded as if I had passed a test. "So you shall. Come inside." She glanced over my head, speaking to someone behind me. "And you too, girl."

I spun to see another woman close to my own age grinning at us. In the instant I met her eyes I felt something that was beginning to be familiar. I had felt it with Veronique and Lapère, even if I had not truly noted it. I knew this woman would change my life and felt as if I already knew her. Strange indeed.

She was short and stocky, with straight brows and a long nose that somehow suited her soft chin. Her clothes were no finer than mine, though her bodice and overskirt were a deep blue while mine were mismatched browns. Her demure cap rested atop her flaxen hair, and I suddenly felt judged for not having bothered to cover my head today, or even for not doing any more with my dark tresses than keeping them from my face.

"Who is this, Madame?" the other asked, looking me over, eyes pausing at my belly. "A client?"

"A new friend," Lapère answered, gesturing for us to enter. "She wants to learn, like you. Mademoiselle de Vin, this is Mademoiselle Deshayes. She is also a student of mine."

"Catherine, to friends. I'm sure if Madame Lapère has invited you into her confidence, you must be an interesting person," Deshayes said with a bow. In the same way warmth radiated from Lapère, something sparkling and entertaining surrounded Catherine. "What's your trade? Palms or potions?" She thought I was one of them already. That was something.

"Neither as of yet. But I read the tarot on occasion," I muttered. "What about you?"

"I'm learning to read hands. I have a few clients so far, but not enough to afford to live on my own. If I ever want to get out of my mother's house and away from my brothers, I may have to get married." Catherine sighed dramatically. "Or maybe I'll have a relation die and come into money. How do you pay your way in the world? You don't look married."

"I act," I said awkwardly, wondering if that was an insult. Reminded of money, I pulled my coins out and offered them to Lapère. "I forgot to pay you for the other day. For the materials."

"Put that away. She won't take it if you're even close to being a friend," Catherine clucked. "Though she should."

"Not everything needs a price, Catherine," Lapère said, shaking her head as she moved to the pot heating above her fire. "Claude will pay me back some other way, I'm sure. Stew's almost ready. Did you bring the bread? The others will be here soon."

"Others?" I echoed in shock. A single student arriving as I came to beg instruction was one thing, but more than that was another entirely. "I can come back another day. I don't mean to interrupt."

"Tonight is the full moon. Every month, I open my house to students and friends to gather and meet. It is an auspicious thing that you chose today to join us," Lapère said calmly, and I felt something tremble inside me. "It's not mere chance you're here. This is the beginning. For you and for us. Now, we'll wait for the others in the garden."

I rushed out the back door into the oasis of green, my mind reeling as I followed the witch. A few braziers were burning to give light to the garden as night fell, and candles were set on the table too, along with places for five people. "How did you know I was coming?"

"The good Lord has blessed Madame Lapère with great gifts," Deshayes answered, coming up behind me and placing a comforting hand on my shoulder.

"I know not what hand your good Lord played in it. I don't presume to speak for him," Lapère demurred. "And to answer you, Claude – the world is always speaking, you just need to be quiet enough to listen. Something Catherine here is still learning."

"I don't have the patience to listen to the world when it tells me things I don't want to hear," Catherine shrugged. "But she's right. If you knew to come today, you were listening too. Be it to dreams or the wind."

I had known. Something had told me, after watching the wedding procession, to wait until today to come. Had some spirit been speaking to me? Was it the same as the dreams I had that guided me?

"I want to learn to do it better, and…" I sat heavily on the garden bench, breathing deep. The moist scent of earth and green

herbs filled my lungs and calmed my heart. I had come looking
for magic – no use being nervous when I'd found it. Especially if
I was meant to find it in this secret, beautiful escape. "Whatever
I can do to have a place like this one day, that's what I want to
learn," I mused aloud.

"That's not terribly ambitious of you," Catherine replied. "I'm
going to have a much finer place. Madame Lapère has told me.
She says my house and my garden will be the talk of Paris!"

"Marie is here," was all the reply Lapère made as the door
opened into the garden.

"Another new apprentice? Thank heaven. I was getting sick
of your face alone, Catherine," Marie (I assumed) declared as she
burst in like a summer storm. The lanky, blonde woman with
a long face kissed Lapère twice on each cheek before plopping
herself down on the bench beside me, the beautiful round breasts
barely contained by her bodice bouncing as she did. She extended her hand to me. "Marie Vigoreaux," she said with a smile.

"Claude de Vin," I replied.

"I hope you have more sense than this one," she said with a
glance at Deshayes before she turned to Lapère. "I need more
hops and thistle to keep my milk in. This child is sucking me
dry."

"I'll get some for you when you leave," Lapère said kindly.
"Madame Vigoreaux here is a wet nurse, in case you were wondering."

That meant Marie was married and had already borne her
own child. It was possible that she was nursing someone else's
child because her own had died. A sad, but common, occurrence.
I looked her over and tried to guess. To listen to that quiet

voice within me or on the wind... There. I felt it. Sadness and emptiness lurked right there behind her straight spine and brash exterior.

"I'm so sorry," I said as Marie's tragedy touched my own spirit. "About your child."

Marie stared before nodding in acceptance of my pity, then looked to Lapère. "I see she's already outpacing dear Catherine here."

"At least I know that nettles will help your milk," Catherine chuckled.

"Only if you boil them," another voice interjected from behind us and I spun, my breath catching in my throat.

It was Veronique. Of course. She too was a student, and part of me had hoped coming here might mean seeing her again. "It's you," I grinned.

"It's me," Veronique smiled back, beautiful as a wildflower. "I knew I'd see you again."

"You and Mademoiselle de Vin have met? Interesting," Catherine said, looking bored. She turned to Marie. "You could also try alfalfa too. For the milk."

"I'm not a fucking horse," Marie snapped the way a familiar friend would.

"I don't know: with that long face of yours, you could be mistaken for one," Catherine hissed back while Veronique brought food over to the table and set it in front of us – bread, butter, and a whole hard sausage – as Lapère fetched bowls for the stew.

"At least I don't have a weasel's eyes and disposition," Marie sniped back, and Catherine laughed. She turned to Veronique. "Did you bring it?"

"Yes, of course," Veronique said before handing a small tub to Marie. To my shock, Marie unlaced her bodice right there at the table and pulled out her breasts, huge and heavy with milk, from her chemise. My mouth went dry and slack.

"Thank God," the exposed woman said before taking a smear of what looked like lard onto her fingers and rubbing it on her red, raw nipples with a groan of relief that made me blush. Veronique sat across from me, and I could feel her watching me as I avoided looking at the exposed woman beside her.

"Jesus, woman," Catherine chuckled. "You could have waited!"

"You'd understand when you have a welp on you half the day, gnawing at you to live," Marie replied. "The little thing already has teeth!"

"Did you infuse the balm with selfheal?" Lapère asked. I looked up to where the elder woman had appeared with the pot of stew. She filled our bowls and it smelled amazing, with chunks of vegetables and even some meat. It felt like it had been forever since I'd had something so fine.

"I only had yarrow," Veronique said. Finally, Marie righted her chemise and bodice, thankfully, and the four of us all stilled, waiting for something from our host before we ate.

Encouraged by our attention, Lapère took the lard from Marie and pulled a few sprigs from a low-growing plant right by her feet, with purple-green leaves and flowers. "Leave this in it and bless it under the full moon tonight, calling on Our Lady for healing. It will work even better."

"Thank you, Madame," Marie said with the deepest of respect. I looked again at the assortment of women around me, all of similar class and age to me, who wished to learn things that were forbidden. Secret arts that might cost our immortal souls.

"No charms or potions in that – just blessings," Lapère said as if I had spoken my fear aloud. "Everyone eat up."

And so we did, as night thickened above us, and it tasted more incredible than it smelled. My stomach was grateful, and the food made me feel strong and brave. "So you all come here to … learn about herbs and fortune telling?" I asked innocently between bites.

"Well, it's certainly not for the company," Catherine muttered, and Marie kicked her under the table.

"Doesn't it feel nice to already be the best-behaved student?" Veronique asked me with a smile. "And yes, we're all here to learn something that will take us farther in life."

"Don't be so mysterious, Pelletier," Catherine snorted. "Call it what it is. We're here to learn magic. All of it – the herbs and the palmistry and what charms and spells to sell when the reading is done. There's good money to be made in sorcery. If you're careful."

"She means if you don't call it that. What we do is fortune telling and helping those fortunes along. The rich always want to know if they're staying rich or getting richer," Marie added. "And they're willing to pay to make sure they get what they want."

"We also help people," Lapère admonished warmly, casting a look to Veronique and then back at me. "We serve Our Lady in what we do, or we should try to. In turn, we seek our own rewards."

"I would not think that the Blessed Virgin had such an interest in sorcery," I muttered, thinking of how I had heard Lapère mention *Our Lady* before. The women around the table smiled conspiratorially.

"The Blessed Virgin is only one of her names," Veronique explained. "You'll learn the others if you stay."

"If I stay and learn to be – what? A healer or a fortune teller??" I demanded, pulse rising. Fear seized me of what these women could truly be. I had come looking for witches, but what if they were all I had been warned of – lecherous, shameless whores of the devil who ate the flesh of babes and danced with demons under the moon? I gulped. "Or a witch?"

"Finally, someone says it out loud," Catherine muttered. "Here I had been calling myself a divineress."

More suspicion filled me as I looked at the faces of strangers around me. They were witches, all of them. Brazen affronts to God. Was this their coven? Were they seeking to ensnare my soul? Would I be made into some sacrifice for them? Or forced to dance naked in thrall to demons and sign away my soul in the devil's book? The thought, surprisingly, did not fill me with disgust or terror. Such a thing would be quite an adventure.

Or were they simply women, the kind I had known all my life, from villages to convents to the slums of Paris? Women who knew the hidden wisdom of plants and palms, and all those other secrets I had always felt whispering to me from the shadows. Women that I had always wanted to join. That would be a great adventure too.

"We have many names too," was Lapère's calm answer at last. "'Witch' is a word men use when they encounter a woman with power they don't wish her to have. Which is any."

My fear disappeared in an instant, and I knew the voices crying out about blasphemy and evil in my mind had not been my own, but echoes of men I had heard all my life – and always mistrusted.

"You have power, Claude. We all do," Catherine said, more serious than I had yet heard her. "Or, to be more honest, you *could* have power. Those with the least power – who are not seen or respected – can wield more than you know. They can be the spider at the center of a web, or the one who lurks and waits to strike. Both have power when they take it."

"And you will show me how to take it?" I asked the women around me, barely above a whisper.

"And how to share it," Veronique said, somber and low. "What do you want to be? What do you wish Our Lady to give?"

Those green eyes held mine, and I felt as if I was already under a spell, summoned and seduced by the circle I had stumbled into.

"You can always walk away, Claude," Lapère said gently. "To move through a crossroad like this is your choice."

The world awaits you, Claude de Vin.

The air around us stilled. This was a test: the first step into the mysteries that would change my life if I let them. I thought of that prophecy and I thought of the walls of the Palais-Royal and the meager applause of the theater. I thought of that dark, aching pit of memory inside me and of hidden gardens and misplaced love, and I wanted to find a way past it. To change it. I felt the power they spoke of in the air around me, like currents of water I could reach out and touch. I looked at Veronique's eyes and wanted to see them every day.

"I want to stay," I said, chin high. "I think I should do well as a sorceress."

"Oh, I like that," Marie said, grinning. "May Our Lady of Sorceresses bless you."

I wanted to say 'amen' to that, but the word felt wrong for whoever it was they praised. "I wish to know Her too," I said instead.

"Then seek Her when it feels right and when you are in need," Lapère said, offering me her hand. She looked up to the sky, and I saw that the white disk of the moon was visible above us.

I took Lapère's hand and Catherine took my other. She reached across the table and Marie grasped her fingers, and Veronique completed the circle. Around the trestle table where our stew still steamed, surrounded by the plants and under the glowing moon, the circle of women that had welcomed me felt more like magic than anything before in my life.

"Seek Her in the wild places, serve Her by helping women who need you and all the downtrod," Veronique continued as a shiver went up my spine. It was an invocation.

"Seek Her at the crossroads, find Her in the night," Catherine went on. "Let Her guide you through the dark places."

"And let those who serve Her guide you and help you as well, like keys to all doors." Marie took up the charge. "Seek strength in your sisters."

"She is the growing green and the black of decay," Lapère intoned, and I felt power – there was no other word for it – surge through my hands from the other women and up from the earth, filling my body and blood. "She is the change of the moon and the fury of the storm. She is the destruction of the fires and the waters of life. She is in us. She is life and death. She is in you."

"Amen," Catherine whispered, and the others echoed.

"Amen," I said as well, feeling no guilt now in acknowledging so blasphemous a prayer. Was it blasphemy to honor this lady of the witches who wore the mask of the virgin mother? "In Our Lady's name," I heard myself whisper as if the words were born from within me.

"She has great plans for you, Claude," Lapère whispered, catching my eyes, and I knew I was the only one who had heard her. Was it even she who had spoken? "The path is long and dangerous through the woods. Trust it."

I held my breath and nodded. I would trust this guide and this circle, and if I was smart and strong, I could keep that darkness at bay and walk in the sun. That had to be possible.

"Can we finish eating now?" Catherine demanded, and the world tilted back into normalcy.

I blinked, wondering if the moon had moved because everything was bright. Veronique smiled at me over the table and passed me a hunk of bread. I settled in to listen and learn from the conversation around me and learn who it was I had joined on this journey.

Lapère was a widow and Veronique shared her house. Both worked as midwives and healers throughout the Court of Miracles and the poorer districts of Paris. There was no difference for them in using herbs to ease a broken heart or to soothe a headache. Their clients came to them to have their palms read or their wounds tended to, though they trusted Lapère more due to her age.

When Catherine commented how much better they could do if they served women in another part of town, Veronique argued that what they did would not be allowed in such places. They were needed here, especially by the women who had nowhere else to turn. The poor, the fallen women, and the whores deserved care too, Veronique said, radiating kindness that I could barely comprehend.

Marie Vigoreaux was not so idealistic. She was married, but saw her husband infrequently, as she was required to live in the household in which she served. She was just beginning to learn how to tell fortunes and hoped as fervently as Catherine that this would be her route to prosperity and fame. Her husband, a tailor, had no idea she came here, nor did Catherine's large family, who she complained of but hoped to support.

Catherine already told fortunes wherever she could and seemed to know everyone in Paris, either personally or by reputation. She spoke of other practitioners of magic, women and a few men as well, with varying degrees of approval, though she seemed willing to work with all of them, if it meant finding new clients. She caught my attention most, however, when she spoke of the court of the King and his nobles. She knew their names and lineages, and I wanted to draw all that knowledge from her like water into a sponge.

We spoke of the King's wedding, and she wanted all the details of what Louis had looked like in the procession, for they had missed seeing him. I was proud to tell the tale and relate how I had once seen the Duc d'Orléans at the theater too. Catherine read the palm of a minor baroness the other day, and the woman had promised to return for a love charm to use on the duke himself, but Catherine had refused, given how impossible it was to enchant royalty.

I answered questions when asked and found myself joking as well. I liked making the other women laugh, for usually my wit was too caustic for my mother's or Thérèse's tastes. This was different. I wasn't a servant or a burden here: I was an equal. Here, we could laugh together, and I even felt comfortable enough to let my eyes linger on soft pink lips as they continued to smile at me.

The women spoke of herbs, debating on what other ingredients were good for salves. Some were names I knew, others were new. Then the talk turned to palms; no formal lesson, but there was discussion of planets and the moon too, and Catherine swore she knew an astrologer who said the marriage of the King had been conducted under an inauspicious sky. Soon enough we were talking of the new queen, Marie-Thérèse.

"I've heard she doesn't want any of the Mazarinettes in her household after her husband tried to marry one of them. Is that true?" Catherine demanded, turning to Marie.

"The Mazarinettes? You mean the nieces of Cardinal Mazarin?" I echoed. I'd heard the term since I came to Paris, but did not know their story well.

"Yes. Five Italian sisters, all beauties and the darlings of the *précieuses*," Marie sighed in reply. That term I did know – the *précieuses* were the wittiest women in Paris. They presided over salons, reading poetry and honing their rhetoric and minds. Françoise Scarron might have been one, if she were not so serious and devout. I would have killed to be part of such rarified company.

"I can't remember which one was supposedly closest to marrying Louis," Catherine explained to me. "But she's been sent away to marry some Italian prince. Dreadful. Marie, have you heard anything about what the Queen will do to the rest of them?"

"Why the hell would I know about the queen?" Marie sighed back.

"You work for a Marquis!" Catherine cried, slamming her small hands onto the wooden table so that our empty wine cups clattered.

"I nurse his child who he never sees, and no one speaks to me," Marie snapped back. "Even if they did, there is nothing to tell. They'll never go to court, much to his wife's despair."

"Which means you're in a good position to help her!" Catherine argued, and Marie rolled her eyes.

"Some of us have to keep our jobs and our heads," Marie said.

"And you'll be stuck as a glorified cow for a Marquis forever if you don't take a risk!" Catherine countered. This was clearly an old argument.

"I won't shit where I eat, I've told you before," Marie said and held up a hand to stop more arguments from Catherine.

"You two will be the death of me," Lapère sighed.

"They'll be the death of each other too," Veronique said to me conspiratorially.

"Why don't you clear the table while you argue," Lapère suggested, and the two friends obeyed. "Veronique, can you show Claude the garden?"

"I would like that," I said, though it made my heart race a bit to have moments alone with the taller woman. Catherine and Marie continued squawking at one another as I rose and followed Veronique among the barrels and beds of plants.

"Here, for the headache you'll have if you listen to them more," she said, plucking a sprig of rue with delicate little clusters of leaves, and handing it to me. "Rub it on your temples, but only at night. If you do it in the sun, it leaves a nasty little rash."

"I didn't know that," I smiled, tucking the sprig between my bodice and chemise and not looking away from her for too long, then remembering myself.

"You'll know all their secrets soon," Veronique replied.

"Some of them are so alike; how do you tell them apart?" I asked as I knelt next to a bed, touching delicate, scalloped leaves about as long as my finger, green on one side and silvery on the bottom. It looked almost identical to another plant a few feet away, but the second plant was a paler green all over.

"You learn the subtle differences in the smell, the leaves, the feel of them," Veronique said, kneeling beside me so our legs nearly touched and I could feel her warmth. She lovingly touched a branch of the first plant. "Not just physically how they feel, but the way their souls speak to you when you ask them."

"Plants have souls?" I asked back with a laugh, but as I touched the leaf once again, my hand inches from Veronique's, I felt something. A whispering pulse at the back of my brain. "Oh."

"Tell me what this one says to you," Veronique whispered, her face close to mine. I had to close my eyes to not stare at her, and in doing so, I made myself concentrate on the little bit of life between my fingers.

"I see the moon and women, they're aching and... dreaming," I whispered, words tumbling from my lips before I could think what they meant. When I opened my eyes again, Veronique was smiling.

"Mugwort. Best gathered under moonlight. Bringer of dreams. She eases monthly troubles and other women's woes," Veronique recited, her own eyes drifting over my face. She was prettier than Thérèse in the silver moonlight.

It dawned on me that this was the first time I'd thought of her since I arrived. It made me feel guilty; like she still held a string tied to my heart and would tug it at any moment. And take me away from Veronique.

"Is there a charm to soothe a broken heart? Or to make you stop caring for someone who no longer cares for you?" I asked, trying to sound casual and failing.

"Wash in an infusion of pansy and yarrow," Veronique said. "Yarrow is that one over there, with the bundles of white flowers. Another witches' herb."

I looked at the plant she had indicated and leaned closer to her to pick a sprig. It was the same flower the crone at the crossroads had sold me when I was led here. That fact would have left me in wonder were I not almost pressed against Veronique...

"Already down in the dirt." I fell onto my ass when the sound of Catherine's voice and laughter sounded throughout the garden. "Sorry, didn't mean to alarm you."

"Of course not, Catherine," Veronique said with a soft scowl, offering her hand to help me up. It was so soft I nearly stumbled again, but I managed to recover myself. I forced my attention to something else and found myself looking at the farthest corner of the garden, one that was already deep in shadow as the sun sank in the west. There were vines with white flowers hanging like trumpets and stalks of tall purple flowers I vaguely recognized.

"What are those?" I asked.

"Oh, those," Catherine said with a wicked smile. "*Those* tend to do more harm when you don't know how to use them."

Veronique clucked at us. "You'll learn which of our friends here can help you or hurt you, depending on many things. Those can hurt much more."

I shivered as I looked at them, something once again whispering to me through the cool evening breeze. "Poisons, you mean?"

"They defend themselves," Veronique countered, meeting my eyes. "They have a right to live and grow, and if you cut them down and use them without regard for their power, they see to it you're repaid."

"I've never thought of it that way," I whispered and thought of being taken from that convent garden in my youth. I wish I had been able to defend myself then.

"Everything has a right to defend itself," Catherine said, a twinge of sadness in her voice.

"Though I'd warrant there is a difference between kicking away a rabid dog and sending it to the grave with a sprig of wolfsbane," Veronique warned.

Catherine rolled her eyes. Another old debate. "Depends on the dog, I'd say," she countered. "Don't you agree, Claude?"

I looked back at the deepening shadows in the corner of the garden – to where death waited among the leaves – and thought of the dark that awaited me at home. That sin that had been planted years ago and refused to be uprooted.

"Maybe it depends on if it's already taken a bite," I murmured. I wondered when I would learn the names of those plants hidden in the corner. And if I would ever need to use them. "When will I learn what they are, or what any of this is?"

"We will start tonight," Lapère declared from the door of her house, Marie by her shoulder. "Our bellies are full. Now, to fill your minds."

"Some of which are emptier than others," Catherine teased, looking at Marie.

"If you're so wise, Catherine Deshayes, tell me the difference between tansy ragwort and Saint John's wort. And the use of both."

"St. John's wort grows midsummer, close to Saint John's day. Tansy grows later in the summer," Catherine replied without missing a beat. "They are both yellow, but the flowers of Saint John's wort have five petals and tansy has many. They both bring luck, but Saint John's wort can bring happiness and revive the melancholy in a tincture."

"And yellow tansy will make you awfully sick if you eat it," Marie added smugly.

"I was getting there," Catherine said. Lapère met my eyes.

"This is the most important lesson, Claude, and the first one. All magic can heal or hurt, depending on how you use it. Poison is in the dose, as they say. The same is true with magic. You must be careful either way."

She held my gaze, and other words came to my mind. *The cost is blood*, she had told me. From that dark corner of the garden, I felt other whispers. There were souls rooted deep in the earth calling out, and I feared I knew now the tools by which I might pay that cost.

I RETURNED HOME WELL past dark, making my way up the shuddering staircase to our door. My mother and I lodged on the top floor of the house, while another family took the bottom. The roof slanted so that in places it was hard to stand straight, but I liked how it made my little corner of the parlor almost like a cave where I could hide. There was no hiding now though.

"Where have you been!" my mother cried when I entered. Her face was red and there was a bottle in front of her. And the house was a disaster.

"I didn't know I was needed," I muttered back, avoiding her eyes. "There was no performance. I went out into the city."

"And left me here! I needed the money – that money you hide that you think I don't know about!" I hardened my expression. So that's why she had torn our humble rooms apart. "I have debts, Claude! And needs! So you better have been out there in the city finding some work to support us!"

"You have work!" I cried. "Good work that would keep us fed if you did not see fit to gamble it away," I said aloud at last. "Or did it go to drink or gallantry? Don't think I don't know the things you do when you go off alone and leave me to clean up after you. And now you want more from me?"

"I want you to support me like a good child should! Or I may be forced to do things you will scoff at if you don't," my mother cried, her face colder and more serious than I had seen in years, and all my courage disappeared.

"You wouldn't…"

"He's still in Lyon, where you disgraced me. Disgraced us both." The words made no sense. She could not mean she would send for him. She could not think that it was I who was to blame.

"You were the one who dragged me out into the street," I whispered, as the room began to spin around me. Hadn't she? The day was a blur, and I kept it that way in my mind. I refused to let it focus in my memory, because if it did, I would have to remember what had come before it. The deep, sucking void of horror that would consume me if I let my mind touch it.

"I don't know what you're talking about," my mother snapped. Suddenly, she was right in front of me. "You're the one that made a scene. Told all those wicked stories about a good man when it was *you* who ruined things," she went on. "I worked so hard to build a life for us, and you threw it away in an instant."

"I – I didn't!" I gasped, fear choking my breath, heart racing as I fought the darkness of my memories. I was back there again, unable to breathe. One candle burning in the dark… "It was him."

The slap stopped my thoughts and brought me back to the present as sharp, silvery pain cut through my panic. My mother glared down at me as I shrank before her.

"You will find more work and keep us secure, Claude," my mother commanded. "Unless you know some charm to restore my fortunes at the tables," she added with a scoff.

"I'll find a way," I breathed, inspiration sparking at her words. She had given me the way I could save us, if I learned fast enough. The spell on Arnault had worked quickly. I hoped the one I would soon beg Lapère to teach me to change her luck would work even better.

I T TOOK ME TWO days of instruction before I was ready to cast the spell. I followed Lapère like a shadow, through every spare moment, learning all she would tell me of herbs and roots and charms for luck. Veronique took over when she was called away, testing my knowledge and adding some of her own. I only told Lapère why I was in such deep need of a spell that would turn around a gambler's luck, and even then, I did not tell her everything. She did not need to know how dire the threat was, but I think she sensed the truth with some inner eye I had yet to hone.

That skill could wait. I just needed my mother to win back the funds that would keep us secure. After that, I might learn other arts or turn my thoughts to larger dreams of the wider world. I wanted to change my fate and rewrite the story of my life, but to do it, I needed to survive.

This is how I found myself at the edge of a cemetery, scraping dirt into a pouch that held vervain, basil, and most of the coins I had been able to save and keep hidden from my mother for the last month. Catherine had offered to come with me, to complete the charm in the waning light of the moon, but I had refused. I did not want a witness to my desperation.

What would my mother say if she knew I was here, with the stench of death from the charnel house in my nose and cold chills running up my spine? What would my father think? He had believed in magic and his cards, and I had asked their advice before undertaking this. Eight of Batons. Nine of Coins. Strength. Clear indications that wealth was to come quickly if I did this. So here I was, begging leave of the dead to borrow their power.

Dirt added to the pouch, I rushed away from Saints-Innocents and back towards the center of the city, keeping to the dark edges of the street. I was dabbling in black arts and that was a crime. I could not be caught. Luckily, no one took notice of me, and I sighed in relief when I reached a crossroads.

"Our Lady of Shadows, our Lady of Flames," I whispered, holding the pouch close to my lips. I felt the air change, felt something powerful well up from the earth beneath me as the sky itself turned its gaze to me. "Our Lady of Keys, unlock luck and prosperity for she who holds these coins. Return them ten-fold, and ten-fold again."

Was I asking too much? Who was I to ask at all? What right had I to such a petition? *The same right you have to live and breathe free*, a voice within me replied. *The same right you have to choose.*

I felt the coins inside the pouch, cold through the burlap. I smelled the herbs and the earth. I envisioned a crossroads like the one before me: one road behind me, two more branching out. In one direction lay ruin, in the other, riches. And I chose that road. As Lapère had told me to do, I let the power flowing through me seep into the coins and charm them with this one, singular choice. I saw the paths that could be taken, and I decided where the fate of these coins would be.

I knew when I opened my eyes that it was done. I could feel the power in the coins like heat radiating up my hand, and excitement and hope filled me as I rushed towards home. I was giddy as the night air tousled my hair, and when I arrived in our flat, dirty and breathless, I did not even care that she berated me. I gave her the coins and lied that I had earned them. She didn't care how, not in the moment, and the lie gave me cover for my time at Lapère's. I had accomplished one thing at least.

It only remained to be seen how long it would take for the charm to work.

CHAPTER 5

THE MAGICIAN

THREE DAYS AFTER I cast the spell, Alix Faviot's luck turned so spectacularly that it was the talk of our little corner of Paris. She had swept into a gambling salon with my charmed coins and been unable to lose at cards, dice, lots, or any other game. Her debts were paid. Thérèse left us, as we knew she would, but Arnault was so impressed by my mother's renewed fortunes that he allowed her to take on more of Thérèse's lead roles. My pride in my accomplishment was only eclipsed by my amazement at how powerfully the charm had worked and how it affected me too.

My mother's turn of fortunes meant more acting for me, painting my face with charcoal to become a wrinkled matron to fill the cast. I must admit, I enjoyed having more time on stage to make the audience laugh. Yet the applause was nothing compared to the power that I felt waiting for me, like a gathering storm on the horizon. I had more time, now that Thérèse was gone, to escape the theater and revel in the companionship and magic I had found in Madame Lapère's small coven.

Thanks to the concoction of pansy and yarrow I had used, I did not miss Thérèse at all. I went to Lapère's as often as I could, not only to learn whatever she would teach me, but to share the space of whoever was there. My instruction in magic was unlike my lessons in the convent or learning by doing in the theater. Here, my mind was respected, and so was my potential. I felt fellowship with these women – these fellow witches – that was unlike anything I had experienced. It was like I had known them forever, but the experience of being part of a circle such as this was entirely new.

Lapère made me feel safe, as I imagined a grandmother would. I didn't know for sure, as I had never known one myself. She had a gentle, hard-won wisdom about her as steadfast and subtle as the plants of her garden. I learned in my second week under her guidance that she had been a mother many times over, but her children had all gone out into the world or the grave. We, her students, were her daughters now. Catherine and I mused on the mystery of letting children go – of parents that set their offspring free to live as they wished rather than relying on them to keep them afloat. Both of us wished our mothers were more like Lapère.

By my third week, I knew the most about Catherine, if only because she liked to talk more than all the others in the circle combined. It was she who told me to begin minding the phases of the moon and encouraged me to find a friendly priest to assist me (advice I did not take). She believed in the power of blessings, not just from Our Lady, but from the proper Church as well, and she went to Mass dutifully every Sunday. I couldn't understand that, but I still went to Mass too, when I remembered, to hear the organ and choir and feel less alone.

Marie was much less devout, claiming always that she was needed back at her Marquis's house in the Marais. The neighborhood was right on top of the Court of Miracles, but more aristocrats were acquiring property there while it was cheap. Marie complained that her Marquis's house was drafty, old, and crumbling. To me, it was a wonder she lived in such a place and did not see how lucky she was.

The Marais was a fashionable district for sure, but nothing compared to the streets close to the Seine and the palaces, where we all would walk, pointing out various notable people. I'd begun to learn the names of the nobles and courtiers that filled the city. After the King's wedding, they fascinated me all the more, and I was determined to learn their histories and secrets as much as I was devoted to memorizing the properties of herbs and flowers.

Even though Marie served a Marquis, she knew little of his world and soon my knowledge outstripped hers. I liked it when I was the one who knew things; who reflected the power and importance of those of higher class.

Veronique liked gossip the least but knew the most about the craft we all sought to learn. She'd studied it for many years before even coming to Lapère. Oftentimes, when I repeated my lessons to myself in the dark hours of the night, it was Veronique's voice I heard.

Ragged edges and square stems will ease stomach and mind, mint and nettle and balm, where it grows in the shade. Flat and plain for a wound, small like parsley for a fever. Foxglove can start a heart or stop it. Wild carrot for an aching head, but be careful: the water hemlock is as deadly as hellebore and looks the same.

It was Veronique who took me to the Jardin des Plantes for the first time. It was a wonder, this new garden of blooms and shrubs and trees from all over the world, open to the public for us all to enjoy. In the golden sun of September, we walked up and down the rows, and she gave me her herbalist's secrets like a new catechism.

For the sweetness of new love, press rose petals in your shoe, and your true love will follow you wherever you go. On the new moon, sweep out the house to cast out any lingering traces of evil that has been done there or malicious spirits.

In my dreams that night, the green of the gardens was the same as the green of her eyes. The rose petals were her lips. I had forgotten Thérèse entirely by then, and her place in my life had been subsumed by the witches who now delighted my days. And the secret, sinful niche she had occupied in my most wanton dreams now belonged to Veronique.

By the time one month had passed – a month of prosperity and learning and new avenues – the dreams she inspired nearly edged on my waking thoughts. So much so that I wondered if I should cast some new spell to cleanse myself of such uncouth desires… But I didn't want to. I cherished the way seeing Veronique made my heart leap and my stomach flip.

Perhaps I was enchanted. Was it possible to tell if I was? Would I undo it if I knew?

ONE MONTH INTO MY mentorship with Lapère and our strange little coven, I decided to voice such a question.

"Can people who have been charmed or had spells cast upon them discover it?" I asked as we sat in the garden in the fading light, waiting for the moon. Summer had yet to release us from her grip, and the air was warm and sweet here, and the sky was shades of pink and purple above.

Lapère looked up from where she was plucking yellow mullein flowers from a stalk to dry them. All parts of the plant were excellent for ailments of the lungs, but the flowers were useful in spellwork too. Veronique was working with the soft leaves of the plant beside Lapère, and my eyes were transfixed by the deft work of her hands.

"There are ways – the egg test is one," Lapère said thoughtfully then nodded to Catherine beside me to explain. It was not that Lapère did not know; this was her way of teaching and testing her students.

"You can roll an egg over the body of someone you suspect is cursed," Catherine recited. "Break it in a bowl, and if there's blood or anything else in it, they're cursed, and you will need to do an uncrossing."

"That sounds like a good way to waste an egg," I muttered, and it made Veronique smile. "What if you suspect something other than a curse?"

"You could divine it," Marie suggested through a yawn. She was splayed at the table, resting her head on her arm. She'd been up late for the past few nights, nursing and tending to the Marquis's babe, and she was exhausted from it. "All sorts of ways you can do it. Drop some milk in a glass of water and look at the shapes. Tea leaves. Or the clouds."

"How can you know you won't just see what you want to see?" I asked. I trusted my cards to give me glimpses of the unseen; clouds and leaves less so.

"You see what you need to see in such things," Lapère answered. "Our Lady is always speaking to us, always sending us signs. We must only listen to hear."

"Are you worried about being cursed?" Marie asked me with a chuckle. "I didn't think you had any enemies."

"I'm planning for when I do," I smirked back, continuing to crumble the dried herbs in my hand. Lapère had harvested them at midsummer when they had the greatest power. Now, the scent of mint and vervain was thick in the air as we pulverized the brittle leaves so they could be set aside in jars. They would join the many others Lapère kept in her stores.

"When other actresses start hexing you?" Marie teased, but it stung.

"I have other ambitions," I replied, hoping to sound aloof and mysterious.

Even in this company, the things I dreamed of seemed out of reach and impossible. Not the wanton dreams of touch, no. The dreams that were even more secret than that. Of elevation beyond the careers serving the elite like Catherine and Marie hoped to achieve. I wanted to *be* them. I wanted to feel like I had when

Louis had looked at me every day, but the gates to high palaces and courtly intrigue were closed to someone like me.

"Whatever you have planned – the best course is to protect yourself in any way you can," Catherine said. "Amulets. Wards on your house. Charms in your pockets. Prayers. Keeps you safe."

"Nothing can keep you entirely safe," Lapère warned, voice warm but firm. "What we do is dangerous, and we cannot mistake our power over some threads of fate for control over everything. The world is too big for that, and there are always forces at work that may hinder you. Even just the ill will of another can act like the evil eye and cause trouble."

"Not even the wisest of us can control everything or protect everyone," Veronique added with a deep sadness I had never heard from her. "And magic cannot do miracles," she added with a pointed look at Catherine.

"Isn't this the Court of Miracles?" I smiled.

"They call it that because all the beggars that go about the streets pretending to be blind or lame come home here and are suddenly 'cured,'" Marie explained sourly. "I thought everyone knew that."

"I didn't," I muttered into the mint in my lap. "I found magic here. It felt like a miracle to me."

"I have a friend who claims he can turn lead to gold," Catherine piped up, but I could feel Veronique looking at me and my blush deepened.

"I doubt that sincerely," Lapère said. "Men – I assume this is a man?" Catherine nodded. "Men have been attempting such wonders for centuries and none have succeeded."

"He puts on a good show though. He'll be at the harvest festival tomorrow. The one I was telling you about in Versailles. And he has other magic too – the kind that maybe can do miracles, as you say." Catherine spoke almost as a challenge.

"Does he now?" Veronique's voice was more amused than convinced. "I should like to see that."

"Versailles is barely a village," Marie scoffed. "And it's out in the woods."

"The king has a hunting lodge there," I said, excited to know something others did not. "He adores it and retreats there whenever he can. More folk are moving to the village to get work there. I hear people talk about it."

"When you're lurking in the Tuileries?" Marie sniped. My friends knew of the habit I had acquired recently of walking as close as I could manage to the open gardens and courtyards of the palaces by the Seine. I liked to listen to the conversations I could hear, as I did before and after performances at the theater. It was all knowledge.

"I should like to see the village anyway – and this wondrous conjurer of yours," I declared, raising my chin high and proud now.

"So would I," said Veronique, and I could not help but grin. "We shall all go together?"

"Some of us have places to be at night," Marie groaned. "Alas."

"And some of us are too old to frolic in the forest," Lapère added. "The moon and I will converse alone, while you have your amusements."

"You won't have a performance, will you?" Veronique asked, and I shook my head.

"Even if I did, I would not miss such a night."

I DID, IT TURNS out, have some duties the next day, but the performance was early in the day. I would have plenty of time to find Veronique after and make the journey by cart out of the city, a transport that Catherine had assured us would get us to the sleepy village of Versailles in time for the evening festival. It was a celebration of the last harvest, to be held under the full moon.

It sounded to me like a witches' night, even though nearly all who attended would call themselves good Christians. The more I considered it, the more apparent it was to me how much the practices of the country – the blessings of fields, the superstitions, and the old songs and stories – seemed to come from a distant age under older Gods than Christ. I mused on what the night might bring as I entered the back of our theater and made my way to get ready behind the grimy sheet.

I had expected solitude, but found Yvette weeping in the corner. Yvette was the one who had taken over for me in my smaller parts, and before that, she had amused the audience with dances and miming. She was not as pretty as Thérèse, but her charms were ample enough that she had attracted the attention of many men, including the stagehand I'd seen her with over a month ago. After she'd used strawberries as a love charm.

"What's wrong?" I asked the girl, whose face was blotchy and wet with tears.

"It's nothing!" Yvette cried, standing to leave. I didn't blame her for such shyness. We were not friends. But I didn't like seeing another woman in pain. I stepped in front of her and grasped her arm gently.

"Has someone hurt you?" I asked, fearing that her bold stagehand had turned on her. She shook her head weakly. "Has someone died?"

"If only," she grunted and wrapped her arms around her middle. Around her belly. Maybe it was that secret voice whispering to me, or an educated guess, but I knew in my soul what her burden was.

"Oh," I whispered. "You've taken on a passenger."

"And it will ruin me," she whispered as fresh tears filled her eyes. "He won't marry me! He said he would."

I felt another crossroads before me.

A woman – a girl, really – had come to Lapère's house a few nights ago. She had been desperate for help, clutching Lapère's hands as she fell before her and begged. Veronique had quickly taken me out to the garden, but even from there, I had heard her say that she had no money and that the man she worked for had seduced her. If his wife found out, she would be cast out on the street by her employers and her family. And so, Madame Lapère had given her a mix of herbs that would expel the child from her womb and asked no payment. She'd told her, if it did not work, to return, and she would take more drastic measures to help. Afterward, the girl had wept tears of gratitude.

Now Yvette was in the same terrible situation, and I had a choice. I could tell her and risk everyone's welfare if we were found out. Or I could let her suffer.

"I know a woman that could help," I whispered, and Yvette's face lit up with gratitude. "On the Rue Saint Lazare. Look for a house with a red door and tell her you know me."

"What are you two talking about?"

My stomach clenched in fear as my mother burst in.

"Nothing!" Yvette cried and scurried away. I wondered what my mother had heard or knew, for her face was dark and foreboding.

"What sort of woman were you telling her about?" my mother hissed. "What have you been up to these weeks?"

"Nothing!" I protested, voice choked. She could not know. This secret was mine, not another thing she could exploit and command.

"What are you hiding? Where have you been getting off to lately?" she pushed. "Don't think I haven't noticed that you've barely been at home."

"As long as I'm giving you my wages and you're lucky at the tables, why do you care where I go?" I snapped back, and her face fell. Had I hurt her? "I'm sorry, I know you love me—"

She shook her head. The words I had put in her mouth – words of hope for why she was concerned – were not the truth. "Luck can change, Claude," she said darkly.

My stomach fell. "How much have you lost?" I asked in horror. I had been a fool to think the spell would last indefinitely.

"Curtain in one minute!" a voice called, and my mother's face transformed into one of calm composure. Always the actress.

"It will turn around. If not, you'll do your duty," the great La Faviot declared. "We will talk more after the performance. You'll tell me where you earned those other coins, finally, and you'll go back—"

I could not listen anymore – I was too angry. So I pushed past her to take my place. I wasn't even in costume, but it didn't matter. No one would care.

Panic and rage hovered around me in turn throughout the performance, as I went through the motions of acting and playing my part. I was only delaying my doom with these spells for her, but what else could I do? She wouldn't accept the answer that I had no other source of income and I had just saved. Life would be easier if I did have some other job – something to free me from her.

I had to think of something to get free before she did the unthinkable and wrote to her husband for aid. The memory of him lurked in my mind, poised to strike and devour me if I dared turn and look at it. So I didn't turn. I disappeared into my role and my duties and I didn't look. At least, not behind me.

I looked at the audience, the sea of laughing faces that had come to our theater to forget their cares. I saw men with smartly trimmed beards and beautiful women with hair of every color. Blonde, brown, black… And golden red.

I nearly dropped the jug I was carrying when I recognized the freckled, lovely face beneath that rosy hair. It couldn't be. But Veronique caught me staring and grinned. And my heart surged back from the edge of the abyss. My prayers had been answered.

I knew what I had to do. I rushed from the stage, dropping my shawl and cap in the wings before the bows were even over and heading to the street as fast as my feet would carry me before my mother could see me go. I could at least see my friend, and maybe she would keep me from being taken.

Veronique was waiting for me in the street as the audience ambled out into the night, most of them likely on their way to a tavern or salon. She was radiant, dressed in the same greenish bodice she often wore. It matched her eyes and made it seem like she had brought the garden with her.

"There you are! The famous actress!" Veronique called, taking my hand with a smile.

"You didn't tell me you were coming," I gasped.

"I wanted to surprise you. If I had told you, I wouldn't have seen that pretty look of shock on your face," she said. "You were very good."

"I'm mediocre, at best," I countered, looking around nervously to see if my mother had emerged to chase me down. "You don't need to flatter me."

"I thought you were a very convincing maid. Don't be so hard on yourself."

"I wish I was a real maid, sometimes," I blurted out nervously. "I'd rather tend to a real lady than this pack of trollops—" I spotted my would-be captor coming out the side door, her face like thunder. She'd had the whole performance to sober up, which made her even more dangerous. "Shit."

"Who's that?" Veronique asked, following my gaze.

"My mother. I don't want her to see me," I confessed, panic rising again. "I need to hide. I have to—"

"Then she won't see you," Veronique replied and pulled me towards a shadowed overhang. It wasn't really a hiding place, but

Veronique came close to me and whispered in my ear. "*Our Lady, blessed and unseen, cast us in shadows, oh, Heavenly Queen.*"

The words made me shiver as Veronique pressed against me. I felt the shadows thicken around us, embracing us as I repeated the prayer in my own heart. Veronique, who I had admired for weeks from afar, was chest-to-chest with me. I could feel her breathing, the ghost of her exhales against my cheek. Her eyes sparkled with life and mischief in the shadows and that was like magic too.

I barely noticed moments later when my mother walked right by as if we were not there.

"How did you…"

Veronique winked. "I asked. She answered. Now, let's go. Catherine is waiting, and you know how impatient she can be."

Veronique pulled me after her through the streets, her hand tight on mine, wisps of red hair flying behind her, so alive and joyful. We ran, laughing through the shadows and past the shops, and we…

We were free.

THE LITTLE VILLAGE OF Versailles was full of revelry that night. The air smelled of trees and rich earth, hay and animals; not the shit and sweat of Paris. The white moon was bright on the horizon, and we could see where people had gathered around fires and torches to sell and celebrate on what would surely be one of the last warm nights before autumn came.

Catherine had met us near the western gate and we'd paid a coin each to be hauled like so much hay far outside of the city by some friend of hers who was bound for the fair. There were stalls set up in the village square, next to carts and open cooking fires, people of all sorts hawking food and goods.

Catherine dragged us through the crowd, and I clung to Veronique's hand, her red hair lit perfectly by the fires, freckled skin golden. I wished I could tell her how perfect she was. Somewhere in the distance, musicians played the recorder, lute, and drum as people whooped and danced.

"There he is!" Catherine cried, bringing me back from my foolish dream and tugging us towards a crowd of people gathered around a man standing on a table as if it were a stage.

The magician was dressed in a black robe, not unlike a priest, but his aura was quite the opposite. With long, light hair and a striking face, he held the attention of the crowds with pure charisma as he pulled a flower out of thin air.

"Do not look away, Mesdames et Messieurs!" the conjurer cried. "See how a humble flower can become – a thing of gold!" With a flourish, the plain bloom transformed into a glittering one made of something that could be mistaken for gold in the dancing firelight. The crowd cooed in amazement.

"*This* is the great sorcerer?" Veronique asked in a whisper.

"Wait," Catherine snapped. "And be quiet."

I chuckled as the magician began more tricks with rings and coins, keeping up a colorful commentary that delighted the crowd. I'd known many an actor in my day, and this man reminded me far more of them than of the witches of the Court of Miracles. He was the sort of character who could make any room into a theater.

"But these tricks and trivialities are just the beginning, my friends!" the man cried. "This is but a taste of my gifts! Would you like to know the real sorcery I have learned?"

The crowd yelled back in the affirmative, and I found myself joining them.

"I have learned the secrets of the stars! The paths of the planets! I have learned the forbidden ways of the mystics of the East, who can conjure smoke from the air!" The crowd gasped as a burst of smoke erupted from his hand. An impressive sight, if one didn't spot the bit of paper in his hand that no doubt had caused the puff.

"You, there, young man!" he called. "I see in your eyes that you yearn to be in the arms of a girl with golden hair! I can make it happen! I have potions that will ensnare her heart and charms that will kindle her fire. And you – good Madame! I see in you that you are owed money! I have a powder to place in your debtor's shoe that will have them paying double!"

"Then give it here!" The woman laughed, tossing the sorcerer a coin. In return, he conjured a little bag from thin air and threw it back to her. I wondered if it would work and how he knew her needs. Was it the same way Lapère had known me before I walked through her door? Was it something he had seen in the stars? Or was it all a confidence game?

"Most fantastic of all – I have learned the secrets of the philosopher's stone!" the man – no, the alchemist – cried. "I know the secret to turning iron into gold!"

"Do it now then!" someone called.

"Oh, if only I could, my friend!" the sorcerer lamented with a deep bow, hand to his chest. "The process is complex, requiring months of distillation and ingredients that are hardly common. But if you, good sir, wish to help me for a modest sum, I will return your investment five-fold when the gold is created. Who among you is ready to invest?!"

At that, I rolled my eyes, as did Veronique, but Catherine was transfixed. "We're going to find some wine," Veronique told her.

I was happy to follow Veronique once again, and soon enough, we found ourselves side by side at one of the long tables at the center of the market, cups of red in our hands as the world bustled around us.

"So you *don't* believe he can turn iron to gold?" I asked as I sipped.

"I believe he'll convince enough people that he will earn his meals for a few weeks," Veronique replied.

"How can people be that foolish?"

I had heard claims about the philosopher's stone, and legends of the men who had discovered it, or killed themselves looking for it. Alchemy always struck me as different from the magic of the earth, the sorcery that was innate to the world. What was the point in transmuting something already beautiful?

"Do you know the secret to reading palms and telling fortunes?" Veronique asked, surprising me by taking my hand in hers.

"I've learned the basic lines," I stammered, eyes on my own palm. "Heart. Head." I pointed to the two lines directly below where my fingers ended. Veronique nodded that I was correct. "Life line." That was the long one that circled the base of the thumb. "And the line of fate." I indicated the fainter line crossing through the head and heart lines.

"Very good. But that's not the secret."

Veronique rubbed the center of my palm with her thumb and I felt it in the core of my body. I tried to concentrate on her face and mouth as she spoke, but that proved difficult as well.

"No one really wants to know the future," Veronique said, tracing the long, arcing life line that sat like a halo radiating from my thumb, making my skin prickle. "No one wants to hear about the love they will lose or the dreams that will never come true. They want to hear that everything will be alright. Most people *want* to be lied to."

"That can't be true," I stammered, though I knew immediately it was. I lied every day because it was what was needed and expected of me. It was the only way to survive. Veronique traced another line on my palms, a shadow of pity passing over her face. "Not of everyone at least."

"I've yet to meet anyone that looked at the future with no fear. That's what we sell them when we divine for them. It's the same thing that charlatan sells when he tells them he can turn lead to gold: hope." Veronique paused, her finger ghosting over my palm again, the sensation making my head spin. "You'd be a good reader, you know, with all your training as an actor."

"I would rather really help people," I replied in a daze. "Not lie to them."

"You sound like Catherine and Marie," Veronique said, her eyes twinkling. "They think if they learn enough herbs and spells, they can do what that man promises when they read a future: see the problem, then offer the solution. It's smart business. A good way to get paid twice."

"You don't like that?"

Veronique shook her head. "It's easy enough to sell a love charm or call in a debt, but most of us can't offer such easy solutions. Most people have bigger problems. I want to help them in real ways."

I thought of the women who came to Lapère because they had nowhere else to go; women like Yvette, and the people who sought her out for remedies because they could not afford to let a doctor bleed them. That was the good Veronique wanted to do.

"I feel what we do..." I hesitated to speak the word *magic* in public, even after such a display. "I think it can offer real hope and real solutions. It's helped me. Though it might not have been enough."

Veronique raised an eyebrow but did not let go of my hands. "The craft is part of nature, and nature is unpredictable. We cannot always know how seeds we plant will grow or how long they will thrive. Especially when the working is for someone else," Veronique countered. "And what happens when what we promise doesn't come true?"

"What do you mean?"

"I can mix a love charm or tell you which plants and stones will protect you, but I'm just one person against the will of the world. What if I fail and you blame me instead of fate? What if something I can't control goes wrong?" Veronique cast an eye to the crowd still gathered around the conjurer. "Men can get away with selling alchemy in the streets. But women? Well, we get blamed for all the evils in the world already. Original sin and all that. We have to be careful. My mother..."

Veronique swallowed, her beautiful face falling in regret, and my heart swelled with pity and worry. "You lost her?" I asked, holding back my curiosity about what it would even be like to have a mother you cared about losing.

"She did what we did too. Witchcraft."

It made me shiver to hear her say it aloud, and not from the excitement of her hand still holding mine. "What happened to her?"

"We lived near Rouen. Things are different there. Less tolerant than Paris. My mother was a midwife – a healer. She gave out charms and told people which prayers to say to protect their crops or what potions would bring fertility. She helped everyone. Then, when one farmer's crops failed one year, he blamed her. The whole village came for her."

"They killed her?" I asked, aghast.

"She died under torture." I could see the stark memory in Veronique's eyes. They were usually so bright. Now they were barren of joy. "That is how it is done, with witch hunters. A confession is not valid until there is torture. The things they do are hideous. Worse than any deal with the devil they could accuse us of. I didn't learn until years later what had happened – I was sent away to family here. She died before she could teach me what she knew."

"Why learn from Lapère if that's what got your mother killed?"

"Because it is her legacy. I will not let evil men take that from me," Veronique replied, life and fire returning to her as she straightened. "It is because of her that I know enough to be careful. It's safer here in Paris, but it's still dangerous to offer too much. Unless you're a man. They don't get burned as often." Veronique looked down to where her hand still gripped mine. "Please promise to take care of yourself as you follow this path, Claude."

"No one who matters would miss me if I was burned," I shrugged.

Veronique met my eyes. "Are you saying I don't matter?" She said it with a teasing smile, and my heart jumped to my throat.

"Why do you two look so dour?" I nearly fell off the bench, pulling my hand away from Veronique's as Catherine spoke.

The smaller woman took a seat across the long table with – to my great surprise – the conjurer and another woman I did not know. "Claude, Veronique, this is Adam de Couret. The sorcerer," Catherine said. The man nodded, and took my hand, pressing a dramatic kiss to it before I could stop him. Veronique pointedly avoided the same fate. "And this is Marie Bosse."

"Good to meet you at last," Bosse said. She was stout, with dark brown hair piled on the sides of her head to give her a rather bullish look.

"You've heard of me?" I asked, terrified at the prospect of being known by a stranger.

"Mademoiselle Deshayes had to rub it in that Madame Lapère had taken on another girl, even though she refused to instruct me any further," Bosse said, acidly. "Luckily, sweet Catherine filled me in when she could. At least, before I found Monsieur de Couret."

"You weren't interested in what Madame Lapère had to teach," Veronique noted calmly. She clearly knew this woman and did not seem to like her. "You made that very clear."

"Well, I guess Claude here will be content as a nursemaid or hedge witch living in the slums," Bosse sniped.

"I'm going to do more than that," I whispered. I just wished I knew what it was.

"Now, now, my Madame Bosse, that's unkind. Not everyone has sights as high as you," de Couret said soothingly, drawing all the attention back to him like he was a lodestone. "We can all be friends and students of the mystical arts, can't we? We all serve the same masters."

Bosse huffed and relented while Catherine gave me an apologetic look. "Don't get him started on Asmodeus and – who was the other you claim to summon?"

"Astaroth!" de Couret exclaimed.

"Aren't those demons?" I laughed in shock, sure he was joking.

"They are powerful forces of sorcery, happy to be invoked and to do my will," de Couret said with a grin. "Would you like to know how to invoke them, dear lady?"

"I won't pay you any money to find out," I replied, and the table burst out in laughter.

"For shame! I would never charge a fellow practitioner!" de Couret cried, clutching his heart dramatically.

"If you aren't going to charge me, you don't need to perform for me," I purred back. "I'm an actress, good Monsieur. I recognize a fellow practitioner of that art too." The women laughed again, and de Couret grinned widely, his façade finally falling away.

"I like you, Claude," he said, the affected way he had spoken fading away to a rougher Gascon accent. "I think you will go far."

"We all will," Catherine smirked. "And I still would like to hear of your masters and mystic arts, Adam." She gave Bosse a look and received a scowl in return.

"He's my find, Catherine," Bosse hissed. "He'll teach his conjugation *to me*."

"Dear ladies!" de Couret laughed, pleased to be fought over. "I can educate all of you in the mystic arts! The moon is full. The night is still young. Let us drink more wine and discover magic! But first, I will show you how to make your dreams come true! Come!"

De Couret sprang up and bounded to one of the bonfires crackling in the center of the market. With a flourish, he pulled a few leaves from his pocket. Bay, I noted. From another pocket, a small piece of chalk.

"This is an old charm," Veronique muttered, taking a leaf and the chalk. "You write a word or a wish down, burn it in the fire, and it will come true." I watched as she scrawled something on the bay leaf and tossed it into the fire.

"Of course, you could summon power in the light of the full moon to enact that wish more quickly, but let us start with wishes," de Couret grumbled, annoyed that his lesson had been stolen.

Catherine took the chalk next and did not hesitate at all to write her wish on her leaf of bay. Then Marie Bosse. Soon, it would be my turn, and I was at a loss. I couldn't think of a single wish or word that encompassed all I wanted or needed. I certainly couldn't write the desire that sprang to mind when Veronique smiled at me, the firelight dancing on her face...

"It's all quite secret, Mademoiselle," de Couret purred in my ear from beside me as he handed me the materials. I wondered if he did have some power to discern a secret thought. "Wish with all your heart and it will be answered."

I scribbled the one word I could think of and tossed the leaf into the fire, where it smoldered and curled into itself before becoming ash. A strange thing for a wish to do. I'd rather it be a seed to grow.

"Come, let's have another round," de Couret cried, and like magic, a fresh bottle of wine emerged from his sleeve.

I kept myself next to Veronique, warmed by the wine as de Couret held court in the firelight, watching him feed on the competing attention from Catherine and Bosse as they batted their eyes at him and loosened the laced of their chemises so their chests could enjoy the cool night air and de Couret's blatant ogling. It made me laugh and I drank more wine.

How long had it been since I had stayed up into the night with friends? I wasn't sure I ever had. Carousing and laughing as the liquor flowed was something my mother did, not me. Maybe she knew something.

Each story de Couret told was more fantastical than the last. He'd studied with the poisoners in Italy – he had met Juliana Tofana herself, he said, before she had disappeared. He had met moors in Spain, and pygmies on a mysterious Greek island. He told a tale he had from a sailor, who heard it from a merchant, who claimed there was a city hidden in the jungles of the Americas built of gold, for it was the heathens that had learned the true secrets of alchemy.

It was Catherine who returned (when had she gone?) to our table with a full jug of wine in one hand and a cup in the other, handing the cup pointedly to Bosse and the jug to de Couret. "Should we all go somewhere quieter? Perhaps more private?"

"Indeed! It is time to work our spells!" de Couret cried. In a blink, I found myself stumbling from the benches in the square as we made our way towards the moonlit woods, wine in hand, as de Couret bragged of escaping crocodiles and pirates in Venice, while the rest of us guffawed.

It felt dangerous to follow such a man away from the crowds and into the woods, but it was the same sort of danger that had given me such a thrill when I'd taken dirt from graves and called on the powers of Our Lady. It was an invitation to a hidden magic. Who was I to say no when Veronique took my hand? I could never be afraid with her beside me.

We found ourselves in a glade of oaks and pine, the moon so bright above we needed no fire. I relaxed on the mossy ground with my cup of wine as Veronique sat beside me.

"I was going to say we should play a game and drink whenever he spews more nonsense," Veronique snickered. "But I think we'd die that way!"

I laughed and leaned against her, heat filling my cheeks. "What if we drink whenever Deshayes or Bosse tell him how *fascinating* he is?"

Veronique snorted, and I dissolved into giggles as we plopped down on the grass, wine sloshing, and drank again as the trio beside us kept laughing as well.

"Is it true, Monsieur, that in Spain they have a special beetle that they grind to make men especially *vigorous*?" Catherine said brazenly, licking her lips and leaning into de Couret. Veronique and I stifled our hysteria at the sight.

"Oh yes, Mademoiselle! Though I myself have never had need," de Couret grinned, puffing out his chest. I grabbed Veronique's knee in glee. "I have a man in Provence who supplies it, and I have, on occasion, sold this marvelous powder to a poor, afflicted man and relieved him of all his troubles. I believe one even promised to name his son after me."

"What would happen if a woman took your Spanish Fly?" Bosse asked over a hiccup, her eyes half closed.

"Oh, it would make her wild with lust, in the most unbecoming fashion!" de Couret said, a wicked grin spreading across his face. "I should not tell you this, but not even a week ago, a great and infamous courtesan attempted to ingest some of this powder – having procured it from an inferior seller, not myself – and she was sent into such a carnal state, she exhausted three paramours in one night! Her servants were terrified!"

"How do you know that?" I asked, forcing myself not to imagine that woman fucking so wildly she could not stop.

"Again, I should not say, but I, being an expert in this field and well known for my gifts, was sent for." De Couret made deep eye contact with Bosse, who swayed unsteadily, entranced by him. "Only *I* knew how to satiate her. It was not simply a matter of making love, oh no! I had to summon powerful spirits, rub her fevered body with milk mixed with nettle, and only then was I able to fuck the madness out of her."

"I don't believe you," Bosse drawled, eyes drooping.

"I do," Catherine purred, snaking her arms around de Couret and giving Bosse a gentle push. The woman fell back onto the grass like a sack of flour, completely unconscious. "Guess she can't hold her drink."

"How convenient," Veronique whispered to me, lips grazing my ear. I was too awestruck to speak – by the story, by the brazen behavior in front of me, and by the soft temptation of Veronique against me. Catherine, either forgetting Veronique and I were there or not caring, turned de Couret's head and kissed him deeply, and he welcomed it.

"Shall I show you personally how I cured that woman, Mademoiselle?" de Couret asked as Catherine pulled him towards her while Bosse began to snore.

"Tell me your spirits' names and then make me scream them, oh wise one," Catherine purred and straddled her mark.

"We should go," Veronique hissed, tugging at me to stand up and leave. I knew she was correct, but it was a fascinating sight to see Catherine take what she wanted so boldly, right there in the woods, like a pagan of old.

"I can't believe she's so bold! Bosse is right there," I muttered, tripping as I stood so that Veronique had to hold me close to get me to stand. The curves of her body were soft and solid at the same time, pressed against me as she smiled and met my eyes.

"Oh, I can believe it. This was all her plan – seducing her conjurer so she could conjure, making sure there was no one in the way," Veronique said. I wasn't sure how, but we had moved somewhere else, and yet, I was still holding onto her and she had not pushed me away. "She's doing old magic under the moon tonight."

"What do you mean?" I asked, thinking how the silver light from above made the curves of Veronique's cheeks seem rounder.

"De Couret isn't wrong; to make love is a powerful thing, and it can amplify spells and desires. Or be a spell itself," Veronique explained, her eyes mysterious as they stared into mine. "Watch and see. Soon, something will go very right for Mademoiselle Deshayes."

"I wish I could summon such a power," I said aloud before I could think better of it and I pulled myself away from Veronique's warm arms. The grove spun around me. "I wish I could command the elements to make me … more."

"What would you wish to be?" Veronique asked kindly. It made my head swim to think of all my dreams; of palaces and riches and how I could never see my path into those locked halls. I only ever pretended at being a lady, and more often, I pretended to be a maid to one.

The idea hit me as the moonlight shifted and the stars began to glitter more brightly above us.

"I'd like to be a lady's maid," I declared. "I know how to style hair and trade gossip. I could live in a decent house with decent people and make my own way."

"You'd be wonderful at that," Veronique said, and once again, her beauty and kindness made me dizzier than the wine.

"I can't have what I want," I sighed. "I can't make love to seal a spell or cast some charm like that." I thought of the bay leaf that had begged for one thing – freedom. And remembered with shame what I had almost written.

"You can, Claude," Veronique said so kindly, grasping my shoulder. She kept touching me. Why did she have to keep touching me? "You can ask for that."

"I don't like men," I blurted out, pushing away her hand. I looked listlessly towards the clearing we had left and caught the sound of moaning on the warm wind. "I can't fuck for power. The only man I'd ever let touch me like that is the goddam King himself."

"It doesn't have to be a man."

I spun to Veronique again and the world tilted, pushing me towards her. I stumbled into her arms, looking at her face in wonder because something there had changed. "What?"

"I wouldn't even let the King touch me," Veronique breathed. "But I don't think I require magic tonight. The wish I made is already coming true."

"What did you wish?" I asked as those beautiful eyes sparkled in the moonlight and the arms I had longed for pulled me closer.

"To kiss you, sweet Claude. And taste you in every way." Her lips met mine, and the world shook with thunder. No, it was my heart, beating so hard that I quaked as the kiss deepened and Veronique's tongue flitted against mine.

"I didn't even dare to dream of this," I sighed as I pulled away. "I haven't let myself want this for so long…"

"Want. Ask. Let it be given," Veronique replied. I kissed her again, hungrier than before. The woods spun around me, my wine-soaked senses singing with joy as we tumbled to the grassy ground and my back met the earth. We kissed frantically, my body awakening and the pounding of my heart echoing down into my belly and between my legs. My hands groped over her body but met fabric wherever they went.

"I want to see all of you," I begged. "I want to taste you too."

She smiled again, rising with the moon behind her, and unlaced her bodice while I fumbled with the fastenings of her skirt. We were clumsy, our fingers numbed by the wine, and we laughed as our heads collided while we tried to work together. But then suddenly, she was free and pulling her chemise over her head and...

"Oh, you're perfect," I sighed as her pale, freckled skin shone in the moonlight. I took in her gorgeous, pert breasts and the long expanse of her abdomen down to her thighs. Before I could even think, my mouth was on her, sucking on her hardened nipples, then trailing sloppy kisses down her belly and to her thigh, nuzzling my face against the curling hair above her cunt. She tasted like honey and spices when my tongue found her and she made sweet sounds, like a bird at dawn.

"Yes, there! That! More!" Veronique called, encouraging me. I was so proud and amazed that I could have this and I could give this. I could take the thing I had not dared to dream of. I had always wanted to serve, to bring joy and contentment, and finally, I had found the way I could that felt so good. I added my hands to my work, and she welcomed my fingers inside her by convulsing against my mouth. So perfect, so rare, this pleasure I could give.

I felt it when she came, all through her body, the way she shook and sighed. It was magnificent and made my own cunt ache with desire even more. "Perfect," I whispered again as she looked up at me, eyes half-lidded in the moonlight.

"So are you," Veronique said, and for a second, I didn't realize she meant me. "Let me see you too."

Our positions were reversed, and it was her hands undoing my hair and her lips against my ears and jaw. She kissed my neck as I looked up to the starry sky and let go of all my fears. She was as quick with my bodice as she had been with her own, and in moments, my skin was exposed to the cool air of the night and the light of the moon smiling down from above. I fell back again, parting my legs to wrap around her, sighing as she kissed down my body, then gasping as she took one of my nipples into her mouth. Pleasure like I had never felt coursed through me, intoxicating me more fully than the wine.

I writhed and twined my hands into the red hair that now fell free and wild about her shoulders. I could barely catch my breath as desire and feeling swept over me, and Veronique moved down my body. She touched me – the wet, aching core of me – but hesitated there.

"Don't stop," I begged. "Do with me what you will, but don't stop."

She obeyed and found me with her mouth. I let forth a sound like none I had ever made, my body responding with ecstasy as she did as promised and tasted. Never in my previous, clumsy encounters in the dark rooms, under covers, and in stolen moments, had I been touched and devoured like this.

I was flying even as I arched against the earth, made light and weightless by the swipes of her tongue and the suckling of her lips as she held apart my thighs. I panted, feeling my soul rise with the wind around us. It was magic, the way she touched me and the heat of my response, and I wanted her as much as I wanted every wish.

It was everything, this pleasure, as it rose and crested and sang. It was the moon above us and my exposed breasts heaving in the night air. It was the way her gentle fingers slipped inside me and pushed and how I cried out and shook. It was magic, rising around us, commanding the paths of fate to change. It was ground against me as I felt myself become the fertile earth as the stars wheeled above and Veronique hummed and licked against my sex and the way everything in me burst like a thunderclap as I came, calling out to the heavens above.

I saw everything as the climax pushed me to another place of being. I saw my future and the strings of fate holding me back from it. With the power of my pleasure and the moon calling to me and the earth embracing me, I cut those bonds and I bent the path ahead of me. Towards halls of gold and grand designs, I bent my fate, and the climax lifted me again.

Time stopped meaning anything as we tangled together among the oaks, the night wind embracing Veronique and me as we lost ourselves in the pleasure we had so long been denied. It was not a sabbath or an unholy rite, but it was sacred, nonetheless, what we found there under the moon, protected by Our Lady in the shadows, sighing into the night.

CHAPTER 6

THE LOVERS

W E WOKE BEFORE DAWN, wrapped in one another's arms, blushing and bashful. My head ached and my joints were stiff from sleeping on the ground, but it didn't matter, because Veronique did not run away when she saw me in the light. We dressed before anyone could find us and stumbled past the other unconscious members of our band. Catherine and de Couret were half-clothed a few feet from where Bosse was still snoring. The joy I felt stifling my laughter with Veronique as we stumbled through the morning dew was something I wanted to keep forever.

The woods and the village were quiet and perfect, the air fresh as birds sang in the alders and green surrounded us. It felt sacred, not just from the magic we had worked, but by the way the light of dawn caressed each leaf and stem with tender love. We kissed with the same reverence, safe there among the trees and protected by the loving embrace of the earth.

I didn't want to go home to the tight, twisted streets of Paris that stank of piss and death. Nor did I want to face my mother's wrath for disappearing for a full night. Whatever magic we had worked last night, I prayed it kept me from ever returning. I had tasted freedom in Veronique's arms and could not return to my cage.

We ate warm, fresh bread to break our fast as we waited for Catherine to revive. Eventually, she did, and we rode back into the city with her, while de Couret stayed (to Catherine's annoyance) to make sure Bosse made it home alive. Veronique did not mind that I went with her back to Lapère's house rather than my own. I still tried to retract my hand from Veronique's when we entered, but she wouldn't let go.

Lapère was waiting in the front room when we entered, stirring porridge over the fire, tea already steaming on the table. She looked us over, noting our entwined fingers and how I blushed. To my shock, she smiled, warm and kind. "Well, that took long enough," she muttered, and Veronique grinned beside me.

"You knew?" I asked.

"I always know," Lapère said, handing us the cups with a playful scowl. "And I'm not so old and blind I can't see what's in front of my eyes. Take this. Fennel and peppermint, for the hangover. I trust Catherine's conjurer was entertaining?"

"He puts on a good show, but he boasts of conjuring demons, dabbles in alchemy, and trades in Spanish fly," Veronique answered, sipping the brew she had been given. I did the same as we sat at the small table by the fire.

"Leave it to a man to waltz into danger in so many different ways," Lapère chuckled. "His possession of a cock will keep him safe, as long as he doesn't start hawking inheritance powders and tries to be discreet."

"He is the furthest thing from discrete I've ever seen," I chuckled over my tea. It helped my headache with each sip. "What's an inheritance powder?"

"Dangerous business best left alone," Veronique chastised, straightening her spine.

Lapère shook her head sagely. "You know there are plants in every garden that can hurt or even kill. The poison of hellebore or wolfsbane is quick and violent, but these powders act much slower and are far harder to detect."

"What does that have to do with inheritance?" I shivered at the idea that such deadly things lurked innocently among the flowers and trees.

"It is said that, in Italy, there are women who use it to slowly kill their husbands. The disciples of Tofana," Lapère went on as Veronique's frown deepened and my jaw dropped. "It makes these men seem to only be growing ill naturally before they expire. When they die, there is no suspicion, and the inheritance is theirs."

"Surely a woman would only use such a thing if her husband is cruel," I said.

"One would hope," Lapère replied darkly. "Marie is here. I'll get some bread for you all."

Sure enough, the door opened, and Vigoreaux swept in, scowling and looking tired. "I can't stay too long. The Marquise has me at her beck and call today. I only escaped under the ruse of getting her something for the headache losing her maid has caused her."

"Something has happened to your mistress's maid?" I asked, sitting up at sudden attention. Marie looked curiously between me and Veronique, who was also rapt.

"The little bitch ran off with her lover in the middle of the night. Left the household in chaos with no one to take on her work!"

"I can replace her!" I exclaimed, nearly jumping from the table and giving Marie a shock. "I know how to do everything required!"

"You're an actress, not a maid," Marie balked.

"She knows all the popular hairstyles and fashions! Claude is as discrete and well-mannered as can be," Veronique argued with a grin, and Marie shook her head in amazement.

"You'd be saving my ass if you're willing to take the job," she said slowly. "But I warn you, the Marquise is as demanding as she is cheap. Do you want a mistress like that?"

"I want a new start," I replied, breathless. "I want freedom."

I thought of the night before, drunk and spread out on the ground, filled with magic and dreams, and that moment like lightning when I had resolved to set myself free and command my own fate. It had been magic. It had been a beginning.

"Well, get yourself washed up and come back with me," Marie said at last.

Lapère looked me over with a knowing smile. "I'd offer you some lavender for luck but I don't think you'll need it."

I WAS HIRED ON the spot by a relieved Marquise Michelle-Françoise de Termes. She was a thin, sallow woman with cornsilk hair and long features who did not care that it was her wet nurse who had brought me to serve her, only that I was willing to start work that very night. I would be lodged in the de Termes home, and what a home it was.

The house of the Marquis was so grand, I could barely understand it. How could Marie have complained about a place like this? There were walls of white stone and a grand gate that admitted visitors from the street into a quaint courtyard. Off that were entrances to the stables and kitchens and servants' quarters, all on the ground floor. There was even another courtyard and garden through the kitchen, and I adored it from the moment I saw it. The Marquis and Marquise lived on the upper floor, and their rooms were on opposite sides of the house from one another, separated by drawing and dining rooms with painted and plastered walls hung with art and arms.

It dazzled me, even though the air was stagnant and the floor creaked. I was to have my own room adjacent to the Marquise's. It was barely more than a cupboard, but it had a bed with a clean straw mattress and it would be mine alone. No one could hurt me there, and that felt like magic.

Luck remained on my side when I snuck home, making sure to confirm my mother was gone before I hastily gathered my meager possessions. I felt a pang of regret at the chaos I would cause for my fellow actors when I left my short letter at the theater explaining my roles would need to be filled, but I felt equal satisfaction at the rage it would cause Arnault. When I thought of my mother's reaction, I felt fear first; fear of her rage and disappointment. Shame at myself for abandoning her. But those could not overcome my joy and the thrill I felt to know I was free. She could take care of herself now.

That night, Veronique and I made love in Lapère's smoky, stifling attic, and it was heaven. Sweaty and sated, I fell asleep once more in her arms. Everything was as I had hoped and prayed. Like magic. Even so, I had dark dreams that night: of prophecies and prices paid in blood.

T HE FIRST FOUR WEEKS of my employment as chambermaid to a Marquise were nothing like I had dreamed. My duties were both more boring and more exhausting than I ever could have imagined, and yet, I was deliriously happy to undertake such a challenge. I still went whenever I could to Lapère's for instruction in Our Lady's mysteries and skill, and I was educated daily on what it meant to serve a noble Lady, no matter how modest her fortunes were.

The Marquis Roger de Termes was a minor noble whose only real claim to glory was his family's distant vineyard in Burgundy and a crumbling château there. He was bad with money and desperate to be admitted to court. The former made the latter unlikely. The Marquis was also desperate to have another child, as he was disappointed with the daughter the Marquise,

Michelle-Françoise, had provided him with, something she re-fused to take any blame. Indeed, how could a man so miserable at making love be expected to produce male heirs?

This was all according to his wife, who was quite ready to excoriate his reputation to her new chambermaid within the first few days of my employment with her. Michelle-Françoise was a fourth daughter of a great house and deeply annoyed to have her considerable dowry wasted on a man who could not even maneuver them into court. I learned, after many weeks, that it was not just bad fortune that kept the de Termes family from court; the Marquis's father and grandfather had been on the wrong side of the Fronde as well.

"Idiots, all of them," the Marquise sighed as I prepared her gown for one fall evening. The windows of the manor were open to let in the fresh air that had been rinsed by the early fall rains. "Never was there a more foolish cause than that uprising. We are not England!"

"What does England have to do with the Fronde?" I asked in interest. I knew that the English had restored their king to the throne after he had lived for many years in Paris, thanks to Louis's charity.

"They cut off their king's head and let their parliament rule," the Marquise lamented as I helped her into her yellow overskirt and tied it at the back. "It was the Parlement of Paris that started the troubles. My father-in-law was one of those greedy fools who resented the power Cardinal Mazarin asserted on behalf of the young king."

"By power, you mean taxes," I asked carefully as I fetched the bodice of the dress, which was embroidered on the front with flowers and birds.

"They thought their names and their army's success gave them the right to rule," Michelle-Françoise answered. "They were wrong. They drove the King and his family away, but God granted Mazarin and Queen Anne aid from Spain. And the rebellion was crushed at last."

"Did you see any of the fighting?" I was truly curious. I had been in the country for much of the conflict, far off from the battles and danger.

"I was here when the Prince of Condé took Paris under siege," the Marquise answered with a shiver. "And when the King's own cousin, La Grande Mademoiselle, started firing cannons from the Bastille."

"I've heard about her. Anne Marie Louise d'Orléans." I uttered the name like a spell. "Is she the Duchesse d'Orléans now?"

"No, that title awaits whoever has the misfortune of marrying the King's brother, who is always the Duc d'Orléans," the Marquise corrected gently. "But Anne Marie will be *Mademoiselle* until the new Duke has a daughter. She's not made many friends at court since she returned from exile, that one."

"Really?" I cinched the laces of the bodice, flattening the front of my mistress's chest, so that she had to sit straight and stiff at her vanity when I began to add more pins to her hair.

"She was not invited to Louis's wedding to the Infanta and tried to sneak in! I'll ask Madame Sévigné at supper tonight," my mistress went on as I arranged her curls. "She's always good for gossip, if nothing else, and I have heard the Comtesse de Soissons will be there."

"She's one of the Mazarinettes, is she not?" I asked as I pinned another one of my mistress's curls carefully in place. The vivacious nieces of the great Cardinal Mazarin were as good as princesses, it was said, given that their uncle had, along with Queen Anne, practically ruled the country for over a decade while Louis was a child.

"Yes, the second one, and the most ambitious. Poor Cardinal Mazarin. He did such valiant work to secure the King's marriage. Now, the rumor is that he's taken to his bed with exhaustion that cannot be cured," the Marquise sighed.

"I'm sure the doctors are helping him along," I muttered, and my mistress turned to me in shock. "I'm sorry, Madame. I don't trust the fancy doctors. They killed my father."

The Marquise narrowed her eyes at me. "Bled him to death, I assume?"

My mind flashed back to a miserable, dark room that smelled of death, listening to the priest give last rites while I sobbed and begged the doctors to stop making it worse. "He could barely speak when he died, he was so weak from their cures."

"I hear that Mazarin has the best doctor in Paris," my mistress said slowly. "And all he prescribes for the poor man are enemas and emetics. That means water up his ass and potions to make him shit himself. All that, along with the bleeding."

"None of those cures have ever sounded very healthful to me."

"God save us from the men trying to heal us, then," my mistress sighed. "Once I'm done here, you're free for the evening. I shan't be back until well past midnight. I'd stay later, but we must make appearances at the All-Saints Mass tomorrow."

"Thank you, Madame. I'll make sure to be back by then."

The nights when my new mistress dined out with friends were the best time to slip away for a few hours to Lapère's house to dine and learn and practice small charms and palm reading. And, when we could slip away, to lose myself in Veronique's body. It was always too brief, but I knew it was temporary. My cards told me so.

"Would you like me to prepare you in any other way for dinner?" I asked carefully as I finished with the hairstyle and hooked on the Marquise's pearls. She looked over her shoulder and gave me a wicked smile.

"Of course."

I retrieved my cards from the little cabinet where I slept. I shuffled the cards, thinking how impressed Catherine had been a week ago when I had brought them to Lapère's – at first. In the end, she had declared fortune telling with the cards was too accurate. It was better to use a client's hand or something like a glass of water because, in her mind, the less the client could discern themselves, the better chance a reader had of telling them what they needed to hear to keep coming back.

The way my new employer had become instantly reliant on my readings made me beg to differ, but I kept that to myself. The cards felt like a secret between me and my ghosts, one I didn't need to share with other witches.

"Cut," I ordered, putting the cards before the Marquise, and she obeyed. I drew the first card: the Two of Batons. "Someone at dinner is, perhaps, beginning a new business or endeavor of some sort."

"I'll have to keep my idiot husband from investing," the Marquise muttered.

I drew another card: The Seven of Cups. "This means that someone has almost too much, so many options they can't decide…" My mistress nodded and I pulled a final card, this one upside down. "The Queen of Cups, reversed. Someone is jealous…"

"That will be the Comtesse de Soissons. She's still mad that her illustrious uncle didn't marry one of them off to the King. As if Louis would have married that Italian slag when he could have the Infanta of Spain!" The Marquise laughed. "Of course, you must know the real reason that he wasn't allowed to marry a Mazarinette."

"I don't," I replied, putting the cards away in my pocket as I straightened my lady's gown one more time. She was using the tone reserved for her most salacious gossip.

"Some say Mazarin is the King's real father," the Marquise whispered. "Queen Anne spent years trying to conceive with the old king. No one thought a child would come. Mazarin enters the picture; then, like a miracle, Louis the God-given arrives, healthy and perfect!"

"That would be quite the scandal," I whispered back, grinning at the idea. "But it can't be. The King is chosen by God. He's so glorious."

"Glory doesn't come from blood, it comes from power," the Marquise replied, somewhat bitterly. "Perhaps one day soon, we'll be back at court and I'll be able to judge for myself."

"I hope so," I said genuinely. There was nothing I wanted more for my new employers than for them to rise in the ranks. My small exposure to them, to the world of salons and grand entertainments and the politics of court had enthralled me as completely as the magical secrets of Lapère's garden. I knew with the utmost faith that the latter could help me grow closer to the former.

T ONIGHT, THE PATH TOOK me back to the Court of Miracles with Marie Vigoreaux beside me, gossiping about Catherine's latest schemes and how, to our shock, her bid to set up a regular business selling fortunes and a few charms on the side had begun to bear fruit, albeit slowly. Maybe she had worked her own magic under the moon that night with de Couret.

"She says de Couret has a priest he's met who offers to bless certain objects for her or pass them under the communion cup to imbue her sachets with extra power," Marie told me with a laugh. "She can charge a lot for blasphemy, if she finds a client brave enough to ask for it."

"What about her plan to secure herself a rich husband to finance her endeavors?" I asked back. Two weeks ago, Catherine had latched onto the idea that she could not succeed in her plans without some man to support her, or at least house her. "Have her love spells not worked?"

"Oh, you know she gets love from several men, in several positions," Marie cackled. "But that's not the same as a husband who will support her."

"Like yours supports you?" Marie rarely spoke of the man who had given her his name, and whose child she had borne and lost.

"You mean my tailor who won't repair my own torn skirts?" Marie sighed. "He has his own interests and perversions. I don't care. It keeps his cock out of me most of the time."

I didn't press the issue. Soon enough, we arrived at Lapère's house. The moment I stepped inside, I felt that something was different. The table was set for supper, but with more places than usual.

"Who else is coming?" I asked as Lapère turned from stirring a large pot of stew over the fire.

"My husband, I hope, and whatever other guests he brings," Lapère said with a sad smile as Veronique came down the narrow stairs. I looked between her and Lapère in confusion.

"Your husband?" I stammered. I had thought her husband was long dead.

"It's All Hallows, Claude," Veronique explained calmly. "This is a dumb supper, where we invite the dead to join us on this night, when they are close."

"I knew you could find some way to shut Catherine up," Marie chuckled, but the idea had shut me up too.

I'd heard of dumb suppers, especially when we passed through Brittany, but never been to one. The idea of sitting down for an entirely silent meal with the dead, who were provided their own portions and places at the table, made me shiver instinctually.

"Oh, is the novice scared of ghosts?" It was Catherine who had entered and spoken, seeing how I had gone pale.

Veronique came to my side and took my hand. "I recall you refusing to gather graveyard dirt a few months ago out of fear that a restless soul would follow you home, Catherine," she snapped.

"No more arguing, girls," Lapère said and gestured for us to sit.

The silence began. We broke the bread that Catherine had brought, and Lapère ladled the rich stew into our bowls. It was beef, something she usually couldn't afford, but this was a special evening.

With none of the usual conversation, my eyes drifted to the empty places at the table, one beside each of us, as if we could bring our dead to the gathering. I closed my eyes as I ate, trying to feel if they were there. I did feel *something*. As if someone was standing at the door, or watching from beside me: that creeping sense of being seen by someone outside of your vision. It wasn't dangerous. There was no pit in my stomach or shivers like I felt walking by a churchyard at night.

It felt more like being inside the church in the quiet moments between Masses, when the building was full of whispers and echoed with safety. I had been a child when my father had taken me to the Cathedral at Aix-en-Provence, one of the great gothic cousins to Paris's Notre Dame. The light through the stained glass had been magic to my young eyes, and I had felt seen and safe with him holding me up high. His hands had been strong and stable. He had smelled of lavender and musk.

The taste of salty tears mingled with my bread.

I looked up from my food to see that the faces of the women around me were equally somber, some with eyes closed, others with a distant, loving look. We continued in silence for the entire meal, remembering, as the dead sat beside us. In the end, like a wind through the door, I felt love like a breeze against my skin, reaching out to me with regret and pride.

After supper, I disappeared upstairs with Veronique, not caring what the others might think or say. We were all witches together, blasphemers, and sinners in the eyes of the same men who would call what Veronique and I did a crime. They dared not judge us for our passions any more than they judged themselves.

Still, my lover and I were quiet and quick as we held each other in the dark, bodies shaking as we kissed and caressed. She made me come with her fingers and I bit down on the rough linen of her shirt to stifle my cries before I paid her the same attention.

What mattered even more than the pleasure was holding her after in the small, stuffy space where she slept. Holding her and thinking of the strange supper we had shared.

"Did you think of your mother tonight?" I asked softly, my head against my lover's breast.

"Yes," she whispered back, as if she might weep again. "Who did you think of?"

"My father. He died twelve years ago," I replied. "I miss him every day."

"Do you think he'd be proud of you?" Veronique asked thoughtfully. "I wonder if my mother would be proud of me throwing myself into the craft that cost her life. And being with someone who—"

"Is equally as sinful?" I asked, and Veronique looked askance at me when I chuckled. "I think my father would be glad to know that, for the first time in years, perhaps for the first time since he left me, I'm truly happy. I've found my path and I have you. What parent would not want joy and progress for their child?"

"Is that why you still have not spoken to your mother after a month apart?" Veronique replied, and I sat up in consternation. I made the choice not to talk about my mother, just as I had made the choice not to visit her. I had no idea how she was coping with life on her own and I refused to care.

"I should have said what *decent* parent would not want those things for their child," I muttered. "My mother probably hasn't noticed I'm gone."

"I doubt that," Veronique chided. "More likely she's worried sick that you left without a word."

I laughed at that. "She's worried I left without leaving money. If I'm lucky, she's run off to—" I couldn't even say it. There it was again, that horrible black pit, swallowing up my words, erasing my memories so I would not have to relive them. "Someone else who she can burden."

"What if something's happened to her? Or she thinks something has happened to you and doesn't know you're alright?"

"Why do you care?" I snapped back, ire rising. "I left her behind for a reason."

"It's never as easy as that, Claude, you know that." Veronique looked as pitiful as she did beautiful with her mussed hair and clothes askew. But for the first time, I was less attracted to her charms than I was angered by her foolishly kind words. "You're lucky to have a parent alive."

I laughed again. "Not this one."

"You should forgive her, for whatever offences she's caused you," Veronique offered, and when I looked at her, her eyes were wide and kind. "You don't know what she's suffered. I can't bear to think of how you might feel if something – if something happened to her and she went to her grave thinking you hated her. Asking forgiveness of a ghost on a night like this is not a substitute for finding it in life."

"You think I have to ask for *her* forgiveness?" I bit back, my rage breaking the dam. Had she heard nothing? "She should be on her knees, begging mine!"

"Maybe she would be if you'd bother to speak with her!" Veronique protested. How could the woman who I'd sinned with look so innocent when she spoke? "It's been over a month, you have to talk to her!"

"I don't want to talk about this anymore," I declared. Veronique did not understand. No one could understand.

I didn't look back as I rushed down the stairs and into Lapère's parlor. Marie and Catherine were still there, huddled in conversation over a jar of salve. "What's that?" I demanded, noting that Lapère was standing to the sides, looking worried.

"It's something a young practitioner should be careful with," Lapère sighed pointedly. "It's a balm of various ingredients – which I won't share the names of – that can help a soul into a journey beyond the body."

"It's flying ointment," Veronique darkly said from behind me. "It's dangerous stuff. Why do you have it out?" I felt her glaring disapprovingly into the back of my head.

"Because these ninnies were talking about that idiot conjurer de Couret offering them some," Lapère sighed. "I was telling Marie it's dangerous for anyone nursing. You don't want anything in there to pass on in the milk."

"We don't know that for sure," Catherine argued, but Lapère took back the ointment. "Come on, Madame, tonight is supposed to be the best for scrying and peering into the beyond!"

"If I thought you were actually interested in what you might see there, I'd consider it, but for now, you should be safe," Lapère said and set the jar back in its place.

"I look. I see more than you could ever know, Madame," Catherine said grimly, watching as Lapère walked away. Lapère's eyes were on the fire, so she did not see when I took the jar. I had no doubt that she knew I pocketed it, but I did not care. I was tired of being told to be correct and cautious.

"Marie, we need to get home before it's late. The Marquise will be eager for me to help undress her, and little Françoise gets hungry at midnight," I said, walking pointedly to the door. "Catherine, walk with us."

I didn't bid Veronique adieu, and I kept my back straight as I left the house, trusting my friends to follow.

"Well, that was abrupt," Catherine huffed. "What are you—" She stopped as I held up the jar, then grinned.

We scurried to the de Termes house and slipped inside the dark kitchen. Marie and Catherine took the flying ointment from me, and I rushed to work. I barely made it to the Marquise in time to meet her when she stumbled in. I had to practically catch her in the front hall and help her into bed, making sure to remove her jewels and stays before she tumbled into bed and immediately began to snore. Evenings with her husband always made her drink.

I, on the other hand, was not tired at all. I crept down to the servants' quarters and Marie's tiny room. I was not shocked that my fellow witches had started without me, but I was shocked by the state in which I found them.

Catherine and Marie were nearly naked, most of their clothes discarded on the floor. Marie was sprawled on her bed, arms akimbo and eyes half-closed, muttering to herself and stroking her glistening breasts and abdomen lazily. Catherine was leaning precariously on the wall, the little pot of ointment in hand. She swayed as she saw me.

"Claude, is that you?" Catherine called, loud enough to wake the other servants. I seized her, covering her mouth as I did, only to see that her pupils were so wide I could barely see the irises.

"Claude?" Marie asked distantly. "Give her some. Let her fly too."

Catherine giggled into my palm, pulling me with her as the door closed behind us. "Yes, good," she sighed when I let her go. "Join us. It's beautiful, Claude. I can see them all. Take off those rags and join in."

It would have been the right and upstanding thing to leave. I could see Lapère and Veronique scowling at me in my mind, warning me to be careful and not toy with things I did not understand. Maybe this was something else Veronique could never understand herself because she was too afraid. Well, I had left my mother's house to be free, and I would not let someone else control me in turn.

I stripped down to my chemise and Catherine handed me the pot of ointment, her body undulating as she did so, her eyes looking past me. "Rub it under your arms or neck… Anywhere the skin is thin…"

"Put it in your cunt," Marie interjected, and I looked over to see her greased hand working between her legs, her hips squirming. "It feels so good there."

I dipped my finger in the salve of fat and beeswax then rubbed a glob under one arm and then the next. Then over my breasts and chest, because Marie was right. It did feel good. It felt good to touch. Catherine was next to me and she was warm, and the ointment smelled like green things and melted in her hands and she rubbed more on me.

"You need more," she giggled and pressed my fingers into my cunt with hers. It made me groan and I shuddered. I liked this. It tingled and warmed me. It made the flickering candlelight softer.

No. Brighter. And the shadows… They were dancing.

"Can you hear them?" Catherine asked from where she had collapsed beside me, her hands trailing over me. When did I sit down? "The shadows. They're talking."

"They're singing," Marie moaned. "Oh, they're calling us and singing. Summoning."

I wanted to laugh and say they were mad. But I could hear them too.

Whispered songs, calling through the night, lifting me up by my arms. The spirits and shadows and demons wanted me to dance with them and I wanted to join.

So I did.

We did. We joined the circle and danced. I swayed to the beat of the distant drums, my body echoing their rhythm as hands moved over me. In me. Were they mine? Were they the shadows? There were fingers deep in my cunt, wet with the ointment and my arousal, and yet, I was dancing still. My fingers were somewhere like velvet and it shuddered. I felt like I was coming, but it was so very different from earlier tonight. The pleasure peaked and I cried out and became the song.

I left my body behind and the dance of ecstasy would not end. I flew.

I floated through the sky, high above Paris. I could see the towers of Notre Dame and the fortress of the Château de Vincennes and the curve of the Seine. I was above the clouds, racing under the moon with a cavalcade of other untethered spirits around me, all bound for the same place. A circle. It was a circle. Someone was holding my hand tight as we danced around a fire that was also Marie's little candle, and my soul and body sang, and I dreamed. My body moved as if I was being fucked and flung about by the shadows and I came apart.

I saw the stars, whispering and singing to me. I saw lovers tangled together, rutting in the dirt. I saw tall shadows crowned with antlers. I smelled blood and earth and touched the dirt and trees. I heard the drums and I saw a light. I rushed down the path into the woods to chase it. Woods far from Paris, to the west and the setting sun. My path. I had found it.

My mother was there. Not my mother as she was, but as she should have been, beatific at the base of a tree where I suckled her breast and tasted her sweet milk. She laughed and called me greedy. I was, because I was full and ecstatic. My father was there too, his body becoming one with the ground and rotting away, mushrooms for eyes and moss for his beard. I screamed but it was muffled. There was a hand over my mouth, pulling me away. A calloused hand I knew that made me want to scream all the more.

"Don't take her." Was that Catherine's voice? Was it her putting a knife into my hand? The darkness was pulling me down. "Fight him, Claude."

I stabbed the darkness. Again and again. My knife slipped into the heart of the horrible thing and blood drenched me, hot and slick, and I laughed. I ran again, naked and free and flying, following the light of the star that became the moon and then the sun... The glorious, blazing sun was so bright.

It blinded me.

It burnt me.

It turned me to grateful ashes, and the winds swept me into oblivion.

THANK GOD FOR THE rooster the cook kept. The mangy thing started screeching before anyone else in the house stirred and could find me and Catherine splayed naked on Marie Vigoreaux's dusty floor. We were entangled, as Veronique and I had been so many times, and my cheeks burned to think what we might have done last night. My thighs and womb ached as if I had spent the night in ecstasy...

I grabbed my clothes as the others stirred and rushed back to my room, my head still spinning from the journey my spirit had

taken the night before. I wondered what the others had seen and
what the strange visions I had experienced meant.

I washed myself in the basin, taking care to clear all the remaining oil from my skin, and brushed the dirt from my hair. I
thought all the while about what I had seen. Veronique would
be a better interpreter than anyone else, save Lapère, but I didn't
want to tell them what we had done. Not a moment of it. It was
all shameful, was it not?

I shook my head. I was my own woman, finally free of my
mother's control, and yet here I was, worrying again about
disappointing someone else. Someone I loved. But she would
frown at me to hear I had done something so dangerous, that
I had dreamed ecstatically of blood. Not to mention waking up
next to others in such a state.

Veronique and I had made no promises to one another. We
did not even speak of what we were or whisper words of love.
To define our trysts or name our love affair would be like casting
molten gold into a mold, taking something radiant and exciting
and untouchable and rendering it into a thing that could be stolen
and broken.

I pulled out my cards for answers.

Two of Swords: blindness. Four of Cups: refusal of the gifts
before you. And The Tower. I had drawn that card several times
in the last week, and I had always interpreted it as a reassurance
that my time with this destitute Marquis and his petty wife was
limited, and that soon enough, I would find a way upward to a
better position. But now, with these other cards and the visions
of the night before, I could not help but grow cold. Something
was coming that I was trying to ignore.

B ECAUSE I DID NOT want to look at my future any more than
I wanted a confrontation with Veronique, I threw myself
into my work. For a week, I attended to my mistress carefully,
not leaving the house for several days, and I avoided my friends.
I had exchanged one awkward look with Marie when she had
brought the Marquise's little daughter in for a visit, but we had
not spoken of flying together, and I had no idea where the others
of my circle were for a few days until I came to the kitchen for
supper and found Catherine there, grinning, next to Marie.

"I found him," Catherine declared, grabbing my hand and
pulling me to their place by the huge stone ovens where the
manor's bread and food were baked. "Just like I saw that I would."

"Found who?" I asked, lost.

"You'd know if you'd bothered to talk to me, silly girl," Marie
chided. "Catherine had a vision *that night*: of a husband wreathed
in jewels."

"And I've found him. Antoine Monvoisin," Catherine grinned.
"He's a jeweler and merchant. Richer than anyone in my family
has ever dreamed of being!"

"And he's asked you to marry him?" I gasped. "After a week?"

"Of course not, you ninny," Catherine sighed. "But he will.
I'm going to let him think he's seduced me, show him a night
like he's never dreamed of, then insist he marry me to preserve
my virtue. If I'm lucky, I'll have a babe in my belly by then too."

"That's—" I didn't have the words. I knew Catherine was ambitious, but enough to ensnare a man so ruthlessly? Last I had seen her, it had been waking up next to her after a night of things I half-recalled. Things Veronique could not know about.

"He's a good Christian. He'll fall for it. I'll have to start going to Mass with him every day, and won't that be a good place to make friends who need some guidance from a proper *Madame*." Catherine let out a giggle.

"You have it all planned out," I said. "All from what you saw that night. It's beginning to come true."

"I saw a house, a grand one, with lines of ladies out the door," Vigoreaux interjected. "As if I was flying above them, and then, they were dumping gold into my lap. I was drowning in it."

"That doesn't worry you, the drowning?" I asked, memories of how I had felt that blood on my hands coming back and making me shiver. "Catherine, was what you saw good?"

"He chained me with gold, the man I saw," Catherine grinned. "Choked me with it until I was in ecstasy, but I slipped out from him and took to the skies. Like a phoenix, wreathed in fire. What could that mean but glory?"

"Doom?" I scoffed. "I saw things too."

"Don't be such a worrywart," Catherine said, waving away my concerns. "You partook of that blessing with us, if I recall correctly."

"Do you not remember?" I scoffed. In the week since, fragments had come back from that night, visions of bodies twisted together that made me dizzy. Not just with the magic, but with a strange, dangerous desire for more.

"Oh, I remember a very good night," Catherine said with a wink to me, licking her lips. "You give yourself to that power that showed us those things and you'll see your rewards too. You need to stand up and take them. And come back to Lapère soon. She's been fussing and worrying. So has your Veronique. She's been unbearable."

That made me blanch. "She's not—"

"We haven't told her about what we did," Marie said, taking my hand reassuringly. "And we won't. What happened is a secret for the three of us alone."

"I'll come soon," I muttered. It made my heart warm that Veronique was worried for me, though it felt wrong to keep a magical secret.

"Claude," came the voice of a valet, echoing with annoyance. Had he heard us speaking of magic? Was I doomed? "The mistress wishes to see you."

"Isn't she taking a visit from her friend?" I asked back.

"She said to bring you to her. There's something she wants to show Madame Colbert."

I looked between my friends, who nodded for me to move. "Go, little Claude," Catherine whispered. "Seize your destiny."

I smiled at the idea despite myself. If I was to be dismissed or disciplined, my mistress would not do it in front of a guest. Perhaps she wanted to refer me to Madame Colbert's service. I knew that this social call had been quite a coup for the de Termes family, as Colbert was married to an important man in the government. The Marquise had sneered to me privately that the husband was a *noblesse de robe* – from a family who had bought their titles and positions in the government, rather than a *noblesse d'épée* like the Marquis and Marquise who came from ancient lineages – and much less money.

I entered the salon, by far the finest in the house. It was hung with tapestries and furnished with handsome chairs and delicate candelabras, as well as a gilded fireplace. All of this made the space warm and inviting as the November rains dripped outside the window. I gave a curtsey to my mistress and Madame Colbert, unsure of if I should speak.

"Ah, Claude, you have not met Madame Colbert, the Marquise of Seignelay," my Marquise smiled, her tone tense. She was trying very hard to impress the woman, going so far as to use the title her husband had bought for them.

"It is an honor, Madame," I said, curtseying again. "How can I assist you?"

"Your mistress and I were just enjoying a game of cards," Madame Colbert said, indicating the fine deck laid out on the table between them. "And, of course, discussing our interests throughout society. And my dear Marquise de Termes let slip she has a maid that can use such cards to uncover secrets."

Heart pounding, I looked between Madame Colbert and my mistress, who gave an encouraging nod. "Yes, Madame, I can read cards. Palms too. Though I'm better with cards."

"Oh, what a delight!" Madame Colbert cried. She snapped for the valet and signaled for him to bring a seat for me, and I blushed. It was a high honor to be allowed to sit in the presence of those so far above me in rank. I took my place at the inlaid table and the cards were thrust into my hands. They had the same familiar pictures I knew so well and the colorful images were a comfort. "Now, tell me everyone's secrets!"

"I don't know about *everyone*," I stammered as I began to shuffle the cards. "Here. Cut them how you like and then put them back together." Madame Colbert did as she was told and I drew the first card, hand shaking. My mistress was watching me like a hawk, and I felt like a mouse, hoping to avoid death in her claws.

"The Knight of Coins," I said as I looked at the painted image of a man on a horse, holding a green club, a single coin set in the sky like the sun. "You know a man who's involved with money…"

She had to know I was using the knowledge I already had of her husband, for she looked unimpressed. I drew another card and set it on the table.

"Coins again. The Five of Coins," I said hesitantly. "This means greed. Keeping money to oneself." Madame Colbert's eyes narrowed further and I drew yet another card. "Seven of Swords. Someone cunning and dishonest."

"What are you implying, Claude?" my mistress laughed nervously. My heart beating in my ears, I pulled another card and looked at it without showing the other women. Instead, I took Madame Colbert's hand and looked at the lines of her palm, letting the world whisper to me as Lapère had tried to teach me.

"I don't speak of your husband, my Lady," I murmured, letting words flow through me. "He is honest, but someone above him is not. They are hiding something. Money, perhaps. Hiding it from the—" Madame Colbert was pale and staring at me as I turned over the final card: an upside-down Emperor. "From the King."

"I knew it," Madame Colbert hissed. "Fucking Fouquet and his Cardinal."

"Everyone knows Mazarin has been enriching himself for years," my mistress laughed. "But Monsieur Fouquet? Really?"

"Oh, I'm sure of it, and your little sorceress confirms it!" Madame Colbert crowed. "Thank you, Claude. Here, for your troubles." She drew a purse from within her skirts and gave me several of the coins within.

"You may go," my mistress said with a genuine smile, and I obeyed. "Do you really think that—" The door closed behind me before I could hear the rest. It didn't matter. I had done it – served my mistress and endeared myself to a powerful woman.

I rushed to my room, head buzzing with possibilities of what could be next. Catherine and Marie had always said that it was among the nobles that the most money could be made, and they were right. I had more coins hidden in my room now than from a month's wages! It was only the start – as long as I could tell my mistress and her friends what they wanted to hear. Would I be able to help them too?

I shivered to think of Veronique's warning about doing spells one could not guarantee, but she was so idealistic. It was why I was so in love with her, but were her ideals mine? Could I follow the morals of someone who did not understand why someone like me would do anything to climb out of the muck and mire? Who did not understand my scars?

I WAS UNEASY THE next day. I had expected to sleep well, happy with the possibilities the future held. But dreams had tormented me – dark dreams of knives in the dark and muffled screams. I had awoken with the sense of being watched, a familiar terror of what might happen if I turned my back. I pushed the fear away and the thoughts it inspired. I was being irrational. I was safe. No one could find me here.

All day, I was distracted as the feeling grew. Lapère would tell me to listen to my intuition, to hear what Our Lady whispered. But what if the message was doom? My mind was still spinning that evening when I ate my supper in the kitchen, deaf to the gossip of the other servants around as I chewed my cold bread.

"Claude!" I jumped as someone pushed me and (apparently) repeated my name.

"What?" I demanded of the cook who had called me.

"Your friend is in the courtyard!" the cook sighed.

I looked out the door to the servant's yard and saw, to my shock and deep relief, Veronique. This was what had been coming. She looked grave, wrapped in her shawl to keep off the rain, but still a beautiful sight. I had missed her.

I rushed to her, pulling her with me to a secluded corner of the yard, under an overhang, chickens pecking at the worms around our feet.

"What are you doing here?" I asked, fear rising as I noted other servants peering at us from the kitchen. They were gossips, all of them, and I would not give them more fodder. This job meant too much to me.

"I haven't seen you since All Hallows! I've been worried," Veronique said, looking downward. "I didn't mean to drive you off like that."

"I haven't been driven off," I sighed. "I just needed time on my own. You don't know how it hurt me that you couldn't understand what my mother has done to me."

"Whatever it is, I know you can forgive her," Veronique said pitifully, and I grabbed my hand away as she reached for me.

"Did you not hear me?" I cried, wrenching myself away. Why could she not understand that my mother had poisoned anything between us so long ago?

"Claude, she cares for you. She's been looking for you!" Veronique burst out, and fear exploded in my gut.

"How do you know that?"

"I heard that a woman had been asking after you in the Court of Miracles and I found her the other day," Veronique confessed, ignorant to how I had begun to shake. "Claude, she at least deserves to know where you are."

"Did you tell her?" I demanded, mouth dry, mind racing. "Did you tell her where to find me?"

"Of course I did! She's your family, Claude."

"Family are the ones who protect you!" I cried. "You've damned me!"

"Don't be so dramatic. She was worried," Veronique sighed. She was still lost in her ideals and I could not bear to look at her.

"All she wants is my wages to gamble away. Unless..." I couldn't comprehend it. Fury whited out my vision as I ran inside, leaving Veronique to gape after me.

"Claude, what's happened?" I think it was Marie who asked it as I rushed up the servants' stairs to hide in my little room – the one place that had been mine for the first time in *years* – and try to regain my breath.

It would be alright. It had to be, didn't it? My mother would not dare come begging at a fine house, demanding my attention and money. Would she?

"I think she must be in here," came a voice on the other side of the door. The Marquis de Termes's voice, and there were steps behind him.

"Roger, this is my private room. Surely we don't need to let people in here, especially peasants," the Marquise said. I wanted to hide. I wanted to scream. There was no way out...

"There you are!"

The door flew open, and my mistress was there with her husband beside her, looking concerned.

"Claude, please come out: your parents are here to see you and speak with us. You've been dishonest," the Marquis said, and I stumbled forward, looking at the two faces behind him in utter despair and horror.

My mother looked smug and satisfied, but it was not her face that made me cower. It was the man who loomed beside her, the face of all my terror, the one that sent that black, screaming void inside me into utter panic. My stepfather. The nightmare I thought I had escaped made flesh.

CHAPTER 7
THE DEVIL

H E WAS SMILING KINDLY, like always. Everyone who met Giles Faviot remarked on that smile and what a kind, soft-spoken man he was. Often, they would wonder how he came to be married to a harpy like my mother, but then speak of what a charitable thing it had been for him to take on a widow and her daughter. None of them suspected what he had done to that daughter.

"Claude," he cooed when I stumbled into the room. "You look well, thanks be to God. We have been so worried for you – your mother and I."

"So these are your parents, Claude?" the Marquis asked, and I knew the recognition and worry on my face would make it impossible to lie.

"Yes," I whispered.

"Of course we are, and we're so relieved to have found our daughter," my mother said, drawing on all her experience as an actress to sound close to tears. "We have been looking for her for weeks."

"We did not know she had family," the Marquise said, drawing closer to me. For the first time, I was truly grateful for the way she always needed to be on the opposite side of an issue from her husband. "And she has been of great service in this position."

"Of course; she is a good, obedient girl," my stepfather said, and it made my stomach turn. Monsieur Faviot looked humble and contrite. His hair was long and pale, in contrast to his brown coat and hat in his hand.

"When she chooses to be," my mother hissed. "Not so much when she disappears without a word to her family or her previous employer."

"If you mean to disgrace her by revealing she worked at a theater, we know this," Madame de Termes sneered.

My stepfather shook his head kindly. "No, of course not. We are happy to allow her to continue her work here."

My heart leapt.

"Continue? As if you have the right to stop her?" My mistress scoffed and her husband sent her a glare.

"They do, dear wife," the Marquis snapped. "Or he does. He is her father—"

"Stepfather!" I cried before I could stop myself.

The Marquis advanced on me with a face like thunder. He did not like to be interrupted or reminded of any instance when he was wrong. "You are old enough to know the law, girl. This man is your only male relative by marriage, and therefore, all your property is his. Not your own."

Rage like fire sparked inside me and I opened my mouth to protest the base injustice of it all.

"Don't speak," Roger de Termes admonished. "It is to him we must pay your wages – if we continue to pay them. What she has done by lying about this is tantamount to theft."

"What?" I yelped. "No! I didn't lie. That's my money!"

The Marquis's slap was sharp and controlled. He could have done much worse and I knew it. Even so, his wife gasped and pulled me back.

"Roger! Claude is not to blame here. She surely had reasons to conceal that she had family." The Marquise forced me to look into her eyes, begging me silently to confess why I had lied. But what was the point? I was a daughter and thus a *possession* of the man who stood in place of my father. All I could do was let her see the tears that began to fill my eyes and my unspoken plea for protection. I saw her heart break for me.

"Monsieur Le Marquis," my stepfather began, obsequious and gentle. "We beg of you to keep Claude in your service as well as you can. I have been ill of late and just returned from work in the country, needing the care of my family."

Lies. All lies. He had been waiting for my mother to break and open our house back to him so he could return to the horrible way things were before, in Lyon.

"You need the money, is what you mean," the Marquis drawled, unimpressed. "And it seems my wife has grown attached to this creature."

"As I told you, Monsieur Le Marquis, Claude is a good girl, just misguided. We ask only that she stay with us at home as many nights as she can manage, to help my poor wife in maintaining the house when she can."

"Fine. Take her now," the Marquis said before I could protest or scream. My mother seized me, squeezing my arm so hard it would bruise, and dragged me away from the Marquise. For her part, my mistress looked sad to see me go.

"Have her back by ten tomorrow. I need to be dressed," the Marquise called after us, a glimmer of hope as I was hauled out to the street and towards my doom. I had been abandoned by my mistress and thrown into fresh horrors with no protection from *Our Lady*. I had been betrayed by the one I loved.

I waited to weep until I was out of sight of the house, turning to my mother with a sob. "How can you do this? You horrible, greedy woman."

She raised her hand to strike me as the Marquis had done, but my stepfather caught her hand. "Alix, compose yourself!" he admonished, gentle as ever. "And let go, you're hurting the poor child." He stepped in between us, pulling me from my mother's grasp with the gentlest of touches and taking my hand in his.

He was a candlemaker by trade, my stepfather, and the work had left his hands with the strangest of textures, rough in some places and burned to smooth nothingness in others. I knew those hands so well, and even though I had pushed so many memories into that black abyss inside me, I could not forget those hands and how they felt on my skin. They called all those other memories up from the dark and I wanted to scream right there on the street.

Instead, I froze. I went limp and compliant as I always had before. I was no longer Claude the maid or the witch. I was a coward.

"There you go, coddling your precious little Claude like always, as if I'm not the one you married," my mother said. "Go ahead and forgive her! Pretend she didn't nearly *ruin me*."

"You should apologize to your mother for the disrespect you have shown her, Claude," my stepfather reprimanded. I wonder if Veronique had wanted me to apologize too. Had she known what she had brought upon me? Would she grovel to me when she found out? "Claude, did you hear me?"

Obey. Do as you're told and it will all be over quickly. That was the only thing I knew how to do when his grip tightened on my wrists. "I'm sorry, Mother. I was wrong to try to hide away," I muttered numbly.

"That's a good girl."

I pushed down a wave of nausea at those words and spoke no more as we made the trek from the Marais to our house. To another prison. Seven years ago, when I was barely sixteen, we had come to a place like this in Lyon, and for a few brief moments, I had thought it was a fresh start. We were in a bustling, cosmopolitan city, and while I was sad to leave the convent where I had spent the last few years, it was an exciting place. The man my mother had married had been so kind and complimentary to me when we had met weeks before. Surely, he would be a good new father to me…

I had been such an idiot. When I had realized what sort of man Giles Faviot really was, I hadn't run. A fool and a coward, as always. Alone.

We came to the crossroads that would lead us home and I tripped, my knees crashing into the mud, my hands splaying out before me.

"Clumsy," my mother sneered as I looked up from the muck to a small tuft of green. In the wet days of fall, something was growing in this dark little street.

Seek her at the crossroads. The words from months ago echoed in my mind. *She is the green of growing and the black of decay.*

I recognized the herbs in front of me. Lemon balm and tansy. Perhaps the last sprigs of the year. One was excellent for bringing on calm and a deep sleep, the other good for ulcers and rheumatism. But not too much.

"Claude, are you hurt?" my stepfather asked.

"I'm fine, I just saw these and—" I looked at his clear blue eyes, hating the sweetness there. "You said to Madame de Termes you were ill. These herbs here could help, if you let me make them into a tea for you."

"Such a thoughtful girl," he smiled. He did not stop me as I picked them, then helped me up as I tucked my prizes into my apron pocket. I thanked the crossroads and gave a silent prayer in my heart.

The house was even worse than I remembered it. The fire was dead and it looked as if it hadn't been cleaned in weeks. There was no food to be seen on the shelves, but I noted there was a jug of wine. I doubted there was much left.

"Alix, we have these wages from our dear Claude. Go out and buy us some fresh bread," my stepfather instructed, and my panic jumped.

"It's so late, go in the morning!" I protested, and to my relief, my mother didn't argue. That was good. Maybe she knew not to leave me alone with him. "I'll get to work cleaning up, if you don't mind helping."

She did mind, but she didn't complain. Now that we were off the street and she had no audience to play to, my mother was a shadow of herself. She made a weak effort to help me with the fire, bringing wood as I lit it afresh. All the while, my stepfather sat at the table and watched. It was my turn to be an actress now, I reckoned, and so, I smiled at him as I boiled what water we had left from the barrel.

I cleaned and swept and emptied the chamber pots out the window, all while he watched, looking away from the way he smiled when I had to kneel or get on my hands and knees. When it was time, I steeped some of my herbs in the hot water. By then, my mother had already begun to drink, and the look on my stepfather's face had changed.

"You must be tired, Alix," he said to my mother, his eyes on me.

"You both must be," I countered. "Here. This is best drunk before bed."

"When did you become a doctor?" my mother slurred, and I ignored her. My stepfather took the cup graciously and drank deep.

"That's very good. Thank you, Claude." He smiled at me like a wolf sighting its prey.

"I'm tired, and I'll need to wake up early to go out for food." I tried not to let my voice shake. I prayed for the herbs to do their work. Make his eyes droop. Make him yawn.

"Of course, get some rest," my stepfather said.

I went to my little cot under the sloping roof, barely more than a burlap sack of rotten hay. The bed on the other side of the room was not much better. I didn't undress or even wash. I laid down fully dressed, wrapped myself in a blanket, and pretended to sleep.

And I listened. I listened to the creak of the floor as my mother stumbled to the bed. Then, thank heaven, the sound of a yawn, and the scrape of a poker in the fire. Another creak. More footsteps. Then he was in the bed with her.

If the tea had done its work, he would sleep the night through. He wouldn't wake the way he had for so many years. He wouldn't creep across the room and kneel beside me and shake me awake while he covered my mouth.

It had always been important to him that I was awake. I had learned that quickly in those first weeks here. It was never enough to simply touch me; he had to see my eyes when he did it. He had to know I was being quiet because I had been ordered to be so, and because the fear had paralyzed me.

Then, I had stopped being afraid. I had stopped *being* at all. When he came at night, I had gone so deep inside myself that I had felt nothing. I'd been little more than a warm corpse for him to abuse.

I began to shake as the memories from that pit inside me began to rise, creeping across my mind like the monster had done across creaking floorboards for years. He didn't want to let me escape. He didn't want a victim who laid there like a limp doll while he groped me, so it had escalated. He had started finding me at home when my mother was gone. My body recoiled in on itself at the thought, bile rising in my throat.

There was only one such day I had not consigned to the abyss in my mind. The last day, when my mother had come home early and found him with me bent over the table, my skirts raised high...

My mother had called me a whore. She had accused *me* of seduction. She had dragged me out into the street and called me a disgrace, and I had screamed back. She had made me go to a priest and confess my sins. But discovery had been enough for her to drive him away, for a while. Disgrace had driven her from Lyon. In desperation for money, she had joined the acting troupe and we had followed them all over France. Now, her greed and blindness had led him back to us.

Now, I was a prisoner again.

I could run. It was dangerous, but I could. But where would I run to? I could throw myself at the mercy of our good King and be thrown onto the street for impertinence. I had nothing of my own, and anywhere I went – to Marie or Catherine, or even Lapère – they would find me. It would take too long to find work and start again. Unless I truly wished to be a whore, I would starve before I found my way. I was trapped.

I didn't sleep until I heard them both snoring. And even then, it was uneasily, muttering prayers and spells in the dark. *Lady of Darkness, Heavenly Queen, hide me in shadows and keep me unseen.*

I CONSIDERED RUNNING AGAIN when I took coins from my stepfather's purse and went to buy bread in the morning. That was my money, but if they caught me after taking it, I could be arrested. So I came home, before dawn, to find the candles already burning in the twilight.

My mother looked hungover and thunderous. "You little thief," she hissed when I entered, swatting me. "Thought you could take our silver and run off."

"I was buying you food!" I cried, rushing away.

"Leave her be, Alix." My stepfather's voice was weak. I looked to see that he was rising from bed, bleary-eyed. "She's just doing her duty."

"Do you plan on escorting me to the Marais today? So I can continue to do that duty?" I asked. *Like a prisoner*, silent on my tongue. "I need to be going soon."

"You'll go when you've done your chores. There's barely any water in the barrel. Go take the bucket to get some more," my mother snapped. We drew our water from a fountain far down the street. It was a long, cold walk this time of day, but I would not mind the time away.

"You go, Alix," my stepfather ordered.

My heart froze. "It's not a bother, I can do it," I sputtered.

"You've already done enough, sweet Claude," he countered. My mother squawked in indignation.

"So you want me to break my back while *she*—" The blow to her stomach reduced the insult to a pained grunt and she doubled over. My stepfather looked down at her, his hand still in a fist.

"Claude knows how to obey, Alix. She has remembered, even after you spirited her away. Learn from her. Do as your husband bids you," he said, all kindness gone from his voice. All the strength and bravado were gone from her too. "Go."

My mother rushed from the room and I was left cowering, inching towards the fire. I had almost made it, almost survived...

"You look like you're still feeling unwell," I stammered. "Let me make you more tea."

To my relief, he didn't argue and returned to the bed.

"I will expect you back tonight before the strike of twelve," he said calmly, the frame creaking as he sat, eyes fixed on me. "I know I can trust you to make the journey there and back without getting lost."

There was a threat in those words, and so I nodded. "Yes, Monsieur."

Too soon, the tea was ready, heavier on tansy this time. It would make him ill and tired, but not soon enough. My hands shook as I mixed it; my stomach turned and the fear rose within me.

"Thank you, sweet Claude," he said as I handed him the cup. "Now, come here."

I shuddered as he reached for me, hating the way his hand lingered on my wrist, his patchwork-textured fingers rubbing against my pulse point. "You need to rest. Let the medicine do its work."

"I will, I promise it, my dear, caring nursemaid," he said with a rasping laugh, pulling me closer. "But it's been a while since I've seen you."

"I'm right here," I protested softly.

"You know what I mean, silly girl." His voice was always as sweet as honey in moments like these, as his grip on my wrist tightened enough to be a command. "Let me see you, Claude. Show me how beautiful you are."

His eyes were so clear and bright when I looked up at him, sparkling with the reflection of the candle flames in the twilight. Candles he had made and shaped with those hands. Around those lights was a void. A shivering, buzzing pit of black that I felt closing in around me. "Yes, Monsieur," I whispered.

"Call me Papa," he ordered, and the pit in my stomach merged with the black shadows. My ears hummed, my skin shuddered.

I forgot everything and let the dark take me.

I DON'T KNOW HOW I made it to the de Termes house. I blinked once, and I was walking down the street. Again, and I was in the kitchen. Someone was asking me a question. Who was it? The housekeeper, Madame... I couldn't remember her name. I was standing in front of the fire and the droning noise in my head was still so loud. I was outside of my body, where time could not touch me. Where nothing could touch me.

I reached for the kettle on the fire. Someone cried out, but not before the hot iron seared my fingers.

I gasped as the world whooshed back into focus.

I looked down at the red, throbbing skin, pain grounding me in the now.

"What?" I stammered, looking at the housekeeper.

"I said, are you going to be sick?" Madame Lafarge (yes, that was it) snapped at me. "Or can you do your job and take this tray up to Madame de Termes?"

"I can." I grabbed the tray, the burns on my fingers smarting as I carried it up the servants' stairs.

Madame La Marquise was already awake when I entered, but she was simply lying in her disheveled sheets, staring at the ceiling. "Ah, you made it back," she said numbly.

"I'm sorry. I can go if you're not ready." I didn't even know if she had rung for food or if I had been ordered up.

"I'm ready. It's fine," she sighed and pushed herself up. She was in her dressing gown, no robe. In the mornings, despite how lovely her bed was with its soft sheets and creamy curtains, she always looked so common and normal. No jewels. No silk. Today, she was just another very tired woman whose shit and piss I'd have to carry like anyone else's. "I don't like not having you close at night," she said as I placed her tray of bread and butter beside her.

"I'm so sorry, Madame, if I could stay, I would—"

"My husband prefers not to fuck me when someone can hear," she went on, and I snapped my mouth closed. Was that why she looked so exhausted? "He went to work to bring about a son last night. Miserable business. If I could make his cock shrivel and fall off so I never had to endure that again, I would."

It felt like falling in front of those flowers again, the words were such a shock. And such an opportunity.

"I can't make it fall off, but…" My mistress raised an eyebrow as I began, careful and calculated in my words. "But I know a woman who deals in certain herbs. She could help."

"Is she the one who taught you how to read palms?" Madame de Termes asked, her voice curious and not at all angry. I nodded.

"How much money would she need to make sure my husband never gets it up again?" she asked, her eyes sparkling. "Or would you do it? Can you curse him so that he never has a son?"

"I've never done a curse," I answered honestly, and as I did, I felt my blood grow colder. "But I very much would like to try one, if my lady would allow it."

"I would relish it. Get my purse."

I WAS HALFWAY TO Lapère's when someone grabbed me from behind. I spun, striking out automatically with a cry before I saw it was Marie Vigoreaux who had followed after me, her blonde hair wild and her cheeks flushed.

"For God's sake, Claude, I've been calling your name for three streets!" Marie exclaimed, her eyes wide with concern. I had not bothered to look at myself in my mistress's many mirrors, but I could nearly see my reflection in Marie's eyes and face. I looked awful and felt the same. "What happened?"

"Veronique led my mother right to our door," I confessed. At least Marie had the kindness to look offended. "She came last night – with her husband. They demanded my wages and dragged me home to stay there at night."

"God, I hate men," Marie spat with more venom than I had ever heard from her. "Do you know that my husband demands an accounting of everything I'm paid? I keep nothing I earn from the Marquis. At least he lets me stay out of the damn house."

"At least he doesn't—" I stopped myself before I said it because I didn't know if my barb was true. Monsieur Vigoreaux could very well take his rights as a husband over the protests of his wife, like so many did. "I need to get to Lapère's."

"What for?" Vigoreaux asked.

"I need to do a curse," I said flatly and I was glad when my sister smiled. I felt stronger, with her beside me.

"That can be a dirty business," Vigoreaux replied. "I mean that literally. Dirt. Piss. Nails and bones. Dead animals."

"Will it work?" I had been crawling through filth for years. I wasn't afraid of a bit of blood and bone.

"Depends on what you want to happen to him." I admired that Marie knew it was a man who deserved my ire. We spoke no more until we knocked on Lapère's door. As usual, she opened the door before the second rap on the wood.

Her face was somber when she saw me and she looked at me with pity in her eyes that made my guts squirm. She knew I had been hurt in the past and had been hurt again now.

"Come in, girls. I have some porridge warm," Lapère commanded. "You look like you could use some comfort."

I was about to thank her and accept before I saw Veronique. She was practically hiding in the corner, eyes expectant and worried. Worry that I would be mad at *her*. Anticipation for when I'd tell her that it had all turned out the way she had hoped and I had shared a touching reconciliation with the woman she had led to me.

"I need some herbs for my mistress," I said to Lapère, pointedly looking away from Veronique. "Something to stop a man from getting hard and performing."

"Is she that tired of the Marquis?" Marie chuckled, but Lapère looked suspicious.

"There are things that can help with that," Lapère said slowly. "Much more is known of remedies for when a man can't perform. You must be careful with such preparations, though. Cherry bark and valerian may help, but it has to be taken regularly."

"A hex then," Marie said for me, with a tone that made me think there was something about her husband I didn't know. "A spell to wither a prick and keep it hanging useless. I think you'll need some of his hair for that. Better if it's from close to the object of the spell."

"Marie Vigoreaux!" Veronique cried. "Surely, I did not hear you contemplate aloud placing a curse on your employer? You could be arrested!"

"Oh, are you so scandalized?" I hissed, spinning to pin her under my gaze. "It is at the request of his own wife – a woman who should be allowed to decide what happens in her bed and life but has *been denied that right*."

Veronique's face fell, and it satisfied me to see the pain there. "I'm trying to protect you both," she muttered. "If you start on a dangerous path like this—"

The door opened and cut her off. Catherine sauntered in, taking in the grave faces throughout the room. "Has someone died?" she asked, looking at me, then Veronique, before understanding bloomed in her face. "Or are you facing the consequences for doing the thing I warned you not to do?"

"You knew?" I gasped. I was ready to throttle her.

"I heard a woman was looking for you, but *I* know you well enough to know it was none of my business," Catherine spat at

Veronique before turning to me, the anger fading from her face. "And then I had a dream about you last night, Claude. And—"

"You dreamed about me?" I asked as she placed a tender hand on my cheek and my anger evaporated.

"Claude, I'm so sorry," the smaller woman said to me, all her cunning and ambition set aside. It took everything in me not to fall at her feet weeping right then. I couldn't break now, because if I did, I would never put myself back together.

"Claude needs something to keep a man from, well, acting like a man. A potion or a curse, we don't care," Marie said, and I think she was beginning to understand too. "We can do both."

"Neither is guaranteed to work," Lapère said, more pitying than a warning.

"If you're caught dosing the Marquis's food, you could be burned for that. And if you get a dose wrong—" Veronique said.

"I could kill him," I whispered, ice prickling in my veins, as I finally turned to Veronique.

"You should think about this, before—" she began but stopped at the fury in my face.

"Before what? Before I need to come back for wild carrot and rue and mugwort when it fails?" I spoke, and the room darkened as I did. I advanced on Veronique, my pulse thundering in my ears. "Or should I wait for when *those* don't work? When I have to go upstairs and let our dear Madame use the tools hidden by her bed we don't speak of? When I have to scream and bleed and endure more shame *because of him and a choice you both took from me.*"

Veronique looked stricken now, as realization dawned in her eyes. "I didn't know."

"I should not have had to tell you!" I screamed. "I ran from that woman for my reasons, and you should have let me stay hidden! I should not have to tear open my wounds for you to let me live my life in peace! But here we are, so let me bleed for you."

"Claude, it's alright. We'll protect you," Catherine said, reaching for me. I wrenched myself away, tears streaming from my eyes.

"You cannot protect me from what's been done!" I screamed, my hate and rage exploding at last. "You cannot protect the girl he raped when she was fifteen! You cannot protect the idiot who could not even stop him this morning! All your power and potions are useless now!" I let out a wail and shattered at last, falling into Catherine's arms. Marie embraced me from the other side as we sank to the floor, and Lapère knelt and took my left hand. Finally, Veronique took my right.

I could not look at her through my tears. I could barely think as I sobbed out all my pain, but it meant something to hold her hand and to be held. The pain was less, encircled by these women in Our Lady's sight. Catherine petted my hair as my breath finally steadied, soothing me like a child.

"We will protect you," Catherine repeated. She hooked a finger under my chin and forced me to look into her eyes, and her expression was more serious than I had ever seen it. "And we will make the man who hurt you pay the price."

I RETURNED WITH MARIE to the Marquis de Termes's manor. If I had my way, I would have slept for hours after my explosion and confession, but women such as us had no luxuries, especially not the luxury of time. Marie was not a terribly warm or nurturing person, despite being employed to nurse a child, but she made an exception for me and held my hand as we walked home. She also had kept Veronique from trapping me alone. She had tried to apologize, but I hadn't wanted to hear it.

I did my work for the day. I dressed and pampered the Marquise and whispered in her ear that I would need a lock of her husband's hair to complete his punishment. I read her cards and saw no more children in her future, at least soon, and overall, that seemed to please her. I felt numb and empty when I was excused for the night and dragged my feet home through the street. I should have been afraid to walk alone in the winter night with no protection, magical or otherwise, but in all honesty, I would not have minded being stabbed by some ruffian on the street. I would welcome any delay, even death.

In the pocket beneath my skirt, I carried herbs from Lapère – her strongest sedatives that would hopefully make Monsieur Faviot sleep long and deep, if nothing else. I had not been able to sneak into the garden for anything else, especially from the corner of poisons in the back, but I had thought about it all day.

Maybe I could find more tansy. It was late in the year, approaching winter, and so little grew wild right now, especially in the city. If I could make it to the Jardin des Plantes, perhaps I could find some lilies or yew. Maybe soon, Louis would open up the gardens of the Tuileries to the public as a gift. Our good and gracious King did that sometimes. The King was perhaps the only man I could bear to think of without cringing or wanting to curse every member of that sex.

"There she is," a deep voice whispered from behind me and I stopped in my tracks. Was this it? Was death here to save me? "Good to see you again, Claude."

I turned to see Catherine for the second time that day, alongside Adam de Couret. The conjurer. "I'm glad we found you," Catherine said.

"Why were you looking?" I asked, my sense of self-preservation finally rising. I knew this man, but I did not trust him, and I did not want someone else to know my business.

"My dear Mademoiselle Deshayes here – soon to be an esteemed Madame of her own household –" de Couret began, ever the performer, "invited me to help her accompany a friend home. I told her that it is unsafe at night in these dark streets, so I came prepared!" With a flourish, he pulled a lantern out from under his cloak, already lit.

"He's being dramatic," Catherine sighed. "I went to find him for advice. He's a wise man, and I told him you're undergoing a trying period with your family." She gave me a meaningful sidelong glance – as if to assure me that my secret was safe – as we began to walk.

"Ah yes, family. No one can hurt us more," de Couret sighed, and he sounded surprisingly somber. "My father was a drunk. The cruel kind. You'd think that much wine would have made the aim of his fists worse but…"

"I'm so sorry," I said, and meant it. "What happened?"

"He fell into a pigsty," de Couret answered with a cold smile. "Brutal animals, pigs. Did you know that? They'll trample you, if you're lucky, but if you're drunk, making a fool of yourself in the night – well, they're always hungry. There was little left of him to mourn. Not that anyone in our family would."

"Did you push him in?" It shocked me to hear Catherine ask aloud the question I had harbored as well.

De Couret gave a devilish grin and shook his head. "My mother never took credit. And for our part, we children heard the cries, but we assumed it was an animal who lost its way. We weren't wrong."

"Is that what inspired you?" Catherine went on, glancing at me once again. "To this trade in inheritance powders, as they are called."

"My dear Mademoiselle," de Couret smirked. "Are you speaking of those loathsome Italian concoctions? Or of the dangerous tools of an alchemist that have, on occasion, freed a poor wife of a boorish husband?"

"They're real?" I asked, my heart beginning to race. "These substances?"

Catherine smirked. "Arsenic has been in the arsenal of many women and men of influence since the days of Rome. And that is only one such blessed element. When placed in the right hands or supplemented, it can be quite useful."

"Sounds very dangerous," I muttered, noting that de Couret and Catherine were exchanging looks.

"Only if the dose is wrong," de Couret said. "But these powders can also simply bring about sickness. A lingering illness that seems natural and can be cured with a long visit to the country for fresh air. Far less violent than other means of dealing with family."

"There are things like aconite and belladonna," Catherine went on, leaning close to me in the night and taking my hand. "But they are violent and conspicuous. These powders are far more subtle. They are rare too. Monsieur de Couret is lucky to have access to them."

I looked up into her eyes, and there was the same look there as before – dark and determined. It was a look Veronique would have pulled me away from and judged, but she was not here. "Such remarkable things must be very expensive," I said slowly.

"There is more of worth in this world than money, Mademoiselle de Vin," de Couret said. We had stopped at the crossroads by my house again, and I felt a twinge of power run up my spine. "Such as favors and connections."

"I wish to build a better life for myself," Catherine declared, straightening her spine. "To do that, I need fine ladies coming to my door, clamoring for fortunes and solutions."

"Solutions I will help find," de Couret added. "But we need someone with access to society to lead them our way. The welfare of any such agent is a sound investment."

I looked at them: Catherine watching me, eager and dire, and de Couret with his lamp held high, the sputtering flame making the light dance over his face. "Monsieur, the light you offer," I began. "I appreciate it, but it may spread sparks. Don't you worry who it might set ablaze?"

Did he not care for his soul or the lives and well-being of the one I would use this powder on?

"I care that I am warm and can find my own way, and lead those who need it," de Couret said with a shrug.

"And some people deserve to burn," Catherine added, and as the light blazed in her small, dark eyes, she smiled at me.

"I agree," I whispered.

De Couret smiled and bowed, taking my hand as if to kiss it. Instead, he pressed something into my palm. A glass vial the size of my thumb. Holding it sent a thrill through my bones. For the first time since I had seen my stepfather's face yesterday, I felt something like hope.

I nodded to him and the man bowed, stepping back to allow Catherine to embrace me. "Start very slow, along with the teas and the hex," she whispered into my ear. "Be patient and trust."

"This could send us to the gallows," I whispered back. "If you tell someone…"

"I won't, and neither will he or you. We trust each other, Claude, as true sisters in Our Lady must," she said. "I do this for you. For justice."

"Thank you," was all I could say.

I walked the short way home, tucking the vial into my bodice before I mounted the stairs. The sight that met me when I opened the door was bleak, but not unexpected. My mother was passed out already in the bed, rumpled with a bottle beside her, and the place stank of piss and shit. My stepfather looked grim in his seat by the table.

"I did not think you would be coming home so late, Claude," he said, but with some difficulty. "My ailments have continued."

"That's why I was late," I said with a sweetness I could not believe. "I stopped at an apothecary to fetch you some remedies. The man said they may take some time to work, but I'm sure they'll help."

I watched as he looked between me and my mother, who muttered and stirred on the bed, not lost enough that he could take a chance. He seemed to doubt me until he gripped his stomach and grimaced.

"Yes. Good girl. I'll take that remedy straight away," he muttered.

I didn't even hide it from him as I boiled water and mixed my herbs in his cup, the ones from Lapère. I was more careful though when I turned my back to him and added the smallest dash of white powder from the vial as well.

"Here, Papa," I said as I brought him his cup of poison and placed it lovingly into his hands. "Drink up. This will make it all better."

CHAPTER 8

JUSTICE

I WAS NOT – despite the warnings of every holy book and holy man – struck down for my sins upon crossing onto the hallowed ground, not that I had been very worried. God was already punishing me enough in other ways, I did not think he would keep me from his house.

I was glad of it, for I loved churches. I had adored churches as a child and even as a young woman in the convent. Maybe it was because they were all the same and it felt like coming home. Even this simple parish in the Marais was familiar in so many ways. The hard wood of the pews found a way to keep you awake and alert and penitent, whether you sat or knelt. The gray columns and colored glass. The scent of the incense and the Latin sung into the echoing space as the priest performed the rites. The chapel in the convent of Sainte-Cécile had been all stone and stained glass too, and I had thought it was magic how the sun made it glow.

The convent garden had been right next to the chapel, and in the spring, the wisteria climbing up the side would turn into a waterfall of light purple. It had been under that fragrant canopy that I had first kissed the girl I had loved for a year. It had been a game (we had said so), a game of kisses, so that we would not be shocked when our real loves swept us away to marriage. Her lips had been thin and inept against mine, but I had loved it and loved her. Sweet Marguerite.

I thought about those first kisses as I avoided looking at Veronique across the church. It didn't surprise me that she had been invited. She was Catherine's friend too, and had known her longer than I. When the wedding ceremony was done, Catherine would be Madame Monvoisin. She claimed she liked that name far better. *Mon voisin* – my neighbor, it meant. And she was destined to be, if nothing else, an interesting neighbor when she moved into the home of the man who knelt beside her at the altar, Antoine.

I thought of their wedding night to come and wondered if it would be an event of any particular note, given that Catherine had already taken the man to her bed. If her spells and potions were working right, she was already pregnant with his child. Was the man in love with her, I wondered? Or was he enchanted by her carnal charms? Was there a difference?

The priest raised his cup over the altar and said his spells to turn it to blood as I tried to concentrate on the ceremony and keep my mind from drifting to carnality in general. Since I had been forced to return home, the very thought of anyone's touch made me sick for fear it would bring back memories of *him* I could not bear. All the better that I had seen Veronique so rarely in the weeks since her betrayal, my confession, and the resolution to protect myself.

Adam de Couret was nowhere in sight in the church. Not surprising. The man spoke so much of demons and alchemy that I doubted he would feel welcome here, or at the marriage of one of his lovers. He had many, just like Catherine. He had invited me to his bed more than once as our acquaintance had grown in the past weeks, but I had declined for many reasons. My conviction that the sole man in the world whose touch or attention I would ever tolerate was my beloved King had only increased in the weeks of my captivity.

Soon enough, the holy rite was done, and my friend Catherine Deshayes was truly gone. She rose from her knees Madame Catherine Monvoisin. It was a name, according to Vigoreaux during a drunken reading of her friend's palm, that all of Paris – nay, all of history – would know. That had been too much for any of us and we had laughed. I recalled it vividly because it was the first time I had laughed since *he* had returned to my life.

The crowd followed the newlyweds out into the church square, and I thought of the other times since I had started poisoning my stepfather that I had wanted to laugh. The impulse was there when I saw the man who had hurt me so much vomiting up his guts or laid out in bed, struggling to breathe. It made him angry that he could not touch me, I knew that. It also pleased him that I was the one caring for him in his infirmity while my mother gambled away my wages. He'd ask, once in a while, to *see* me, and I would comply, displaying myself outside his reach because 'I did not want to tire him.' He would call me his good girl, then I'd add more toxins to his tea before I escaped to bed or work.

My mistress had been kind in allowing me to attend the wedding of a friend today, as she had great sympathy that I was caring for a sick parent as I still attended to her. She was more than grateful to me because my spells on her husband had worked as well as my poisons on my stepfather, and she was free of his attentions lately. I had dreamed last night that I was speaking to her of her miserable marriage and her face had become Catherine's. I hoped it was not a portent. I wanted my friend to find some happiness. Even if she was marrying a man for his pocketbook, she deserved that.

"Congratulations, *Madame*," I said as I greeted the couple outside, smiling genuinely. "And to you as well, Monsieur Monvoisin."

"They are warranted. I have secured a fine, good woman as my wife!" Catherine's new husband guffawed. "And soon, she will fill our home with sons!"

"Or daughters," I countered, and the man shrugged.

"Which do you think will come first, tell me!" Catherine laughed and – in front of everyone – presented her hand. "Of course, I know what I have prayed for, hoping God will grant. But it is no sin to peer into the future that the Good Lord has written for us."

I gave a crooked smile as I looked at her palm. She was giving a performance, and a good one, to all her devout neighbors in this new parish of Saint Paul. She would be taking clients soon in her respectable house, and she wanted it clear to all that she offered to see the paths laid out by God. She would offer prayers and petitions to saints when her clients worried over their prospects. Nothing *unseemly*.

"I see more than one child," I told her honestly, noting how her palm had subtly changed from the last time I had looked – or maybe I was seeing different things. "Four. At least."

"Well then!" Catherine laughed as her new husband puffed up in pride at his prophesied virility.

"But the first…" I looked at the curve of the small mark crossing her lifeline. "A girl. But a strong one. Very much like her mother."

Catherine met my eyes, her pretenses falling away as a wistful smile played on her thin lips. "Really?" I nodded, and her smile broadened. "What shall I call her?"

I thought back on the church and memories of better days. "Marguerite. You will call her Marguerite."

I stepped aside for the next well-wishers, though I felt Catherine's grateful stare following me. In the crowd, I found Marie Vigoreaux, a pillar of calm among the crush, observing everything.

"Will you ever marry, do you think, Claude?" Marie asked without ceremony.

"No. Never."

"It's a dangerous world for single women," Marie replied. "Without protection."

"Our Lady protects me," I whispered back, glancing at the carved image of the Blessed Virgin at the front of the church. "And I protect myself."

"Claude?" I turned to see Veronique standing behind me, looking penitent and worried. "I'm glad to see you out and about."

"I have my liberty during the day," I replied stiffly.

"And?" she pushed.

"As I'm sure you heard me tell Marie here, I protect myself. And it works well so far."

I didn't like the relief in her eyes, the way she absolved herself visibly to know I was safe *now*. "That's good. I'm glad. I hope to see you soon, perhaps during Advent?"

"Perhaps."

I did not wait for another word; my anger was still too fresh. I turned and left, noting from the corner of my eyes how she tried to speak to Marie. I was not required to go back to the Marquise until supper, which meant it was as good a time as any to make an appearance at home. Perhaps I could convince them I could be trusted to spend a few nights at the manor...

I did not expect to find my mother arguing with a man in the street at the foot of our stairs when I approached. He wore black and a wide hat and carried a leather case. A doctor.

"Won't you even look at him!" my mother was yelling at the man. "He's been declining for a month!"

"I told you, Madame Faviot," the doctor said firmly, as I edged closer to the conversation. "I will see him when I know I will be paid."

"We have money! Or we will, when—" Finally she saw me, and her face transformed. "When this one is paid! Claude, tell the man you will get your wages soon."

The frost in my veins returned and I straightened my spine. "I wish I could tell you, Monsieur, but my wages have been paid these past weeks directly to my stepfather or into whatever account he has created for that purpose."

Indeed, it was a great mystery to me where my meager income went, as it was an arrangement not deemed fitting for a woman to know. The only money I had was a collection of coins back at the manor in my old rooms, all snuck to me by the Marquise as payment for secret services.

"That won't do," the doctor snorted.

"What of your wages from the theater, Mama?" I asked sweetly, knowing they were already in a card den somewhere, or perhaps they too were being paid to her husband if the glare she gave me was any indication.

"From what you have told me, it sounds like he is afflicted with flux," the doctor drawled, explaining to me something he had clearly told my mother. "He would benefit from bleeding, but I must be paid up front. I know it's grim, but if things go wrong, it *is* hard to collect a debt from a dead man."

"We have honor, sir!" my mother squawked, and I rolled my eyes.

"We will speak to him, sir, and call on you if we have need," I said, and confidently turned the doctor towards the street. "In the meantime, I will continue to attend to him. As will his dutiful wife."

The doctor strode away down the street as my mother leveled me with a glare. "Are you content to let the man that supports us die?" she hissed at me.

"He has not supported us for years, if I am not mistaken," I replied, calmer than I expected myself to be. "Whatever fortune you think he has hidden somewhere, it hasn't done us any good."

"I am thinking of *my* future, you ignorant little cur," my mother said, her hand flying back. "You'll be gone soon enough. He'll tire of you or you'll run, and then it will be up to him to support me."

"You can support yourself, if you keep sober long enough and stop gambling away all you earn," I said, and for the first time in a long while, I looked at my mother with pity. "You have a career. Hell, you could find a rich patron to keep you, if you wanted. I know you have no problem opening your legs for the men with money. Why rely on that man up there as if he's your life?"

"We swore vows," my mother said, her voice small. I thought back to the marriage I had witnessed this morning – the solemn ceremony, the incense, and the chants as two souls were bound. It was supposed to mean something, wasn't it? This morning, I had known it was little more than a ploy by my friend to advance herself. And I remembered a similar ceremony, watching my mother swear herself to a man who was not my father and the love I had seen on her face. We had been so hopeful then.

"How can you possibly still love that man?" I asked in awe and horror. "After everything? After all the ways he's abandoned you?"

"You're young. You don't understand." Maybe she was drunk again. Maybe she had lost her mind. I wanted to not care. I wanted to tell her she had been tricked by a terrible man who only wanted to worm his way into her household to hurt another, but maybe my mother was broken just like me, in ways I didn't understand.

"He'll make a turnaround soon," I muttered. "I'm sure of it. The winters in Paris have always been hard on him. Maybe you could take him back to the country and it will do some good. Go wherever he was hiding in Lyon."

"I wish we could," she slurred, slumping down on the stair. "I wanted the doctor to bleed him and make him better! I wanted to be the one to save him and then – then he'd look at me the way he looks at you."

I stared at her and thought back to Veronique's words and how they had angered me on All Hallows. How I had exploded at her for suggesting I forgive this woman or try to understand what she felt or had been through. Despite myself, compassion for her wheedled into my cold heart.

"Would you really leave, if he was well enough to travel? If I sent you my wages, would you both go?"

"Is that what you want?" my mother asked back, eyes bleary.

"It could be," I replied, but I didn't want to think on it further. "Let's get inside."

Our rooms smelled of sickness. They had for weeks. It was a wretched scent of shit and sweat and decay. No matter how many perfumes or flowers I hung, nothing drove out the stink. Of course, the dried foxglove I had hung was not known for its perfume, nor was the hellebore.

"Is that you, sweet Claude?" my stepfather called from the bed. "How was your—" He broke into a fit of wet coughing.

"The wedding was fine," I replied. "It was a wonder to see two souls so joined. I am happy for them." I looked at my mother. She looked as miserable as the man in the bed. Was she so sad to see this monster suffer? Was *I* sad to see that I had caused such misery in a man who had done so much worse to me?

Was I prepared to end that misery?

I T IS GROTESQUE AND unnerving to see a person die before you swiftly. It's worse to see it happen slowly, even if it started as your design and deepest desire. I watched Giles Faviot suffer from day to day, knowing I was behind it. My mother filled her husband's gullet with brandy, thinking it medicine, but he could barely keep it down. I took any excuse to leave the house of the dying, even on a cold December night.

I had told my mother I was going to get more medicine, and it had not been a lie. I wrapped my shawl close around my shoulders as I walked through the snowy streets. It had been two weeks since the wedding. Two weeks of constant work at the manor and at home, and I was tired. I was especially tired because the inheritance powder de Couret had given me had run out, and I could not contrive a way to get more from him.

I also could not decide if I wanted more. Wanting him to stop touching me and suffer for his crimes was one thing. Watching him die slowly was another…

Maybe it was better to offer a real remedy. Maybe if I truly healed that monstrous man, he and my mother would be so grateful, they would leave me to my life. Maybe she would take him back to Lyon and it would be done, like she said.

Lapère's door, surprisingly, did not open right away when I knocked. More surprisingly, it was Veronique who stood behind it, and she did not let me in right away. "Claude," she said, hesitant. "What are you doing here so late?"

"I need some herbs," I replied, trying to look inside. Why was she keeping me out? "Where is Madame Lapère?"

"Claude de Vin?" I was not expecting to hear Thérèse du Parc's voice from behind Veronique. I pushed inside to see the old object of my love and obsession sitting at the table with Lapère, while my most recent paramour stared worriedly between us.

"What are you doing here?" I demanded of Thérèse before I could think. Before I could see her look down in shame and touch her belly. "Ah, Monsieur Molière has afflicted you the same way as Armande Béjart."

"Monsieur Racine, actually," Thérèse said, haughty as ever.

"She needed a certain kind of midwife," Lapère said, somber. "I was telling her that it would hurt. She'll need to rest after and I can't guarantee anything."

I could see now that Thérèse was pale and looked stricken. "And I was telling her I understand. I cannot have this child. I will endure."

"Keep drinking that then," Lapère said of the tea in front of her. "It will relax you before we go up."

"Do you need someone else there?" I asked automatically, meeting Thérèse's eyes as a friend for the first time in months. She nodded stiffly.

Veronique watched from the corner of the upstairs room while I held Thérèse's hand and Lapère did her work. It was a messy, dangerous business, letting the herbs and her tools free Thérèse's womb. She bit her lips rather than screaming, sweat collecting on her brow as she locked eyes with me.

"It will be alright," I whispered, pushing away a few locks of the blonde hair I had styled and admired so many times. "It's almost over."

Thérèse gave a cry and her eyes rolled back, the pain pushing her into unconsciousness. Perhaps that made it easier. Veronique looked at me from the corner, and I could not help but think that, even in this dark room, doing such secret, sinful things, she was still beautiful. Her face still radiated with the kind light that had entranced me from the first moment I had seen her.

In a few more moments, it was done, and I let Thérèse's hand drop as Lapère washed her bloody hands in a basin and took something she had collected to the fire and placed it among the flames. I watched as she said a solemn prayer, closing her eyes before finishing and returning to the bedside.

"I'll watch her. You go with Veronique downstairs," Lapère ordered. "She will give you whatever you need."

I wanted to protest, for although Veronique knew part of my situation, she did not know all of it, and I still did not know if I could trust her. Or maybe she was the only one I could trust. Of all the witches within my circle, she was the one I still loved with too much of my foolish heart.

I knew where to go and Veronique followed me. I felt her presence as I still felt the smarting of my hand where Thérèse had gripped so hard. Suddenly, we were alone in the parlor, and Veronique was behind me, reaching for my shoulder. She gasped when I spun and kissed her.

She tasted as I remembered and felt the same too: like coming home, familiar and warm and perfect. She embraced me fiercely, grabbing tight around my waist, her body pressed hard against mine. "I missed you," she cooed as I kissed down her throat, her breath catching.

"I missed you too," I almost wept, all the love and desire that my anger had pushed away surging back. I took her by the wrist and pulled her out the back door into the cold, quiet garden. It was not fully dark, for the moon shone brightly above us, reflecting on the plaster and stone and patches of snow and frost. I grabbed her and kissed her again, pinning her body between mine and the wooden table where we had first dined together.

I was starving. It had been so long since I'd touched her. Since I'd *wanted* to touch another soul. I worried I'd never feel desire again but the fire stoked inside me. Every sweep of her tongue and squirm of her hips ignited me.

She gasped when I pushed her onto the table and knelt before her, but it became a beautiful, soft moan when I lifted her skirts and kissed those milky thighs. Her skin was so soft here, the scent of her so pungent. She was wet for me. She *had* missed me.

She was quiet; she had to be, holding back her moans when I began to lick her, feasting as she bucked against me. I'd missed *this* – making her writhe, making her swell as I sucked and devoured, letting her flutter around my fingers when I filled her up. It made my own body tingle and sweat to know I gave her such pleasure. When she came, spasming against me, her thighs rigid against my cheeks, I felt alive like I hadn't for so long.

I grinned when I pulled back, looking down at where she lay, debauched, on the table, and I wondered if my face glistened in the moonlight.

"Claude," she whispered, her hand coming to my thigh and beginning to pull up my skirts. "You're so beautiful. Let me touch you too…"

Let me see you, Claude. Show me how beautiful you are. Hands on my thighs. Inept, rough fingers inside me. Pain. Shame. Him.

I jumped from the table and ran. I would have screamed but I couldn't breathe. I collapsed in the darkest corner of the garden, fighting for each breath as terror and memories pushed down on me.

That's my good girl.

"No!" I cried aloud, gasping, and then… Hands on my wrists. Someone shaking me. Grabbing me. Oh, God, he was going to do it again.

"Claude! Breathe! It's me!"

I blinked. Veronique was right in front of me, her hand on my cheek, forcing me to breathe in time with her.

She was weeping.

"I'm sorry," she whimpered, because now she saw. Now she knew how he had broken me. She pulled me to her breast and I wept too, ashamed. "Claude, I'm so sorry."

"He broke me, Veronique. He ruined me," I sobbed. "I can't even think of being touched because of him. I don't know if I will ever be free of what he's done."

"Claude, look at me," Veronique said, finger under my chin. "You are not tainted or ruined or broken because of what he did. Look here." She directed my eyes to a plant with dark greenish-purple leaves and a five-petaled flower of white.

"Hellebore?"

"They call it Lenten rose because, so often, it is one of the first flowers, blooming in the dark hours of Lent, before anything else. But look at it right now – in the longest nights of winter. It is alive and blooming and it's beautiful." She looked from me to the flower, expectantly. And I felt a spark of hope. "Even in the dark, things live and grow and bloom."

"Did you have to choose a deadly plant as your example?" I asked dryly as I leaned down and plucked one of the white flowers and examined it. "It's a beautiful flower that can kill and destroy. Like I can."

"Claude, a hex does not make you a killer," Veronique countered. Still so innocent.

"I've done more than hex him," I said at last and found I hated myself for how it would sound to her. "I thought I could make it better by making him sick," I confessed through a sob.

Veronique shook her head, eyes bright in the moonlight. "Did it?"

"I don't know," I said honestly, my head spinning with the worry and guilt that had also been pushed away by her love. "He hurt me so much. For so long. Is hurting him so different from what you and Lapère do for those women and their babes?"

"Yes, it is," she said, firm and certain. "We help women. We free them and let them make their choices. Hurting him, or not healing him if he's sick, that's not the same. It's violence in answer to violence and—"

"I've been poisoning him," I corrected and I hated how sad it made Veronique look when I said it. "I thought there was no other way. I wanted to make him suffer but... Maybe there is another way."

"There is always another way," Veronique said, so earnest and still so hopeful. "We told you, we will all protect you. We'll do a banishment. I'll show you how. We'll send him far away. Your mother too."

"What if it's too late? What I've done to him…" I thought of the pathetic sight of my stepfather, pale and sickened, barely able to walk, and all by my hand. "What if I've killed him?"

"Purge him of it," she urged. "Emetics. Induce a fever." She rushed into the house again, gathering dried herbs and other medicines from the many jars that Lapère had. "Get it all out, then let him begin to heal."

"I don't know if it will work," I protested, my head spinning at such a change. All that mattered was that he would be gone sooner this way and the stink and burden would be gone. They would both be gone if I could do this.

"I believe in you," Veronique said, pulling me to her for a swift kiss and gifting me with her smile. I wished so dearly in that moment that I could see not only myself as she saw me, but the world. She saw such good in things, even in the worst people. Maybe I could live up to who I was or could be in her eyes.

I T WOULD BE HARD to watch, I told myself as I rushed home. The herbs would make it worse before they made it better. Healing is often like that. The body must ignite itself in fever to burn away the sickness. It will expel that which offends it in the most violent of ways – coughs and sweat and vomit and shit.

Doctors balance the humors and let blood to do the same thing. I recalled the blood flowing from my father's arms with such vivid clarity as I scaled our stairs that it was like a vision.

Perhaps it was, because when I entered our house, it was blood I saw. A scene like my father's deathbed, but now it was my mother, frantic, with a bowl below her husband's sliced arm.

"Help me!" she screamed when I rushed to the bed. My step-father was pale, eyes half closed, muttering feverishly. "I tried to bleed him but I can't stop it!"

"You idiot!" I yelled, dashing to the wardrobe to find whatever clean linen I could and tearing it into a bandage. "You may have killed him!"

"I was saving him because you refused to help!"

"I came with medicine, and now it will not be enough!" My heart was pounding as I bandaged his arm with steady hands. I was always calm in times like these, when crises exploded around me and everyone else lost their minds. "You need to go to the marquis – my Marquis!"

"What?" She balked.

"Go to my lord and tell him I need money for a doctor. Go right now," I ordered. "Beg him. Tell him it is urgent. Tell him he can reduce my wages! Just go get the money and fetch the doctor!"

For the first time in my life, my mother did as I asked and raced from the house to find help. I didn't know if she would be fast enough. I wondered, as I heard her steps disappear into the night, if I should have told her to summon a priest too; for her husband's final confession.

I busied myself bandaging, stoking the low fire, and boiling more water. It was not the right time to give him the herbs I had now, but it might be too late if I waited.

"I'm so thirsty," my stepfather's strained voice came from the bed. "Please, sweet wife, bring me some wine," he groaned as he tried to rise, and I rushed to the bed, pouring him some sour red into a cup and lifting it to his lips.

It was an instinct to obey him and tend to him, even now. Maybe it was an instinct for him to reach out and caress my arm, so loving. Then again, he had called me wife. "Thank you, my dearest," he muttered. I could see the fever upon him and the glassy confused tint in his eyes.

"Don't overexert yourself," I murmured. No use arguing now.

"I am so sorry I have been such a poor husband to you, dear Anne."

I froze at the name, confused, but a suspicion sparking in my mind. "Anne?"

"Have you forgotten your name, Madame Faviot?" He laughed weakly. "My Anne. My mistress of silks and sweetness. The best wife in Lyon."

So that was why he had been so content to stay away in Lyon. He had another family there… That meant my mother could send him back, but not follow herself.

"Do you think you deserve to be taken back into our home, after abandoning us?"

"It was you who made me go!" he protested, demeanor changing, darkening. "You believed a foolish girl's tales. Elise is a child, she did not know what she was saying!"

It was like the floor was gone. Then everything else. I was alone in a void, my body trembling, my heart racing, and memory choking me. *She's just a child, Alix.* He had said that so long ago. When I had protested to my mother that I could not be alone with him. *She doesn't know what she's saying.*

"Remind me, how old is our Elise?" I heard myself ask, from far away.

"What a thing, to not know your own daughter," he scoffed. "You've always been too busy for her. I've known other women like you, you know. It's a good thing I watch out for her. She's thirteen, Anne. How could you forget?"

"Thirteen."

My hands stopped shaking, and the room came back into focus. I saw clearer than ever before.

Thirteen. A girl of thirteen waited back in Lyon. Another me. How many had there been before me? How many might there be after?

"I'm still so thirsty," my stepfather sighed. "More wine."

"Let me make you some tea instead," I replied, sweet and calm.

I filled the cup with hot water first, then gathered my friends, the flowers and leaves I had learned to trust. No inheritance powder now. Nothing to make him ill or to save him. Foxglove aplenty first, and then the sprig of hellebore from my bodice. That winter flower, grown in a garden of poisons.

I let it steep. I called on Our Lady. The mistress of death and shadows and ghosts who waited at the crossroads. I felt Her with me. Righteous and terrible.

"Drink," I commanded as I pressed the cup to my stepfather's lips. He took a swallow and gagged at the taste. "More." I poured

the tea into his mouth, forcing him to take down more. I did not
relent, even as he sputtered and choked. I made him drain the cup
– every drop and shredded leaf. He looked sick at the taste, so I
made more and did the same again, watching sweat appear on his
brow.

"What – what medicine is in that, Anne?" he asked blearily,
coughing between words when he had drained the second cup
of brewed death.

"I am not Anne," I replied, calm and dark. Finally, his eyes
widened and he saw me. His pupils were uneven, his breath
shallow.

"My sweet Claude," he rasped, coughing again as his face grew
red. He was beginning to shake. I smiled as he did. "My most
loyal nurse."

"Indeed," I replied. "I have done all I can to rid this house of
pestilence."

For the first time I had ever seen in all the miserable years I
had known the man, fear entered his eyes. He grabbed his chest
and then gasped in agony. "I need – oh God – my heart. Claude,
help!"

"Do you believe in hell, Giles Faviot?" I asked softly, taking in
the way he had begun to writhe and twitch. His heart had to be
pounding so fast now, his guts seizing as they tried to expel the
toxins. It was too late. His body had begun to betray him.

"Claude?" he hissed, grabbing for my hand. His muscles were
spasming, his fingers twisted into an inept claw that I batted
away.

"You put me in hell the first time you touched me, did you
know that?" I looked over to the miserable cot I'd called my bed.

"I pushed it away, all that hell, but it's still in me. All the darkness you brought into my life. And now..."

"I can't – can't breathe!" he gurgled, his face turning a rainbow of colors. With another cough, a small amount of blood seeped from his mouth. I leaned close to him, and I wondered with a smile if he felt the same crushing fear right now that had choked me for years.

"I will not let you put another girl in hell," I whispered and watched his terror. "So I will send you there instead."

I could smell it before it happened, death seeping into him as his bowels emptied and his blood bubbled into his mouth. It was a foul, ugly death, his face turning purple, his hands clawing at his body and his eyes never leaving me until they turned glassy. He went limp, and it was done.

I burned the flowers I had hung, thanking them for their warmth and their help on this dark night. It was a strange thing, to be alone with the corpse, to feel the echoes of pain and confusion in the room still, mingled with a sense of quiet and peace. I composed myself, calling on all the acting I had learned from my mother, and sat myself by the bed.

It was not hard to weep. I had but to think of how I was free now and how I had perhaps damned myself forever. I thought of the poor child this man had hidden away somewhere and wept in relief that she was safe. I wept for the way Veronique would look at me when she heard the news.

I even wept when my mother burst in with the doctor and I saw her agony. I wept because she could have saved us from this.

"There was nothing I could do," I said. Or lied. "He grew more feverish and—"

"I will call the coroner and the priest," the doctor said, unexpectedly kind as my mother fell next to her husband's bed, hand clutched over her mouth. Maybe it was to keep out the smell or to help her breathe through her sobs. I offered her some comfort, guiding her by the shoulder out the door and into the cold night air, crisp with the smell of fresh snow.

"It's over," I said calmly as she collapsed outside the door weeping.

I let the snow mingle with the tears on my cheeks and closed my eyes. For what felt like the first time in months, or perhaps even years, I breathed deep and free.

"It's over," I sighed again into the night.

W HAT WAS DONE WITH the body could only charitably be called a funeral. Giles Faviot's corpse was thrown in the charnel house at the Saints-Innocents cemetery, tossed among hundreds of other piles of bones to rot away on sacred ground, if not necessarily in it. Latin was read. My mother and I looked solemn and dutiful, and then, it was done. It felt like any other winter day in the grim, wet streets of the city.

Seeing to my late stepfather's affairs was equally underwhelming. At last, the money he had been hiding from us came into our hands, and legally, my mother and I were free women. We came home from seeing bankers and lawyers, and I cleaned the house while my mother drank, sprawled beside the table.

"I should burn that bed. Burn everything here," she said when I was done.

"The rent is paid through next month," I declared calmly. "You can find other lodgings when the theater pays you, if you hold onto the money. I will return to the Marquise."

My employer had been extremely relieved that I would be returning to her service fully. She had neglected any pretty words of sympathy for my family's loss, and it had made me respect her more.

"Oh yes, it's always been so easy for you to walk away. To leave me," she spat, but she sounded sad, not bitter. "You don't care what will become of me!"

"You have never much cared what became of me," I shot back. "You can take care of yourself. The consequences will be yours now if you can't." She opened her mouth to berate me. "Do not call me an ingrate or a foolish child. I am a woman grown and I am free of you. You may hurt yourself all you wish, but it is no longer my burden."

"Do you truly hate me?" she asked with the audacity to look hurt. "I did not think you would blame me for this."

"Blame you?" I truly did not know what she spoke of or why she looked like she was about to weep.

"I killed him. You were always his favorite, and I killed him trying to do what you did and take care of him. Now you throw me aside."

"If I thought you were the reason he was dead, I'd be thanking you," I replied softly, and her face fell in shock.

"Claude, it is a sin to say such a thing," she slurred. "He only ever cared for you." I sighed, truly too tired to argue the truth with a drunk who never cared for me except when she needed me.

"You are free to send word to me by letter if you are in need," I told her. "But I am no longer bound to you. The bonds of law that kept me here died with that awful man, and you have forsaken any bond of blood or love. So do not seek me out."

I left without another word, letting the burden of her slip from my heart. The pain was still there, the ache, like the pain that comes from standing after spending too long on the floor. My heart still smarted and ached from all the harm she had done and the deep, tarry pit of memories of what she had allowed to happen to me still waited in my gut. But I would not allow her to add to them. I wouldn't let her push me deeper.

I left her alone in the house that had been my hell and walked free into the streets. I had work to do for my mistress.

T HE DE TERMES HOUSE was preparing a grand New Year's party the next day. Nothing compared to the glittering fêtes going on at the palaces and country châteaus, but still unlike any party I had ever seen. The Marquis hoped to ingratiate himself with more of the rich merchants and businessmen of Paris, trading the prestige of his noble name for their money and investments in his lands and businesses (or something of that nature). His wife was annoyed at having to mingle with more of the noblesse de la robe or, worse, tradesmen, but she would still entertain them with a glimpse into their future. That was my task.

I would read their palms and cards. So would the friends I had told my mistress of, friends who wished to expand their lists of clients. Marie would make her debut as a divineress, much to the Marquise's delight, and I was on my way to enlist Madame Monvoisin. I owed her a debt. First, I had to learn where her new house was, and to do that, I needed to visit Lapère.

This time, the door opened before I even raised my hand to knock. Lapère's face was unreadable as she looked me up and down before Veronique rushed to pull me inside.

"Where have you been?" Veronique demanded. I felt myself beginning to shrink under her worried gaze. "Did it work? Is he—"

"He's dead," I said, plain and calm as I could manage. Even so, Veronique looked so horrified I had to turn away from her. "My mother tried to bleed him on her own," I muttered, repeating the now-familiar lie of what had accelerated my stepfather's death. But Veronique knew it had been me that caused the illness.

"Claude…"

"Do not say you are sorry," I whispered. "He was an evil man and the world is better without him in it."

"He was still a person," Veronique replied, and when I dared to look at her, I hated the disappointment in her eyes. Disappointment at my callousness and lack of pity. Disappointment in me for doing what I had to in order to survive. "He still deserved—"

"He deserved to die the first time he defiled me," I countered and looked to Lapère. I could see in her eyes that she knew what I had done. There was no admonishment or judgement in her face like there was in Veronique's. Perhaps there was respect.

"A price in blood indeed," Lapère muttered, and Veronique scoffed.

"This is not what our art was meant for," Veronique whispered, shaking her head in disgust, looking down on me, as always, from her perch of righteousness. "Did you expect us to toast you?"

"No more than I would all the children you've kept from being born," I shot back, and Veronique went pale.

"That's different and you know it," she whispered.

"Why? It is all sin upon sin," I sneered. "I have lost count of the crimes against God that will damn me, according to the law and the church. You are just as guilty, only you fancy yourself an angel of mercy, when I have been one of judgement."

Veronique stared at me, pain and disappointment written over her face. I knew then that I had broken whatever it was between us. Another price for freedom.

"I needed to learn where Catherine's new house is. My mistress would like to hire her for a New Year's party," I said as calmly as I could.

"She lives on the Rue de Beauce, near where it meets the Rue Bretagne. You'll find her there tonight," Lapère told me, turning to Veronique as she opened her mouth to protest. "Claude is doing her duty to her lady, Veronique. That is all."

"I thought we understood one another, at last," Veronique said darkly. "I thought you had resolved to heal him."

"Fate chose my path instead," I replied, thinking about the absolute certainty I had felt pouring poison down that monster's throat. I had not thought of myself in those moments or of revenge, but of another girl like me who I could save. And if I told Veronique of that, she would still condemn me, even after all her own crimes and sins. "A path I am glad of, despite the price."

When I turned away, I knew I would not see Veronique again for a very long time.

I SET OUT INTO the cold to the Rue Bretagne, racing away from the woman I still loved, because she could not love me back now, after what I had done. Indeed, Catherine's house was bustling when I arrived, a regular salon of conjurers and workers of the craft filling her parlor. I found her in the corner laughing next to Adam de Couret, her hand running up his thighs.

"Where is your husband, Madame Monvoisin?" I asked without ceremony as someone handed me a cup of mulled wine. Catherine laughed when she looked up and saw me.

"He's been called off on business, to – I'm not sure where," Catherine said.

"A noble man, off supporting his dear wife so she can entertain her friends," Adam called to the room, raising his cup in a toast.

"Would that dear wife like to do the same?" I asked. "My mistress, the Marquise de Termes, seeks to employ a fortune teller for her New Year's fête tomorrow. It will be full of rich women with palms itching to be read and to hand you gold."

I found myself laughing at the way Catherine's face lit up, and de Couret's, as well. "I would be delighted," Catherine said. "I'm so glad you thought of me. That bitch, Marie Bosse, was lording over every divineress in Paris that she was engaged by some baron."

"Will she need a magician as well?" de Couret asked, grinning.

I sighed. "Alas, not yet. If anyone requires a demon or someone to encourage their more blasphemous tendencies, we shall not forget you, Monsieur de Couret."

"I'm changing that name," he declared. "Our dear Catherine, the kindest of neighbors, has been called La Voisin by a few, and I too desire a title that will entrance all and roll off the tongues of the mighty and mystic. I am now and will go down in history as Adam *Le Sage.*"

"The Wise indeed," I chuckled. "I like it."

"As do I," Catherine – *La Voisin* – said with a devilish smile, looking me over. "I am surprised to see you here making such an invitation, however, given your circumstances. Unless they have changed."

"It is because they have changed that I feel bound to make such an invitation to my friends." I put meaning behind the words, and Catherine's smirk spread into a grin. "He's dead and buried. I am free."

"Indeed you are, my friend!" Catherine cried, jumping up to embrace me. "May he rot in hell like he deserves," she added, whispering into my ear, and my heart jumped. This. This was the joy and approval for what I had done that I wanted. That I deserved. "Cheers!"

I tapped my cup to hers and drained it, then downed another when Le Sage toasted me as well, making a sly remark about how effective his products were and how good it was to know that. Another cup, and the house grew louder and more crowded.

Another, and I was with Catherine alone, laughing about how all we had dreamed months ago when our souls had taken to the sky was happening. She was curious to know how I had seen her handing me the knife that would free me.

"I have more, if you want to look again," she offered. Through the haze of more wine and the delicious drunkenness of freedom, I nodded.

"I'm done with the past," I lied. I couldn't run from that screaming pit of memory and pain inside me, nor the whispers in my soul that I was now a killer. Now, I could never be redeemed. As if that had ever been possible before as a witch and a woman whose lusts were an affront to God. It was a blessing that I did not serve him.

"That's the spirit, Claude. On to greater things. On to glory!" Catherine laughed and seized me. We fell into a bed; whether it was hers or someone else's, I didn't know. I heard the door lock and my bodice was coming off. I didn't scream when she touched me to rub the salve over my skin, and that was a victory. The knots around my mind and spirit that had been loosened by the wine unraveled with the ointment, and I flew.

Once again, I was above Paris and in my body at the same time. Once again, I felt my heart race and my body clench as ecstasy filled me, then glee. I was more aware this time, somehow, of how we touched, and how her oiled skin felt against mine as we writhed together. Flew together. She was not near me in the sky while I raced towards the woods in the west once again.

Woods, beautiful and green, where a knight hunted for a doe: a poor, pitiful thing. She lay down before his knife, and it glittered gold. Behind me, an owl called, and I turned. It was a beautiful bird, and it lifted me in her claws, each one piercing my body so deep I cried out, but not in pain. It was pleasure and ecstasy as the owl carried me, and then I carried her. I anointed her as the sun rose. As it bathed us in light, pleasure filled my earthly body. The little death took me as I gave both of us, owl and witch, to the glorious sun as sacrifice.

CHAPTER 9

THE HERMIT

1661

VERONIQUE AND I RAN away from one another in different ways. She went far away; I retreated inward. For the first time in my life, I was alone. No parent to control me or guide me. Even with a coven of friends and a needy employer in a crowded, chaotic city, I was an island of solitude as the tide of time rushed around me.

The weeks where I had held a man's life in my hands had passed like centuries, but the next months passed like a heartbeat. When the year turned to 1661, my stepfather's body was still growing cold in the ground and Veronique Pelletier lived in Paris. By February, she was gone, far away from me. Because she knew I had put that body in the ground. She had finished her apprenticeship and knew all Lapère could teach, or so Marie informed me. So she had gone back to Rouen to, as she said, do some good in this world. That message was a barb meant for me alone.

It hurt, perhaps more than anything else in that dark season. The sting of her judgment made my isolation all the more bitter. I didn't understand her righteousness and I resented it for what it had taken from me. Didn't we all want to serve ourselves? Perhaps goodness was a luxury I had never learned to appreciate. Our Lady was a bringer of winter and death as much as she brought spring and new life. Why could I not serve both? Catherine and Marie used their magic and skill to advance themselves, and I did not judge them for it. In fact, I was jealous that, as I drew more and more into myself, they became bolder and freer. I was left to tend my wounds and learn to be human again like a soldier coming back from war who jumps at any sound like the echo of cannon fire.

Marie weaned Françoise and left me alone in the service of the Marquise de Termes. I was happy for Marie, even if I could not follow, because she finally began to make her way as a divineress for the ladies of Paris who were so curious about their future. Catherine's business thrived as well, with more people every day coming to their doors for fortunes told over the table, and spells and cures delivered under it.

I was melancholy all the time in those months, as the void Veronique had left in my life and the horrors I had seen and wrought tried to consume me. When we gathered in the garden or a parlor to call on spirits, or clasp hands in a circle, I felt their power and glory growing. I was happy for my friends, or so I told myself, but I was lonely even in their company.

I could have done the same and joined La Voisin and La *Vigoreaux* as a competing witch. There was certainly enough business among the well-heeled of Paris. They told me so many times as our diminished circle met under the full moon and learned at Lapère's feet. But I didn't want that. I did not wish to be outside the palace walls. I wanted to rise *within* the noble ranks, somehow. I knew there had to be some magic that would earn me a place closer to the court and the King whose face I still saw in my dreams. To achieve that, I was content to wait and learn, in shadow and silence.

I hoped that when winter thawed the cold in my heart would melt away too; that I would be able to forget what I had seen and done in my darkest days. The memories – the ones I had pushed away for so long and the new ones I had forged – would not leave. They haunted me. Waited for me as I walked carefully through each day's duties and trials, like a swamp that would swallow me down if I strayed off the path. I had to be careful: a man might brush past me in the street or the Marquis would give an order too loudly, and I would freeze or fall. My breath would leave me and I'd be in the dark once more.

The nights were the worst, at first, when I'd see Giles Faviot's pale face in my dreams, bloody and dead, but he would still reach out to me.

After weeks of torment, I went to Lapère, who aided me with a spell to cut the cord of his influence on me, even though he was dead. Under March's new moon, with candles anointed with herbs and a string, I unbound myself from the pain of what he'd done. Or began to.

It was in those bleak days that Lapère told me the stark truth of witchcraft: that magic often takes time. That there are ills and wrongs in the world that no witch can prevent or undo.

Only time could heal me fully and bring me to something new. If I wanted to use the freedom I had killed for, I would have to work for it. I would have to be patient and wait for seeds deep in the earth to grow. If I could do nothing else, I could wait.

Lapère encouraged me to find joy again, and I tried as spring brought life back to us all. I helped her with the work Veronique no longer could, watched as she brought children into the world, and tended to the sick and heartbroken. I learned more charms, read my cards, and did my work diligently. I devoured books at night when I could not sleep – until my candles ran out. History and myth, learning of the times when Our Lady had worn the faces of goddesses, and witches had spoken prophecies to heroes. I read of kings and heroes and felt some relief.

When I had a day to myself, I would go to the woods west of the city, as close as I could come to the village of Versailles. There was something about the quiet woods between the lodge and the little hamlet of Trianon that brought me peace.

The smell of alder and birch and oak and ash soothed me; growing things and wet earth and moss were my comfort. The quiet let me breathe, far from the stink of the city. I wanted to bury myself in the earth some days, but I settled for letting the trees hold me up for a while as I rested. As I healed and hoped.

Never, in those days, did I see another person in the woods, though I knew the King hunted there. I kept up the hope I might, that I would get a glimpse of the secret, vaunted world of royals who never had to feel this way. The closest I came was a huge stag that I saw rush through a glen. That night, I dreamed of the arrow that would end its life, and I was that arrow.

I T WAS STRANGE TO be so lonely when my job was to serve another person; to sleep feet from her in my little cubby behind the wall. Madame de Termes was happy to have me back in her service, and she did enjoy talking to me about all the gossip of the court. I consumed it with relish, and bit by bit, I learned more of her world, or at least, her place on the edge of it. I studied the papers and listened to gossip wherever I could, hoping it could be of advantage to our household. That April, the news from court indeed took a turn that would affect my life, and every life in France.

Cardinal Mazarin, the man who had ruled France while Louis was still a child, who held more money and power than even the King himself, was dead. He had been ailing for months, but unlike his mentor Richelieu before him, Mazarin had not left an obvious successor to his power. Thus began the dangerous competition of who would succeed him as chief minister and head of government.

As chief minister of France, everything had come through Mazarin. Each matter, from the army to the sewers of Paris, had been overseen by him to some extent. In all the vast bureaucracies, he had been the one at the center. He had, along with his family and favorites, reaped great rewards for his works, for a good deal of gold meant for the crown and the state had gone into his own coffers. Or so Madame de Termes declared, though she was also convinced Mazarin was Louis's true father.

This was a rumor I refused to believe. I walked every week near the grounds of the Louvre and the Palais-Royal, as well as taking my secret journeys to Versailles, always hoping for a glimpse of Louis or any of his family. I had seen the Duc D'Orléans several times on the way from the theater. He was nothing compared with Louis, but he too possessed an aura of glory.

Louis, though… I only saw him from afar, never close enough to examine. A lacy cuff. A heeled shoe of blue satin. A plumed hat atop dark hair. It thrilled me every time I was even close.

Now, Louis faced the first great challenge of his personal rule: choosing who would take Mazarin's place. The city caught fire with gossip about this matter which would affect us all, and each overheard conversation or rumor about the matter made me feel closer to the King. Just the idea of knowing something – of being in a world that the King affected – warmed my frigid heart that summer.

Who would succeed Mazarin in his duties, though? The administration of France could not function without such a man at its center. It was as fraught an issue as the succession of a new king, with endless debates and many competing camps; but they were all bound to be disappointed. Because when it came to choosing a man who would run France for him, Louis surprised everyone: he would do it himself.

There would be no Cardinal or minister hiding behind the throne; no one standing between the will of our sovereign and the machinery of the state. Louis had been king for sixteen years, but now, he would rule as no king had before and increase his glory. The first matter of business was to, according to a scandalous rumor shared over and over again in the drawing room of the de Termes manor, rehabilitate a treasury Mazarin and his cronies had left rather empty.

This did not mean the battle for control of the King and the court was over, or that the divide between competing candidates was healed. The King still needed allies, ministers, and treasurers. The scramble to replace Mazarin at first elevated one of his most famous protegés, Nicolas Fouquet, to Superintendent of Finance. The Marquis de Termes vehemently supported him, for he was a friend. Fouquet's family had been merchants just generations before, and now, he was one of the richest and most powerful men in France. Roger de Termes saw Fouquet's elevation to control the treasury as an opportunity for him to finally erase the stain of the Fronde from his family's name and regain a position at court.

For my part, I was dubious of a man whose family had taken a squirrel as its coat of arms. It was fitting, I had to admit: a small but fierce and determined little beast known for hoarding treasure. Fouquet was powerful and generous with his plentiful gold. When he came to dine with us once (a truly exciting event for the house), he reminded me powerfully of men like Adam Le Sage or other actors and swindlers: self-made men who dazzled those around them with their charisma, but who were dangerous to trust. Of course, there was also what my cards said about him, for he was the subject of many readings.

My mistress, the Marquise, hated Fouquet on behalf of her friend Madame Marie Colbert. Jean-Baptiste Colbert was Fouquet's chief rival, and man and wife were obsessed with bringing about the downfall of a man they saw as an upstart. It dawned on me slowly that Madame de Termes had a friend who saw the King and attended court all the time, a friend who came to visit more and more frequently. Not to see her, but to see me and gain secret insight into her husband's enemy.

Marie Colbert returned, again and again, to have me read her cards and palm and confirm that someone in her husband's orbit was betraying the King. For a few brief days that June, when I joined Lapère to gather herbs under the high sun of Midsummer, I dared to dream that I could do more for Madame Colbert than tell her fortune. I could do what Catherine and Adam Le Sage and even Marie did – offer her a solution to the problem of Fouquet through magic. Lapère discouraged that idea when I brought it up, claiming that a man like that would seal his own fate. I didn't want to leave it up to him, but it turned out I had no control at all.

Madame de Termes became nervous as her husband ingratiated himself more and more to Fouquet, and the Marquis noticed his wife's growing friendship with Madame Colbert. The last time she visited that summer, she requested the name of any other fortune teller who might give her insight, and who might have other skills of use when Roger de Termes cut me and his wife from her life. So I sent her to La Voisin, and Catherine called in Le Sage.

Curses were tricky things. I knew that well. They could recoil back on the caster, or, like any magic, have unintended consequences. So I was grateful, in a way, that someone else would curse Nicolas Fouquet.

It was quite a thing, I was told, for Madame Colbert's servants to catch a real squirrel for the spell. But the little thing died under her knife all the same, and the body was strewn with baneful herbs as dark spells were spoken by Catherine and Le Sage, then dropped discretely near Fouquet's gardens.

When I heard from the Marquise that we would be attending a fête at Fouquet's new estate – an event that was rumored to be the grandest party the nation had seen in a generation – I could not sleep that night, thinking of the curse. The only charms I cast or prayers that I said to Our Lady (and God, for good measure) were for protection. I wore rosemary and lavender in my bodice, which made me feel safe, and, if nothing else, dampened the smell of a city in summer. In August, every noble in Paris, even those out of favor like de Termes, flocked to the estate of Nicolas Fouquet: Vaux-le-Vicomte.

I was beside myself when the Marquise said I would be going with her. It was a dream that I – the girl who had watched the court from the wrong side of locked gates and curtains, who had looked on the King but once and dreamed of being in his presence again – would accompany her to the party. I did not care that I would be sleeping on the floor of the great kitchens with dozens of other servants, or that I would be required to cook and serve, if needed. I was going to see the King.

I HAD NEVER SEEN a place so beautiful as Vaux-le-Vicomte. No one had. The de Termes house in the Marais in which

I worked and lived was old, outdated, and drafty. This château in the country was new, sparkling, and perfect. It had taken three years to build, in a style that mirrored the Louvre and other palaces, but with a great dome at the center like no one had ever seen. I certainly had never experienced such a marvel of architecture outside of a basilica.

The manicured gardens went on forever, planted so that they resembled green tapestries. The grounds were filled with fountains and flowers and rows of perfectly manicured trees. The halls were lined in gold. The chandeliers sparkled with crystal. Every column and cornice was carved and embellished. The floor was made of black and white marble like a game board. The walls of the château themselves were decorated with frescoes and portraits, the likes of which I had never seen, and all of it was set in the pristine, perfect country, where the air was clean and the flowers bloomed.

Yes, the crowds of guests meant there were not enough chamber pots, and soon the air inside the château was pungent with the scent of too many people, but what else would one expect?

The château was heaven to me, even though I only had the briefest glimpses of the gilded halls. This was what paradise had to look like: the pinnacle of beauty on earth (at least, to my amazed eyes). No one, courtier or servant, noble or peasant, had ever seen such a residence, for nothing had ever been built like it. This new château was a bold declaration by Fouquet of his power and his wealth. This man was unquestionably Mazarin's heir, and his glory could not be rivaled by anyone in France, even the 23-year-old monarch who arrived to fanfare.

That was his mistake: trying to outshine the sun.

I didn't see Louis's arrival – I was with the other servants, attending to mundane duties. But all of us rushed to try and get a peak when we heard the King himself had joined the party. I rushed from window to window, pressing between servants to get a look through the new Venetian glass at the man who ruled us all. Would it be different than seeing him at the wedding? Would he have changed in the year since I had seen him?

Only in that he was even more glorious when my eyes finally found him. It made me tremble to watch him from that crowded gallery. Later, when I snuck into the gardens to catch another glimpse, my heart pounded at the magnificent sight of the man who I thought about so often, he felt like an old friend. I had inched closer and closer metaphorically for months, and now, I did the same literally, whispering my charms of concealment, and plucking rue from the garden to keep me safe so I could see him better around the edge of Nicolas Fouquet's perfectly trimmed hedges.

When I had seen him a year before at his wedding, Louis had been shining – grinning and triumphant. Now, he was gracious and poised. When he looked at a courtier, he gave them every bit of his attention, and I felt warm watching it. Something changed though, in the few unguarded moments when he thought no one was looking. I saw those remarkable dark blue eyes survey the riches and wealth Fouquet had displayed, and look … perturbed. The King was annoyed. Perhaps even angry.

Louis was polite to Fouquet when the host arrived. Too polite, perhaps. It was then I was sure that the man was doomed – because there was danger in the King's eyes. I had to leave when the crowd turned so that I would not be caught. I ran back to the kitchen with gossip on my lips that everyone else agreed was true. Fouquet had gone too far. Louis was a hunter, someone said, and he had spotted prey.

No one slept until hours past midnight, and when I finally did lay my tired bones on the cold, newly-laid stone of Fouquet's kitchen floor, I could think of nothing but Louis and the splendor I had seen around him.

I closed my eyes and saw the beautiful women in their gowns of every color, like flowers in a garden or jewels in a chest. The men had been equally as dazzling in their long, embroidered coats and lacy cuffs. There had been tables of sweets and fruits, and dinner had been course after course of the finest game and most delicate confections on plates of gold and silver. There had been music from viols and flutes and trumpets, and a stage set up with acrobats and dancers. Molière had been there with a company to present a new play, *Les Fâcheux*, though I had avoided any contact with actors who might know me. The gardens had been filled with lanterns and light when the sun set. At the end of it all: fireworks. It had been as beautiful as a dream, as magical as any night I had spent with witches beneath the stars and moon.

I wanted to keep it. I wanted to stay.

When I slept, I dreamt of Louis's distant face, but he was on a riverbank, and I was in the water. The current was strong and it pulled me away. I called out for him, begging him to save me, but he did not hear. Hands, dead hands in the water, pulled me back down.

I did not like that omen. I did not like what my cards told me when we returned home, despite the Marquis de Termes's ebullient pride at being a friend of so great a man. I drew The

Tower three times in one day, along with the Five of Cups and the Nine of Pentacles reversed. Ruin and hardship awaited. I told my mistress as much and she fought back tears. I did too, for we both knew it would be a long while before we saw the King and court again.

FOUQUET WAS ARRESTED IN September and thrown into a cell at the Château de Vincennes. He was accused of stealing from the crown, for how could a man below the King entertain so lavishly and build a château that eclipsed every royal palace? It was more complicated than that, according to the Marquis, and the trials and procedures against the man would drag on for months, if not years.

The details of it all didn't matter. What mattered was the story, the rumor. All of France knew within a few days that Fouquet was a criminal and a swindler, so he was. No one was happier to spread this story than Colbert, who became Louis's new Superintendent of Finances and set about funding his King's goal to etch his name into history. Marquis Roger de Termes, on the other hand, did not fare so well.

My employer, idiot that he was, defended Fouquet publicly, which infuriated his wife, and cost him as much as his family's support of the Fronde. By the time the queen gave birth to a new Dauphin in November of 1661, we were once again relegated to the fringes of noble society.

The darkness of that winter was profound for all of us. Marie's husband and Madame Lapère took ill as the snow began to fall. It took all of our skills as a circle, as women who knew the secrets of healing, to keep those we loved alive.

My mother fell sick as well. It was Thérèse who knew where to send for me to let me know that Alix Faviot was refusing all care from doctors and friends because she only wanted me. The message came while I was at Lapère's house, nursing her and praying into the night that the woman who taught me magic might live.

Would I be brave or good enough to say the same prayers over the woman who had given me life? My conscience berated me loudly about how I still had a soul and it would be wrong in all ways to stay here when I was needed. That conscience sounded very much like Veronique's voice. Could I live with the guilt and the shame if my mother died, if I did nothing?

It turns out I could, but barely. My grief and shame and resentment froze me like a statue, and I refused to go to my mother's side. It helped my guilt afterward that she did not die, of course. Somehow, she pulled through, but not thanks to any prayer from me.

I mourned like it was a death, even so; because after a year of running from it, I had to accept I would never see my mother again. That the woman whose skirts I had clung to as a child had caused me greater harm than could be spoken, and I, in turn, had been willing to do terrible things because of it. I mourned for the mother I should have had and the women we would never be.

The winter held onto my spirit like ice. I went through the motions of living and striving, but more often than not, I found it all hollow. In the spring, we spent a great deal of time away from Paris on the de Termes family lands in the country. I was grateful, for that was the only place I felt alive again, the place where I could feel magic. I wandered the woods of Versailles like a ghost as summer bloomed, then faded to fall.

Madame Lapère told me over and over that "magic takes time". But there is also a magic to time itself of the most potent kind. It can obscure crimes and heal pain. It can make an enemy or a lover disappear entirely. It can transform despair into strength, but only when you are not watching.

CHAPTER 10

THE MOON

1663

"**I** SAW THE OWL again," I told Catherine as we lounged in her bed, the moist light of a spring morning beginning to seep through the shutters. Soon, her husband and daughter would wake, and I'd have to go home.

"You and your owl," she drawled as she stretched. "I've told you what it means."

"If it meant what you said, I wouldn't keep dreaming of her," I replied, rolling my eyes. "I have enough wisdom. I've won it hard enough."

"Fine, then; ignore the expert," Catherine shrugged as she put on a chemise.

I didn't remember much of the flight of the night before, besides the bright vision of an owl flying to the moon. It was the same one I'd seen many times in my years of witchery. I still did not know what she meant – except that she was waiting for me.

"If I didn't, you'd make me pay you," I replied.

"You can't afford me, lady's maid," Catherine sneered.

I rolled my eyes as I found my shift and replaced it over my body, making no effort to hide. While Catherine had seen every inch of me, there was never desire in her eyes when she looked at me, and I appreciated that.

In the years since I had lost Veronique's favor and my stepfather had reminded me of how hateful touch could be, I had only been with anyone when I was flying, if you could even call it that. Most often, it was Catherine, but a few times, Marie Vigoreaux had joined. What we did under the influence of that potion was never about desire or lovemaking, but I had found the influence of that potion was the sole way I could bear to be touched by another.

We never spoke of what our bodies did while our souls took those journeys and saw beyond the bounds of everyday life, and I was grateful for that too. Catherine and Marie never asked about the condition of my soul or the aches of my heart, and I didn't care about doing such things with married women. My heart was a locked garden, overgrown and wild with poison.

"What did you see?" I asked as I began to lace up my threadbare bodice.

"I saw myself snaring a deer and stealing it from a hunter," she replied with a shrug. "I think it means I'll take another client from that bitch, Bosse."

"Why don't you just curse her?" I asked and earned a glare as I slipped into my petticoat. "Ah, yes. Because she'd return it to you? I didn't think you'd be so circumspect."

"I use my energy on increasing my fortunes, not trifling with jealous fools who will destroy themselves," Catherine replied with all the confidence of a woman who believed she would become the premiere witch in Paris. I tied on my pocket and then donned my woolen blue overskirt.

"Don't make yourself a target for her, even so," I warned, reaching into the pocket through the slit in my skirt and checking that the protective charm I kept there, made of dried rosemary and an old needle, was still there. There were murmurs lately of persecutions in the country, more arrests in the Court of Miracles.

"Better to be a target than fade away," Catherine said. "When was the last time you worked any spell at all?"

I frowned and looked away. Perhaps she had not meant it to be cruel, though Catherine never minced words or spared anyone's feelings. "I don't need anything," I muttered.

"How long are you going to keep lying to yourself?" Catherine said, tired and annoyed. "You've hidden yourself away for what – two fucking years now? Serving that useless Marquis is not what you're meant for."

"Why do you care what I'm meant for?"

"Because how are you going to send the richest women in Paris to me if you keep languishing out in the country or hiding in that crumbling house with your disgraced Marquis?" Catherine gave me a cold smile, and I was glad of the walls around my heart. Otherwise, I would have been insulted.

"I can't magic myself a new position," I pushed back and received a scoff in return.

"How exactly did you conjure the job you have again?" Catherine asked, and I sprang away from her to grab the jacket of my dress. I had never felt as powerful as I had that night in the woods with Veronique. Ever since she had left, my magic felt so small. Or maybe it had been shut away deep inside me, like so much else.

"I don't have access to that kind of power," I replied. "Or the right to ask for it."

At that, Catherine laughed fully, and I met her pitying eyes. "Have you learned nothing? We are witches. We do not ask for power: we take it. We do not wait for the world to change: we walk the path to somewhere new. When you are in the darkness, make a light."

"Hard to do when you don't know where to find the flint or tinder," I said bitterly and left her staring after me in disappointment.

Her laughter lingered with me as I walked home through the streets of Paris, where life for the day was already well underway. Bakers were at their ovens, fishmongers led their carts, and the servants and soldiers who kept the city safe and working made their rounds. I felt alone among the crowds, as friends called out to one another and the world woke up. And yet, to my surprise, I felt alive for the first time in...

I didn't even know how long.

The sting of Catherine's words was like cold water that had awoken me, and I looked at the world around me as if I was seeing it for the first time in an age.

The spring sun was bright, the breeze was fresh, and the sky above was the brightest, most inviting blue. The Marais was crowded with women on their way to dressmakers, their sleeves like the bells of a foxglove, drooping from their arms. The men in their plumed hats and heeled shoes with gold buckles bowed and smiled, and for the first time in years, I felt like I was meant to be among those people, not just an observer from afar. The ones that moved from these crowded, dusty streets into golden halls like I had seen at Vaux-le-Vicomte. The world that I had been told awaited me, on whose periphery I had lingered so long.

I had served the Marquise de Termes dutifully for over two years; chained myself to a boulder that refused to move, even as the world changed around us. But now, as I strode through the crowd, Catherine's words echoed in my head like a spell. I thought of the owl flying west... West towards the palace. Towards the King. Even towards the country house where the de Termes family was bound tomorrow. I would cast my spell there, I decided, where I could gather what I needed.

I KNEW THE SORT of spells that required magic words and poetry. I had worked hexes and charms while holding the hands of sisters, chanted over candles, and even looked at the entrails of a mole for signs once (Catherine's idea). That sort of magic had its uses, but it did not suit me when I worked alone. What I was good at was stepping into the garden by the manor, where the cook grew a few herbs and vegetables, and asking the plants there how they could help me.

The mint spoke of luck and riches. A fresh start. The early shoots of garlic whispered of magic and life growing from the dark. The dandelions between the flagstones and in the corners were there for resilience, unconquerable life, and the ability to grow wherever the sun touched. And there - the first lilies, white as the moon. The symbol of the kings of France. Like the lily that I had stolen from beneath Louis's carriage before I even knew what magic it could hold. All these I gathered, and took to the crossroads near the church of Saint-Eustache at night, as the waxing moon hung high in the sky.

I had always felt power in this place, for the great church nearby held a lovely chapel to the Holy Mother, and the Blessed Virgin looked out from her alcove above the door, blessing me. Our Lady waited here in her many forms, as the virgin above the place where the roads met, and the earth and the road itself. The Mother who was the journey's end and beginning.

"Show me the road. Take me somewhere new," I whispered, and the wind rose around me, the trees and grass whispering. Power like I had not felt for a long time welled up from the earth beneath me. I clung to the plants in my hand and filled them with my will – with my vision of the world I wanted to reach. I knew I could not place myself there alone. I needed someone to help me. Someone who, perhaps, would ease my loneliness too. "Bring me the one who will help me to fly, who I will help too. The one who will soar with me."

In the dark, far off, an owl hooted, and it felt like an answer.

I placed the bouquet at the crossroads, keeping one sprig of each offering to tuck into my bodice against my heart. Then I nodded in reverence and returned home. It was simple. The spell was cast.

Magic, I have found, can be many things. It could be as simple as a cup of tea or a borage bloom in your hand. Rarely do witches gather to dance about fires under the devil's thrall (though, I cannot say if this was entirely untrue, as I do not know all witches).

More often, our work was what Lapère called small magic. Charms and spells whispered to the wind, a trinket passed under the sacrament at communion, herbs and trinkets in a pocket that would nudge fate in one direction or another. What I had done was closer to that than a grand ritual, but it felt powerful. I slept that night with hope buzzing in my skull because I knew I had begun something, though I did not know what it was.

Two days later, when I was told that I would be accompanying my lady and her husband to visit a new relation of the Marquis further in the country, a thrill went through me. His cousin's new father-in-law was, apparently, a man of title with no sons, and Roger de Termes saw an opportunity to ingratiate himself. This was something new. Movement.

This was a seed I had planted finally beginning to sprout.

To my disappointment, the first few days of the visit were both busy and boring. The château was finer than the country house the de Termes family kept, and it belonged to an uncle who had finally relented to the Marquis de Termes's persistent requests for a visit now that his daughter was married.

The Marquis de Mortemart, Gabriel de Rochechouart, was over sixty and liked to speak of his youthful friendship with the old king, Louis XIII, as well as complain about his daughters, the eldest of which was now married to de Termes's distant cousin. I heard from the other servants that all the daughters were witty and beautiful, educated in poetry and rhetoric alike, the epitome of the *précieuses*. I heard from my mistress that it was no use trying to make her look beautiful in comparison to this young woman in particular.

Servants were expected to keep to the kitchens or our own quarters when we were not needed, which was all well and good much of the time. I liked that you could learn all a great family's secrets after a few hours spent fireside with one of their maids or valets and a bottle of wine. In this case, I learned that my own master's ambitions to swindle money for his failing estate from the Marquis de Mortemart was destined for failure, which depressed me and sent me wandering to the gardens on our third night there. Anything was better than another restless night in my little bed in the servants' quarters, conversing with the spiders.

The moon above was full and high, a silver coin against a sky of blue velvet and diamonds. Or so I thought. My mind was still on the riches and finery of the courtly world. I wandered the winding paths, breathing in the scent of the earth and leaves wet from afternoon rain. The moisture seeped through the rough wool of my shoes, and the chill made me pull my shawl closer.

I noted the lilac bushes just ready to bloom and smiled, wistful that I would miss their scent when we had to return to Paris in a few days. Then, out of the shadows, I heard... weeping.

They were not moans of pain or even despair. Whoever was crying in the garden, tucked behind the unpruned shrubs, was angry. These were tears of fury and sadness. And it was a fine lady crying them.

I came around the shrub to see the woman crumpled on a stone bench beneath a barren arch. She was well-dressed – or had been, for she looked as if she had been undressing before running out here. What was making her cry, looking up to the sky in rage?

"How could you do this to me now?" she asked the stars, and I became worried about hearing too much.

"Madame," I said softly. The lady jumped up, turning to me and wiping her face. "I'm sorry to intrude! I heard someone crying and I was worried."

"Who are you? I don't recognize you from dinner," she demanded, sniffling to regain her composure.

"I am lady's maid to Madame de Termes."

"Oh. You poor thing. I can't imagine how dull that is," the woman scoffed with a tone that left me no choice but to laugh. "Forgive me. I didn't think it was possible to be such a gossip, and yet do nothing to be part of the gossip. I guess my dear husband brought her and her smoked ham of a husband here to remind me of our future exiled from the court."

"Monsieur de Termes does look a bit like a ham, you're right," I chuckled.

"But he's stupid and sheepish, so more of a side of mutton," she went on. I laughed again as the woman retook her seat on the bench. "Would that his cousin, my useless husband, was as easy to herd."

So, this was the newlywed daughter. "Is that why you're crying? Your husband wants to emulate my master and avoid court?"

"He has wanted that since he hauled me to our wedding," the other Marquise sighed, patting the bench to indicate I should take a seat next to her. "He hates the politics and the scheming. Says it's unchristian. Since we've been married, he hasn't allowed me to return. I brought him here in hopes my father would convince him to see some reason before I lost my standing entirely. But that's not worth shedding tears over now."

"Then why do you weep, my lady?" I asked once again, and she turned to me in the moonlight.

I had heard that the young bride was a renowned beauty, and I could see that now. A long, straight nose sloped down from her large, expressive eyes. Her mouth was a perfect cupid's bow above a chin with the slightest cleft, and her cheeks were healthy and round. Her hair was undone; in the sun, it would have been a golden color, but in the moonlight, it was silver. Those deep blue eyes met mine and her pretenses fell away.

"I'm pregnant. My husband's efforts have borne fruit, and he knows it now," she said with a forlorn tone. "He'll use it as the final excuse to rip me away from court for good. He's overjoyed that the good breeding stock my father promised him is proving fertile. Now I must resign myself to a life of obscurity."

"You're not alone in your despair, my lady," I said, moved to kindness by her despairing face. "I haven't met many, but I've yet to meet a Marquise happy to be bearing her husband an heir." I hoped she didn't mind the joke, and indeed she smirked.

"Maybe we aren't excited to be walking smokehouses for little hams," she shrugged. I liked her irreverence and spark. Which made it all the more tragic to see her so sad.

"Are you sure of your condition?"

"It's my second time pregnant," she confessed. "The first time was a lover when I was just past seventeen. He was ravenous for me in those days, and I for him."

"Young love." I wondered why she was telling me such a scandalous thing, but then I remembered my place. No one would believe rumors spread by a servant. Or maybe she trusted me. I had known this beauty for less than five minutes, but I wanted her to trust me. "Did you have the baby or lose it? Or something else?"

"I lost it," she replied, holding my gaze. "My mother knew a midwife who had certain skills. She was going to take me, but I went riding and... I didn't have to see that woman."

"I know women like that," I replied softly, giving her a confession that could easily lead me and my friends to the stake.

"Alas, I think it's too late for that," the beautiful Marquise sighed. "If I lose this one, my stupid husband will be right back on me to get another. At least that part doesn't last too long. Unlike this exile will."

"It might not," I offered to the dejected woman. She deserved some hope. "May I see your hand?"

"For what?"

"A look at your future, of course," I said with a smile.

Divination was not about knowing the exact shape of the future, but more often about giving someone a kernel of hope or guidance.

The young Marquise offered me her right hand, palm up, with a dubious expression, and I took it. The feel of her soft skin against mine sent a jolt through me. I had read many palms and touched others over the years since Veronique, but this... It felt intimate the way those fleeting moments with her had. Magical.

"Can you even see?" the noble lady asked, looking up to the full moon above us and the sparse torches that lit the garden.

"It's not always about seeing with the eyes," I replied as I peered at the lines of her hand. In truth, it was difficult to make out the markings, but what I could see and what I could feel – what the wind whispered to my soul – told me enough. "You shan't be kept from court for long. You have greatness in your future."

"I always thought so," she exhaled sadly. "How will I attain it married to a dullard who sees little more value in me than a prize mare?"

"You keep him off you and keep him away," I said with a careful shrug, tracing her palm. She had marks showing she would have many children, but not necessarily by the man she despised. Something inside my gut told me I needed to tell her more. "There are ways."

"Are there? Might your mistress be privy to these? I notice there is no heir to her husband's title yet." There was a curious sparkle in her eyes. "I'd be happy to know what sort of magic she uses."

I smiled slyly. "What makes you think I mean magic?"

The beautiful young Marquise wrapped her fingers around mine. "I know what sort of tricks fortune tellers offer. Do you know any that might drive a man away entirely?"

"I could make him disappear, if you wanted me to. Or I could at least try," I answered before I could stop myself, and the interest in her face flared.

"That's a dangerous thing to tell a stranger," she said, looking me over more carefully now. I wondered how I appeared to her: my dark hair a contrast to her gold, my plain servants' clothes in stark relief to her fine silks.

"Then let us not be strangers," I smiled. "My name is Claude de Vin." To further charm her, I plucked a flower from a pot beside us, one of the first carnations of the year. "I am happy to meet you—"

"Françoise-Athénaïs de Rochechouart de Mortemart," she recited like a litany. "Or I was born a Mortemart. Now, I am Marquise de Montespan."

"Françoise-Athénaïs," I echoed, letting the name play on my tongue. "That's beautiful."

"Call me Athénaïs. My friends do – at court, at least. It's a boon to be named for a goddess when the King fancies himself Apollo on earth."

"Pallas Athene." She nodded, and a new warmth began to fill me. "The protector of Athens, and the wise. Her symbol is the owl."

"You're educated, for a maid," Athénaïs noted. "Knowledge of the gods and of how to drive an unwanted husband away. That *is* knowledge you have used before, correct? Not just gleaned from books and fevered fantasies?"

"I have worked certain charms for my mistress," I answered, still wary. "And others."

"Have they succeeded?" She was holding her breath, hope igniting in her eyes. Veronique had always warned me about promising too much, but if this woman was my destiny, I wanted to promise her everything.

"They have. But I will warn you, these endeavors often take time," I couched. I had already promised too much. "And my mistress can be protective of my time and attention."

"That's a diplomatic way of saying she knows she has someone special in her service," the Marquise grinned. I could see such fire in her now, and it was captivating. "I bet you won't say who she's had you casting spells for."

"I have no idea what you could mean," I smiled slyly. "I offer advice and prayers, and a bit of herbal knowledge."

"To think my idiot cousin has been hoarding a sorceress," Athénaïs said with such admiration it made me want to laugh. "And such a beauty too," she noted with a smile that took me aback. It had not been since Veronique that anyone had bothered to call me beautiful. I had forgotten what it was like to even want to be seen, and how charming it was to be reflected in a pair of pretty eyes.

"You are too kind, Madame," I muttered, blushing. "I am happy to be of service as much as I can."

"I'm not kind, not in the way demure ladies are supposed to be," she snapped back, like a boast. "My husband very much hates that I refuse to be kind to him at every turn and speak my mind, but I cannot be other than what I am. And I shall not be kind when it comes to you – if you are all you say."

"Madame?" I asked, suddenly terrified.

"Oh no, sweet one, I will not be unkind to you. Never," she said, and I believed her utterly. "But I think I'm about to be quite a bitch to your soon-to-be-former mistress. At least your master will get his investments."

I found myself grinning at her in the moonlight, my heart surging. I could not tell her, but I knew, then how well a spell could work when given enough time. She was magic come into my life again. She would change everything. My lady. My new hope.

My Athene.

T HE GODDESS ATHENA WON Athens from Poseidon with her wit. Athénaïs de Montespan won me from her cousin's household with an expert deployment of money and charm. I was not party to the details, but when we returned to Paris, I was in Madame de Montespan's service, much to the Marquise de Termes's chagrin. I promised her any assistance of a prophetic nature she needed, even though I knew she would likely fade from my life after this.

The Marquise de Termes would send my things when they returned to Paris, but I didn't have much. I traveled with my cards and those were all I needed. Athénaïs promised that a maid of hers would be clothed as such, and so, it was not important for me to bring more. I was excited by that idea – the thought of dressing like the ladies I saw in the street. Even in my time as an actress, I'd never worn fine costumes or gowns. Perhaps I'd have something

now. Thought of silk and brocade buzzed in my brain as we rode
to my new home.

I rode next to the driver – a man named Jean Luc who served
as a valet and manservant to the Marquis – not inside the carriage.
Jean Luc was friendly to me because he was glad to have another
soul to speak to. It was just him, a housekeeper, and a cook until
now. It was a coup for the Marquise to have snagged herself a
maid, at last, he said, and was probably allowed because she'd
finally been bred. I hated hearing Jean Luc speak of her that way,
as I hated any time a man regarded a woman as nothing more
than a source of heirs, but I forgave him, as he was only restating
what Monsieur de Montespan had said.

I had not yet spoken to the ostensible head of the household
where I was now employed. The Marquis de Monstespan had
given me a quick look and a nod before we left, and that was all.
In general, he struck me as a small man, not only of stature, but of
vision and mind. He was square and stocky, his face etched with
a frown that made him look older than his years. One of those
people that sucked the joy out of any room.

The Marquis de Termes, while weak-willed and useless, had at
least had some vivaciousness to him – a trait that had to have been
carried in the blood he shared with Athénaïs. But my lady's dour,
scowling husband could not have been more ill-suited for her. It
was little wonder she was in despair to be carrying his child.

We passed through the gates of Paris, and I could not help but
smile. It was always a thrill for me – coming back to this city at
the center of the world. This was a city where great minds and
artists convened to shape the future, and where even the most
miserable of beggars came with their eyes on the hope of a better

day ahead. I was one of the few lucky ones who had found my way up from the slums into a fine manor, and now, I served a woman who had but one goal – to remain in the highest reaches of society. I would help her get there and stay, as much as I could. We reached the house late in the evening, but luckily the rain had held off and kept the streets clear. The Montespan house was near to the Louvre, almost in its shadow. It was smaller than the manor of Athénaïs's cousins. More money bought less in the shadow of the King, and people who lived here were not expected to spend much time at home, but in court. I had walked by the door that eventually led me into the house many times, as I had wandered near the palaces and dreamed. Now, I was thrust into the freshly-plastered front hall and left behind by Monsieur de Montespan and Jean Luc to take in my new home.

The house was newer, but it felt strangely empty, I noted first. There were furnishings, yes, but not enough of them. The same was true of the tapestries and art – they were present, but sparse, and those I could see were not of the pedigree that I was accustomed to in my old manor. It was as if this was just a place where they slept and rested, not a home where they lived. It was cold too, with scant fires and candles lit to welcome us.

"It's miserable, I know," Athénaïs said as she joined me in the hall, looking where I looked. "You're probably thinking you've made a terrible mistake. I know that was my impression when I was dragged here after my wedding. Did you know the brute didn't even want to spend money on cushions for us to kneel upon at the church for our wedding? I had to use a cushion meant for a dog under my knees. The first of so many humiliations."

"I gather you were not given the opportunity to choose your husband?" I asked sympathetically. There were many things about the lives of nobles I envied, but the lack of choice in marriages, especially for well-born daughters, was not one of them.

"I tried, and fell madly in love to do it," Athénaïs replied with a shrug of her elegantly exposed shoulders. "Louis de La Trémoille, son of the Duc de Noirmoutier. He was a beautiful idiot."

I laughed, and it encouraged her to grin back at me. "You mean he was easy to command?"

"He listened to his cock, and that cock listened to me," Athénaïs sighed wistfully. "Poor cock. It was short and fat, but it got the job done well enough. It had more sense than his head. Didn't go off getting in trouble it couldn't handle."

"What did the head do?" I chuckled.

"Got its owner into a disastrous duel, which saw him exiled to Spain. I guess it was for the best," Athénaïs said. "His father was a leader in the Fronde. I didn't know that when I seduced the son. Could you imagine me married to a person tainted like that? My cousin – your former master – was barely involved, along with his father, and they'll never be admitted at court for that crime."

"The King still hates the frondeurs that much?"

"If you were a ruler and your subjects had tried to kidnap you and then rebelled against you, wouldn't you resent them?" She raised her brow and her eyes sparkled.

"I would never forgive the betrayal," I answered. "At least your husband is loyal to the crown. That's something?"

"If only he weren't a cheap, miserable bore who hates the court," Athénaïs replied. "Come, I'll show you to our rooms. If all goes well, we won't be in them often."

I followed her up the stairs to a chamber that I would have thought belonged to a second daughter, not the lady of the house. The bed was small, the furniture was old, and the windows looked out into a tragically neglected garden. The only indication that this was a lady's room was the overflowing wardrobe.

"Help me change out of these so I can rest," my mistress commanded. "We're to visit court tomorrow. You've already proved useful. My husband deigned to tell me in the carriage that he would allow me to see my friends there with a maid as a chaperone. Can you imagine?"

"Tomorrow?" I asked in shock and excitement. For years, I'd dreamed and fantasized about stepping into the elevated halls of the nobility and seeing the King's court, but it had always been this distant, impossible thing. Now I was to go there tomorrow?

"You're about the same size as me. We'll put you in one of my older dresses, if you don't mind. You'll look fine," Athénaïs said with a wave – as if it was nothing to dress me up like one of her kind. "Get me out of these stays first."

"Of course," I muttered as I rushed to unlace her, marking how she relaxed when released.

"God, these ache," she groaned, cupping her breasts through her linen chemise as I loosened her skirts and removed them. "And they haven't even had the decency to get bigger! At least this babe could do something useful for my figure before it ruins things."

"They will, don't worry," I reassured her. "Do you know how far along you are?"

"The midwife said two months," she shrugged. "Not long enough. Can you tell me if it will be a boy?"

I blinked, biting my lips. Such predictions were tricky and bound to disappoint. "Not with certainty. No one can know anything for sure until birth."

"Damn," she sighed. "I'm torn. If it's a boy, it will mean that my stupid husband will be satisfied and leave me be, but if it's a girl, it would be a nice way to spite him. I guess that's a worry for another day. We have other things to use your gifts for."

"Do we?" I asked as I searched for a robe for her.

"Your old mistress confirmed that you have a talent with spells and with cards," Athénaïs grinned, guiding me to the right drawer to draw out a blue silk dressing gown. "What sort of spell will send my husband away? And I do mean off somewhere in the country leaving me alone, not in the grave. Not yet, at least."

"Either is an option." I was glad to receive a smirk in return as I placed the robe over her shoulders. "I'll need some part of him. Hair or something else. Also some wax and a few other things."

"I could have you arrested for even saying that you know," Athénaïs said in wonder. She was perhaps an inch smaller than me, so when she looked up at me through her thick lashes, I could imagine perfectly how successful she was as a flirt at court when she used that teasing tone and look. "I won't. I'm just shocked you're so honest about it."

"Oh, Madame, I have friends who are far more overt and honest about their spells and they do good business," I said with a shrug.

"I could enlist them to help you. Magic works better when it's done by more than one person."

"Can't I be the one to help?" She asked the question earnestly, looking at me with wide, beautiful eyes and a curious smile.

I considered her – how eager and single-minded she was in her goals. How fearless. I admired that. "We'll wait until the moon is waning more. Then we'll banish him together."

"Excellent," Athénaïs said with a contented sigh. "Now, Michelle-Françoise told me you have cards you read. Read mine now. I want to prepare for tomorrow. I've been away too long. All the other maids of honor will have usurped me by now."

"Maids of honor?" I asked back, impressed.

"I had a place in the household of Princess Henrietta, until my unfortunate marriage," she explained.

"*The King's sister-in-law?*" I had understood Madame de Montespan to have a position at court, but not one so high. That would mean I'd be in proximity to women with power and rank as I'd only ever seen from afar. I was going to faint from nervousness.

"Yes: *Madame* is what we are meant to call her. And her husband, the Duc d'Orléans, Philippe, is simply *Monsieur*." She said it all so casually – as if I'd learn quickly. Suddenly, the etiquette and titles of the world I was to enter were daunting. "Do you have those cards?"

"Of course," I stammered, fumbling in my pockets for the worn deck Father had bought in Marseilles all those years ago. "You shuffle them."

We sat on Athénaïs's too-small bed as she did as asked, and my mind strayed to where I might be sleeping. I doubted this under-staffed and half-furnished house had beds set aside for servants. "Now what?" she asked as she handed the cards to me again.

"We'll look at everything to start." Reading for a fine lady was nothing new to me now, though as always, the cards were different from palms – more open to the reader's questions, interpretations, and anxieties. Harder to lie about, as Catherine would have said.

I set out four cards in a row and turned over the first. The Moon.

"This is you," I said, smiling at how apt the card was. "Bright and adaptable."

"Reflecting the light of the sun," she murmured. "I know that already. Next."

"This is something challenging you," I said of the next card before I turned it. "The Queen of Swords. A woman – a passionate one. She follows her whims and feelings above all else."

"Henrietta," Athénaïs said. "She's my way back in, but how to charm her is the question. Is that the next card?"

"The solution, yes." I turned the third card and revealed The Lovers.

"She wants a liaison?"

"Perhaps," I said as I studied the card. "Perhaps she is lonely or unfulfilled in some way. Is her husband – Monsieur – a good match for her?"

"Her husband prefers to fuck young, handsome chevaliers, not his wife. Her tastes, well… There are many rumors. Who knows what is true?"

"This is the final result," I offered and turned over the last card. "Nine of Cups. An abundance of opportunity and happiness. A good card."

"Well, that's good to know," my mistress smiled. "Gives me some ideas."

"I'm glad to help," I nodded.

"Go fetch some food for me and feed yourself. Whatever the cook has on hand, as long as there's bread for the ravenous little thing in my belly," she said. "Then we'll wash up for bed."

"Of course, Madame." I curtsied as I jumped to obey, and it made my mistress chuckle.

"I've forgotten how nice it is to have a servant. If nothing else, I'm glad to not be alone in this house. Don't take too long, Claude."

I liked hearing her say my name. Despite how this house was poorer than my previous residence, I liked my new mistress more than my last. I liked how she made me feel like an old friend. While the prospect of a day in court tomorrow was more than daunting, I was excited to enter the fray at her side. She had great plans - the mistress my spell had brought. As I ate and fetched her dinner, I thought back to the first time I had entered another home where I instantly felt welcomed and at ease: Madame Lapère's.

I had been the one whose fortune had been told then, and I still remembered the words. *The world awaits you, Claude de Vin.*

CHAPTER 11

THE EMPEROR

LEMPEREVR.

THE MARQUIS finally deigned to speak to me in the morning, before we left the house. He caught me as I was going from the gardens to his wife's room with flowers in hand, hoping to bring some color to the dreary chamber. I did not like the way he blocked my steps in the hall and looked me over.

"She's made quick work of you," the man snarled, taking in the gown Athénaïs had dressed me in earlier that morning. The neckline was lower and the fabric finer than anything I had worn before. The sleeves were wide, the front flat and embroidered, and the skirts wide and sweeping. When my mistress had put the dark blue damask over me, it had felt like armor. Now, under this man's withering gaze, I felt naked.

"She wanted me dressed in a manner befitting the court," I muttered. "Your wife is very generous, Monsieur."

"My wife is a whore flinging herself back into the brothel, and she's dressed you to match her," Monsieur de Montespan said, shocking me into silence. "I let her steal you away from de Termes because she's with child, and she needs to be watched. She's sent away everyone else. Calls them spies. But she likes you, and so *you* will keep her in check."

"I do not think Madame is so easy to keep in check, nor that I even could."

"I do not care what you think, girl. You are to go where she goes, watch what she does, and report back to me. Especially if she tries to make a trollop of herself at court," the man commanded. "Do you understand?"

There was nothing in the man's face to show he expected me to do anything but obey, so I gave a nod and curtsey. "Yes, of course, Monsieur," I lied with a demure look.

"Get back to work then," he growled, and I rushed to Athénaïs's room.

She was still lounging half-dressed when I came in, and her face fell when she saw my expression. "The brute found you then? What sort of braying did my ass of a husband subject you to?"

"As you guessed, I will be expected to report back to him on all your activities at court," I shrugged. "I agreed, for all that he'll let me."

Athénaïs smiled. "Good."

"You know I intend to lie?"

"Why do you think I was so eager to bring you into my service?" she said with a shrug, bringing attention to her pale, bare shoulders. "A woman willing to refer me to abortionists and work spells for me on the first night we met is the exact person I need by my side to retake my place at court and punish the man who wants to keep me from doing it."

I smirked to myself as I set down the flowers I had picked for her room. The first carnations of spring – pink, red, and white. They were a flower of gods and kings, and a good charm for protection and healing, even though they were laid on many a grave. Common, but powerful.

Athénaïs did not know the half of it when it came to me. There was darkness and sin in me that would be my doom if ever anyone learned of my crimes. For the first time, it made me feel powerful to know those shadows were there.

"I am beginning to think, Madame, that nothing could keep you from your ambitions," I smiled back. "And I do like the sound of punishing unworthy men."

"Then we are quite the pair then, are we not?" my mistress purred. "Get me dressed then."

"Of course." I approached and helped her up from her chaise and stood behind her as she looked at herself in the murky mirror against the wall. "But first, something for good luck protection."

I plucked a carnation bud from the bouquet I had brought. It had been hard to find much in the overgrown, neglected patch of plants that took up the inner courtyard, but I had stood in the quiet and asked the few things that managed to grow in this harsh place what they might offer, and a ray of sun had shown me the flowers.

I showed Athénaïs the little bloom, and she smiled. "May this protect you from unfriendly eyes and words," I said.

"Is that from our garden?"

"Even in forgotten places, beautiful things can grow. This one will bring you strength and remind the court what a captivating beauty you are," I told her as I traced the petals over her round cheeks, down her jaw, and to the nape of her neck. I tucked it into her hair, keeping my eyes on hers in the mirror as I did. "Though you need no charms to do that, my lady, a little magic is always welcome."

"If any of those bitches try to steal you from me like I did from de Termes, I will gut them," Athénaïs sighed, and I had never felt prouder. "You were wasted on her. I won't make the same mistake."

"I am sure you won't."

I T WAS SUCH A strange thing to simply *walk* to the court of King Louis the Fourteenth. For my entire life, the palaces and nobles of Paris had loomed over me, as commonplace as the sky and just as impossible to touch. Like my friends, I had worked and strived to get closer to the high ranks of society for years, only to tumble back down again and again. Now, with a borrowed dress of borage blue, I walked next to a Marquise right through the gates of the Louvre, and no guard or noble gave me a second look. We needed no carriage or invitation, we were just *admitted*. It was that easy.

Indeed, on days when the King was in residence and accepting petitions, it was easier to at least get close to his presence for us born of the third estate. Many a day, aggrieved Parisians gathered to wait and see if the court would be open to them and if they would have the chance to plead their case to a minister or official, and perhaps, if they were lucky, to throw themselves at the mercy of the King.

At one point recently, the rumor had run through Paris that the bereft family of Nicolas Fouquet had thrown themselves at Louis's feet to beg mercy for the disgraced minister as he rotted in the dungeons of the Château de Vincennes. It was not granted. Some said the fact it was so easy for the King's subjects to reach even members of his court was one reason the King preferred to spend his time at palaces and châteaus outside the city.

But he was here today; the flags raised above the palace said so, and my heart jumped to think I might glimpse *him*. Of course, there were other nobles and royals I would see today as I did my job of lingering behind my mistress like an attentive, quiet shadow, but the King was the only constellation in this firmament I would have any chance of identifying. It made my stomach twist to think of it as we made our way through the garden and courtyards.

The Louvre was older than the city of Paris, some said. So old, no one even knew the origin of the palace's name. It had simply always been there: first, as a fortification when Paris had been contained on the old Île de la Cité in the Seine, then, as a castle, and then, a palace. It was sprawling, with a long gallery connecting it to the grand Tuileries Palace across the royal gardens. The carousel, where soldiers and chevaliers would parade on horseback, dominated the front courtyard. Today, Musketeers were drilling in the wide space, decked in their blue and silver tunics, ready to defend their King.

We made our way to the grand entrance – Athénaïs confident and me wide-eyed and amazed, trying to take in the details of the creamy limestone walls and carved ornaments that seemed to cover every surface. It was grander than I had ever dreamed…

Then, without ceremony, we were admitted through the front. Like it was nothing. Like I belonged there, because now, by magic and Our Lady's grace, I did.

"Home," Madame de Montespan sighed in contentment as the other courtiers followed through the doors. I could not say anything in response – I was too busy staring in unchecked wonder at the opulence that surrounded me, trying not to faint from joy.

To my eyes that had only ever seen churches, or looked from servants' corridors and through windows into the refined spaces of the elite, the vast entrance of the Louvre was like walking into a dream. Gone were the muddy streets of Paris with refuse piled on the sides. I was in a hall taller and grander than any place I had ever been, save a cathedral. But there were no gray stones and somber saints here. The columns and doors were carved with stone flowers and swirls, the floor was polished marble, so firm and cold I could feel it through the soles of my shoes. The glass in the windows was clear and let in the watery spring sunshine. And the great staircase stretching above us looked like a road to heaven.

"Isn't it lovely?" Athénaïs said as she noted my awe. "The King has invested a great deal in beautifying this old place, but there's only so much he can do."

I wanted to laugh to hear such a sumptuous palace called *old*, but I also knew it was true. This had been the jewel in the crown of Henry IV, Louis's grandfather. It had been this beautiful for a century.

"Mademoiselle Athénaïs!" a trilling voice called from across the hall, and a tall woman dressed in elegant pink dripping with gold trim and pearls rushed towards my mistress. She clasped hands with Athénaïs and kissed her on each cheek.

"Jaqueline! You know I am Madame La Marquise de Montespan now!" Athénaïs laughed.

"Well, it has been so long since you have shown your face at court, I cannot be faulted for forgetting!" the other woman replied, and there was a slight note of mockery in her tone. If my mistress heard it, she did not let it diminish her brilliant smile.

"I have been enjoying the countryside to hone my wit and plot my ascendancy. And gain new allies," Athénaïs replied and glanced at me. "This is my new companion. Mademoiselle Claude... des Œillets."

I commended myself on making a serviceable curtsy upon hearing my new title. It would not do, I knew, to be a woman at court in any capacity with a simple and short common name like de Vin. I liked the new title my lady had given me. Mademoiselle des Œillets, the lady of the carnations. I was her flower, plucked to be her magical charm.

"I am pleased to meet you," I said politely.

"This is Jacqueline de Roure, Vicomtesse de Polignac," Athénaïs said of the woman who returned my curtsey with a dignified bow. "Have we missed the levée, Jacqueline?"

"Indeed. Though I'm sure that was all in your plans," the Vicomtesse said with a smirk. I decided I liked her. "He's already out and about, perfect time for you to make your entrance. And I must say, you look lovely."

"Enchanting," I added, admiring my work on Athénaïs's ensemble and styling. She was not as ostentatious as the Vicomtesse, but she was striking. The light blues she wore accentuated her beautiful skin and golden hair, her necklace was placed perfectly to draw attention to her décolletage. I had concocted a bit of rouge to make her cheeks a bit pinker. Not enough to make her look like a made-up actress (which would be a scandal), but enough to accentuate her ample beauty. As we ascended the stairs, men and women of the court looked at her and whispered. Only a few looked at me, but as always, their eyes drifted past me to more interesting things. Just as I liked it.

We entered a great gallery, and once again, I was struck dumb at the sight. The ceilings were painted with frescoes of angels or gods (I could not tell which), and the walls were decorated with inlays of gold. Everywhere I looked, I saw silk and crystal and painted porcelain and beautiful faces in the latest fashion. The men were as outrageously dressed as the women, if not more so, with huge cuffs to their coats barely containing the swaths of lace around their wrists. They wore colorful stockings and high-heeled shoes with shining buckles, vests with gleaming buttons, and feathered hats above their long, curling hair.

And all of them – men and women – turned and noticed when Athénaïs entered, laughing at some remark from her friend I had not heard. Her laugh was like a song, echoing through the gallery and pulling every eye towards her. I had not seen the queen enter, but I wondered if she stepped into the room with anything like the confidence and power Athénaïs did. She ruled that space when people looked at her, transmuting the weight of their gaze into her power. Like magic.

The people in the room moved towards her like the tide had changed, some drawn like iron to a lodestone, and I watched and curtsied as nobles and their hangers-on made their greetings for a while until we had a moment of peace.

"Is she here?" Athénaïs whispered to the Vicomtesse slyly as we walked the gallery.

"Do you mean *Madame?*" Jacqueline snorted. "Oh yes. With her gaggle of hens by the window there."

My eyes went to one group of women in the far corner, positioned beside a window to catch the light perfectly on their silk and jewels. Their dresses were all in light shades of cream, gold, and pink; their wide, puffed sleeves and flattened chests made them look like so many pastries set around to decorate the only lady in their midst wearing red, her hair and neck bedecked with more jewels than her entourage. They were there to make her stand out.

"That's her," Athénaïs murmured, leaning into me. "Henrietta of England, Duchesse d'Orléans, second only to the queen in rank. *Madame.*"

Madame was strikingly beautiful, much like Athénaïs, but of a different breed. Her hair, curled into so many perfect ringlets to frame her face, was brown, and so too were her eyes. Her nose was long and straight, befitting her long face and quirked smile. She held herself above it all.

"You can tell she was raised a princess," I replied quietly. She was serene and poised, as only the noblest could be.

"She thought so," Athénaïs said under her breath as we drew closer. I was given the impression that the women around Henrietta were trying very hard not to see us. "Though I must note that her people murdered her father and she was in exile for much of her life. Only once her brother was restored to the throne of England was she married off to Philippe."

"She gave him a child fast enough," Jacqueline added. "Though the Comte de Guiche might have some thoughts on that *speed.*" It was some private joke that made Athénaïs and the Vicomtesse snigger.

One woman, right at the elbow of the Duchesse, finally caught sight of us and leaned in to whisper to Henrietta behind her fan while casting a withering look at Athénaïs. "That one isn't one of your admirers, is it?" I asked as the lady continued to stare daggers at us as we approached.

"The Comtesse Olympe de Soissons," Jacqueline said. "The most successful of the Mazarinettes. According to her. Though she has other ambitions."

So, this was one of Cardinal Mazarin's famed nieces. The Mancini sisters were all said to be beauties, but I was not impressed by Olympe. Her chin was weak, tucked too close to her neck, and her eyes were set wide in her face. Her hair was a plain brown color, not deep and rich like Henrietta's, nor close to black like mine.

"She hates me for being smarter and prettier than her," Athénaïs said of the woman as I observed her. "She is our target."

"Target?" I echoed softly but there was no time to explain: we had arrived at the battlefield. Henrietta looked up and gave a brilliant, if forced, smile.

"Athénaïs! It has been too long!" Madame said as she embraced her old friend, her ladies looking on in various states of undisguised contempt. "How is married life?"

"A delight, of course! But my husband agrees it is a crime to keep me from all of you and did not wish to be greedy," Athénaïs replied easily.

"Can he afford to be greedy?" the Comtesse de Soissons purred. "I had heard his fortunes were sparse." It was impressive, that the woman was ready to hurl an insult so quickly.

I looked the Comtesse over. She was in a pink dress that complimented Madame's but did nothing for her golden skin. She was taller than Athénaïs; gaunter, as well, like she had been carved from brittle wood. And her dark eyes were sharp and cunning. I did not like her.

"Why no, Madame La Comtesse," I said with as much deference and obsequiousness as I could muster. "The Marquis de Montespan is one of the most generous men I have ever met, and was so concerned with his wife's virtue and care that he has sponsored my entry into court as her companion." I made a show of looking about the room. "I see no other ladies of the court can afford such a retinue."

The women muttered to one another, a few of them giggling in the direction of Madame de Soissons, who turned her searing gaze onto me. "And who are you?"

"Claude des Œillets," I said with a curtsey, the new title rolling off my tongue as I realized that now, beside Athénaïs, I could be anyone I wished. These women did not know I had been born in the country and raised in the gutter. They did not know I had been broken and defiled and forced to kill. *They* saw me for what

I was now, and what I had raised myself up to be. A lady of the court, or at least companion to one.

"A pleasure, Mademoiselle," Henrietta said, extending her hand. "It is so rare that a lady should have ladies of her own."

Out of the corner of my eye, I saw Athénaïs smile. She was special now, thanks to me. In a stroke, her return to court had transformed from one of possible disgrace and lowered rank to proof that she was elevated now. I could tell Henrietta was intrigued. She held my eyes, her soft fingers clasping my own as I curtsied deeply to her.

"And are you a relative of Madame de Montespan?" the Comtesse de Soissons asked, but I had no time to reply.

A footman flung open the doors of the gallery and the assembled nobles all stood straighter. "His most serene and glorious majesty, Louis Dieudonné of Bourbon, King of France and Navarre," the valet cried, and the court bowed as one, myself along with them, as the King himself entered our midst.

I trembled as I held my curtsey, waiting for the most powerful man in France, or perhaps the world, to pass. I saw his feet first, in perfect ornate heels of blue velvet accented with gold. They were so clean – as if they had never been worn before today. I had heard for years that the King was renowned for his shapely ankles and calves, and what great pride he took in them, and indeed, encased in their delicate embroidered stockings, they were striking.

My eyes trailed up to the silk ribbon below his knees and the incredible material of his great coat, blue damask trimmed with lace and thread of gold. There was an entire ornate embroidered garden of decoration on that cloth. I held my breath as I dared to look higher, but I was too slow. He passed and we rose at his nod.

I was still shaking as I rose, though I had not even seen the King's face.

"Magnificent," Athénaïs breathed beside me. I saw the unchecked admiration in her eyes as she looked after the monarch as he strode through the gallery, letting each noble see him and bask in his gaze.

He was followed by a large retinue of footmen and ministers, as well as a man beside him, who turned to give the Duchesse a kind look and a bow. He looked like a softer, haughtier version of the King, and I knew it had to be his brother Philippe, the Duc d'Orléans. *Monsieur.* He took a young lady in white by the elbow from the crowd that had entered with the King and pushed her towards Henrietta.

The woman who walked towards us looked markedly nervous as the court looked after her. She wore white and gold, a perfect complement to her pink cheeks and blonde hair. The very picture of innocence and decorum.

"How kind of our King to return my lady to me," Henrietta said with undisguised contempt so that all her ladies might hear as the woman approached. "Mademoiselle de La Vallière, how good of you to join us."

"I am sorry. I was detained, Madame," the blonde mademoiselle said with a bow to the Duchesse. So, she was another of her appointed ladies, a member of her household as Athénaïs had once been and hoped to remain.

"Were you at prayer?" The Comtesse de Soissons said coolly. "We all know how devout you are. How magnanimous of our

King to allow you to enter with him after you stayed for additional confession and meditation on sins and penance."

The woman – perhaps I should have called her a girl, for she looked as overcome as one – looked ashamed at the comment and turned her attention to me and Athénaïs rather than reply. "Ah, my dear Madame de Montespan. We have missed you."

"Louise, you know lying is a sin too," Athénaïs said. I was shocked that she had taken the same acid into her tone as the other women. It made Mademoiselle de La Vallière blush.

"Do you know if the Queen will be joining us today?" the Comtesse de Soissons asked sweetly. It was another jab I did not understand, but it made the poor La Vallière look even sicker.

"My beloved sister is feeling ill," Henrietta replied before La Vallière could speak. "Perhaps I should call on her later today, with my dear maids of honor, of course. As we all so love our Queen."

"How kind of you, Madame," Athénaïs purred. "I am sure your very presence will lift her spirits."

"You must join us," Henrietta said with a grin, and Athénaïs puffed up in triumph. The Comtesse frowned.

"Athénaïs is not a member of your household, nor the Queen's – not anymore. It would be a breach of etiquette to bring her," Soissons said. "The Dowager Queen will be there too, and we know how *she* feels about Athénaïs. Alas."

"Tell Queen Marie Thérèse I shall pray for her, and her child," Athénaïs replied, not missing a beat. "Claude, come with me. We have one more introduction to make."

"Yes, Madame," I murmured, confused. I followed Athénaïs as she wafted gracefully away from the Duchesse and her ladies. "I fear I shall need to hear the story of why Mademoiselle de La Vallière is so clearly detested."

"She has what we all want," Athénaïs sighed to me. "The heart of the King. One day, I will steal it."

I stared at my mistress. I was accustomed to women of ambition, and I knew Athénaïs treasured the court and the games of intrigue and politics there, but to hear her say so boldly that she sought a position in the favor of the King himself filled me with shock and not-a-little dread. To play games with nobles was one thing, but to play games with the King…

The King. Who was looking at us – or at least at Athénaïs. And moving our direction.

I was going to be sick. Or collapse. I was sure of it. Louis, the King who had smiled up at me from his carriage as flowers rained down on his wedding day. Louis, who I had hoped to spy from afar so many times, but had so rarely seen again. The King of France, God's chosen on earth, was walking gracefully towards *me*.

"Do not speak until he indicates you may," Athénaïs whispered to me. "If you have a spell of some kind for bravery or calm, cast it now."

"May Our Lady protect me," I exhaled. My heart pounded and my vision swam as the King and his entourage of courtiers approached. I could see the curls of his dark brown hair, the arch of his brow…

I dropped into the deepest curtsey I could manage while keeping my composure, lower than my mistress beside me, who did not seem at all terrified. She was smiling up at Louis like she was thrilled to see an old friend.

"Our dear Mademoiselle de Mortemart has departed and returned to us even more resplendent as Madame de Montespan." The King's voice was measured and warm, both circumspect and inviting. Not at all the frightening tone of a man who could command armies to march for him.

"Any such splendor is a mere reflection as the moon is to the sun, my King," Athénaïs said and extended her hand. The King took it – the most elegant of gestures – and helped her to rise. I dared, at last, to look at his face. He was beautiful, perhaps the most handsome man I had ever seen (for I could not be pressed to recall any other man at that moment). Looking at him, at this being who I had worshipped and watched for so long, who was now within arm's reach of me, was incredible. I felt a pull to him, a force around him like no one I had ever known, like the power I had experienced in only the most ecstatic moments of magic.

As if he felt my common gaze fall upon him, the King's attention turned to me. My chest tightened, and I worried that my palms had begun to sweat. This was Apollo, the sun at the center of the court, and he was looking at *me* with curiosity. I was so accustomed to going unseen that the absolute focus of that divine attention stole the words from my slack mouth.

"Your Majesty, this is my new companion who has come to court with me, Claude des Œillets," Athénaïs said for me. To my shock, the King extended his hand to help me rise. I took it on reflex, and I swear I will never forget the texture and strength of those hands the first time I touched them.

"It is an honor to be here in such shining company," I managed to say and thanked every little borage blossom sewn into my shift for the courage they gave me. "Your Majesty."

"You have already found the most amusing and delightful among us as your guide," the King said with a smile towards Athénaïs.

"Indeed, I am blessed by her attention. No lady I have ever met is as fine…" I swallowed as I felt others look at me. "If only because I have not yet met your beloved Queen or mother."

"Oh, she's very good, Madame de Montespan," the King said with a sly smile.

"You have no idea," Athénaïs replied. "She is an enchanting find."

"You will have to bring her to Fontainebleau," the King said, and my heart leapt. I could see Athénaïs stifle a grin. "The rains are meant to return and the city will be a mess of mud. We have missed you so at my entertainments. And at the tables."

"If my King commands it, I cannot refuse," Athénaïs said. "We shall be there."

"Excellent," Louis said. His focus was still upon us entirely, so much so that I had forgotten anyone else was there. "We shall be delighted to see more of you again, Madame La Marquise."

The King nodded and moved on through the gallery, and I felt as if my bones had left my body. Perhaps Athénaïs felt the same, for she grabbed my hand in triumph, squeezing it tightly.

"The first steps are taken," she whispered to me.

OUR DAY IN COURT was one of small talk and gossip, parading through the galleries and the gardens at the center of the Louvre palace, and trying to catch the attention of the right people. It was hard to keep my concentration on the people. I spent half my time gaping at the interior halls of the palace – room after room of carved columns, inlaid wood floors, enameled walls, and fantastical frescos on every ceiling. The people were as beautiful, each trying to outdo the others in their dress and accessories. I was happy that my position as a maid meant I was expected to be coy and quiet and unobtrusive. I was not skilled at the doublespeak and elegant etiquette of court yet. But my mistress was.

Athénaïs was a master of her craft, and I understood fully now why she could not bear to be separated from this place. She let people come to her, attracted by her laughter and wit, and she held her own in every discussion, no matter the topic, from politics to poetry to everything in between.

I tried to keep up, and I was at least able to comment intelligently on the latest works by Molière or Racine. I kept to myself that I had once pined for Racine's now-famous mistress, Thérèse du Parc, but I knew other secret gossip of the actors that I hinted at enough to draw interest, including the rumor that Molière's lovers, the Béjart sisters, were not sisters at all, but mother and daughter.

Supper was served long after the sun had gone down, after the King had been presented with dozens of dishes to taste and enjoy. It was a sumptuous meal, richer than anything I had ever encountered, with glazed meats and fresh fruit and spring vegetables, tarts and cakes, eels and oysters, and, of course, wine. When the King was done eating, it was time for his ceremonial farewell to the court where he entered his private chambers with his most trusted courtiers and servants.

In the morning, the inner circle would be present for the levée, to watch the king rise from bed and dress him. The same was done for the Queen, with the highest ranking lady of the court – Madame, in this case – present to give the queen her first article of clothing. I was informed by Athénaïs that the role of attending a royal as they used their golden chamber pots with velvet seats was highly sought after, as it meant speaking to the powerful in the most intimate of moments.

Athénaïs explained all of this as we stumbled back to her house in the dark of the night, Jean Luc escorting us with a torch.

"I don't think I'd much like matters of state being brought up to me while I was taking a piss," I laughed, my gait unsteady as I made my way over the cobblestones with sore feet. I was not accustomed to the heels worn by everyone – man and woman – in court, and my feet were paying the price.

"I don't think I'd like that if I were King either," Athénaïs said as we entered the front hall of the house. She leaned on me, hopping as she took off her shoes and sighed in relief. "Or Queen. But no one talks to her."

"Do you often dream of being queen?" I asked with a smile, and she grinned back.

"I dream of being the most powerful and revered woman in the court; no one says that has to be the Queen." It was here, alone in the shadows, she could confess that deepest ambition, one I had already guessed.

"I think you shall be," I said as I smiled at her elegant profile. "But what lady is it now?" I liked her idea of taking off the shoes that had been pinching me all day, so I did the same, then followed her as she ascended the darkened stairs.

"You were there watching everything that happened, quiet as could be. I bet you already know," Athénaïs grinned. "A little spider in the corner, like you were at my cousin's house."

"You saw me watching?"

"Only because I'm smarter than most and bother to look past what's in front of my nose," she said with a shrug as we entered her room. I took to lighting a few candles as she began to undo her hair from the combs and pins that held it in place. "Now, tell me what you observed, and we'll compare."

"I would say Henrietta is more powerful than the Queen now, for she's there to play the game. And everyone hates Mademoiselle de La Vallière," I began – starting with the most obvious. "You included."

"We all suspect she's become Louis's mistress," Athénaïs sighed. "Come unlace me so I can breathe."

"She doesn't seem to enjoy such rumors or attention," I murmured as I obeyed, loosening the laces at the front of Athénaïs's gown and lifting the overdress off her. Next came the lacy undershirt and stomacher, and then the bodice and petticoats.

"Louise de La Vallière is a mystery to me, I must admit. She's quite intelligent, especially for a girl of nineteen, but she's also pious. It's not just the veneer of faithfulness we all put on: she sincerely means it. When she fails to take communion, it matters to her. The same is true of the King, and when they both abstained... It's clear they are in some state of sin together."

"How scandalous. I had thought you nobles were above us common folk and our licentiousness."

"Oh no, I think we're much worse," Athénaïs said as she sat before me and nodded to a brush for me to attend to her hair. "We speak so much of virtue, and yet, don't care at all about keeping ourselves from sin. I think Mademoiselle de La Vallière is the one woman at court who truly cares for her soul, aside from the Queens."

"Which is why she's such beguiling prey," I sighed. I had heard of the various women who were said to compete for the King's affections, much to the disgrace of both Queens – his wife, Marie Thérèse, and his mother, Anne of Austria. Part of me had, perhaps, thought it would not be true; that the monarch was better than a common man following carnal impulses.

"It would seem so," Athénaïs agreed. "Louise was brought in to curtail Louis when Queen Anne thought he was spending too much time with Henrietta. Or was it Marie Mancini? I can't recall, honestly. This was in the first year of his marriage, after Marie Thérèse was pregnant."

"Really?" I settled myself in to listen, delighted to at last hear the gossip of the court from one within the court. "She was installed on purpose."

"She was being pursued by the Comte de Guiche – the greatest seducer at court, he's in exile for a while now, I think – but Louis was encouraged to spend time with Louise to save face for both of them. Then Henrietta allegedly started sleeping with Guiche, and Louis and Louise became enamored. My guess is you're right about the attraction to her purity. Louise was and remains a contrast to Henrietta and the Mazarinettes. She's the one woman at court who didn't want to be pursued by our lovely King."

"Was it Louise that he found in a convent?" I asked, recalling one of the more outlandish tales I had seen circulated in a pamphlet a year or so ago. I had not thought it was true.

"Oh, that dramatic nonsense," Athénaïs groaned. "The little fool was so overcome by her conscience after some dalliance with Louis – perhaps after he finally took her virginity before any husband could do so – that she ran off to the convent of Sainte-Périne in Chaillot. Or maybe it was after their first fight. I heard it all from Henrietta at the time, who was upset about the Comte de Guiche discarding her in favor of her husband."

My jaw fell. I was beginning to have a hard time keeping track of who was rumored to be fucking who and who was actually embroiled together in sin. I wished I had a chart. "So she did go to a convent?"

"For a day. Louis rode off after her and convinced her to come back, like the great romantic he is," Athénaïs sighed. "One thing we all agree on is that Louise de La Vallière was not worth such an effort."

"Including the Comtesse de Soissons? She hates her in particular, I gather," I said, and Athénaïs nodded. "She and her sisters were all rumored to be Louis's lovers at some point."

"Perhaps. The bitch certainly hates me," Athénaïs said. She was trying to make it sound like a joke, but there was weariness there. "She was delighted when I was wrenched away from court by my husband. She will be the greatest obstacle to me securing a place in Henrietta's household again. After Louise snagged Louis under her nose, Olympe will tolerate few rivals. But I need that position – and the money it pays – if I am to stay in court. And I have to secure it while my bore of a husband is about."

"The moon will be dark soon enough," I said as I slowly brushed out her golden hair, marking its silken texture between my hands and how the candlelight made her skin gold too. "When it is, I'll cast the spell to drive your husband as far away as we can."

"Hopefully, we'll be back from Fontainebleau by then," Athénaïs said, rolling her neck and absently massaging her chest. I tried not to glance at her round, luscious breasts, but she made it hard not to do so. "Or maybe not. The King does love his estates outside of Paris. He makes everyone come to him so he can keep an eye on them all."

"Close quarters mean more control," I agreed as I placed Athénaïs' hair in a loose plait and thought back to the composure and poise of the monarch. The way we had all bowed to him and in doing so, elevated him in every way. "I think the King likes things he can control. He's a hunter, after all, isn't he? He wants to take down the wildest of does – the ones he shouldn't be able to catch and seduce. Like La Vallière."

"This is why I have you beside me," Athénaïs said as she rose and turned, placing a hand on my cheek. "You and your cards and your cunning eyes see the secrets of the court. When we go to Fontainebleau, you will take those eyes everywhere and find how I am to make my way back into Henrietta's good graces again."

"I will try," I said, losing my words as I lost myself in her lovely eyes. She was like the King, in her way, my new mistress. She made me feel seen and important when she looked at me. Not as a scrap of charity, the way attention from Thérèse or my mother

had made me feel, but true respect and regard. It made me ready
to do anything for her.

"There's my girl," Athénaïs smiled, and to my shock, she
pressed a quick kiss to my lips. It was fleeting and sweet, a gift
from one friend to another, but it left me struck dumb as she
turned and made her way to her bed. "Get some rest, Claude,
we have a lot to do tomorrow. I think I would like to have a
proper bath drawn, perfumed with whatever you recommend to
entice all the court to me. As long as it doesn't do the same to my
husband."

"Yes, of course, Madame," I stammered as I retreated to my
room beside hers, my fingers upon my lips, thinking of the
softness of her kiss.

I dreamed of them that night, as well as Louis's eyes.

THE NEXT DAY WAS indeed busy, with visits to dressmakers,
milliners, and jewelers – including Antoine Monvoisin.
Athénaïs spoke with the husband while I met with the wife,
procuring a few herbs from her garden that I couldn't find
elsewhere. La Voisin was grateful for the business, but made me
promise to share her name with at least three ladies at court in
exchange for a gift of rose oil mixed with lavender to anoint my
lady.

I used a good amount of it in the bath that was nearly ready
for her when we arrived back at her house. Jean Luc and the
housekeeper looked annoyed at having to haul the tub upstairs to

her room and fill it with scalding water, but neither I nor Athénaïs cared much. I stripped down to my shift to help her wash and she took off everything.

It was my first full look at the perfect curves of her body as she sank into the water and I helped to scrub her, and then lathered her with oils and perfume. She made lovely sounds of pleasure at the heat and relaxation, and spoke of how, at the palaces, there were entire rooms and pavilions dedicated to baths for the royal family or those in their household. She lamented that soon her figure would be changing with the growth of the babe, and I assured her it would still be beautiful. I meant it.

In my room next to hers that night, I clutched a ribbon she had worn to hold up her stockings that day, of blue satin. It still smelled of her, of roses and sweat. I held it close and thought of that promise, of what I had left unsaid by not telling her that she would remain beautiful to me, no matter what. It was true, and that should have frightened me, because nothing good had ever come of my infatuations in the past. Thérèse had not wanted me, Veronique had judged me. But Athénaïs… She was different. She had to be different.

I could feel myself falling more into her thrall each day, and I relished it. It had been so long since anyone had ignited my interest and passion like her. So long since I had dreamed of kisses and soft skin. I let my hands and mind stray in the dark, Athénaïs filling up my dreams. It was a strange thing, to want her to succeed in seducing the court, to hope she might give her love to another, but she deserved pleasure and power, and I would give it to her. I caressed my cunt, her ribbon tangled in my fingers, and thought of her pleasure and smile.

I'd enchant and ensnare for her because she had already ensnared me, I thought, my mind as frantic as my hand on my sex. It had been so long since I had touched myself, so long since I'd been touched, and my desire for my mistress, for those round breasts and pink lips, was so fierce, it barely took anything to make me come.

I gasped into the dark as I did, twitching and letting the little death unravel me, and pushing all my desire and lust into the ribbon.

Like a spell. All for her.

CHAPTER 12

STRENGTH

T HE CHÂTEAU DE FONTAINEBLEAU was radiant when we arrived, almost as much as Athénaïs's face when she looked out the carriage window to see it. The forty-mile journey south from Paris had been long, but the anticipation had kept us alert. As we rolled through the avenue of trees to the great entrance of the country palace, the hours in the shaking carriage seemed a small price to pay.

The creamy stone and steep roof reminded me of the Louvre or Vaux-Le-Vicomte, but there was something more relaxed about this place. It was an old château, used by kings and courtiers for centuries, but it had always been a retreat in the woods, not a prison inside a city. The easy curves of the great stairs at the front and the streams, fountains, and gardens surrounding it were welcoming as much as they were grand.

We arrived at the perfect time – Athénaïs's design – later rather than early, so more people were there to see Madame de Montespan exit her carriage with me and Jean Luc trailing behind. I was surprised when the servants escorted him, but not me, to place luggage in our rooms. I was instead ushered into the glorious front hall and gallery beside my lady. I was even more surprised as we were presented to an older woman in a resplendent gown and jewels that were somewhat out of fashion, but nonetheless beautiful. Her hair was silvering and her eyes were sharp and dark. She had a familiar long sloping nose and a sweet cupid's bow mouth. There was only one woman to whom the courtiers would bow so low.

"Her most serene Majesty, mother of the King, Anne of Austria and France," Athénaïs said as she presented me, and I sank before the Dowager Queen who had ruled France alongside Cardinal Mazarin for all of Louis's youth. "My Queen, this is my friend and companion, Mademoiselle Claude des Œillets."

"It is an honor, Your Majesty," I said, hoping not to stumble over my words. The Dowager Queen looked over me with little interest and turned her attention to Athénaïs.

"You have brought a maiden companion, but not your husband," Queen Anne said, and Athénaïs gave a gracious nod.

"He woke this morning with a malady of the stomach that prevented him from traveling," my mistress said.

"Something he ate must have disagreed with him," I confirmed.

Indeed, it seemed something had made it into the Marquis's food – perhaps a narcissus mixed in with the onions – the night before, keeping him very close to his chamber pot. Athénaïs had been ecstatic at the news and given me a knowing look.

"Being a good and loyal subject and husband, my husband insisted I attend, as requested by His Majesty the King, and my dear friend, Mademoiselle des Œillets, is here to make sure I am attended."

"How charitable of everyone," the Dowager said and clearly did not mean it. With another nod, we were excused and passed on to join the others milling about the gallery.

"She doesn't like you," I muttered as we made our circuit of the gallery, nodding and smiling to the other nobles who had come to parade for each other and the mother of the King.

"She doesn't like anyone," Athénaïs replied with a soft chuckle. "In fact, I think she rather favors me compared to how she feels about others. Just look."

We turned to watch as Olympe, Comtesse of Soissons, sailed into the room, a young woman trailing her. Apparently, she did not want Athénaïs to be the only one at court with an attendant. That made me smirk, but the way Queen Anne barely lifted her hand to greet the Comtesse was even more humorous.

"She hates all the Mazarinettes for their attempts to seduce her son," Athénaïs whispered to me as we watched Soissons turn and scowl as she left, hissing a comment to her maid. "But she hates hypocrites and sinners the most, I think."

It was at that moment Louise La Vallière arrived alongside Madame and Monsieur. The Dowager Queen greeted her son warmly and her daughter-in-law with at least an illusion of respect, but she glared daggers at La Vallière, who looked cowed by the situation.

"Do you think she'll stand in your way of being appointed to Henrietta's household again?" I asked quietly behind a fan.

"She certainly won't help. *How* to get into Henrietta's good graces though – that will be for you to help me discover," Athénaïs said.

"Am I to read the Duchesse D'Orléans's cards or palm?"

"You'll read the gossip of her servants," Athénaïs grinned back. "Tonight after supper, you'll wander among them. Because the gossip here is good, but what the servants know is better. You, my dear Claude, can move in both worlds."

It should have been an insult, to be reminded that, for all that I was allowed to walk with Athénaïs among all this splendor and scheming, I was still just a lady's maid – a nobody from the gutter. But I was also an actress, and I had played the role before. I had a mission now. One I was suited for.

A few other interesting characters entered the gallery after us, including a Princess of the Blood who remained out of anyone's good graces. Yes, that was the Grande Mademoiselle, Louis's cousin – his uncle Gaston's daughter, who had stood against her King in the Fronde. I did not like her on principle.

Madame and Monsieur arrived together and yet apart. The secondary royal couple did not look at each other as everyone marveled at them. Duc Philippe was attired even more gloriously than his wife, in a coat of red velvet and gold thread, a sash with a diamond-encrusted brooch, the feathers of his hat and the gilding of his cane drawing the eyes of everyone in the room, male or female, at the expense of his more conservatively-attired wife in pale pink. Henrietta whispered with the Comtesse de Soissons while her husband's focus remained on a dazzlingly handsome man in his entourage who I soon came to know was the Chevalier de Lorraine. Another Philippe, but never to be confused with

Monsieur. Indeed, it seemed to me sometimes that there were only four or five names in all of the nobility.

The nervous anticipation grew in the room, the courtiers all taking places and chittering like birds roosting before a storm. Or perhaps, more aptly, waiting for the dawn. I was nervous and excited too, and so was my mistress beside me. Though she hid it behind a veneer of decorum, I knew her heart.

Louis entered, at last. For the first time since I had seen him at his wedding procession, he had his Queen beside him, looking distant and depressed. The way my heart leapt when I saw him, the thrill of his mere presence reminded me of why I would attend to my tasks. I would walk barefoot over thorns to get to him, and also to get Athénaïs what she wanted. It was a strange tangle of feelings, but as Athénaïs had said of me, I was a curious sort of spider. So that's what I would be.

As I had done for so long, I watched, quiet and observant behind my mistress's shoulder, as the King gave his attention to his court. Women and men bowed to him, all seeking his attention and favor, but few receiving more than a courteous nod or smile. Some of them had petitions or requests on matters of state, which Louis acknowledged but did not answer; this was not the time for such things. And besides, Colbert and other counselors remained in Paris. This was the time for revelry.

I watched and enjoyed as we took in the wonders of Fontainebleau. The gardens and galleries, the delicacies and diversions. The court was welcomed with a true fête – dancers and a new play by Monsieur Corneille. The work was serviceable, but I was honestly sad Molière had been occupied.

The court composer, Monsieur Lully, conducted a march for when the King walked to his seat, and then dances and other music as the party went on. It was a delight, and when it was suitable, I remarked on the weather, the deliciousness of the food, and the mediocrity of the play when asked. For the most part, though, I was quiet.

I watched Athénaïs as she moved seamlessly from group to group, accruing invitations to dinners and gambling tables, fielding flattering compliments and sly insults with equal aplomb. No one here said exactly what they meant, because the rules of the game they were all there to play prohibited such honesty. It took me a while, but soon, I could tell which Comtesses really meant it when they said they had missed Athénaïs presence and which ones resented the competition of her return. They all wanted what she had lost and sought to regain – an official position in Madame's household. Or in the Queen's. Such positions not only came with prestige and pay and dedicated apartments in the palaces, but also access to the royal household at all times.

I mulled on the contradictions of the maids of honor of the Queen and other elite ladies as Athénaïs and I retired to our quarters long after midnight. For years, I had been a maid, a servant to a noble. Mere servants were not enough for royalty, however; they needed other nobles to serve them, not mere mortals like me.

Of course, it was intimate to serve someone. There was a level of trust that came from what I saw of my lady in her unguarded moments, from all she confided in me as I undressed her. There was unspoken trust with the person who truly saw a noble without all their armor and artifice.

"I've never been this tired after such a celebration before," Athénaïs groaned as she fell into bed. "And don't tell me it's because of the pregnancy. Until I can see it, I'm going to pretend it doesn't exist and enjoy a nice relief from my courses for a few months."

I chuckled as I arranged the sheets over her and removed her slippers. "I'm afraid to say your babe likely won't tolerate that. They have a way of making themselves known."

"I could barely eat at supper after starving all day," Athénaïs sighed. "I'm desperate for a fuck, but the idea of inviting any of those useless, simpering courtiers here for a tumble is just as repulsive. And it wouldn't do me any good."

"Then sleep," I consoled her, still smiling at her forthrightness and how honest she was about what she needed and why. "I'll return soon with more useful information than any marquis or count could ever provide you."

"Don't get caught, little spider," Athénaïs murmured with a smile as her eyes fell closed. I did not need to assure her that I wouldn't be. I changed into plain clothes befitting a lowly maid, whispered my spell for concealment, and anointed my wrists with four thieves' vinegar I had brought. I breathed in the acidic scent, punctuated with rue and garlic, and set off into the dark halls.

The servants' corridors in any great house were easy to find once you made it to the kitchen, so that was where I started. Though it was long past midnight, there was still activity there, with cooks stirring dishes that would be served tomorrow, and a few other maids and footmen relaxing next to the huge fireplace.

What was left of the grand meal that had been served hours before was laid out on the central table for anyone hungry to pick at. None of the other servants gave me a second look as I meandered through the warm space, making a show of taking some food and reclining by the fire next to the valets in fine livery, gathered to gossip among themselves.

"We had an entire carriage full of trunks just for his clothes," one footman was saying to the other, clearly incensed. "Well, his and the chevalier's. All of us had to ride in the wagon with Madame's things."

"How can you stand working for a sodomite like that?" the other footman scoffed.

"The sodomite pays twice what any other household does. Even this one!" the footman scoffed. "And he pays that much so that all I complain about is the carriage rides."

The first speaker took a draught of wine and his companion shook his head and crossed himself. I chewed my delicate cake and moved on. I knew the rumors about Monsieur – how he would attend private parties in gowns and doted on his male favorites, but I had never heard such explicit naming of his sins.

I picked up a basket of linens as I left the kitchen, slipping into the hidden passages reserved for servants and stewards so they could move about Fontainebleau unseen and quiet. I didn't know my way, but I walked as if I did, and no one stopped me, and eventually, I found the right corridor that took me to the rooms of the royal family. During the day when they were in residence, these quarters were open to their household and courtiers, but now, in the dark of the night, only servants could enter. And spiders.

There was still a tumult of activity in Monsieur's rooms – voices of men and the clink of bottles filling glasses. I peeked through a cracked door and was unsurprised to see the King's brother in a gown of gold, entwined with the Chevalier de Lorraine on a divan. Other men around them laughed and embraced as well, and I could not help but smile sadly. I was like them, in my converse way.

It was quieter near the other bedrooms, and my heart sank that I was too late to eavesdrop on some gossip between Henrietta and her ladies that I might use for Athénaïs's ends. We had more days remaining in Fontainebleau, of course, but I wanted something I could bring her now.

I drifted from door to door, listening for voices or movement, holding my breath, and sending up soft prayers. I needed this.

"Almost!" My heart lurched into my throat at the sighed exclamation from the other side of the door. "Yes, right – right there!" The voice was strangled and frantic and unmistakably female. A lover nearing the peak of passion. Could it be Henrietta with some paramour – satisfying her while her husband also took his pleasure elsewhere?

Whoever was doing the pleasuring made a muffled obedient sound and the voice... was not male. I pushed the door open enough so I could peek through to the room beyond. The sight thrilled me in many ways.

Henrietta was at the edge of the bed, her fine night dress hanging off her body, one pert breast exposed as she watched the woman between her legs. Her brow was knit, her skin flushed, and her hips were moving frantically as she chased the climax that Olympe de Soissons was trying to give her. Trying poorly, it had to be noted. Her mouth and tongue were at work, but she was hesitant, too careful, and clearly not lost in the ecstasy of the beautiful woman she served. That's what this was – a service, not passion. Not enough for Madame.

"Harder!" Henrietta yelled, and her lady-in-waiting halfway obliged with the fingers she was pumping. The princess brought her own hand to her cunt, batting away Soisson's inept mouth and rubbing furiously as she was fucked. Faster and faster, the Comtesse matching her ferocity at last, until finally, she cried out and arched her back, her orgasm overtaking her.

Henrietta didn't see how the Comtesse withdrew and wiped her hand and face as soon as she could. She didn't see her maid's scorn. But I did, and that was all that I needed. I closed the door quietly and scurried back to my duties, smiling wide.

I WOKE EARLY, MY back sore from the small bed in my room adjoining Madame de Montespan's. I fetched her breakfast and had it ready for her when she rose half an hour later, accompanied by groggy moans.

"You would not believe the dreams I had, Claude," Athénaïs yawned as I came to sit at the edge of her bed with her tray. "I never thought having a child in me would make me dream so vividly of all the ways one could get put there."

"I had quite a vivid night as well," I drawled back, enjoying how sweet and soft this formidable Marquise looked in the morning.

"Oh, you wonderful thing! What news?" she demanded as she sprang up from the pillows.

"For one, I can confirm every rumor about Monsieur."

"So can every person in France with eyes or ears," Athénaïs grumbled back. "I need to get to Henrietta."

"And you will, because she shares the same vice as her husband," I replied with an easy smile. Athénaïs's dark brows raised high. "Or the inverse of it. I saw her—"

"With a woman?" Athénaïs finished for me, interest and glee in her face. "As a lover?"

"Would you like to know who?"

"You're just teasing me now, you little minx. Of course I do."

"I must say it looked like she was as poor a companion in bed as she is at court. Strange, really, since you've told me the Mazarinettes were all trained in seduction and lovemaking by the Cardinal himself. Or did I hear that from someone else?"

"The Comtesse de Soissons?" Athénaïs cried, grabbing me. "She was fucking Henrietta?"

"Well, she was trying," I replied, thoughtful and honest. "If someone were to offer Madame a more enthusiastic or skilled lover, perhaps the Comtesse could be replaced. And one who provided Henrietta with *satisfaction* might be elevated."

"And who would you suggest?" Athénaïs asked, more serious now. I could no longer meet her eyes. I took her hand and looked at that instead, reminding myself of my devotion to her and what we had promised to do. I was bound to her by a spell I had cast, and a heart I could not control.

"It could be me, if you made the right... introduction," I murmured.

My mistress gasped. "You'd do that for me? Commit such a sin?"

I had to laugh at that. "I have committed sins much graver, be assured. To serve you in such a way would be an honor and I—"

"Have you done it before?" My eyes shot up to meet hers at the fascinated tone in her voice, and there was no judgement in her face. "Have you been with women?"

"Many times," I confessed softly and moved to release her hand. Athénaïs tightened her grip before I could.

"Do you like it?"

"I do, Madame, it is… my preference." I swallowed down my rising anxiety, waiting for some black pit of fear to bubble inside me. But my shadows stayed put in my heart as Athénaïs gave me a fascinated smile.

"I think, then, dear Claude, that you should not be wasted on a self-important bitch like Henrietta. That will be my task," Athénaïs said slowly. Her hand swept up my arm, over my shoulder, and to my cheek. My heart was pounding as I lost myself in her determined gaze.

"*You* wish to seduce her?"

"I wish to, but I require instruction from one devoted to me and practiced in these arts." I almost swooned to hear her say it aloud. The only thing that stopped me from falling was her, my Athénaïs, leaning in and kissing me.

I think I wanted to kiss her from the first moment I saw her; wanted to feel her melt into my mouth and catch the sound of her sigh on my tongue. She was so welcoming, so hungry, and I realized distantly that it had been such a long time since this glorious woman had been truly kissed by one who adored her.

"My lady," I whispered as our lips parted, meeting her blue eyes and finding delight there. "How may I serve you?"

"Do to me what must be done for Madame," she commanded with a smirk. "Then we shall see what I have learned."

I ignored the spike of fear that the second order gave me and turned my attention to the choking lust I felt when I looked at her. With shaking hands, I removed her chemise, lifting it to expose her naked body in all its supple, welcoming softness.

"Tell her she is beautiful," I sighed, running my hands over Athénaïs's flushed skin. "Tell her she deserves to be pleasured by one who is starving for her."

Her eyes lit up at that, thighs parting subtly and drawing my attention to the dark hair above her sex, a different shade from the golden locks of her head. "Take off those clothes, Claude, or I won't believe you want to be here."

I had never undressed faster, spurred on by the thrilled, powerful look on Athénaïs's face as I revealed myself to her. As soon as I was bare, ready to kneel before her, she seized me and kissed me again, pulling me towards her in unexpected desperation. This was the first time in so long I had touched another with nothing clouding my mind, and yet, her lips were as intoxicating as any wine, and my mind swam as my flesh hummed in desire. Her skin against mine ignited me, as I pressed my body against hers in the bed.

"Do you starve for me, Claude?" Athénaïs cooed as I kissed down her throat, the need to touch and taste every inch of her overcoming me.

"More than you can know," I whimpered and took her tight nipple into my mouth. It made her cry out softly, but not in pain. I thrilled at the friction of her belly against my breasts, of her legs seeking to wrap around me.

"Show me then," Athénaïs sighed and grasped my hand. "I will show you too."

She guided me to her sex, revealing the wetness there. She was dripping, and it was for me. I would make her come for me too.

I parted her thighs and took my honored place between them, adoring her cry when I set upon her with my lips and tongue. She was sweet and pungent in my mouth, responsive to each lick and nuzzle. Soon enough, her hips were pumping, chasing after her pleasure.

"God, that's good. No one has ever done this to me," she babbled, and I smiled against the roundness of her thigh as I added a hand to my work. "Oh, heavens. Claude, yes…"

I filled her with my fingers and she screamed into her pillow as I began to fuck her properly, licking fast at her most sensitive places until she convulsed around me, pleasure tossing her body like a leaf on a stream.

I caressed and kissed her as she came down from the climax, making my way carefully back up her body and cradling her face. She was undone, bleary-eyed, and smiling. I had given her that.

"That was a wonderful first lesson," Athénaïs sighed. "Now, I will see what I have learned."

"Madame, you don't have to," I protested as she pushed me onto my back, dark panic rising in my gut and buzzing in my ear. Orders to be still and obey echoed from the back of my mind.

"I want to, Claude. I need to." She kissed me and my fear eased, but not entirely. "Shall I begin as you did, with these pretty tits of yours?"

"I—" The words choked in my throat as she sucked a nipple into her mouth, her tongue and teeth both playing with the tight nub. She was methodical in it, caressing me with her hands as she suckled and drove all thought and reason from my mind. "Yes, Madame, yes, that's right."

"Spread your legs for me," she whispered, and I complied instantly, my head lolling back. It felt like flying, like part of my soul was exiting my body – the part that was afraid and wanted to cry out for her to stop. "Oh, you're lovely."

He'd said that too. The man who had broken and ruined me. But the hands on me were delicate, not blunt and rough. She was not him. I was safe. I knew it in my soul. Even so, my heart was pounding, my breath was ragged, my body tense with both desire and fear. "Please," I heard myself whisper, desperate for her to touch me once again. Thank heaven, she did.

"Oh my," she murmured as her fingers discovered my wetness, tentative and curious. "It feels so different from attending to myself and yet…" She pushed a finger inside me without warning and I gasped, my body beginning to quake. "You're so *tight*."

"I…" How was I supposed to form the words to tell her of my fear and shame, and how traitorous my body was for wanting her to keep going? How I was close to coming from just the feel of my mistress within me, and yet, how afraid I was to let go?

"I am ahead of myself," Athénaïs laughed warmly, charmed by how she had undone me already. "I think this was next. I must admit, I have always wondered what the taste would be." She pushed my thighs apart and gave a light, experimental lick at my cunt, her finger still teasing within me.

I bit down on my raw sound of pleasure, but I could not control the way my body began to writhe and respond. I was reeling. I was overcome. My body was so tense, I was ready to snap at the right touch. And touch she did, teasing me with the tip of her tongue, fast and slow in turn, and finding those places inside me that made me groan and buck as she slid out and in. I wanted so much to let go, but I was still so afraid.

"Remarkable and delicious," she murmured. "Do you need more?"

I made a strangled noise that was nothing close to words because I didn't – I *couldn't* – understand what she was asking. All I could do was writhe my hips and pant, every nerve and muscle primed with pleasure.

"I cannot believe I have rendered you speechless with so little effort, my Claude," she went on, and I groaned as she added another finger inside me and her thumb pressed above my entrance. "I want to know how to make you come. How will I do that if you won't instruct me in what you want?"

I wanted to scream as she kissed up my body, trapping me beneath her in a way that made me wild. Didn't she know? She already had me so close, but how could I tell her when even I didn't know what key would unlock me?

"Madame," I begged, my eyes screwed shut as she fucked me and kissed my jaw. "Athénaïs."

"I want you to come, Claude," she panted, and straddled my thigh, rubbing herself against me as she pushed me to a dizzying, terrifying height. "I need you to come."

I shook my head, frantic and lost. I couldn't. If I did…

"Look at me," she ordered, and I had to obey. I looked up into those gorgeous eyes, the blue now almost completely obscured by her wide pupils. Her cheeks were red, and she was so beautiful, and my whole body was screaming for release – but *I couldn't.*

I was weeping, I realized, even as my body chased her hands, even as my own hands grasped her so tightly. Because if I let go, I would fall. The darkness would take me.

"Come," Athénaïs commanded. "Come for me."

Whatever curse was upon me shattered at those words, and so did I. I came, pleasure whiting out my vision, my body trembling and tossing as my mistress moaned in delight above me and fresh moisture coated my thigh where our bodies entwined. I rode the climax for what felt like forever. I wanted it to be forever because I had not felt so safe in years.

Athénaïs collapsed on the bed beside me, catching her breath as I continued to float in bliss, my mind quiet for the first time in so long.

"A good first lesson," Athénaïs purred. "But I shall need many more, I think. As often as possible."

"Whatever you wish," I whispered back. "I will provide it. Anything."

I was prepared to do anything for her. What did it matter if we were plotting to put her in another's bed? As long as I could be near her, I didn't care. I would fuck and spy and scheme to get another moment like this.

CHAPTER 13

THE WORLD

LE MONDE

I FOUND MYSELF IN the gardens of Fontainebleau on the last day the court was to be there, watching Olympe de Soissons carefully. I had learned all I could about the Comtesse in the previous days. Some things had made me pity her; some had made me hate her.

I walked alone beside a great reflecting pool, my bonnet keeping the spring sun from my eyes, and watched the Comtesse with a cluster of ladies across the water. She always had to be at the center of any group, and unlike Athénaïs, who attracted people around her, Olympe placed herself forcefully where she wanted to be. Like her position in Henrietta's household, where Olympe had wedged herself to get closer to the King, a man who remained frustratingly out of reach for her.

The Comtesse was the second-born of the five famous Mazarinettes. Nearly all of the Cardinal's nieces had been rumored to be entangled with Louis at some point, having grown up beside him. Now, Olympe was the oldest of the Mancini sisters living, as Laure, the Duchesse de Vendôme, had died in childbirth six years ago. Laure's children had been passed off to the youngest of the sisters, Marie Anne, who had been married at seventeen to the Duc de Bouillon, an infamously brutish man. Olympe spoke of her brother-in-law with nothing but contempt, for it seemed Marie Anne was the only sibling Olympe still loved.

The spray of a fountain shielded the Comtesse from my view as we continued by the pool at the same pace. She did not notice me watching. She was only cognizant of the crowd around her, laughing at her every word as their jewels and silks glittered in the sun, brilliant as the water. It was a recent addition to the grounds, added at the King's command. Louis loved these gardens, and that was the reason we were all here: the King was promenading through the grounds, and every companion and courtier wanted to catch a glimpse of him and bask in his divine attention. Especially the Comtesse.

It had been the third sister, Marie, who was most often rumored to be Louis's first great love. Olympe was jealous of that. Marie had been removed from Louis's orbit by marriage to an Italian prince. The fourth sister, Hortense, had nearly been married to Henrietta's brother, Charles II of England, while he had been in exile in France in the 1650s. In a huge blunder, Cardinal Mazarin had not thought the absent king was a good enough prospect (nor had the Grande Mademoiselle, to be fair). When Charles was restored to the throne in 1660, it was too late for poor Hortense.

She had been saddled at the age of fourteen with one of the richest and most odious men in France, Charles de La Porte. If Olympe pitied that sister (who was rarely at court and was just then in confinement with a second child), she did not show it well.

The Comtesse and her entourage turned the corner at the same time as I did so that I could walk slow enough to come behind them as we moved up towards the château and the open doors where courtiers were coming and going. I thought I was doing quite well – until the party in front of me stopped abruptly and bowed.

The King had stepped out in front of them.

I bowed too and it was only Louis who saw it, giving me a gracious nod that allowed me to rise before gifting the Comtesse and her friends with the same courtesy. My nerves fluttered, excitement at seeing the King once again taking over me. Would I ever encounter him and not feel this giddy thrill?

"Your Majesty, your gardens are a wonder," Olympe declared with what I'm sure she thought was a coy and charming smile.

"They are but a taste of what we will have soon," the King replied with a smile that was almost mischievous. "My new gardens at Versailles shall be a wonder to all of Europe. I have engaged André Le Nôtre. He was wasted on that traitor Fouquet."

"All things you create and touch are wonders, sire," the Comtesse purred. I didn't mean to roll my eyes, and I certainly did not mean for the King himself to see me do so. I froze when I realized my error, wondering if it would mean my exile and death. Then, to my shock, the King laughed softly.

"Do you enjoy my gardens, Mademoiselle des Œillets?" the King asked me, and suddenly, every eye was upon me as I walked cautiously toward the gathered crowd.

"They are beautiful, sire."

"But?" he pressed. How had he heard the unspoken remainder of my thoughts? I met the royal eyes and prayed he was merciful with those who spoke honestly.

I forced my voice to be steady. "But the variety is disappointing. Have your gardeners forgotten that the iris blooms this time of year? Or the humble petunia?"

A beat of silence passed as the monarch considered me and the court waited for his response. And then, he laughed again, hearty and warm. Real. "I have said as much myself! I am very near to having to make an official proclamation for the gardeners to put in a kitchen garden as well. I don't see why I'd need to ship peas in from miles away when I can grow them right here."

"There is still time to plant them for summer, sire," I replied. "We are done with the frost."

"And how they shall thrive in your presence," Olympe cut in, her laugh as false as the King's had been warm. "What else do you wish to plant, Your Majesty?"

"Well, I had considered—" The King's words faded as he caught sight of someone behind us. In an instant, his eyes went from those of a gardener to those of a hunter. "You must excuse me, Madame La Comtesse. Mademoiselle des Œillets."

We all turned to see what prey our sovereign had spotted, though I already guessed. Sure enough, sweet Louise de La Vallière had emerged from a garden path with Henrietta. The

Duchesse looked bored with her, then unsurprised when the King offered his arm to her lady.

"Did you know that Louis started conversing with La Vallière to throw off suspicions about him and Madame?" the Comtesse hissed towards no one in particular before her eyes fell on me. "You are Madame de Montespan's companion, are you not?"

"I am, Madame La Comtesse," I said with a low, careful bow, the depth of my descent showing my respect for the lady. I saw in her face that it did not go unnoticed. "Though I dearly hope to make more friends in court as I make my way."

"Excellent," Soissons said and gestured for me to follow as she began to move. "Walk with me. Not you," she snapped to her other companions.

The Comtesse did not moderate the speed of her stride as we headed in a different direction than Louis had gone with La Vallière, and I had no choice but to keep up.

"It is indeed beautiful here," I began when we finally slowed near a pavilion and a much smaller fountain.

"You seem to know a great deal about plants, which fascinates the King," Olympe declared, looking me over. I wore a dress of pale green with wide sleeves and a bodice forming a long, tapering triangle of ivory down my front. It was a fine garment, and you could see the lace on the cuffs of my chemise and the embroidery on the overdress, but it was nothing as ostentatious as the concoction of cream and pink trimmed with pearls and gold that the Comtesse wore.

"Gardens bring me great joy and comfort," I replied honestly.

"Teach me about them then. Tell me all that that is," she ordered, pointing at a shrub.

"It would take a great deal of time to impart all I know," I replied carefully, taking stock of the woman before me. She was agitated and, if I was honest, reeked of desperation for any topic she could use to converse with Louis. "And it is knowledge I would only share with one truly interested. For their enjoyment and not for other purposes."

"If you need to be compensated, take this," she said with no hesitation and removed one of her pearl necklaces. "You need more decoration anyway. If anyone asks, I was being charitable to my new friend. Feel free to tell Athénaïs. She'll be ashamed for not outfitting you better."

I took the necklace and put it on, smiling wryly. "I will tell you what you wish, Madame La Comtesse. But..."

"But?"

I bit my lip and looked at my nails, the picture of friendly hesitation. "But I do not think that naming a flower will gain you the King's attention for long when his gaze is so focused on Mademoiselle La Vallière."

Color rose in the Comtesse's cheeks, and her eyes narrowed. "You assume that is what I want."

"I would never assume, Madame La Comtesse – neither what you wish for nor what it will do for your future. I apologize." I made my voice contrite and sincere. "My mind is occupied. I recently had my fortune told by a good friend – one who shares my love of plants and all their purposes. She spoke of the King and how he shall evade any who seek him."

"A fortune teller?" There was the spark I wanted to see in Olympe's eyes. "It has been a while since I visited such a person. Is your friend skilled?"

"She is excellent and, well, she does have a way of helping women achieve their hopes when the future is uncertain. Alas, while she is my friend and provides me my fortune at a discount, I cannot afford her help in that arena. Such assistance is reserved for only the most trusted and richest ladies of the court." I gave a small gasp and covered my mouth at the confession. "Forget that…"

"Other ladies of the court?" Now the other woman's eyes were wide and transfixed. I could see the thoughts rushing through her mind – that her rivals had access to knowledge and power she did not. "Can you make me an introduction to this friend?"

"She lives in the city," I began, making a show of worry. "Perhaps when we all return from Fontainebleau, I can take you some evening. You will need to tell Madame that you are unavailable."

"Believe me, it would delight me to be *unavailable* to Madame for a few hours."

"We will make arrangements when we return to the city," I assured her with a sly smile.

"ALL OF IT IS done," I told Athénaïs as soon as I entered her room later that night. She was still in her gossamer costume from dancing in the royal ballet that evening, a spectacle I had been sad to miss. I had seen the rehearsals and helped her practice, of course, but it would have been a delight to see her dazzle the court with her beauty. Alas, it had been the perfect time to slip away from the palace to a crossroads nearby to bury our wax figure of Athénaïs's husband.

"How soon will the bastard be gone?" she asked, rising on her elbows from where she seemed to have collapsed on the bed.

"You know I can't say for sure," I chided. "Magic is a force of nature; we can't say when the wind will change, only know that it will."

"Well, your other trick worked quickly," she replied, reaching under one of our pillows to retrieve the little sachet she had watched me make with a bit of the Comtesse de Soisson's hair and herbs. It was, in its way, the opposite of the poppet of wax we had made of the Marquis de Montespan. For him, the herbs had been hot and baneful – belladonna, nettle, and mace – driving him away and heating his steps. I'd buried it facing away from Paris to hurry him on his way. For Olympe, it had been all allure and sweetness – rose, almond, and thyme – enticing her to me.

"Maybe that's because of what we did on top of it," I smirked, my heart speeding and skin heating at the very thought of the delights I had found in Athénaïs' bed in recent nights. For her part, my mistress laughed warmly.

"Will we make one for Henrietta when the time comes?" she asked curiously. "Would it make you jealous to cast a spell for another woman to want me?"

"I cannot conceive how the whole court does not want you already," I answered honestly. "I know I must share you. I will have to take comfort in the fact that when it's done, you will come back to me."

Her eyebrow quirked, and she beckoned me to her. I moved to stand between her legs at the edge of the bed, taking in her golden, disheveled beauty as she looked up at me. "Did you enchant me too, Claude? Am I under your spell?"

"No, Madame," I said softly, dropping to my knees before her and pushing her skirts up slowly. "I prayed for you – for a goddess to find me and lift me up. But I would not dream of trying to ensnare you. Your spirit is far too strong." I kissed her thigh as I exposed it, nuzzling her.

"What a sorceress you are," she laughed. "Such magic you spin with that silver tongue."

"It is good for other things too," I whispered before I set to work serving her. Of undoing her, so she would know how to do the same to a princess, hoping all the while she would come back to me when she was done. The way she moaned and moistened – the power of her climax when I made her come – promised me she would.

"I HAD THOUGHT WE were going to some slum," Olympe said in surprise as our carriage rumbled to a stop a safe distance from Catherine Monvoisin's house. "This is quite respectable."

"She is a good Christian woman, my friend, and married to a jeweler. Though she makes money of her own," I answered. It was a precaution for the Comtesse's reputation and dignity for her carriage to wait here as I took her to my friend, not that her coachman would care where she went. The Comtesse did not want her rivals to know of her advantage over them, more than she cared for her reputation.

"How do you know this woman?" Olympe asked as we wove through the crooked streets of the city, the ones that had developed over years, fanning out like roots in the soil from the center of this huge, ancient city.

"I learned of her from a friend, and she has helped me find my way," I replied innocently. "La Voisin is an answered prayer."

"I hope you are right," the Comtesse muttered.

Soon enough, we were at the doorstep of the woman I had known as Catherine Deshayes, and like our mentor Lapère, she opened it before we knocked. In this case, it was likely due to her watching for us since I had warned her we were coming via a letter the day before.

"Mademoiselle des Œillets," Catherine said smoothly when she saw me, my new name sliding easily over her tongue. "And – oh my – Madame La Comtesse." She gave a deep, deferential curtsey.

"You know me?" Olympe said in surprise.

"You are known by all who look to the palace," Catherine replied. "Though your beauty is not done justice by your portraits and the papers. How may I be of service to two fine ladies?"

It was a wonder Catherine didn't wink at me when she said it, but Olympe drank up the flattery. "I hear you can tell me my future."

"I can see what path God, in his wisdom, has laid out before you, and where that path might lead if certain choices are made," the divineress replied cannily.

Catherine was good at this: better than Vigoreaux or Bosse or any of the other women of her ilk who tried this trade. She had unmatched ambition and no shame in sweetening her words with lies, piety, and flattery to win her clients over. Adam Le Sage had taught her well.

"Come in, come in, my dear ladies."

In La Voisin's parlor, we were treated to cakes and cider after we shed the heavy, dark cloaks that had protected our expensive dresses and identities. Catherine gave me an approving look upon observing my finery. I could hear a child laughing above us in the house and for the first time, I noticed the swell of Catherine's belly with another addition to her family. I wondered if it made her happy.

"Let me see your hand, Madame," La Voisin said to the Comtesse, and was eagerly obeyed. Catherine made a great show of saying a quick prayer, looking to the heavens, and crossing herself before she began to examine her new client's palm.

They trust me more when they believe I'm speaking for God or channeling some holy gift, I recalled Catherine telling me over our third glass of wine many months ago. *They can tell themselves what I do isn't witchcraft when I cloak it in prayers and piety.*

I had wondered aloud what the difference was, really, between a priest blessing a rosary or medallion and me making a charm for protection. There had been no answer.

"You are close to greatness on many sides," Catherine began. "From your birth and your marriage to your current place."

Olympe looked dubious. Everyone in Paris knew that about her. "Go on."

"You have a son and he…" Catherine's eyes went out of focus, a sign that this might be a real prophecy, not a show. "He will achieve greatness on the battlefield."

"The battlefield?"

"He will be safe, worry not," La Voisin assured her. "Your battles – the ones that lie before you, Madame La Comtesse – those are far more dangerous. More fraught."

"What shall I be battling for?" the Comtesse asked, now agitated, and Catherine's brows furrowed. "What is wrong?"

"Oh, Madame La Comtesse, I must be mistaken. You are a happily and successfully married woman," La Voisin began, reeling her prey as Olympe leaned closer. "There could not be any reason that I see a fight for love in the future. For a great man! Surely, it must be your husband. If his affections have turned away – oh no, I cannot suggest it."

"What if they had?" the Comtesse said, voice dark and serious. "What if I wanted to bring a man's love and affection back to me? Or if I had a rival I wanted to drive away?"

"One thing at a time, Madame," Catherine said with a smile. "There are ways, of course, to achieve such things – through our good Lord. I can say prayers for you. I know a priest who will bless something to give to your husband. Just to start."

"To start?" Olympe echoed, and I saw the sparkle in Catherine's eyes. She had her. It would be a slow process, enticing Olympe de Soissons to use La Voisin's aid to achieve her ends when it came to her ambitions. Who was to say what measures would be sincere magic and what would be mere show in exchange for her coins? It would give her hope and keep her distracted while Athénaïs made inroads with Henrietta.

I didn't feel any sort of pain when I imagined what Athénaïs was doing at that moment. She knew what she wanted and so did I. A position in Madame's household would keep us in Paris and at court. It could even lead to more advancement, perhaps bring us closer to Louis and the thrill of his attention…

"Mademoiselle des Œillets, would you mind giving us privacy?" Olympe asked with a glint in her eyes.

"There is more food in the kitchen," Catherine said.

"Of course, take all the time you need." I nodded and retreated to the kitchen, only to find I was not the only one there. I smiled to see Lapère seated at the table, bouncing little Marguerite Monvoisin on her knee.

"There you are. I've been waiting," Lapère cooed without looking up, smiling at the giggling child. "You have not visited my house much of late. The moon has missed you."

"I've been at court," I replied proudly. At last, Lapère met my eyes and gave me a warm smile. "You knew that, though, didn't you?"

"I did. You have done well for yourself," my elder said. "And don't bother telling me this is only the beginning of your rise. I know that too."

"I have a friend who will need a midwife in the fall," I said instead as I sat beside her. "You have not met her but—"

"I'll attend your friend, don't worry," Lapère said. "Would you have asked Veronique for help if she was in the city?"

"Is she still in the country?" My stomach fell to think of Veronique and how I had persisted in avoiding her for so long.

"She's returned to a village near Rouen, to midwife and help women there. She found friends," Lapère said carefully. That meant another circle. Another group of witches in a much more dangerous place for such circles to gather. A risk that Veronique was taking because of me.

"Is she safe there?" I asked, anxiety rising. "Can you see her?"

"My vision does not extend so far, especially without consent," Lapère shrugged, returning her attention to little Marguerite. "But my instinct is to say no. I tried to make her come home, but she said she was needed there."

It might as well have been an accusation, and it stung. But what could I do? She had turned away from *me*. And anyway, I had a new path now, one she would not understand.

"What other news?" I asked tightly.

"Things go worse in our court than the one you frequent," Lapère sighed. "Your King hates this city and wants to scrub it clean. Every time I look to the future of the Court of Miracles, I see an ending."

"I wish there was something I could do." I had heard of the man Louis had tasked with bringing Paris into some sort of order, sweeping away the rot and slums, as if it were so simple. Nicholas de la Reynie, the man was called, and I feared what he would do.

"You do not have the ear of the King yet?" Lapère chuckled. "Don't blame yourself for the choices of others, Claude. That way lies madness."

"Maybe one day, I will have his ear," I said, puffing up. It was a mad thought, but I already had been closer to the King than anyone I knew from the old days could imagine. "Maybe I could still help."

"By the end of the year, the Court of Miracles will be gone," Lapère shrugged.

"What about you? You'll never leave your garden."

Holding the small child, Madame Lapère looked particularly old. Her hair was grayer than it had been when I first met her, her back slightly more bent. She clucked her tongue and shook her head. "I'll survive, as long as Our Lady deems it necessary. Our friends La Voisin and La Vigoreaux keep me busy when women need me."

"Is that why you're here tonight?"

"Yes, someone is coming at midnight, but I came early for supper and company." She smiled as little Marguerite burbled on her lap. "I always enjoy time with the young. You remind me of how grateful I am to be past those years."

I laughed and took a place beside her, comforted by her mere presence. There was something magical in just being near an elder who still knew so many secrets of the hidden world.

"What do you use when you can't find pepper for a banishing?" I asked, and we fell into the ease of old lessons as she gave me her answer (clove, if it could be found, or mustard seed, of course). Soon enough, the other women were done with their private audience, and Soissons and I were on our way after she had paid Catherine with a heavy bag of coins.

The Comtesse seemed determined and elated as we returned to her house, which was also near the Louvre, but much grander. Like many ladies in the royal households, she had apartments in the palace, but did not always use them.

"Thank you, Mademoiselle des Œillets, you are a useful ally," the Comtesse said as I turned towards the street that would take me back to the quiet Montespan manor. "I think you may go far."

"I will take that as a compliment, Madame La Comtesse." I curtsied and left, hiding my face with my hood and considering her words.

She meant that I had shown her I was capable of doing what was necessary, no matter if it was a sin. Not all women at court were so unscrupulous. Some, like Louise La Vallière, truly cared for their virtues and what the priests and bishops said of their sins and souls. Yet, they were just as much a part of the intrigues and politics as the rest of us; helpless creatures who were used and traded, but refused to do any using themselves. They were not like Athénaïs or Olympe or me. We took. We were not the ones taken unless we wished it.

What would Veronique have to say about this world?

The thought stopped me in my tracks right where I was to turn down our street. I had not thought of her for months, as I had lost myself in Athénaïs. That was a blessing, was it not? As it was a blessing to forget and ignore all those terrible things I was capable of – the things I had done that Veronique could never accept. She was not a simpering swan who would let herself become a prize. She would refuse to play the game. She would leave the city she knew to have a chance at helping people before she compromised her soul. I didn't know if that made me resent her or respect her. Maybe a bit of both.

Still, I hoped she was safe, and that whatever circle she had found would protect her.

I closed my eyes and felt the power of the crossroads where I had found myself again. "*Hail to you, Our Lady, Queen of Crossroads and the Night,*" I whispered as the wind picked up and stirred my cloak and hair. "*Protect your daughter, Veronique Pelletier. Keep her from harm in your service.*"

I felt the night breathe as it regarded me, as it acknowledged my prayer. Who was to say if Our Lady would answer me, or if I deserved to ask such a thing? I hoped I was heard. I hoped Veronique was safe.

Content with my petition, I returned home quickly. It was even darker than I had anticipated, and I had to use my key for the servants' entrance. The kitchen was empty, save for the cook dozing by the dying fire. A place he usually would be awake this time of the evening, playing dice with Jean Luc. I kicked his foot and he startled awake.

"Where is everyone?" I demanded as he scrubbed his face.

"Oh, you weren't here for the good news," the cook snorted. "The Master has been called on legal business to the south. He'll be gone for months, and who knows when he'll summon your lady. Doesn't want her to travel too much with his heir in her belly."

"A few months?" I asked, not fighting my smile. "How unexpected."

"Mistress will be happy to hear of it, I'm sure. I know I am," the cook said before yawning and closing his eyes again.

I hopped away in glee. I had good news to share with my mistress in the morn. A gift from me. The spell had worked. I hoped she had good news for me as well.

CHAPTER 14

THE WHEEL OF FORTUNE

I T AMAZED ME HOW easy it was to walk into the palace of the
Louvre alone, without Athénaïs beside me. The guards with
their halberds at the gate seemed there merely for show and the
Musketeers – those sworn defenders of the King and France –
did not give a woman such as me a second look. Perhaps they
recognized me from when I had come before or they thought a
woman could be of no threat, but I still found the lack of security
troubling, given that the King's grandfather, Henry IV, had been
felled by an assassin, as had the king before him. Perhaps safety
was an illusion, like the barriers I had thought stood between the
common and the court.

I banished such grim thoughts from my mind as I made my way through the grand halls and galleries, still awed by their splendor, but noticing more about the place in contrast to Fontainebleau. Even the walls of a palace could not keep out the din of Paris on a busy morning, with merchants yelling and horses thudding past. All the perfume wafting from the courtiers could not fully mask the stench of shit, sweat, and rot from without and from within. No wonder the King preferred his country gardens.

I found Athénaïs entering the grand gallery, glowing with triumph at Henrietta's side. She met my eyes, and I knew we had won. She reached out to me graciously, bringing me to her side as I curtsied to Madame.

"I apologize for my lateness in attending you, Madame La Marquise," I said. I had no idea what excuse had been made for Athénaïs's early presence and did not wish to undermine it.

"Nonsense, it was I who kept Madame de Montespan late last evening," Henrietta laughed. She too looked happier than I had ever seen her. I had taught Athénaïs well. "I was so delighted to welcome her back into my household, I could not let her go so easily."

"My Lady - you have been appointed as a maid of honor again?" I asked, feigning surprise.

"You will, of course, continue to serve Madame de Montespan as her own lady," Henrietta added, and I beamed, this time sincerely. "She was quite clear on that. There will be a stipend for you too."

"I am glad of it," I said, amazed. "It is so good to know my lady will have a place in court, with her husband gone to attend business in the country for some months."

The gleeful laugh Athénaïs gave echoed through the grand gallery, pinging off the crystal and gold so that half the court assembled looked at her in shock. "God bless him, this is the greatest service to me and to France my dear husband has ever done."

The Duchesse laughed in response, and so did I. Outside, in the sky above the city, the clouds parted and the first beam of spring sunshine broke into the room like a ray of hope.

"What merriment so early in the morning?" We turned to see the speaker and all fell into curtsies, even Henrietta. It was proper when the Queen Mother and the Queen herself approached. They were alike, in their way, these two Spanish princesses who had been married to kings of France. Devout and decorous, with the same round cheeks and distinct chins that marked them as aunt and niece. It was the elder that had addressed us.

"I have just been informed that a stray animal troubling my lands has been driven out at last," Athénaïs said without missing a beat as she rose. Henrietta stifled a giggle as the two queens gave each other a look.

"We are on our way to Mass. Will you join us, Madame?" Queen Marie Thérèse said graciously, not trying to hide the Spanish accent that still colored her speech. "And your household members as well."

"Of course, Your Majesty," Henrietta agreed for us all. We fell in line among the Queen's ladies and made our way to the gloriously beautiful chapel. I tried not to gawk at the statues of saints, gilded crosses, and filigree throughout. It was the most decorated church I had ever been in, and all the gilding and gold made me feel far from any presence of the divine.

A few moments after we took our places in the pews behind the royals in a place of high honor (Athénaïs was practically floating out of her seat in glee), the Comtesse de Soissons rushed in. Her face was a wonder to behold as she saw us and knew instantly that something had changed, but she said nothing as she took her spot behind us.

The King was the last to arrive, and we all rose to honor his entrance, bowing our heads as he took his place at the front before the altar, across the aisle from his mother and the Queen, to whom he gave a gentle smile. Behind him, I noticed, was Louise La Vallière, who looked up towards the cross like she was facing her judgment before the King took back her attention. He was like a magnet, and I watched in fascination as that poor woman's resolve to make herself holy again crumbled under Louis's searing eyes.

We all looked up at the priests when they began Mass, chanting in Latin and waving the censers of incense to call down holy light upon us. Magic of their own. I said my amens and aves as I had been raised to do, but I was sad there was not more music. I liked it better when the priest or choir sang. I couldn't understand Latin well, but music was a language we all knew; God especially.

I glanced at Louis and wondered what it felt like to pray as the King – as the nation of France embodied in a mortal man. Did he pray for his people? As God's chosen, were his prayers louder than mine (if I bothered to make them in this stuffy place of idols and filigree)? Or did he care more for what was beside him? Did he pray for absolution for breaking his marital vows, as we all knew he did? Did he feel shame as his devout mother and wife watched him bow his head?

I wondered if I would ever be in a position to ask him. It was a wild thought, to contemplate knowing the intimate thoughts of *a king*. But was it so far-fetched? I was soon to serve in the household of his brother's wife. I – strange, poor Claude from nothing – had spoken with Louis and made him laugh. Now, we stood before the same altar. Would it be so strange for us to speak again?

Would Our Lady – in her disguise here as the Blessed Virgin, looking down from her alcove, her face peaceful as she regarded her children – hear me if I prayed for such a thing, the way God would hear Louis?

I would not find out that day – the chaos of court after church assured it.

There was much to do, it turned out, to make sure Athénaïs was in a position – physically – to attend to Henrietta. She would keep her house close by, of course, but she would be granted an apartment for her use in the Palais-Royal, as well, as all maids of honor to Madame were. She would need new wardrobes for both, of course, and with the income she now had she could, at last, afford it. Or try to. Where she should go and what to buy were a hot topic of conversation.

It was not my job to worry about that – other than wondering if the new gowns Athénaïs fantasized aloud about with the Vicomtesse de Polignac on her arm would be easy to get on and off her and if they would accommodate her belly when it began to grow. How would she handle her confinement and the birth? I found myself wondering as we strolled through the modest gardens between the Louvre and the palace of the Tuileries. How soon would Henrietta know her new plaything was with child?

I hung back from the group of ladies around Madame and found myself in the orbit of another woman who was also left behind by the crowd. None other than Louise La Vallière, the alleged mistress of the King.

"I saw you at Fontainebleau," the mademoiselle said to me when she noticed my staring. "You serve Madame de Montespan as a companion?"

Her voice was soft and demure, and for the first time, I noticed that she walked with a slight limp. Rather than make her seem awkward, it contributed to her overall air of vulnerability and ethereal beauty.

"I do," I replied. "She has done a great deal for me."

"She is lucky to have such loyalty. It is an admirable quality," La Vallière mused aloud. "We all must serve. To do so is a great honor."

I realized, as I looked at La Vallière, that she was already making an excuse for herself, for she knew what I expected of her. She *served* the King, her eyes said. She was a mere vassal, just like me.

"Must we? Without question?" I said carefully, and to my surprise, La Vallière laughed.

"What questions would we ask?" she shrugged. "When God himself will not answer, who are we to question our role? Especially as women..."

"Then we must follow our hearts," I offered, trying to be of consolation as I saw something dark in that woman's eyes. Something I recognized but did not want to see.

"Our hearts are treacherous and sinful," La Vallière declared, her face hardening. "This world does nothing but force us to sin and seek repentance. We cannot trust *our hearts* when they lead us into temptation."

"Ah, there it is," I said softly. She was not a victim. She was a hypocrite. She desired the King, as all did, but called herself a sinner because of it. "You are a romantic."

"I am no such thing, Mademoiselle!" La Vallière gasped, her delicate hand against her breast. "And I will not allow you to spread such lies."

"Claude!" I jumped at the sound of Athénaïs's voice. "I have errands for you!"

"Of course, Madame," I called back, holding La Vallière's gaze. "I must serve too, Mademoiselle. I shall see you again soon, I am sure."

I retreated, wondering if I had made my first enemy at court. It was no matter. As the lover of the King, the poor girl was everyone's enemy.

I WAS NOT ALONE with my mistress until much later that night when it finally came time to undress her. She rushed in as I was unpacking in the new room we would share, close to Madame's in the Palais-Royal in case Athénaïs was needed. With an appetite for a new delight, I was sure Athénaïs would be needed tonight.

"Oh, what a triumph!" she cried as she rushed in. "Everything has gone to plan!"

I had no time to agree before she embraced me and pressed a kiss against my lips. She smelled of sweet wine and perfume.

"I'm glad to hear. It was not too terrible?" I asked when she released me, my head spinning as it always did when she kissed me.

"You're better than her, if you wanted to hear that," Athénaïs smirked, and it made the knot in my stomach unfurl. "She was far more interested in me servicing her pampered cunt than giving anything back. Yet, according to her, I'm the best she's ever had."

"I'm not surprised," I purred as Athénaïs turned so I could attend to her back laces. She met my eyes in the mirror before her as I bent and kissed her shoulder. "You are the most beautiful woman at court, why would you not be the greatest lover? I am sorry I couldn't be there to assist you after."

"You were serving me in other ways," Athénaïs smiled, touching my cheek. "Is Olympe dealt with?"

"For now, we have her in hand," I replied. "I think she may try to curse Louise La Vallière. Should I help her with that?"

"Louise or Olympe?" Athénaïs laughed back as I removed her overskirt. "I'm not sure which of them we want sharing Louis's bed. What's worse – a whore with no heart or one with no spine?"

"The Comtesse de Soissons already has enough power," I mused. "La Vallière thinks herself a saint who is being corrupted. I don't know if the court would benefit from a snake like Olympe taking her place. For now."

"For now," Athénaïs smirked, then sighed as I kissed her neck again. "Henrietta wants Louis to have a weaker mistress if he won't have her. And La Vallière is easy to control."

"Should I protect her then – from Soissons?" I plucked a dried flower from Athénaïs's chemise. The carnation had been there against her breast, my charm to bring her love and lust, all day.

It worked well because it made me think of how I wished to be held close to her breast too...

Athénaïs pouted. "I don't wish to share your talents."

"La Vallière would have me burned if I mentioned my *talents* to her," I whispered. "But that does not mean I can't protect her from whatever Olympe attempts. Or undermine the Comtesse."

"We'll consider it, but first..." Athénaïs caught me in another kiss, this one hungry and warm. She was still mine, despite where she had been the night before and where she had to go. "Will you make me come before I go to Madame? She'll like it if I'm wet."

"Yes. I like it too," I whispered back.

THE SPRING PASSED QUICKLY. Perhaps more so for me as I found myself living several lives. I was busy every day in service to Athénaïs – taking on the duties of a maid, even though very few other ladies at court had a companion such as I. At least, not at first. I observed with amusement that soon after our arrival, the Comtesse de Soissons took on a girl who might have been a cousin as a companion and chambermaid. Her name was Marie-Auguste, and she was nothing compared to me. She crossed herself when I took her to visit the outskirts of Paris for the first time to procure a charm for her mistress from La Voisin. She was sick for days after, and from then on, Olympe decided she would make her own trips to the witches of Paris.

I saw them far more often than the Comtesse knew. I would still see my old friends when I found the time, and met Lapère's circle under the moon. There were new women sometimes, mainly fortune tellers hoping to make friends with the most well-known of their kind in Paris – and, of course, Vigoreaux and Bosse were there too, their enmity growing for one another, but also, I could tell, for La Voisin as her star rose.

It did not go unnoticed in the shadier districts of Paris that La Voisin was doing well for herself. Rumors circulated – started by her, I was sure of it – that her clients included noble ladies now. Her compatriots were jealous. So I helped them.

I had to be careful with how I whispered my friends' names in courtiers' ears, but I found ways to do it, often through the servants that I mingled with as easily as dukes and vicomtesses. That was my great skill: slipping in between two worlds, keeping one foot in both. When a marquise or baroness was said to be unhappy with her husband, I told her maid's friend, who whispered of a man named Le Sage, or how La Voisin or La *Vigoreaux* could help with such problems.

By summer, many ladies in court knew where to go to get their fortune read or even procure a love charm. Some of them went further – they procured Spanish fly to sprinkle in a lover's wine. Who knew if it was really ground-up beetles or just dust? It made them happy, and it made my friends money. Whether or not a potion is real is all relative, anyway: for what is the difference between a tea to bring luck and a poison to bring death, but the speed of the efficacy?

I enjoyed my place at the center of this web of connections, always observant of who hated who, who was seen coming and going from whose rooms, who was in debt to which minister, and what ladies sought favors for their husbands or lovers. It was as tangled a mess of connections as life in the theater, with as many secrets and surprises as the ways of witchcraft. In short, it was what I had been preparing for my whole life, and I thrived in it.

For the first time in years, I was happy. I felt proud of what I had done and where I had found myself. Where I had put myself, raised above so many others who did not ever dream of entering this world and these halls. What did it matter that my friends never praised me for what I had accomplished and all the riches and intrigue it brought to them? I knew my triumph. In mere months, I had achieved what they could not even dream of; surely, they were proud to know me.

The hard part was staying where I had placed myself. I had to be vigilant, keeping enemies and allies close enough that, sometimes, I was not sure which was which, as was the case with La Vallière and Soissons. The Comtesse seemed relieved to be ousted from Henrietta's bed, and I learned at the beginning of the summer exactly why. Olympe's eyes were not only on the King's favor, but the Queen's. She hoped for the coveted position of Superintendent of the Queen's household: the highest a woman at court could rise in terms of titles.

Marie Thérèse, however, was not overly disposed to promote a woman who had once hoped to marry her husband, to say nothing of Dowager Queen Anne, who could not forgive any of the Mazarinettes. The only person who all these great ladies despised more was Louise de La Vallière.

La Vallière was a frustrating mystery to me. She was so devout, speaking endlessly of her prayers and what some sermon she had heard or tract she had read meant for the souls of Henrietta's ladies. She turned her nose up at the gambling that was rampant at court, she refused to gossip about other affairs, and she was never afraid to offer her opinion on how the behavior of Henrietta's husband was a disgrace to the crown and an affront to God. All the while, she made the King break his vows and took carnal pleasure outside of marriage.

The ladies of the court whispered that it was a disgrace that the Queen did not know the King was flouting their marital vows. Wouldn't his mother be ashamed too? Of course, the King's grandfather had been an infamous philanderer and gallant, with an official mistress who received an income and a place at court. Queen Anne, in her devotion to God, had put an end to that, and Marie Thérèse, the Spanish Infanta who had become our Queen, would also not tolerate such humiliation.

It was June, and the court had moved. Much to the disgust of many a noble, we did not follow the King to Fontainebleau, but to the much smaller and humbler hunting lodge of his father, the place Louis claimed would soon be the grandest of his residences, the Château of Versailles. It was there that Henrietta and Olympe would go on the hunt for La Vallière, just as the King did the same in the woods around his lands. Whoever could expose Louise would win the favor of the Queen and perhaps oust her from the King's favor too…

Or so La Voisin and I counseled. All the portents pointed to a great change. I had taken to reading cards and palms for Henrietta in secret, at Athénaïs's behest, for I was the only one trustworthy enough to do it. It was one thing to pawn off a comtesse on a friend, but the future of a princess was something we had to keep close. I was inclined to agree, especially when the readings of my cards and Athénaïs's palm revealed that there might be more to Louise La Vallière's status than before. Athénaïs was unhappy to see the Empress card come up in a reading about the younger woman, but I knew what it meant.

I knew what to watch for as La Vallière skulked and prayed more than usual in the modest chapel at Versailles. She seemed more religious than ever, and in these closer quarters, it was easier to watch her and wait to strike.

I found my church in the forests and incomplete gardens that surrounded the palace, where I liked to walk in the afternoons to avoid the heat and gather what magical ingredients I could find. It was during these walks I missed Veronique the most, as well as Lapère and the friends I had learned these plants with long ago. It was they who confirmed to me what to do – the gambit I would make to move us higher than before. The poppy and the poplar, the alder and the moss, they spoke to me in the twilight as I laid out my cards on the grass. Six of Swords. Three of Cups. The Empress reversed.

THE GAME WAS CALLED Jeu de Volant, and I adored it. It was simple – two teams of women on either side of a net, all of us armed with small rackets, batting a feathered ball back and forth. I'd played a version of it back at the convent when we girls were allowed to exercise, and it had been my loud reminisces of it in front of Queen Anne that had prompted the discussion of setting up a game for the ladies of the royal households. Just as I had hoped and planned.

"Do you really think this will work?" Athénaïs asked as we moved out to the gardens where the net had been set up for us. She was nervously adjusting her bodice – it had to be looser lately to accommodate her belly, much to her dismay.

"I think it has a chance, like all gambits," I replied as I offered Athénaïs a hand to descend the limestone stairs towards the gardens. It was a balmy day, sweat gathering where my hair met my neck, and I was glad to have my mass of dark strands pinned up so that the breeze could touch my shoulders. My dress itself was simple but elegant, plainer than my mistress's, as always, in a periwinkle shade of blue I was told brought out my eyes. The important thing was that it was comfortable enough to move and play in.

"Ah, here we are, my dear Madame de Montespan," Henrietta trilled from beside our makeshift court. She was standing next to the pavilion where both Queens were seated in the shade, Queen Anne's ladies behind her and Marie Thérèse, readying themselves for the game. "Our esteemed judge was worried the teams would be uneven!"

"I still think your ladies have mine at a disadvantage, dear sister," Queen Marie Thérèse said as she examined the racket of one such lady standing demurely before her. "They are all so young."

"My youngest walks with a limp," Henrietta said, aloof and uncaring. "Come here, Mademoiselle La Vallière, and show her Majesty she need not be afraid."

I noted how Queen Anne scowled when the young blonde approached. I did not know if it was because of the insult to La Vallière or because of the impious woman being brought into her presence. La Vallière, for her part, looked ill, but bore the scrutiny with dignity.

"My leg will not trouble me," La Vallière said softly. "I barely notice it."

"She does look well," Queen Anne said stiffly. "If a little pale."

"And your ladies, Majesty, play for the dignity and honor of our Queen," Athénaïs said so smoothly, one would forget who she served. "And, alas, I must give them an advantage by removing myself from the game," she added with a calculated sigh.

"Whyever so, Madame?" Henrietta cried, playing her part so perfectly it was as if she had rehearsed it.

"I have been advised that it is not prudent to engage in such exertions in my ... condition." Athénaïs bolstered her confession by placing a palm on her belly and looking down, the very picture of motherly concern.

"Oh, my dear Madame, we did not know!" Queen Marie Thérèse said with more affection and feeling than I had ever heard from her. It was well known how much she loved children, her own son being the center of her world. "Congratulations to you and your husband."

"Thank you, your Majesty. He is overjoyed at the news," Athénaïs lied sweetly and looked at me. "Claude shall play in my place, if that is permissible."

"Of course, she is the very inspiration for this match!" Henrietta said, then turned pointedly to Louise La Vallière. She had grown even paler, her eyes flitting to Athénaïs's belly and her hands twitching. Because she wanted to place a hand on herself in the same place – I was sure of it. "As an unmarried woman, our Mademoiselle des Œillets should have no such compunctions about a game that will require so much exertion."

It was a challenge; a gauntlet dropped at La Vallière's feet to begin a duel, in front of both Queens. The King's mistress knew the position she was now in. She had begged off concern for her limp, so she could not use it as an excuse, but now, she had to think of her unborn babe – the child of *a king* – and if she would endanger it by playing.

"Is there something wrong, Mademoiselle de La Vallière?" Queen Anne asked, her voice like ice as she looked at the woman before her with the same contempt she would have used for a whore on the streets. Or perhaps more – whores on the street did not sully the bed of the King.

"Nothing, Your Majesty," La Vallière stuttered, before turning away and taking her place on the court. Unluckily for her, it was next to the Comtesse de Soissons, who had observed the entire interaction with a grin.

"Madame de Montespan," Marie Thérèse said, and I looked to see that her face was full of heartbreak, rather than the ire of her mother-in-law. "Sit here by me; you need rest on such a hot day."

A murmur went through the two teams on the court. It was the highest of honors, reserved for the most vaunted and esteemed of ladies, to *sit* in the presence of the Queen. Indeed, the special tabouret – a stool granted to those of rank – was as precious an object as gold at court. This was a coup for the Marquise de Montespan.

"Why, your Majesty, I could not imagine," Athénaïs said, as was expected. But a servant had already brought her stool, and she took it when Queen Anne gave her a severe look.

I smiled as I took my place on the court behind La Vallière and Olympe. The latter's look of joy at La Vallière's humiliation had curdled into a jealous sneer for Athénaïs. How she must have wished she had thought of this. But she hadn't. *I* had planted the seed, and the flowers were ready for harvest.

The game began with Henrietta throwing the shuttlecock up in the air and the teams of ladies rushing to hit it back and forth. There was running and jostling, points scored on both sides, but the eyes of the Queens were on Louise La Vallière alone, and she knew it. So did the woman beside her. The Comtesse de Soissons was in a mood now, seeing Athénaïs seated next to the Queens, and it was Louise who bore her wrath. She stole shots from her and jostled her with her hip, laughing blithely as she did. The women on the other side of the net, the Queen's maids of honor, were happy to help, aiming all their shots at La Vallière and forcing her to rush about the court.

I did not like La Vallière – she was too holy and too hypocritical for my taste – but I did not like seeing a woman who was so weak be pushed about, quite literally, by someone as ruthless as the Comtesse de Soissons. When the next hit was launched at La Vallière, I took the opportunity to dash in front of her and swat the ball away, much to the Comtesse's ire. I met La Vallière's eyes when I scored a point with the hit and saw she was near tears.

"I will take this place, Mademoiselle. I have more experience in the fight," I said, and La Vallière retreated, leaving me beside

Olympe. "Be careful of doing in the daylight what is best left for the dark, Madame La Comtesse," I whispered.

The Comtesse gave a heavy sigh, and I took it for agreement. It was too much to hurt La Vallière in public, or worse, endanger her child. She had been exposed to the Queens, but she was still the paramour of the King. Now she had a connection to him which guaranteed her a place for life. If the child lived and she lived through it.

THE PALAIS-ROYAL – THE official home of the Orléans household, of which Athénaïs was a part – was close to the Louvre, but smaller, for nothing was allowed to eclipse the glory of the King. I preferred it to the cavernous halls of the King's residence, which was soon to be connected to yet more galleries and administrative buildings, so much so that it felt more like a city unto itself than a home. The Palais was warmer, even on nights like this, where I moved through the halls in the waning afternoon sun.

Madame and Monsieur were attending a play tonight, and their retinues were not needed, which left Athénaïs time to rest as the babe in her belly taxed her with its growth – and its effect on her digestion. She was sleeping now, and it was my time to return to the secret places of the city to help her.

It had been a week since La Vallière had played in the game of Jeu de Volant to disprove suspicions of her pregnancy, yet confirmed them all with her expressions and demeanor. If we had needed any more confirmation, it came when the King intervened, as it was rumored that he visited La Vallière twice before the court left Versailles to return to Paris.

It was whispered that the King preferred his palaces in the country because everyone lived so close and it was easier for him to access La Vallière there than when she was serving Henrietta at the Palais. He did not seem to mind the chatter that his sister-in-law was close to dismissing Louise, as it was a disgrace for one of her unmarried ladies-in-waiting to be pregnant. There was another rumor, among the servants, that the King had sent his most loyal agents secretly throughout the city to find a new residence he could buy for La Vallière to keep her in permanently.

I walked through the busy streets of the city and wondered if poor little Louise would be happy in such a gilded cage. I, for one, liked my freedom. I liked that I could come and go as I pleased. I could put on my old, plain skirt of black and bodice of brown and walk among the people. None of them would know that, a few days before, I had been playing games with the Queen herself. I smiled to imagine their awe at who they were walking beside. As they all talked and gossiped about the King in his palace, I could simply walk into that palace. All because of my magic and what I had fought for.

Because I would not waste the freedom I had killed for.

I stopped in my steps, a shadow passing over my eyes and making me shiver. The unquiet dead were here, wandering the streets with all of us as they moldered in the charnel houses leagues away. I had not sat down to a dumb supper for years because I didn't even want to consider inviting the memory of Giles Faviot to my mind, but suddenly, the shadow of him and all the harm he had done and that I had done to him was so real, it choked me.

I was not surprised to look up and see that I was at the crossroads by our old house. The place where he had died by my righteous hand.

I scowled and turned my back on the crumbling wreck and the ghost there. Walking faster than before, I made it to my destination: not La Voisin's house this time, but La Vigoreaux's. Marie was sure to have the herbs I needed. What she also had, it seemed, was an apprentice. There was a woman seated by her door, embroidering by lamplight, who I did not recognize, and she rose to stop me.

"Madame La Vigoreaux is occupied with a client," the woman said, clearly proud to be the one to deliver such news. She looked younger than me; small, with tightly curled black hair and tan skin that made me wonder if she had Moorish blood. It was rare, but not unheard of, especially among those of us that trafficked in magic and other forbidden things.

"I'm an old friend of hers. I'm sure she won't mind if I wait in the back," I replied, but the woman – a girl, really – shook her head.

"A lot of people lately claim to be old friends so they don't have to pay or wait, but unless you're the bloody Queen, you'll need to wait out here for your reading." The woman paused and looked me up and down, maybe trying to see how much I was worth. "Unless you'd like me to read your palm for you. I'm her apprentice, Françoise Filastre. Or La Filastre, as they call me."

"Oh, are you?" I clucked. "Has Marie outgrown Lapère at last, to take on her own student?"

"You know Madame Lapère?" La Filastre said, face going slack.

"I do. But now, I'd like to see what La *Vigoreaux* has been able to teach you." I thrust out my palm into the light, and the younger woman took it with trembling hands. "Be sure to tell me of all the riches in my future if I work the right charms."

La Filastre scowled at my hand. "It looks to me like all you'll ever have is borrowed riches and glory. Ever a student, never a teacher like my mistress," she hissed as the door swung open behind her and I pulled my hand back. This child had no idea what she meant.

"What are you doing here?" Vigoreaux asked without ceremony. "Aren't you busy wiping some princess's ass?"

"Madame has released her ladies for the evening, so I am running an errand for my mistress. You make the best ginger and mint concoction for expectant mothers, I recall." I could not help but smirk as La Filastre gaped at me. I wasn't the Queen, but I was as close as she might ever get.

"If it's for a great lady I am happy to serve," La *Vigoreaux* chuckled before motioning me into her front room. Her client was still there, seated by the fire and wiping her eyes as if she had been weeping, but she looked relieved. And familiar... It was the Marquise de Brinvilliers, a woman I had seen a few times at lesser social functions when I worked in the de Termes household. A noble. I had seen her once at court, for her husband was a notorious gambler and bore, and thus, they were rarely invited to the most elite of events.

"Madame– Vert was just leaving," Marie said, stumbling briefly over the false name before offering the client her hand. "I assure you: next time we meet, I will introduce you to the man who can solve your problems."

We did not speak until she had shown the Marquise de Brinvilliers out, and the three of us, all witches and conjurers of different types, were alone in La *Vigoreaux*'s parlor. It was a finer room than Lapère's, but similar, with shelves of books and jars of herbs. Just teas, of course, nothing nefarious, if anyone came asking. She handed me a full jar from one of the most accessible shelves. "I know you're going to charge me double, since this is going to court."

"Don't be ridiculous," Vigoreaux smiled. "It will be triple."

I handed her the purse of coins I had brought with a smile. "How much will Madame de Brinvilliers be paying you?"

The young apprentice looked worried that I knew who the client was, but Vigoreaux laughed.

"That will depend on what happens to her piece of shit father, I think," Marie said with a shrug. "And that will take time. Not all of us are so impatient with our ascension and tricks."

I felt cold as she looked at me, contemplating the derision in her voice. How could she look at me in judgement?

"Thank you for your help," I said stiffly. "And congratulations on your new student. May Our Lady watch over you both."

I gripped the jar tight under the cover of my short cape as I returned to the Palais-Royal. The streets were growing dark, and now that the Court of Miracles was being razed and its inhabitants dispersed, the whole of the city was less safe. Or at least, I had started to feel that way as a woman alone at night. Even my humble clothes now were cleaner and finer than they had been in my past, when I was invisible on the streets. Now, I had to mutter spells and prayers for protection. And to keep my mind off the uncomfortable reminders I'd had that night.

I looked up to the sky with a frown. Maybe there was something in the stars that had soured things. The King employed astrologers, though fewer than his predecessors. They were concerned with the movements of the planets and constellations in ways I did not understand. I pitied them as they spoke of how a man named Galileo had moved the stars. Now we knew the sun was the center of everything, not us. Their art, in turn, was both ancient and new, yet always limitless and mysterious.

It made me feel small to think of the infinite stars as I entered the Palais through the back. The servants' entrance, but I still entered. I still had a place here, past the gates I had once dreamed of passing. I had ascended in ways my friends had never even attempted because I was not like them. I was different. I was not like the women of the court either. I had a partner who saw me, and we had elevated one another…

I arrived at Athénaïs's rooms, my heart filling with hope at the thought of seeing her, but there was only a chambermaid there, shoveling the ashes from the fire.

"Oh, Mademoiselle!" the little mouse of a girl cried. "Madame de Montespan is in Madame's chambers. She was called for and she told me to have you join her as soon as you were back."

"Of course." I turned and went as quickly as I could toward Madame's rooms. I had never been called there in the evening. What could Athénaïs need? We had not anticipated that Henrietta would need her after the theater.

"More wine!" came a cry on the other side of the door, followed by a crash. A servant rushed past me out of the door as I entered and took in the scene.

Madame was half undressed, draining a goblet of wine as Athénaïs petted her shoulders soothingly. It was an odd picture: two disheveled women in the center of a bedroom covered in gilding and silk. With painted walls and damask curtains, a canopied bed, and intricate furniture, being inside Madame's room felt like shrinking down to play in a box of jewels.

"There you are," Athénaïs sighed in relief as she saw me. "Madame needs help getting undressed."

Madame turned drunkenly to Athénaïs and threw her arms around her before kissing her, sloppy and desperate. My mistress kissed her back before gently pushing her away and giving me a pleading look. "I need help with other things and you know it," Henrietta slurred, swaying.

"Let me assist you," I muttered, coming to the other side of the inebriated princess. I began to unpin her intricate gown as she listed towards Athénaïs.

"Do you think he's going to fuck Racine's slut after humiliating me in front of that whole audience?" Henrietta demanded, stomping her foot. "How dare he bow to her first! A whore recognizing a whore!"

"What has happened?" I whispered, completely lost.

"The Chevalier de Lorraine – Monsieur's favorite – surprised them at the theater and paid all his respect to *an actress* at the expense of Madame," Athénaïs said quickly.

"That preening peacock did it on purpose. To remind Philippe of how petulant he can be when he doesn't get enough attention or gold," Henrietta whined.

"He loves an audience, that one," I muttered as the gown finally came free. There was one easy way to earn Henrietta's favor, and that was to share in her hatred of her husband's lover. Not because he had taken Philippe from Henrietta, but because he was too public about it. "Lorraine is nothing compared to you, my princess."

"Nor is that actress," Athénaïs cooed as we started on Henrietta's intricate stays and panniers. "What was her name? Claude knows all the theater people and she can confirm if this one is worthless."

I raised my eyebrows high as I looked at Athénaïs behind Madame. I didn't realize she remembered my tales of my past in the theater.

"Thérèse du Parc," the Duchesse spit, and I felt the blood all leave my body. Both of the other women saw. "You know her?"

I could have said that yes, I knew her. That once, when I was young and foolish and thought the stage was the way to my dreams. That I had served her with the same fervor with which I now served Athénaïs, before she had cast me aside. I had been willing to risk my soul for her and it had meant nothing. But there was no point to that story.

"Only by reputation," I said lightly, becoming an actress again myself. Just then, the servant returned with the wine that had been requested, and Athénaïs ran to intercept it, leaving me with a near-naked princess in my arms. "She's a viper and a whore, like you said."

"Am I prettier?" Henrietta asked me. Her eyes were watery and unfocused, swimming with the wine. I looked over her shoulder to Athénaïs, who gave an encouraging nod.

"You outshine her like the moon outshines the stars," I said, sincere and heartfelt, because I said it to Athénaïs. I did not have time to appreciate the way she grinned at me across the room before Henrietta kissed me, her breath hot and her mouth uncoordinated against mine.

I froze, but Madame did not notice. She enveloped me, desperate and clumsy as she pawed and pecked at my breasts and neck. Athénaïs was there in an instant, tenderly cupping Henrietta's face.

"My dear Princess," Athénaïs cooed. "I thought you saved such favors for me."

I let out a breath of relief, even as jealousy contorted in my gut. Henrietta squinted between us and snatched the wine from Athénaïs, taking a deep sip before thrusting the cup to me. "I want her tonight too."

"What?" I asked, my shock resurging. Surely, she couldn't want something as common as me.

"Tell your servant to fuck me," Henrietta said as she pushed the cup to my lips so that I had no chance but to drink deep. "You were complaining that you were so tired, Athénaïs: let her do the work tonight." Before I could choke down the entire gulp, Henrietta was kissing me again, chasing the wine down my throat with her tongue and beginning to ineptly undress me.

I looked at Athénaïs, whose expression showed she was as lost as I. She looked between the two of us as Henrietta pushed the bodice off me while she kissed my neck. Months ago, I had offered to please this woman to advance us. Now, she wanted me – or sensed I was available for use. Had Athénaïs told her of our lessons and how I shared her bed? Or was the great Duchesse d'Orléans, once the Princess of England, just drunk and lonely and lustful?

"I cannot presume to order her," Athénaïs said as my heart began to race, even as my body responded to the feel of cold air on my exposed breasts and belly. "You are so beautiful and captivating, Madame... how could she contemplate refusing you?"

There it was. A command without a command, delivered with a plea in Athénaïs's eyes as she stepped closer. I forced myself to smile and drained the cup. Thérèse never even asked me for my service, Veronique had scoffed at my ambitions, but Athénaïs did what needed to be done and asked the same of me. Who was I to refuse her?

"It would be my pleasure to give you yours," I purred as Athénaïs came behind me and pushed my skirts to the floor. She kissed my cheek as she took the empty cup from my hand and whispered in my ear. "Pretend it's me, if you need to."

I would. Bodies were just bodies, after all, or so I told myself. I seized Henrietta and pushed her towards her great bed.

"Stay and watch, Athénaïs," Henrietta called as we tangled on the mattress and I began to kiss her and touch her. "Stay and..." Her words dissolved into a moan as I took her nipple between my teeth and started my work in earnest.

I let myself enjoy it as the wine played through my veins. I let myself relax as I felt Athénaïs watch me, her hands occasionally on my back, her lips on my shoulders. I liked this, if I was honest with myself. I liked to give pleasure; I liked to be seen and to serve, no matter how. The more I thought of it, the more blood pumped to my own cunt and heated my brain.

Henrietta tasted different than Athénaïs, she reacted differently to my fingers and tongue, and I liked learning that too. I liked how Athénaïs touched me as I made Henrietta scream, how one woman's fingers slipping inside me made me groan into the other's wet folds as I devoured her. Soon, there was no difference between one body or another, as wine flowed and voices rose in ecstasy as we came and fucked and touched. And served.

CHAPTER 15

TEMPERANCE

T HE TALK OF COURT for much of July was of the scandal
around the Marquise de Brinvilliers and the shocking arrest of her alleged lover, a lower officer who served below her
husband by the name of Sainte-Croix. It was not that her taking
a lover was a scandal – no one begrudged her the relief from her
odious husband, who, in turn, ignored her and gambled away
his fortune. No one, that is, except the Marquise's very rich and
principled father, Antoine Dreux d'Aubray. As so many rich men
did, he had the ear of the King, on occasion. In this case, he had
used it to teach his unfaithful daughter a lesson.

At d'Aubray's request, Louis had issued a *lettre de cachet* against
the lover, Sainte-Croix. This private document was one of the
most dangerous tools in the monarch's arsenal: a personal, secret
order that could see anyone, man or woman, thrown in the

Bastille with no trial or any other process. It existed because the King's wisdom could not be questioned, and a true and good King, the representative and chosen one of God on Earth, would never abuse such a thing.

But the men who whispered in his ear might. So, while the Marquise de Brinvilliers and Sainte-Croix were riding together in a carriage, Musketeers and guards stopped them in the street and pulled the poor man from the carriage while the Marquise screamed in protest. He was sent to the Bastille, and the Marquise was forced to return to her children and horrible husband.

The affair was all anyone could speak of until the Comtesse de Soissons made the mistake of being seen in the country with the exiled Comte de Guiche (who had tried the previous year to drive a wedge between the King and Louise de La Vallière by taking La Vallière as his bride). Following that faux-pas, Henrietta had dismissed the Comtesse from her household – which was merely a formality, as Soissons was on her way to becoming the official head of the *Queen's* ladies and household. Louise was dismissed as well, but it was also of little note, given how she had been absent from court entirely and it was rumored the King had purchased her a small manor close to the Louvre.

This left Athénaïs free in her reign for Henrietta through the fall, and she relished it, adoring the attention, glory, and glamour that came from serving the second lady of the court...

"I thought she was the third lady of the court."

I stopped in my narrative of the past few months when Catherine Monvoisin interrupted me. Next to her by the fire in the parlor, Lapère chuckled as she held little Marguerite in her lap. "I can't even keep them straight," my teacher added, tickling the babe's chin. "Which is the one you've been playing with, Catherine?"

"Soissons," she replied as she continued to prepare the long table for the meal. "She's furious about that La Vallière woman getting with child by the King. She wants him for herself."

"The whole court knows that," I said proudly. "Except her husband, perhaps. He's usually too busy playing general. Or maybe he wants his wife to have some influence on the King."

"She keeps asking if it's possible to put a spell on the King or a hex on La Vallière," Catherine laughed. "As if I'd be that stupid."

"As if you had that sort of power working alone," Lapère corrected, and we both looked at her in curiosity. "Yes, girls, there are still things an old woman can teach you."

"I never doubted that," I said with a smile as I leaned over to stir the soup on the fire.

"Well, go on then," Catherine prompted.

"Magic means moving the world – pushing it and bending it. Like tilling the earth, it takes force and power. The bigger something is – some bit of fate or circumstance – the more power it takes. One witch alone can only do so much, even with allies among the spirits of nature or the ancestors."

I took a moment to look at the table where we would soon sit for the dumb supper. I had learned in the years since my first that it was not just to connect and remember the dead that we honored them, but for some, it was to thank them for their intervention and protection. That had not sat right with me, for I did not know if any ancestors cared for me from beyond. Or judged me for who I had sent to join them. My living family had not spoken to me in years.

"What of allies among the divine?" Catherine asked, puffing herself up. I did not know if she meant Our Lady or the God to whom we prayed obediently in church.

"The divine works for all who call on it in different ways," Lapère mused, reading the thoughts from my mind as the child cooed. Or guessing them. "It matters not how it is called. It has power. Think of the care and prayers that focus on a King. He is blessed daily, he is protected by guards of flesh and talismans of faith all around. Prayer is a kind of magic after all."

"So the King is protected from spells?" Catherine asked, taking her daughter from Lapère. Hopefully, the little thing didn't understand the conversation.

"Certainly. Far more protected than a random man on the street some client takes a fancy to, less prone to simple charms." Lapère shrugged. "Perhaps less malleable."

"He has a strong character as well," I said, not disguising my pride to be speaking of a man I knew – or at least had conversed with more than once.

"That means to curse him – or influence him – would take, as I said, a great deal of power, however it was gathered. Your friend the Comtesse might focus elsewhere." Lapère leaned back in her chair, looking at the fire.

"She has quite a long list of women she'd like to see cursed," Catherine said, with more lightness than such a confession deserved. She dramatically covered little Marguerite's ears. "Or poisoned."

"Poisoning would be hard at court," I laughed in turn. "I don't think any proper lady even knows where the kitchen is or what food goes to who."

"You don't think there are other ways to get poison to someone?" my old friend asked back, and it was my turn to look askance at her. "A bouquet of flowers dusted with a toxic powder maybe? Or a poisoned glove – or a gown!"

"The sorts of concoctions you'd need to do that would kill the maker of them, if you're not careful," Lapère chortled. "And how would you get it to the intended target?"

"That's what makes it perfect," I said before I could stop myself, and the two women looked at me. "I mean – it can't work and wouldn't kill. That makes it something you could sell to some unsuspecting fool and when it fails, it's not your fault and no one dies."

"My goodness, the nobles have corrupted you," Catherine muttered. "I must tell Monsieur Le Sage the good news."

"You're still consorting with that charlatan?" Lapère asked, shaking her head. "I've heard a few of his investors are beginning to wonder when the money they gave him to buy his supplies will yield the gold they were promised."

"Well, as you said, great magic takes great resources," La Voisin replied. Just in time to interrupt, the door opened and Marie Vigoreaux entered, with her apprentice, La Filastre, in tow.

"Good evening, friends," Lapère said warmly as she rose. There was a look of derision between La Vigoreaux and La Voisin, but I ignored it as I embraced my friend, much to La Filastre's surprise.

"Who else is coming?" the younger woman asked, looking at the table. My guts twisted at the thought. I hadn't asked after Veronique, though I knew nights like this were important to her. It was probably too far for her to come from Rouen and she'd be with her circle there...

"Just us," Lapère replied. Though it was the answer I had suspected – even hoped for – my heart sank. And I knew Lapère saw. "Here, at least. Tonight, we join others throughout France and the world in honoring our dead."

It was a consolation from the elder and I accepted it. As we fell silent and shared our meal with spirits, it was those others like us, women and men who had come before and would come after, that I called. I thought of the innocents that had been burned and hanged for the craft we dared to practice, and I prayed those days were done.

I looked at little Marguerite with hope for what she would learn from her mother and prayed to our forebears that she would never need the baneful and dangerous skills I had acquired in this very house and the dark garden beyond the doors. Perhaps she would live a better life than us. Perhaps wherever Veronique was, she was safer.

A NEW LIFE CAME into the world weeks later, with Catherine Lapère as midwife. She was the only woman I would trust to oversee the birth of Athénaïs's child, despite the protests of the Marquis de Montespan. The man had returned from his duties in the country for the birth of his heir, and I could not blame him. He had wanted a doctor, but I convinced him that a midwife was all we needed for the birth because it would be cheaper.

Athénaïs was glad to go into labor. She'd been miserable in confinement – delaying it as long as possible by concealing her belly with various silks and stays, but by the fall, she had been forced to withdraw from court duties and society. I'd kept her company, of course, reading to her when her head ached, and even making love when the need struck her. My own needs, as intermittent as they were, remained satisfied by her. Never by Henrietta.

While I often was called on to step in for my mistress to *amuse* Madame, she was regularly too drunk or too satisfied to return any sort of touch, and I was grateful for it. My feelings for Athénaïs aside (feelings I refused to name because if I did not name them, their lack on the other side would not hurt me), I preferred her body to Henrietta's – her curves and heavier breasts, even her round belly, full of life.

I also understood her discomfort and how ready she was to give birth and return to court life. I had enjoyed our few weeks alone, and yet, I too missed the intrigue. Luckily, it had been quiet, with the King gone and La Vallière also removed. As I attended to Athénaïs, sweating and yelling in pain in her bed at the Montespan house, the one I had shared with her so many nights, I wondered if La Vallière would labor alone when she brought the King's bastard into the world...

I had seen mock battles and contests, and heard many a man boast of their bravery and fortitude. None of it compared to what I saw from Athénaïs in her labors that night. She was a warrior through the hours of pain, bleeding, and pushing, at last. Lapère and I were there all the way.

I mopped her sweating brow and held her hand while she gripped me for dear life, and I watched in awe as the body of my lover endured and transformed. I held her as she cried out in pain, as I had held her through pleasure and would hold her through despair. Then, suddenly, it was over, and a small, squalling, bloody thing had joined us. A little girl.

I was the one to lay the babe on Athénaïs's heaving chest as Lapère cut the cord and attended to the afterbirth, seeing to it that the bleeding was staunched as the waiting wet nurse helped her. I waited for Athénaïs to weep or speak as she looked down at the shriveled newborn filling the room with her cries.

"A girl," she said at last. "Poor thing."

"She's healthy and strong," I said, leaning close to look into those dark little eyes while Athénaïs frowned.

"She's doomed to a life of this. Like me," she sighed in return. "Cursed to bear and be a man's burden. She has her father's eyes."

"She's still yours," I whispered, but it was not the time to argue. "Shall I show her to him?"

"Clean her up first. Tell him he can pick the name to mollify his disappointment." Athénaïs waved me away as I took the child in my arms. Lapère and the wetnurse helped me clean her, cooing as she objected to this cold, alien world. It was I who swaddled her and brought her to where her father waited in his study, a cask of wine half-empty beside him.

"You are a father, Monsieur Le Marquis," I said quietly from the door.

"Is it a boy?" he demanded with a scowl, striding to me to inspect the little bundle. I wondered if this had been what it was like at my birth. My mother had complained loudly and often of the pain she experienced bringing me into the world, but my father had spoken just as much of loving me as soon as he held me, even though he had wanted a son.

"A healthy girl," I countered, and his frown deepened as he peered at his offspring. "What will she be called?"

"Hasn't my wife decided?" he asked, and his eyes softened as the babe wiggled in my arms.

"She wished for you to choose," I offered. Before he could protest, I pushed his daughter into his arms. The fearsome brute who Athénaïs complained of so often became something else. He looked so huge compared to the girl in his arms. Massive and overcome.

"Marie Christine," he whispered, his voice thick.

It stung to see how he loved this small thing so instantly when Athénaïs had barely been able to look at her. At least one of them cared. He was, after all, the one who had wanted this child. "A lovely name, Monsieur. Shall I call in the nurse?"

"Yes, have her come here. I'll hold Marie Christine for a while."

It was the kindest thing I ever heard the Marquis de Montespan say.

I N THE WEEKS THAT followed, the new parents argued more than ever. Athénaïs's husband wanted her to nurse their daughter, but she was determined to not yoke herself to a suckling infant. My lady was up and about walking within one day, directly against Lapère's orders. In a week, she was back at court. The child had a father and a nurse to watch it, Athénaïs said; she had a life of her own, and despite the pain in her breasts and her healing body, she never let another noble see her suffering.

Only I knew how hard it was on her to go back to her duties – hard on her body, not on her heart. She separated the baby from her mind as easily as if the child had never existed. It shocked me, but it was common. The nobility did not raise their children the way common people did. Children were an ornament to be displayed on occasion until they were old enough to marry or start scheming and intriguing for themselves. Even the little Dauphin, the treasured child of Louis and Marie Thérèse, and their only living heir, was rarely seen at court except on the most formal occasions.

The ballet in which Athénaïs danced with Louis, just two weeks after she gave birth, was not such an occasion. It was a celebration of the old gods, so unchristian that the Dowager Queen had not attended. The court did not care. The King himself danced as Apollo, graceful and beguiling, and we all fell in worship. The crowd cooed in wonder to see Athénaïs so quickly recovered and returned to them.

Jean-Baptiste Lully conducted the orchestra himself, keeping time with an ornate staff he pounded on the ground like a sorcerer in a mystery play. The ladies and gentlemen of the court hooted in admiration in the theater, newly built within the Palais-Royal itself. Despite the November cold, it was warm and wondrous, with a thousand candles burning and gold and crystal all around to celebrate our Sun King's glory.

Athénaïs was in her element after. She kept on her nymph costume, her swollen breasts garnering as much attention as her sparkling wit as men and women milled around her. I watched her fondly from the side, content in my corner, listening and unseen and waiting to be of service.

"She is quite resilient, your mistress." I jumped at the familiar voice at my shoulder, spinning into a deep curtsey before Louis himself. How on earth had I been so entranced that the King himself had snuck up on me?

"She is a wonder befitting your court, Your Majesty," I stammered as I rose. Louis too still wore his costume – golden hose, golden pantaloons, and doublet, and a crown like the rays of the sun radiating from his thick, dark hair. He was magnificent.

"And you, Mademoiselle des Œillets, are a loyal friend and companion to her. Even helping her in her confinement," Louis stated, and my stomach exploded in butterflies. I had no idea that he had even noticed.

"It is my honor. She is very dear to me," I replied with complete honesty.

"More ladies could use such companions," the King mused, looking at me in such a way that I felt like I was alone in the room with him. It was thrilling. "Were you with her for her labor? Forgive me; I ask because I can hardly believe she had a child—"

It was strange to hear the King almost stumble over the words. As if he needed to be concerned for propriety with someone as lowly as me.

"I was, of course," I nodded. "There was a midwife there as well. It was an easier time than many women experience." I was babbling, but the King was smiling.

"That is good to know. You have some expertise in this, even as an unmarried woman?"

I could not lie, so I settled on a different version of the truth.

"I was raised among midwives and wise, caring women and mothers." That made him give a gentle smile that turned up the corners of his delicate moustache. "I have the greatest respect for women who enter that gauntlet and those who help them."

"And you have great discretion too, I am told." I felt suddenly as if I was naked as the King's eyes narrowed meaningfully. "By my dear brother, as you serve in his household."

"Discretion is a virtue we must all strive for in service," I replied, trying not to stammer or wonder what exactly Philippe and Louis might know of what happened in Henrietta's chambers.

"I may call upon such discretion very soon, Mademoiselle," Louis said with a kind smile. I had no idea what that meant, but it felt momentous to hear it. When he left me, giving a courteous nod, it felt like the sun retreating behind a cloud, leaving me deep in shadow.

In reality, I was in a crowded room full of courtiers and they were all looking at me. I was used to seeing nobles look scornfully at others from the corner of their eye. Noting it was a useful skill for guessing who hated or suspected who at any given moment.

Right now, those cruel eyes were upon me because I had received attention from the King, and I certainly did not deserve it. I did not know whether to feel proud to be so perceived or terrified, but I chose pride. I held my head high and wore it like armor as I walked through the glittering theater.

Years before, I had rushed through such crowds, and one day hoped to be one of the elite among them. Now, I was. Surely, some resented my rise, but I was here, nonetheless.

THE CALL FROM THE King came days later, on a day when no one was at court. It was too cold as winter tightened her grip on the court and the holy days of Advent and Christmas approached. The Marquis had become more generous with his spending on heating the house now that a child lived there, and Athénaïs at least enjoyed the warmth for recovery. The ballet had been a coup, but her body was still healing from birth. For that reason, she was sleeping when the man appeared on our doorstep. I knew him.

His name was Alexandre Bontemps: a man of great girth and serious bearing who attended the King himself as his chief valet. He was something of an enigma at court, as stolid and steady as a piece of furniture. He was always there behind the King, but never spoke unless called upon for some duty. When he appeared or did speak, it was because the King himself wanted him to, and all at court knew it.

"You will need a warm cloak. With a hood, for discretion, Mademoiselle des Œillets," Bontemps told me, his voice low and unquestionable, but still friendly. "The journey is, thankfully, not far."

"Of course," I replied.

I alerted the maid to my errand and told her to assure our mistress I was fine before grabbing my cloak. I joined Bontemps in a carriage the likes of which I had never seen: anonymous from the outside, but lavish within. Perfect, it seemed, for transportation of a King who did not wish to be seen.

In mere minutes, we arrived at a fine home; a petit palais, to be honest. Bontemps led me in as we kept our faces covered, and I was shocked to see the woman who greeted me: none other than my previous mistress's most important friend, Madame Colbert.

"Why, Claude! So it is you!" Madame Colbert said with a smile as she pulled me into a quick embrace and kissed my cheek. "I had a suspicion. I'm glad you're here. Hopefully, you can help."

"Is she worse?" Bontemps asked, concern in his rumbling voice. Madame Colbert shook her head grimly.

"I wish they were not so concerned and frightened by doctors," the older woman said. My curiosity was bubbling inside me. I knew who one of 'them' had to be – the King, who had called on me for my discretion – and I had a strong guess who the other was.

"Is she awake at least?" Bontemps pressed. Madame Colbert nodded then gestured for me to follow. I trailed her up the stairs and to a door she pointedly unlocked.

"She's had a headache today – a very bad one. She has them almost daily lately. She says the light makes them worse, so she won't allow candles, but she insists we keep the fire high because she's so cold. I worry that she's feverish again, but as I said, we aren't allowed to have doctors see her..."

"And *I'm* supposed to be a substitute?" I asked with terror.

"You've just served a pregnant woman. The King trusts you to be of use and to never speak of who you see within," Madame Colbert replied. "Though I'm sure you know, as does half the court."

"I will not say a word," I answered, unsure if it was a lie. Perhaps it would depend on what Louise de La Vallière had to say.

The poor woman groaned at the sound of the door, and the stench of piss and stale air in the hot room was overwhelming.

La Vallière was on her side in the bed, the mattress taking the weight of her pregnant belly, stretched by the child of a King.

Whereas Athénaïs had sweated and complained in her final weeks, Louise was pale, her eyes rounded by dark circles. In her hand, she held a rosary, and her cracked lips moved in a soft prayer.

"You have a visitor, Louise. A friend," Madame Colbert said. I wondered if she was the only one aside from servants that La Vallière had seen lately. It made sense that she was there; as the wife to the King's closest advisor, she could be trusted herself. This child was a matter of state because it was the King's.

"I am glad to see you, Mademoiselle," I said softly, kneeling by the bed and placing myself in La Vallière's line of sight. Her eyes widened in shock when she recognized me.

"Have you come to pray for me?" the poor woman asked, her voice a mere rasp. "To pray with a poor sinner? Have you come to tell me of her punishment? Has she condemned me at last?"

"Claude is here to give you some company, sweet girl," Madame Colbert said, deep pity in her voice. "I will leave you two to talk. Claude has recently attended another birth. She can tell you there is nothing to fear."

Louise's face filled with horror, but Madame Colbert was gone before I could protest, and the younger woman seized my hand, pulling me close to her. "God will strike me down in this birth, I know it! He's already begun."

"My lady, no," I whispered instantly and without thought. I was so close to her I could smell the soiled sheets and see her bloodshot eyes. "You will be fine."

"I deserve to die! And this child too. I will be hastened to hell for dragging *him* into sin!" Louise hissed. "It was me! Don't you see? I tempted him and I failed. I have made him betray our good queen. Now I bear his child and that is my punishment. The evidence of my sin will kill me!" She held my hand as tight as her last grip on reason and hope.

"Louise, this is not a punishment—" I began uncertainly. I had felt abandoned many times too and I had found my way. "It is a test. You have been given a great duty to bear, and you are being tested."

Tears sprang to the woman's eyes and she shook her head. "I will fail. I'm too weak. I have always been too weak!"

I could not know if that was true – if she used weakness as an excuse for what she had done with Louis, or if she had been unable to resist him when he had pursued her. Maybe there was no resisting.

"No, a weak woman could never draw to her such power," I said, calm as I could manage, stroking her face with my free hand. "You hold glory in your womb. That means you can call on that strength and endure."

Louise let out a sob, her beautiful face contorting. "How much longer? How do you know I will survive?"

"I don't," I said, afraid I might begin to cry too in the face of such despair. "But I know you can obey. He who we all must obey commands you to live and survive."

She dissolved into weeping but nodded and released the grip on my hand. She rubbed her belly and winced, and I wondered if she or her body could sense some danger awaiting.

"Have you felt pains?"

"All the time," she whimpered.

"That's normal, but I can send for something to help, and the headaches too. It will help you sleep," I said, making a mental list of what I would need – or what I would send Bontemps to procure. "Can I feel if the babe is kicking?"

She nodded again, and I carefully felt over her belly. I was not trained as Lapère and Veronique were, but I knew where to prod to gauge the position.

"Is he alright?" Louise asked with a small voice.

"Not breech. That's good," I answered, putting on a brave smile in the sweltering room. "And it does feel like a boy." There was no way of knowing, but I had a sense that she was right to call her child a boy. "He'll be here soon. I'll speak to Madame Colbert as to what you will need. I'll even go to the kitchen to see what I can make you now. First, you will need a good bath, if you have a tub here. It will bring some relief."

Louise groaned but nodded, and I returned to the hall where Colbert and Bontemps waited with eager eyes.

"Can you help her?" Madame Colbert asked the moment the door was closed. "I have been trying, but she's getting worse."

"I will require a few things – some herbs – and she'll need a bath. While she's cleaning, change all her linens. Everything must be clean and calm for her. I want that whole room full of lavender by the end of the day; it will help her sleep and cover up any smells too…"

L OUISE'S RELIEF WAS ALMOST immediate, with fresh air and a clean body and bed. I worried what it would mean or say of me to send Bontemps to an abortionist and fortuneteller for herbs, so I made the journey myself. Even alone, with no guard or escort, foreboding followed me.

My mind was full of fire, of what it would mean for me and all those I knew and loved if I were to fail at my task for the King. If this child died, would they call me a witch and blame me? Why did I feel like some doom was hanging over me, deepening with each step towards the old Court of Miracles?

Lapère's face was grim when she opened her door. She gave me the herbs at no cost and delivered the dark news: a tribunal had commenced in Rouen. Even as the King employed one in secret to help the mother of his bastard, other powerful men were on the hunt for witches. The danger to us all was deep and growing, but it was not I who was under the greatest threat now, but Veronique and her circle. They had been discovered.

I barely slept when I returned home that night, as worry ate me up from the inside.

We knew nothing, good or bad. Veronique was smart and strong; that was what Lapère told me. She had worked her spells and prayers for the protection of our sisters and friends, but there was only so much we could do. Magic was movement – pushing the world to change. It could feel simple when you wanted to nudge something or adjust a small part of your life close by, but these forces were so strong and so inevitable, it felt like moving mountains to try and enchant the way out of this on our own.

For centuries, witches had burned at the behest of the church beside heretics and others similarly damned. What use was our scant power against the weight of such holiness?

I wondered, as I recalled poor Louise La Vallière, if that is how she felt in her doomed love affair; helpless against so many things more powerful than her: her heart and her king and her God. Unable to fight. Unable to make change.

The thought troubled me into the dark hours of the night as I worried about a woman who had rejected me and all I was so many miles away. At the same time, I worried for a woman who would condemn me to the stake if she knew what I truly was, whose life and child's life I now had to save.

B ONTEMPS CONTINUED TO FETCH me to attend La Vallière periodically for weeks, always with the utmost discretion and secrecy. Quite the farce, given that so many at court knew that La Vallière had taken up residence in the little Palais Brion, but was 'ill.' I told only Athénaïs, for I knew I could trust her. Her reaction was one of pity and disappointment, for La Vallière, and pride that her instrument had been given such a charge.

La Vallière herself improved under my care. I was able to help her headaches and fits, and with advice from Lapère, give her some relief from the early pains. But when a knock came at the door in the dark of the night a week before Christmas, I knew that the child of the King was on the way.

Bontemps looked as worried as I had ever seen him, his face pale and brow sweating even as light snow fell. Madame Colbert was there when I arrived, with a man I recognized but had never formally been introduced to: her husband. They waited in the foyer, stopping their pacing as I entered, the sound of Louise La Vallière's screams echoing above them.

"She won't let the doctor touch her," Madame Colbert exclaimed, grabbing my hand. "We tried to cover her face to keep her from being recognized, but she tore it off. She keeps calling out for *him*."

"Does he know?" I asked, directing the question to Bontemps. He gave a grim, tight nod.

"He cannot be here. This child is a liability and a scandal," Colbert himself replied. "You, Mademoiselle, must swear not to speak of this."

I wanted to roll my eyes at such a charade. As if all of France wouldn't know before the new year that their King had fathered a bastard. There would surely be furious sermons about sin and fidelity, and how adultery was an affront to the Good Lord, but in their hearts, the people would be impressed and inspired by their sovereign's virility. "I will not speak of it," I reassured the minister anyway. "What can I do?"

"You have soothed her hysterics before, I have been told. Do it again," Colbert ordered. His wife balked behind him at such a ridiculous command, as if the dangerous and painful birth Louise was undergoing was some mere malady to be endured, but I nodded in obedience and rushed upstairs.

The doctor was arguing with the maids when I came in.

"She must lay back down and let me examine her!" the man
– older, with limp, gray hair and a bulbous nose – yelled at the
maids cowering at the side of the room. I didn't recognize them
and I would not have been surprised to learn that they had been
hired for this night specifically. Louise was in the corner, her
hands against the walls, groaning in pain. She wore nothing but a
white shift, soaked with sweat... And stained with blood between
her legs.

"Go fetch more water and rags," I ordered the maids when they
looked at me. I was in a finer dress than they were tonight, and I
knew how to hold myself like a noble, so they instantly obeyed.
Perhaps they were happy to get away from Louise's piteous cries.

"Who are you?" the doctor demanded, but I ignored him,
going straight to Louise. She was, once again, so different from
Athénaïs. My mistress had been a lion in her birthing bed. Louise
was the lamb at the slaughter. I pitied her.

"Louise, dear, why are you standing?" I asked as she paused
moaning to catch her breath. Her face was deathly pale when she
looked at me, eyes red from weeping. "Does it hurt less to stand?"
She nodded frantically, then grabbed me as another pain seized
her.

"Have you pushed?" Again she nodded.

"For so long. It hurts. The bed hurts worse. It's going to kill
me..."

"No, shhhh," I whispered. "Stand," I said, wincing at the force
of her grasp. The maids rushed back in with bowls and rags. I
took one immediately to mop Louise's brow. "We need to see
how close you are," I told her gently, and she shook her head.
"Will you let the doctor—"

"No! He wants to look at me! To see my sin!" she wailed, and I heard the doctor huff in derision. "Only a husband should see a woman like this and I have no—"

"I will look, don't worry," I reassured her.

"Who in God's name are you?" the doctor bellowed, having come behind us. "This woman is in distress. If this child does not come soon, it will die! It needs to be attended to by a real doctor, not some fishwife!"

"I serve a great lady," I snapped back. "One who knows of these matters and has seen fit for me to assist here." I was not talking about Athénaïs, but he would not know that. "Louise," I whispered as another pain attacked her. "You remember your prayers. I know you do. You remember your *Ave Maria*. Say it now. Speak it with these good ladies as they hold your hands and I will check on the progress of your son."

The maids looked as confused as the doctor, but they and Louise did as they were told, holding her on both sides to support her as her face contorted in pain. "I can't," Louise whimpered.

"You can. Call on Our Lady, the Virgin Mother: she will see you through." Louise looked at me through the fog of her anguish, and in my soul, I prayed for her strength. And for mine. I had to be strong and calm too. We all had to survive.

"*Ave Maria, gratia plena…*" Louise began, and the maids joined her in the Latin prayer. I crouched down, in an awkward and undignified position between Louise's splayed legs that I knew the fussy doctor behind me would never have attempted. And I saw good news.

"He's almost here," I called. "With a full head of hair already. You need to push. Say your prayers and push."

She did. I did too. *Our Lady, great mother, protect your daughter. Our Lady of the Crossroads, lead us into new life.*

"This is highly irregular! She cannot perform the act in such a position!" the doctor cried. "She needs to be cut!"

"She needs you to shut your fool mouth!" I snapped. "She is strong and will see this through. Show him, Louise." I could not hear his reply over the scream that ripped from La Vallière's throat as she pushed the King's child into the world, and I caught the babe in my waiting hands.

It was a whirlwind after that. Thank heaven for the maids who caught Louise as she collapsed, and the doctor finally being of some use as he rushed to help me with the bloody, purplish creature that was in my hands. One smack to the back and it began to wail weakly. A boy, but much smaller than the last infant I had seen delivered. With a much heavier weight on his shoulders.

The doctor's sole focus remained on the child as the cord was cut and Louise was led, at last, to her bed. One of the maids fled into the hall and I heard raised voices before the door opened again and Colbert himself strode in. Louise did not see him; she was too near to swooning after the ordeal.

The second most powerful man in France examined the boy and seemed relieved before he went to the open door to whisper to Bontemps. No doubt a message to the King that his son had been born.

"Mademoiselle will be fine too," I called after the man, and Bontemps peered over Colbert's shoulder inside. Louise was an afterthought to them now, it seemed, but she would not be for the King. At least, I hoped not.

Looking down at the exhausted woman in the bed, who barely looked up when they finally saw fit to present her child to her, I wondered if she would rather be forgotten. She barely had the strength to pat her son's head before her eyes fluttered shut in exhaustion. The baby was taken away quickly, and I wondered if Louise would even see the child again. Would she want that?

No one looked at me, once it was done. I felt like a shadow as I left Louise to rest and snuck back home. It was close to dawn when I arrived, and Athénaïs stirred in the bed when I fell into it beside her, not even bothering to undress.

"Was it a boy?" she asked groggily.

I looked up at her with one half-open eye. Of course she knew where I had been. "Yes, not that La Vallière will be allowed to raise him."

"She doesn't deserve it," Athénaïs mumbled and burrowed into the pillow. Whether she meant that Louise didn't deserve to have her child wrenched away from her or did not deserve to bear the child of the King, I did not know.

I ACCOMPANIED ATHÉNAÏS TO Midnight Mass on Christmas Eve at the royal chapel. Everyone was there, as usual; many of us with grumbling stomachs in anticipation of the great feast that would follow. Midnight dinners were common at court, and this one would last well into the dawn of Christmas day.

The candles, chants, and prayers in the crowded church were not so different from the ritual I had joined in nights before. La

Voisin had invited many sisters in the craft to her home for the solstice, and we had read palms and drank mulled wine all night as we tended the fires and kept the light alive through the darkness. When the sun had touched our faces at last, it had felt like hope.

From our pew towards the back, I looked through the crowd towards Louis. He was glowing with pride, like the dawn. A true contrast to the shame in the face of poor, pale Louise La Vallière, who had returned, close to the King and in sight of both Queens. They did not seem happy to see her, nor did the priest who sneered at her from the pulpit. She looked ill under all the attention, but there was nowhere for her to flee.

The priest chanted in Latin and the choir began to sing, joy and devotion ringing through the church, echoing with the sermon's hope that a new year in court would bring a new commitment to goodness and holiness; that we would all turn away from the devil and his temptation. Perhaps the Priest knew of the hunt for witches in Rouen and the arrests that had been made. The provincial court would begin trials soon, or so La Filastre had said: she had a friend who had fled Rouen months before to come to Paris and heard the news in letters, but we heard nothing of Veronique except that she was still there.

"You're distracted," Athénaïs chided me once the service was done and the court filed out towards the feast, snow catching in our hair on the short journey from the chapel to the halls of the Louvre.

"I was worrying," I confessed. "About a friend."

"Louise La Vallière does look rather like she has one foot in the grave," Athénaïs chuckled back.

"You sound jealous." I smiled at her. Jealousy was an alien thought between us, given how often she was required to be in another bed, and I as well. "I can assure you, there is nothing to fear."

"I know," Athénaïs smirked. "I honestly cannot see what anyone sees in the simpering false saint."

"She's not who I'm worried about, just so you know," I said as we came to the largest gallery, now filled with tables of sumptuous dishes and drinks. It was incredible – candied fruits, game birds, and pastries built to look like palaces, and steaming cauldrons of spiced wine.

It was customary for the King to taste as many dishes as he liked before anyone else was allowed to partake, and so, we all waited while Louis strolled along the table with Marie Thérèse beside him. The Queen looked forlorn, but dutiful, much like always, her sumptuous gown overwhelming her small frame. Over the head of a suckling pig gilded in gold, I caught the eye of Colbert, and he gave me a respectful nod. Did he know where the King's new son was tonight? Had the King sent him gifts, like the Magi to the Christ child?

Louis was certainly generous with his court. Once the feasting was done, the King moved through the throngs of courtiers with Colbert and Bontemps beside him and valets running back and forth, doling out gifts from the crown. Land was bequeathed, titles elevated, jewels bestowed, and amounts of money I could not comprehend were promised to the most loyal of courtiers. This was also the time for bold members of the aristocracy to beg royal favor for those not present, and more than one pardon for the lesser crimes of inconsequential family members were given out.

Athénaïs had already been enriched greatly by Henrietta with gifts of money and some property, but she beamed when the King looked on her and promised her credit at the finest dress salons in Paris for any robe or costume she might need for the ballet or new shoes. Louise La Vallière was given the deed to the Palais Brion, which she accepted with humble gratitude.

I was not expecting, once the excitement had waned, for the King and his entourage to move in my direction. But there I was, suddenly subject to the glittering light of the sun in the bitter depths of winter.

"Good evening, Mademoiselle," the King said as I bowed before him. He extended a hand to help me rise, and a shock passed through me as I touched his hands. Their softness always amazed me. The hands of a man who had never labored a day in his life were so gentle.

"Your Majesty. I wish you joy on this holy day," I said, hoping that was the correct phrasing. I had not been paying attention to the other conversations. "For you and your family." I meant the Queen, mostly, but I saw Colbert's eyes glint with admiration when I said it. The King gave me a knowing smile.

"I *and* said family are deeply grateful to you, for all your service to the crown and the court," the King replied. To my shock, Louis nodded to an attendant, who rushed to open a velvet casket in front of me. The case held a jeweled brooch like nothing I had ever owned: emeralds and diamonds and pearls in the shape of a flower. Perhaps even a carnation. "A mere token of my esteem, Mademoiselle des Œillets."

"Your Majesty," I whispered, gaping at the bauble. It had to be worth more than all the money I had seen in my entire life, twice over. (Though, to be fair, I had not earned that much money.) "I cannot thank you enough."

"No, Mademoiselle des Œillets," Louis replied, squeezing my hand and looking into my eyes with a sincerity I could not fathom. "It is I who cannot express my gratitude enough. This trinket pales in comparison to the service you have done."

"If there is anything else you need, Mademoiselle," Colbert added, startling me as I had entirely forgotten he was there. "You need only ask it, and the crown will see it done."

I wanted to laugh, for I knew how much the crown could do if inspired. The man before me, looking at me with supplicant, kind eyes, had sent the Marquise de Brinvilliers's lover to the Bastille with the stroke of a pen and nary a second thought at the request of an esteemed bureaucrat. To offer me – a girl who had once slept in filth and starved – the favor of the crown was all the proof I needed that magic was real. For that power had brought me here.

So perhaps it was right to use that power for the sake of others.

"I do have a request, or – a suggestion, on behalf of a friend," I began, my voice shaking. Colbert inclined his head in interest as I fumbled for the right way to make this gambit. "You, my King, are a monarch of the modern age. A man of science and reason, free of superstition."

"A strange way to begin," Colbert muttered, but Louis nodded.

"I try to be, as far as God will allow," the King added. "Go on."

"I have heard recently from a dear friend that she has come under the most absurd of suspicions from the provincial court of Rouen," I continued, calling on strength from the earth far beneath my feet and the air around me and the thousand candle flames that lit the shining hall. "She is but an honest midwife, a woman who helps women, as I have done, and the fools in Rouen are hunting for witches."

"The country courts are full of idiots afraid of their own shadow," Colbert sighed.

"Fear can inspire men to terrible things. Things which could end the very life of an honest friend – and many others," I pushed on. "I know you love your people, my King, and would not tolerate such persecutions in the name of fear and superstition."

Louis looked at me and into me. Right into my heart in a way that made me want to squirm, but I held fast. I had a chance to save people – save Veronique and other women like me – and I had taken it. Or I had revealed myself and I was damned. I would be arrested right here and thrown in the Bastille, or someplace worse...

"You speak true and correctly, Mademoiselle," Louis said, and my heart nearly leapt from my chest. "Colbert, I trust you will see to it that this ridiculous hunt is ended. We are a modern nation, as Mademoiselle des Œillets makes clear. My people should not be persecuted by country fools blaming a bad crop on the devil."

"Thank you, Your Majesty. God bless you," I said, and in my way, I meant it. Seldom did I speak of God or to him, but the King knew him well and deserved his favor.

The casket with my jewels was placed in my hands, and with a final congenial bow of his head, the King was gone, moving throughout the gallery again. Soon, Athénaïs came up beside me, noting the box I held with admiration.

"You're doing better for yourself than I ever could have anticipated, dear girl," she muttered. "Your loyalty elevates us both."

"Both?" I echoed. Had there been some other boon granted?

"Louis wishes us closer at hand, it seems, and Henrietta fears
raising suspicions, so I have been granted a new position: maid of
honor to Marie Thérèse herself." My mouth fell open in shock.
There was no greater honor in court, save a noble marriage or
a new title. Athénaïs grinned at me. "I must be careful not to
outshine her too much... at first."

"The Queen?" Serving as a lady to Henrietta was one thing – a
household where it was expected that all the members should be
witty and formidable, but serving Marie Thérèse would require
piety and discretion – unless Athénaïs intended to make herself
the center of attention.

"How exciting that this is only the beginning." I looked at
Athénaïs's face – full of ambition and fire – and followed her gaze
across the room to the King himself.

It froze my blood, the way she looked at him and La Vallière
in turn. We had risen so far, the two of us, but I feared she had
set her sights higher.

CHAPTER 16

THE HANGED MAN

1664

THERE IS COMFORT IN the changing of the seasons: the familiar months of drab, gray skies that melt into the green of spring and the heat of summer. No matter what happens, the year turns and the flowers bloom and bear fruit, then succumb to harvest and death. One year is the same as any other. It takes many turns of the wheel for a sapling to become a mighty oak, and from one year to the next, it may seem like nothing has changed, because the growth is subtle and small. In truth, while one year may seem like the last, there are great differences.

The spring of 1664 began like the spring of the year before, with Athénaïs pregnant once again, barely given time to recover from the last time her husband had put an heir in her belly and then been chased away. I had worked another banishment, hoping it would once again keep until the birth. It pleased the Queen to have pregnant women among her maids of honor, as long as they were married. She even enjoyed it when they brought their children to visit her chambers.

So Athénaïs's daughter was a brief playmate to the Dauphin, Louis, after his father and Henrietta's Petite Mademoiselle, Marie Louise, to the delight of all. No such joy came to Louise de La Vallière, prohibited from seeing her child and excluded from any formal life at court. On whose orders she was exiled, no one knew, but we suspected Queen Anne. Perhaps the dowager was the force that made Louis visit his wife more in the early months of the year. Anne commented for all of us to hear one day that soon she hoped that Marie Thérèse would follow in the example of her ladies and sister-in-law and become pregnant again, as if fertility was catching.

Henrietta did have a belly swelling with child, though we all could see how it worried her. Her last pregnancy had ended in a miscarriage, and then, of course, there were the rumors about who the real father of the babe was. Some said the Comte de Guiche (a rumor which annoyed his other alleged lover, Olympe de Soissons), some said an anonymous stable groom, and others said Louis himself.

Athénaïs assured me it was Monsieur. She had received a scolding from Henrietta for leaving her bed so empty while in confinement that the Princess had been left with no choice but to bed her husband for several weeks. When Philippe had suggested drunkenly that the Chevalier de Lorraine join them, it had landed poorly with his wife. One man she could tolerate. Two was unthinkable.

So Athénaïs had been called upon again to Henrietta's bed when she was desired, a secret mistress to the jewel of the court, and a rising jewel herself. The rumors about Henrietta and the King – or the others that were said to have shared his gallant company – continued to swirl. Even as Louis played a doting father and husband, the topic on all lips was if Louis would ever name a woman an official *maîtresse-en-titre* and scandalize all of Europe.

The practice of making the King's mistress a true position in court – naming a woman publicly as the crown's paramour and bedfellow and endowing her with power, prestige, and payment, had last been the purview of Louis's grandfather, Henry IV. While that king had been well-known and well-loved for blessedly ending the wars of religion and getting himself murdered, his love of women in all ways and in all places was what many people still remembered him for. It had been a show of power and virility that Henry had fucked anything with legs. His subsequent death at the hands of an assassin – less so.

But Louis's father had married a devout Spanish princess, Anne, and she had put an end to all that. So too, Queen Anne still hoped, would her son's marriage to her niece, a similarly dour princess. But Marie Thérèse had little of her Aunt's spark or spine. Still, she did have the favor of the King for some brief moments.

It was Louis's custom, no matter what, to visit Marie Thérèse every night in her chambers before he retired. I was not always there, as it was Athénaïs, not I, who was a maid of honor, but when I was present, it was a chance to see my mistress in her finest form. She was witty and engaging, but only just enough to keep the King laughing while nudging the Queen on in conversation. They read the latest books, spoke of recent plays by Racine and Corneille, and debated gently on philosophy. Louis was enthralled. For a while.

In April, things changed. He retreated to Versailles with his closest retainers, and left the court behind. The purpose of this visit was, ostensibly, to survey the plans for the many improvements to the château that would soon begin and to plan a great event there, the details of which were secret.

Everyone suspected more, but only one member of a royal household knew the woods and would not be missed at court. This is how I came, once again, to find myself in the forests west of Paris, near the hunting grounds of the King, left by Athénaïs's carriage in the actual village of Versailles, near woods where once I had danced under the moon.

There are tricks witches know to find things. Quick spells and charms for lost objects. Even someone who would cross themselves at the mention of magic would pray to Saint Anthony when looking for something that has been lost. The spell I cast was one of these simple ones. I knelt on the ground with a bowl of dried mallow leaves and my flint and steel. They lit easily with a spark and were quickly consumed by the flame, a cloud of smoke wafting up. I watched as the wind caught the smoke and followed. That was where the thing I needed to find would be.

Sure enough, my steps led me to a mostly deserted area, where the gardens met the woods. I had but a moment to observe my surroundings – the birds singing, the fresh green grass of spring, the buds upon the trees – before steps approached and I hid myself.

It was La Vallière, looking as wan and tired as usual. I felt the usual stab of pity to see her, waiting like a deer that knows a hunter approaches yet cannot run. Of course the King had brought her here, and she looked as if she had come to this specific spot for an assignation. I wondered how long it would be until Louis arrived and I had more proof that he had recommenced his affair. What I would do with that proof was a different question…

"Have you never heard of rouge, Louise? You look dreadful."

I jumped at the female voice. The speaker was out of my range of vision, but I recognized it. Surely though, it could not be who I suspected. Louise turned to the speaker, who stood somewhere near the entrance of the little grove by a fountain. I crouched lower and craned my head to see better as Louise bowed… to Queen Anne herself.

"I was hoping the sun would brighten my complexion on its own, Your Majesty," Louise muttered as the dowager strode towards her and grabbed her by the chin as she rose.

"That will make you as brown as a peasant. You need to look young and alive if you are to keep my son's interest," Queen Anne chided. "He's started corresponding with that Italian whore again. Where have you been?"

"I thought he had turned his attentions to the Queen, as God has ordained," La Vallière protested, and the Queen rolled her eyes in a most unroyal way.

"My niece has the personality of a toothless lap dog," Anne scoffed. I had never seen such venom from the Dowager Queen. She was usually as composed and calm as the statue of an idol. "Now that she's bred again, Louis will turn away once more – *and it must be to you.*"

"But why?" Louise whimpered, her shoulders slumping as if she was crumbling within. "Why can you not tell him to turn to God? Why must I be his conquest? Why must his soul come at the cost of my sin?"

"Do not weep to me, Mademoiselle La Vallière. Do not pretend it was not you who enticed him first and succumbed to your lust, then crawled to me for forgiveness," Queen Anne hissed back, and I covered my mouth so I would not gasp. "I showed you mercy. I taught you how to make him love you rather than see you as another conquest. Because of all the many women he desires, of all the whores and maids and maidens he has defiled himself with, it is you that is closest to God."

"And so I must succumb again? So that we can guide him back to God?" Louise asked, and again, Anne looked entirely annoyed at the young woman.

"So that *I* may continue to guide him and keep this country from disaster. To keep France herself from falling into the pits of sin," the Queen declared, and finally, everything about Louise La Vallière made perfect sense. This paragon of virtue who had given up her maidenhood and soul had not just given into lust: she was the tool of a woman far more powerful than she. A woman who still hoped to rule France as she had when her son was a child.

"What if there is another child?" Louise asked, her head bowed and her voice small. "I don't want to do that again."

"It is a burden and penance you must bear." The Dowager Queen said it so casually there was no room for Louise to argue. "Take this. It will keep his interest in you and make things easier for you too if need be."

The dowager handed Louise a small glass vial filled with some unknown substance, but I suspected its contents: a potion of some kind to inflame the King's lust. Or perhaps even something to keep his heart.

"This is another sin you ask of me?" Louise asked again, her hand trembling.

"When a witch or heretic burns, it is not murder. It is the cleansing of evil from the world," Anne hissed, and my stomach seized. "When a righteous woman like you indulges in lust to save the souls of all of France, neither is that sin. You do *what must be done* so that justice can prevail and righteousness can drive back the darkness."

There was something more dangerous than ambition and cruelty in Anne's eyes now. There was zealotry. This was the woman who had held back the Fronde. That had handed her son the most power a King had ever had over his nobles and subjects, and she wanted that power because she believed it came from her God and that it had to be used to serve him. Louise La Vallière had to submit as well. I saw her capitulation in the way her ivory shoulders sagged, and she nodded like a scolded child.

"I will serve, Your Majesty. With your blessing," Louise said, dutiful once again.

"You will be in my prayers, Louise La Vallière," Anne replied with a false smile. I did not doubt that it was true; the queen would pray vigorously for her pawn to remain in the King's bed and to nudge him in the direction she wanted.

I returned to the village of Versailles through the woods, making sure to thank the mallow and smoke for their service, lingering among the trees for their comfort. I did not arrive back in Paris until late in the evening, but luckily, Athénaïs was home, rather than serving Marie Thérèse.

"You've learned something," Athénaïs declared, reading the dire expression on my face as I entered her room. She was in her usual mode of disheveled comfort, half-dressed with her robe falling from her shoulders. She set down her book and beckoned me to her.

"Louise La Vallière is in Versailles, awaiting the whims of the King, as you suspected," I replied, and Athénaïs clapped her hands in glee.

"I knew that little minx wouldn't give up such a prize, no matter what her confessor orders her to do."

"She is a pawn," I replied, feelings of pity and disgust still competing within me.

"What? Who would be able to control her?" Athénaïs balked. "She refused when Nicolas Fouquet tried to buy her as a spy years ago. Too virtuous, as always."

"It is her virtue and holiness that entraps her. All this time – since Louis first seduced her – she has been the instrument of Queen Anne."

"His mother?" Athénaïs gasped. "But she is the one who wishes him to be steadfast and true. If it was not for Anne, Louise would already be official mistress!"

"She knows her son – knows his desires cannot be met by our dear, boring Marie Thérèse. So if his mistress is a sweet, holy, virtuous thing who reports back to her and can whisper her counsel in Louis's ear, she can evangelize to him when even he turns away from his wife."

"That's brilliant," Athénaïs scoffed. "And it explains why no other lady of the court has been able to hold the King's attention."

"I think she gave her some Spanish fly to use as well," I added, sitting next to Athénaïs on the chaise.

"Well, that's brilliant too." Athénaïs nibbled at her thumb nail. "I have no doubt Louis truly thinks he's in love with that wet blanket of a girl. It's so unfair. It goes against Marie Thérèse *and* makes it harder for everyone at court."

"Why don't we remove her?" I suggested with a smile. "Not Louise. Anne." I did not like my odds as a witch in a court where the Dowager Queen wanted to steer the King towards God, but was prepared to invoke the devil to do so. More than that, I did not want that for Louis. He deserved more than anyone to make his own choices.

"It's one thing to send away my husband, but quite another to meddle with a Queen, Claude," Athénaïs said, but there was no warning in her voice. Instead, there was excitement and perhaps even desire. If we could do this – remove Anne and undermine La Vallière – there was no saying what other heights we might reach.

W HEN IN NEED OF a reading or decision for the future, there were many witches and divineresses in Paris now that could provide. I knew all of them – or thought I did – and all their methods. Some read cards, like I did, or palms. Some read tea leaves, and La Voisin had taken to looking intently at heads and faces. There was even an old baker named Marguerite Delaporte who used a glass of water to see the future. It was not the same as scrying in a mirror or in the reflection of a lake, but a complete fraud.

It was a strange mix of the real and the false, the magic that worked in the great city. There were those like Lapère, or even her students like Veronique, who could see beyond the veil of the world; who could speak to spirits or divine the future. They sold potions and cures as real as anything from a doctor and helped women with their babes, wanted and unwanted, and all other peculiarities of our bodies that were so often forgotten.

Yet my fellow witches also dealt in spells that had no other power but the client's faith in it, and often, that was enough to change things. Maybe that was what it was to be a woman: to find the bits of magic in the things we had to do to survive, even if we knew they were lies. Maybe Louise La Vallière, who found some semblance of love and pleasure with the King while hoping to give her soul to God, was not so different from us. We all wanted power, and there was only so much of it to be had.

I was on a mission to discover how to take power from the Dowager Queen, and there was no better place to start than among the sorceresses who had made me. I was not desperate enough to look for someone like Adam Le Sage with his inheritance powders yet... There was much that could be done before taking such an extreme step, especially when La Vallière's secret ally was old and growing feebler by the day. Or so the rumors had begun to say - rumors I had encouraged among the servants that were spreading bit by bit.

I considered what questions I needed answered as I walked down a new street to Lapère's house, past buildings with fresh plaster on their walls with respectable businesses and rich tenants. There were few homes like Lapère's left here, and most of her students and their imitators had moved to fine houses in the Marais. I was the only one who had moved to the palace; a fact no one seemed to acknowledge or admire, despite how much information and power I gave to my old friends. Then, of course, there was Veronique: the one who had left the city and who did not know what I had become or done to save her.

Or perhaps she would now, because she was standing in front of Lapère's house, pulling weeds from among the flowers blooming in their pots.

I tried to turn before she saw me, but I was too late. At least she looked as shocked to see me as I was to see her.

She was still beautiful, even if the past years had taken their toll. Her skin was tanned and her freckles more pronounced, as if she had been kissed by the sun and the spring itself. Her clothes were still humble, more restrained now, with a kerchief covering her décolletage and a modest cap over her red tresses. But her jade eyes were still clear and breathtaking when she looked at me, full of fondness and regret.

How did I appear to her? I had not changed my costume for this journey, for it was safer now for a wealthy woman to walk these streets, especially in bright daylight. I wore the sapphire blue that Athénaïs favored on me, a dress of silk and damask with puffed sleeves to indicate I did not need ease or freedom of movement. My hair was intricately styled in the court fashion, with dozens of intricate ringlets, and I wore heeled shoes of satin. I was a very different woman than the actress in rags she had met years ago. The one who had driven her from the city with my sins.

"I thought you were in Rouen," I blurted out, and her face fell. Maybe she was expecting a happier greeting.

"I left after I was... freed," Veronique replied, her hands going to her wrist. My stomach fell at the thought of her in chains.

"You were suspected by the court?" I asked, and she nodded. "I heard about what was happening there and I was afraid of that very thing. I'm so sorry—" The words tumbled from my mouth, and Veronique looked at me in wonder.

"*You* were worried?"

"I was. I—" Did I dare tell her that I had been the reason the King himself had intervened and stopped the proceedings in Rouen? Would she believe me? I had shared my rise with my friends – they all knew of my position at court, and Veronique would know too. Would she believe how close I was to the center of all power in France?

"Many good women were jailed with me. Accused of terrible things," Veronique went on, eyes darkening and voice lowering. I took a step towards her and she flinched. Flinched away from me.

"Things that you think I have done?" I asked stiffly, raising my chin.

"Things I will not speak of in the open, lest I be heard and bring justice upon us here," Veronique replied, just as cold.

"Are you blaming me now? For being the kind of woman they thought you were? Because I have used our arts to defend myself and others?"

"And rise high, I have heard," she replied. "You have done well with your cherished freedom. Some of us are not so lucky."

It was like a slap to receive another reprimand from her after so long, and to have this insult to all I had done added to it. "What I have done with my freedom earned you yours," I said and turned before she demanded I explain.

I no longer wanted a reading from Lapère, I decided as I walked back towards the manor where I lived and waited to serve in the palace. Where I had to return to pack for a journey to a great fête held by the King.

I had gone there looking for some sign or guidance for what to do next, and the universe had given it. I had been afraid of becoming what I already was. What Veronique feared: a witch in my power. A woman unafraid of choosing to weave her own web of fate. A spider who had not tasted blood for too long a time.

I T IS AN INADEQUATE word to call the events that took place at Versailles in May of 1664 a party. A ball or gala lasts for an evening, or perhaps a full day into the night. This was a court entertainment unlike anything anyone had heard of. Louis called it *Les Plaisirs de L'Île Enchantée* – "The Pleasures of the Enchanted Island" – the name taken from an episode of a poem by Aristo, a refined and dreamy work that was all the rage. The fête was set to last for *six* days.

The little village of Versailles buzzed with rumors of all that was to occur in the gardens and palace, and all of Paris too. Workers from throughout the city were hired to build the stages for the plays and ballets, and more to prepare the grounds for the grand equestrian parades and games.

Every cook and baker within ten miles was employed preparing the food – baking fantastic pastries and tarts, brewing lemonade and sweetened wine humbly called 'the drink of the gods,' and slaughtering enough game to feed an army. The gardeners were beside themselves, filling every corner with blooms and fruit trees, including dozens of orange trees out of season that would line the avenues and fill the air with their perfume.

I heard about it constantly in both of my circles. Among the ladies of the court, everyone was focused on assembling new wardrobes – terrorizing every dressmaker, jeweler, and milliner in Paris from dawn to dusk. These women were preparing for battle to be the fairest and most fashionable.

The men too spent a fortune on fashion. Their great coats and silken pantaloons were as ostentatious as any woman's finery, perhaps even more so because they had a King to compare themselves to. (Though no one wanted to outshine Louis, for they remembered that Nicholas Fouquet was still languishing in prison for trying to outdo the King.) No, they all just wanted to be seen – to be a star in the firmament of the revels to come.

But there were other ways to put stars in the sky, to make them sparkle and to make them fall. Ahead of the fête, half the ladies in court were seeking out fortune tellers to determine which lovers to take, how long their dull husbands might live, and what rivals they had to fear. I had given up my quest to have a reading done by Lapère, and so, I read for Athénaïs and myself.

The cards were cryptic, but encouraging. The Seven of Swords returned many times, appropriate for the deceptions and backstabbing that was to occur, but so too did the Eight of the same suit, warning of bondage. We also saw the Empress reversed, and the Nine of Cups, for bounty and wealth. It boded well for us; or I hoped it did.

After weeks of hearing the event discussed in every corner of the city, it thrilled me to no end when we entered the carriage to make the journey to Versailles at last. I had been awake until the wee hours the night before, worried that, somehow, I would be excluded. That Athénaïs might wake and finally see me for the poor, pathetic thing I was (or the devil some thought me), and turn me out onto the street.

But no, I was with her in the carriage. An older carriage; the only kind the Marquis de Montespan (still blessedly busy in the country) deigned to pay for. Still, it was freshly painted and the horses' coats shone in the May sun. At the reins, Jean Luc wore a new livery, and I boasted a trunk of new clothes, though nothing to match Athénaïs's. I was ready to be part of something that everyone in Paris wanted to catch a glimpse of, but wouldn't. They would sit in their jealousy while I walked among queens and kings.

The Château of Versailles was small compared to Fontainebleau or Saint-Germain-en -Laye, but the decorations that greeted guests were breathtaking. It made all who had been invited to stay in the building all the more honored to be in this inner circle, for others had to take lodgings in the village or attend each day by carriage. But Athénaïs and I were shown to a beautiful room, befitting a member of the Queen's household.

"I wonder if Henrietta will call upon me," Athénaïs sighed, looking out the window as the valets finished bringing in our trunks and closed the door behind them, leaving us in a moment of quiet intimacy. I liked the idea of Athénaïs bedding Henrietta less and less these days, not that I thought I could keep her affection to myself, but because there was little value in the service anymore (and Henrietta was a stingy, entitled lover).

"For your sake, I hope not," I said.

"She's been listless lately, and her husband will, of course, be at the center of the festivities. Versailles is so small, everyone must practically sleep on top of one another in that little place." She knocked on the wall to make her point. It was thin, despite the fine enameled decorations upon it.

"It won't be for long. When the building is done, it will be like nothing anyone has ever seen," I replied, recalling a conversation I had managed with Le Vau, the architect Louis had confiscated from Nicolas Fouquet. I imagined what the quarters would be like when complete.

"And yet, somehow you'll find your way into all those quiet, secret corners to do your work," Athénaïs said with a smile, as I looked at her over the bed. "Weaving your web."

"Does that make me your Arachne, Athénaïs?" I asked with a smile.

"Does it? Didn't the Goddess of wisdom punish Arachne for striving to best her?" my mistress replied, as educated in the classics as I had endeavored to become in recent years.

"The way I see it, Athena showed Arachne where she belonged and gave her new life," I replied with a shrug. She caught my eyes with her shining blue ones, reminding me again of her beauty, and the cunning and strength she held. "I have always been a spider. Even my mother called me that. It is no hard thing if I can be a spider for a goddess, to worship her and serve her and—"

I stopped myself before I said too much and ruined it all. Suddenly, I couldn't look at her. It was too much. The carved bedpost was more interesting.

"Do you love me, Claude?" Athénaïs asked quietly. Kindly.

"I am surprised you must even ask," I muttered, trying to sound unafraid. I was afraid, though. The last woman I had loved had turned on me when she saw that I was a spider of the poisonous, bloody sort. I held on to the edge of the bed to stop shaking.

"You must know it is returned," Athénaïs whispered, and to my shock, she was right next to me. She was gentle as she touched my face. She was always gentle when she touched me; as if she knew that too quick a movement would frighten me. "How could it not be, after all you have given me and continue to give?"

I was speechless, my mouth dry, even as my eyes dampened. I managed a whimper when she kissed my neck and jaw, then mouthed her way down to the edge of my bodice. "What you will do for me, for us... It amazes me."

"We don't know that it will succeed," I muttered, but my head was spinning. So rarely was it I who was at the mercy of kisses and touches. More often, we tangled together in the dark, or I devoured her like she was my last sustenance. But right now, my body was suddenly screaming for her touch, and I gripped the edge of the bed to keep from falling as my mistress's wonderful hand hiked up my skirts and reached between my thighs. "Even if it does, it will take time," I gasped as she entered me.

"You told me that magic always takes time, to be patient with it." Her voice was loving and calm as her fingers filled me, and I shuddered at the pleasure of it. "So I am content to sow my seeds now for a distant harvest. I trust you to do as needed."

"I will." She had added another finger, and I was so full and tight as she pushed into my wetness. "If you command it, I will do anything."

"Let me see one," she commanded, her face nuzzling against my breasts. I scrambled to loosen my dress enough to scoop one out so that she could take it into her mouth, sucking fiercely and playing at my nipple with teeth and tongue so that I nearly screamed. "There's a good girl."

"I serve you," I said, and it took my mind to a different dreamy place to say it. "I adore you." She hummed against my breast and increased the speed of her hands as I fell back onto the bed, utterly at her mercy and under her spell.

"Then come for me now. As I command."

I bit into her bare shoulder as my body obeyed, the climax hurling me into the firmament where she awaited me.

I felt drunk when I came back down, utterly destroyed and boneless. But not so much that I couldn't embrace her and turn her over onto the bed. Her voice was muffled when I was beneath her skirts and between her thighs, feasting on her sweet nectar, but I heard her laugh and I loved her all the more.

*T*HE PLEASURES OF THE *Enchanted Isle* began the next day. As in the poem, we were companions of the noble hero, Roger – embodied by Louis in the pageant – all gleeful prisoners of the sorceress Alcine on her magical island. There was parade after parade of horses, with Louis at their center in a gold chariot, his steeds bridled with silver and jewels.

There were races and equestrian contests – all bet upon by a court obsessed with gambling. The amount of money I saw won and lost among the nobility in a few days was staggering. Seeing all that gold made me bold enough to try my hand, with basil and clover in my slippers to bring me luck, and I was wise enough to walk away when I had won a small fortune.

We were treated to ballets and promenades, many of which featured the King himself and his favorites – Athénaïs and Lousie La Vallière included (her limp was barely noticeable when she danced, aside from the whispers of the many ladies who hated her). Messieurs Lully and Molière collaborated on a combination of comedy, ballet, and music like nothing anyone had seen before, *The Princess of Elis*. Reaching back to my days in the theater, I found it remarkable for its spectacle, but forgettable for its story. What was all the more entertaining was the new play put forth by Molière: *Tartuffe*.

It was the best work I had ever seen, especially coming from a man who had always struck me as self-important and hungry for fame. It combined the best parts of his farces with scathing satire of the false piety of so many in France. Ostentatious holiness was revealed to be little less than a ploy for power.

I was not the only one in the audience who craned my neck to see how Queen Anne and Louise reacted to the direct attack

on hypocrisy and faith. Their frowns made me nervous that this
would be the sole performance of the brilliant work…

After the premiere, the gardens sparkled with lights and fireworks, as if we were all walking among the stars themselves. Louis
was not just generous with his spectacles, but with his gifts to
all who had made this trek to celebrate how he had moved the
center of the universe here to Versailles. He held what was called
a lottery, though there was no real chance involved. It was an excuse to dole out gifts of money, lands, and jewels to his courtiers,
including Louise La Vallière, who profited considerably from the
game. It was the only way he could gift her with lands and riches
in public and make it seem honorable.

The wide avenues of the gardens were as busy as broad daylight
as we all paraded in the evening air, the court whispering of the
wonders we had seen and were yet to see. The entire entertainment was nominally dedicated to both Queens, but the whole
court knew it was all for Louise. She walked beside Louis, her
smile forced but bright, her posture demure. As if she could hide
that she was the third queen in the royal retinue and the most
beloved.

I had wondered for a year how La Vallière was tolerated when
the Queens were so pious. The bishops condemned adultery at
Easter sermons, nearly looking the King in the eyes as they did,
and yet, their love affair continued so flagrantly. Now I knew
that it was because Louise was a pawn to a Queen, to hold the
King in check.

Anne looked over the proceedings with the confident expression of a woman in complete control. She was serene as an
empress, a queen who had ruled and would never relinquish her

crown. There was a part of me that respected her, and another part that hated her. She held her power invisibly, even now, guiding the King so subtly, no one even knew she was behind the reins. But the murmurs were there about the way Louis had begun to slowly revoke the rights of protestants, the way the borders of France remained closed to those deemed unclean... Was that all her? Was there hope for change if she was removed?

The King's wife would not be the one to do it. That was for sure.

It hurt my heart to see how Marie Thérèse looked at her husband and Louise as they strode down the avenue together, leaving the Queen far behind as her husband paraded with the woman who Louis had insisted be given a formal appointment *in the Queen's household* after she had been dismissed from Madame's. Marie Thérèse was not one for court pageantry and revels, I had learned. She preferred to spend her time in prayer or reading quietly, or doting upon her son, the Dauphin, and the children of her ladies.

So it was to Marie Thérèse that I went after the brilliant premiere of *Tartuffe*. Precious few spoke to her, for her responses were slow and accented. But I was patient, as spiders must be. I emerged from the shadows in the glittering garden to find her neglected and alone as the court milled and mingled around her, but not with her.

Her gown was black and red, a dark contrast to the flowery colors of Louis's courtiers, but perhaps a nod to the customs of Spain. Still, it was an incredible garment: embroidered in thread of silver and gold, accented with pearls the size of plums. It was as stiff as a tapestry and just as heavy, so that the Queen had no choice but to move slowly, trying to seem regal. In my gown of pale green, with creamy sleeves, lined in lace, I was a stark, humble contrast.

"Did you enjoy the play, Your Majesty?" I asked the young Queen as I gave her a deep bow. It still thrilled me that I, who had watched this woman's wedding procession through the city from a dirty roof, could address her, even though I was adjacent to her household.

"I am not one for the theater, as my husband knows. The words do go by too fast," the Queen replied with a sigh. I hoped that the playwright's barbs against holiness and hypocrisy had gone by too fast too. "But the music was lovely."

"Have the other delights of these days pleased you then?" I asked, noting how her hand strayed to her belly where a new heir grew. I wondered if she was thinking of her last pregnancy, when the poor child had died weeks after birth.

"It has been… tiring. You will understand when you are wed," the Queen said, trying to force a smile.

"I cannot imagine how tiring it is to be a mother to a prince and wife to a king," I said, doing my best to draw on the sympathy I truly felt. "Your dear mother-in-law must be of great help and guidance."

"My aunt– I mean, my mother, the Queen. She is a constant reminder of what I must be," Marie Thérèse replied, just as I had hoped. Maybe the charm in my shoes was bringing me luck once again.

"Such a high ideal to meet," I said as I drew closer, matching the Queen's careful pace as we walked. I looked up to the sky, but the lights in the garden were so bright, I could see no stars. "That too must be exhausting."

"I can only pray to God I will please her." The Queen's accent thickened at the words. She sounded so sad.

"She must be so tired too, I imagine," I offered. "After forty years as Queen, then regent, and now dowager and grandmother, to still be such a fixture at court!"

"Forty-eight years," Marie Thérèse corrected. "She likes to remind me."

"With her health in decline, I do worry for her." The words were careful, delivered lightly, but for maximum effect. The Queen's attention whipped towards me and I covered my mouth in a show of contrition. "Oh, I should not have said that. I know she does not wish it to be spoken of near her son."

"Nor me, it seems," the Queen said, and I could see the questions forming behind her brown eyes. "What illness have you heard of?"

And here was the place to pour the most potent of poisons into the queen's ear: the truth.

"I have heard from servants in her household that the doctors come often, but no emetic or poultice gives her full relief from whatever malady has begun to attack her." It had taken me many weeks of listening and gossiping in the lower floors of palaces to learn that. "I didn't mean to upset you, Your Majesty. It is such a noble struggle, even more so if she hopes to spare her son the knowledge. I thought of all the women at court, she would have confided in you, with whom she shares so much. I did not mean an insult."

To make my point, I began to sink into a supplicant bow to show I was throwing myself on the Queen's mercy, but she caught my elbow to stop me. "You did not know. I forget too often that you are unique in your position. Madame de Montespan is lucky to have so compassionate an ally at court."

"We all need allies," I offered. "Even a queen. For you and the dowager, I know your greatest allies are your confessors and God, but you are not alone, my queen."

"That is to be seen," Marie Thérèse mused. "I hope my mother is not alone either."

"I have heard she finds great peace in her visits to the convent at Val-de-Grâce."

The sweet, simple Queen's face perked again. "Yes, that is true. If only she would retire there more often, she might... find more peace," the Queen mused, and for the first time that night, she seemed hopeful. My work was done.

"I hope you find some enjoyment in this evening, Your Majesty," I murmured with a bow. "For you are not alone."

The Queen moved on into the garden dotted with light like it was another sky, and my heart swelled with pride, like a farmer looking at fresh-tilled fields, waiting for the seeds to grow.

I called on power that night, as I took to bed with Athénaïs, the wine and revelry leaving our heads to spin. I floated through another sea of stars, and I called on the sun-bright burst of light within me to make what I had planted in the Queen's mind grow.

The harvest came sooner than expected.

CHAPTER 17

DEATH

To be a witch, Lapère once told me as we walked in the woods years ago to harvest a mushroom that only grew in the wet days of fall, was to know the rhythm of things. Witchcraft was a way of listening to the whispers of plants and the echoes of ancestors and to the song of the very world. A song that, like any other, had highs and lows, verses and choruses. A repeating cycle, on and on.

I had not understood it then, as she spoke of the wisdom of the earth and the seasons, of how all could come and go, of seed and harvest, but I came closer to her wisdom when harvest and harrowing came.

Queen Anne was forced to retreat from her duties at court at the insistence of her niece, and then her son. A certain leniency in morals began to arise in the halls of the Louvre and Fontainebleau when news spread that the Dowager Queen Anne would soon spend more time at the convent of Val-de-Grâce. The King did not yet know that she was ill, that was kept from him; but it meant something to him and us all to not have the imperious eyes of Anne upon us at all times. It was a triumph for the debauched and ambitious and so it was a triumph for me. Like many, I fell easily into new and exciting sins.

It was freeing to know that, while we were all dragged to Mass each week – and sometimes more often, if you had the misfortune to be favored by Marie Thérèse – we could let the devil in when the churchmen looked away. I spent the summer between Athénaïs's and Madame's bed until Henrietta grew large with child and entered confinement, indulging in some depravities we might never have contemplated when the old Queen was nearby. I had never even contemplated that I might fuck a woman in the manner of a man, but Madame knew expert craftsman of ingenious toys and garments (of a sort), and I gained great facility with them in those first heady months as Henrietta watched us. It was a struggle for all of us to keep a straight face in church the next morning.

Many ladies – Soissons, Polignac, and Montespan included, were there to attend the birth of Madame's first son in July. A small little thing named Philippe, after his father. Or supposed father. There were persistent rumors that it was the Comte de Guiche (despite his exile) that had been the sire, or the Chevalier de Lorraine had stumbled into the wrong bed or been involved in some orgy. Or even that it was Louis's child, but it was no matter. Soon enough , the infant was given to his wet nurses and

Henrietta rejoined court, dancing in the ballets and laughing at the center of every party.

The gambling tables were wilder, the parties went later into the night, and courtiers reveled in assignations with those above and below them. Some of the maids and valets despised being used as playthings for their betters, but others relished it and bragged of their conquests. Or those they had seen. The Comtesse de Soissons in particular was a popular topic, as she was said to require several young stable hands each month to fill the void left by the Comte de Guiche, still in exile. The rumor was brazen (she had only fucked *one* servant, and he was a valet, not a stable boy) and never would have been tolerated before, but now, we all laughed about it.

Well, almost all of us. The lapse in morals once Anne was gone had other consequences, which were to be expected, but the ladies and maids of the court were ill-equipped to deal with them. This is where my web of influence and information continued to grow. More than once, a woman would be told in whispers to seek me out for help when her courses were late or when she regretted her choices in the morning. I knew where to send them or what to give them. I kept watch on them and made their excuses when they were waylaid for days, recovering from the end of their pregnancies. I spread out the business to Lapère and her network, just as I spread out the business of referrals to La Voisin and other fortune tellers.

I kept the knowledge of who was with who and who had gone to who to myself, meticulously catalogued in my head, like the lists of correspondences and cures I had memorized at Lapère's feet years ago. This too was powerful, a force I could wield. And wield it I did, in ways petty and significant. I used my knowledge and connections to force the Marquise de Alluye to relinquish her normal seats at the theater in the Palais-Royal to Athénaïs because I knew what her husband had done with his valets – and how mad Monsieur would be to know he had not shared in that bounty.

When a maid came to me begging for help because a cook had raped her, I made sure he was dealt with accordingly without destroying the woman's honor. It wasn't so hard to have someone place stolen jewels in the boy's pockets. It was even easier to watch him be hauled off, screaming his innocence. I think he was hanged, but I'm not sure of it. His victim was happy with the result and after that, I knew everything that went on in the apartments of Louise La Vallière.

She who, above all and much to her distress, thrived the most in this new, freer world.

Everyone knew now that Louise was the King's official mistress in all ways except a public title. Though *maîtresse-en-titre* was not an endowed position with prestige and notoriety as it had been for the ladies who served Louis's grandfather, it was as good as. Louis lavished his lover with wealth and gifts, and it was clear he was utterly besotted with her, much to the jealousy of every other woman in court. Louise was paraded about at the King's side, and Marie Thérèse was forced to watch, which she did in pious, accepting silence. She was relieved more than anyone to be free of her aunt, even though she regularly visited her and prayed with her at Val-de-Grâce.

In the streets, they told stories and sang songs of the King and his pious jezebel. Pamphlets were published and comedies performed that satirized Louise. Sometimes, she was a whore;

sometimes, she was a saint. It all depended on the day and the mood of Paris. No matter Louise's role, Louis remained the hero. Our virile, powerful king. The fact that he had brought a pious, beautiful lover into his bed chamber was worth celebrating, while Louise was worth condemning. It weighed on her, I heard from her servants. She spent hours at prayer, she fasted and sought to repent, but it was not enough to save her soul. She took the hate of the court and the city as her punishment for her sins but continued in them.

I could not decide what I thought of Louise La Vallière, except that she was a fool no matter what she thought or did. She was a fool for not reveling in the attentions of a King who continued to lead France to prosperity and glory, who filled the court with art and life and wonder. Or she was a fool for being so weak as to continue to let herself be ruled by her lusts and by the Queen Mother's orders that she somehow save Louis's soul in the bed of their infidelity.

The ones who hated Louise the most remained Henrietta and the Comtesse de Soissons, and they took turns snubbing her, as did Monsieur, who knew well enough not to cross his wife. When they were set to receive Louise in their private chambers at the Château de Vincennes one day, they made a point to not be there, even if Marie Thérèse was, and they made sure the whole court knew it. Henrietta made the excuse that Vincennes was a gloomy, ancient place that felt haunted.

We all knew when Louise fell pregnant again, her belly beginning to swell even as the Queen prepared for her labors once again. The Queen was snubbed when Louis attempted again to endear Louise to his brother. He took Louise, not his pregnant wife, with him to see Madame and Monsieur at Villers-Cotterêts, a country estate to which they had flown after a row between Philippe and Henrietta on the subject of his lover, the Chevalier de Lorraine.

Henrietta was incensed to have to receive La Vallière – she publicly declared it was because Louise was so scandalous. In truth, it was because Henrietta found Louise to be an incredible bore. It was a signal, even so, that Louis wanted things to change.

Things die back in the fall, as so too did the gaiety at court and my fortunes.

The snubs continued, but were less pronounced. Marie Thérèse entered her confinement; and Louise took that time to disappear, once again, to the Palais Brion. (I wondered how Louis felt to have two women carrying his children at the same time.)

The most important event in the fall for me however was another woman's confinement – the woman I loved. Athénaïs finally gave her husband what he needed from her, bringing forth an heir to the Montespan name in September.

I was there with her again, attending with Lapère as Athénaïs birthed another life. To be there in such moments was the most potent of magic – to watch as Our Lady guided a new being into the world, and to pray to her to protect mother and child. I think Athénaïs willed herself into early, swift labor to be done with it.

The child was named Louis Antoine, and like his sister, he was barely a thought in Athénaïs's mind before she was back at court, taking advantage of the precious few months while Marie Thérèse and Louise, were both waiting to wage the same battle.

She was not the only one. With Louise, the Queen, and the Queen Mother all absent from court at the same time, a hunt ensued that was unlike anything I had seen before. At every court entertainment that winter, women fawned over Louis – dancing for him in ballets, flattering him with their wit, and surrounding him with merriment.

Athénaïs was one of them, of course, and I was happy to be at her side whenever she was close to the King, but she had duties as well, as a member of the Queen's household. We were graced often by the King's presence, and I adored it. Louis was wiser and more amusing than any man I had ever known, and I looked forward to his nightly visits to his wife's chambers, even if he did so on the way to Louise's rooms.

Marie Thérèse and the King were both endlessly amused by Athénaïs's wit and humor, and she continued to rise in favor with both of them, even as the Comtesse De Soissons, still the head of the Queen's household, faltered, falling back on the Vicomtesse de Polignac as her only friend. It would have been easy in that time for Athénaïs to seduce the King; we both knew it, but she held back.

I held her back.

I told her that this was not the time. We had to wait until Anne's grip on Louis was gone entirely. I read her cards and palm and they said to wait. Athénaïs could not tell that these were prophecies of my own interpretation, not just what the tarot and her hands told me. I kept her at bay even when she could have so easily struck – because I had never in my life been as happy as I was serving her.

I did not want it to ever change.

I wanted to keep my place in her bed and her heart. My love for her was as deep as the sea and just as dangerous. I was willing to share her with a vapid, uncaring woman like Henrietta – a spoiled princess who cared solely for her pleasure and prestige. She was young and brash, Madame; not the kind of person who could truly win Athénaïs's affection. She was no threat to my place. But Louis was different. He was not only the King, he was the very light of the court itself. If Athénaïs were to attempt to seduce him and supplant La Vallière... She would succeed and she would be his. I could not compare to a King that everyone in court, man or woman, was in love with.

Even myself, if I was honest. Louis dazzled me. One moment close to him was never enough. Perhaps I did not want Athénaïs's attention to turn to Louis because I would have been jealous of both of them. And what use would she have for me if she was the intimate of the King?

It was not all lies on my part though. As fall turned to winter, my dreams darkened. Death showed himself in my cards, lingering near the Queen of Cups, and I worried for my Athénaïs. I wove spells to protect her as rumors of plague came from the countryside. Athénaïs's husband attempted to call her back to their manor too, but we refused. We were needed for the birth of Marie Thérèse's child in November, after all.

The birth of a royal babe is a very public affair, and a fraught one. This was the third time the Queen had labored as courtiers and doctors prodded and surveyed her, but the first I observed. I had been at many births, including that of the bastard half-brother of this child, enough to form opinions about what was and was not good for a mother and child. Nothing I saw in Marie Thérèse's gilded birthing chamber was what I would have chosen or recommended.

There were no midwives. No women were allowed to even touch the Spanish queen except to mop her brow and hold her hand. A parade of old men in black coats monitored her and dismissed her cries of pain and her fear for her babe. Almost exactly two years prior, she had been in this same bed, and the little princess she had given birth to had been weak and sickly. She had barely lived a month. As I watched the Queen weep and push, and doctors debated if they should cut her or bleed her, certainty overtook me that this child would meet the same fate.

I prayed to Our Lady and the Queen's crucified god that it would not be so… Even for a witch though, there is little we can do against the will of fate when it is set.

The little Princess Marie-Anne was born to muted adulation in the waning days of November 1664. She died a few days after Christmas. Marie Thérèse was inconsolable at the loss. Her household went into mourning, as did the King. It was a loss that changed the Queen more than the previous dead princess because this was one she had to bear as Louise La Vallière prepared to give the King a child too.

Eleven days after Marie Thérèse's second daughter died, Louise La Vallière's second son was born.

1665

"She does not want the mourning period to end. She won't like this," Athénaïs reprimanded. Olympe de Soissons had read the letter formally summoning the Queen and her household to celebrate Candlemas – *La Chandeleur* – at the royal chapel. She was dressed in a gown of red with cream lace, not the black that had been required of every woman who came in view of the Queen since January, and she shrugged.

"Her Grace cannot flout the will of her husband," Olympe said, and there was a clear edge to her tone. "He wishes to celebrate with the entire court."

"The entire court? Even La Vallière?" I demanded, drawing the attention of the Comtesse du Bussy, who, no doubt, would gossip of my impertinence to her windbag of a husband.

"It's possible she has not recovered from her *illness*," Olympe replied. "The King did not mention it when he relayed this to me."

"He told you all this personally?" Athénaïs asked, eyebrow raising. Her black gown made her skin look all the more like porcelain and her hair like pale gold. Olympe looked quite the strumpet in comparison. Even more so when she gave a wicked smile.

"I spoke to His Grace yesterday while my husband brought business to Monsieur Colbert. Something tedious about canons or muskets. Louis was happy for the distraction," Olympe said, and her satisfaction with herself was as glaring as a cat flouncing through a parlor with a fat mouse in its mouth.

"Did you speak to him about your brother-in-law's disgrace?" Athénaïs replied smoothly, and Olympe's face turned red. "I do pity your sister for having to endure such a man as the Duc de Meilleraye. Poor Hortense."

"It is one thing to be despised by the court, but another to be insulted by the King so publicly that it's spoken of in the streets," I added.

The Duc de Meilleraye had dared to question the King's morality and virtue, berating him *in public* for his continued betrayal of his wife with Louise La Vallière. In response, the King had tapped the man's head and noted, "I always knew there wasn't much there." An insult so simple and stinging that the Duc, a detestable man, had left the court and dragged Olympe's poor sister Hortense with him.

"At least *she* has a name to uphold," Olympe snapped at me with a cruel sneer. When I was noticed enough to be insulted, my low birth was always front of mind for those who knew my origin. To my surprise, however, no one at court truly cared.

"Wasn't your grandfather a shoemaker from Sicily?" I shot back, and Olympe balked.

"Stop quarreling on my behalf," came a soft, accented voice from the door to the private bed chamber. We all stood to honor the Queen in her robe, looking pale and tired, her skirts disheveled from kneeling before the crucifix she kept next to her bed. It was a sad sight. "If it is my husband's wish that mourning for our child should end, then let it be ended. He is the King."

"Shall we help you dress, Your Majesty?" Athénaïs asked with genuine care. "We can choose a new gown, something that will please the King."

"The only thing that would please him is if I could put on that woman's face and charms," the Queen sighed in reply. We all knew who 'that woman' was – La Vallière. Marie Thérèse never spoke her name.

"She could never compare to your radiance," Athénaïs argued, a sweet lie.

"And she may never return," Olympe said with a smirk that made me cold. She was up to something, and I did not like it at all.

"We would not wish that…" Marie Thérèse reprimanded, sensing the same malice in the head of her household. "Just as we would never wish any child to be without its mother."

The pain in Marie Thérèse's voice made me wince in guilt and sympathy. We all knew about the King's two bastards by Louise. I knew more than most – the child whose birth I had overseen was kept in a humble house near the palace of the Tuileries, seen to by Madame Colbert and nurses, visited occasionally by his father, but never his mother. The newborn had joined them last week, according to the servants that kept me apprised of such things after his mother had refused to nurse him or look upon him and she recovered from a taxing labor.

"I should like to visit my son for the afternoon," Marie Thérèse declared. "Dress me as you see fit, Madame de Montespan. Madame de Soissons may return to my husband to tell him I will see him at the church. Mademoiselle des Œillets, please alert the Dauphin's household."

With a nod from Athénaïs, I did as I was told, crossing the long breadth of the Louvre to the rooms where the little Dauphin lived, as separated from his mother as La Vallière's children. At least he would grow up knowing who his parents were, not with the false name and pedigree that Colbert had given to Louise's children. My message to the nurse was brief, and I thanked Our Lady that the errand left me free. A creeping dread had entered my mind and I wished to confirm it.

I T WAS STILL A wonder how easy it was to come and go from this grand place after I had watched her walls for years, wishing I could be on the other side. Now I knew exactly how to slip out the back and make my way to the Marais and the house of La Voisin.

Catherine was seeing customers, as usual for the late afternoon. Two women waited in the street, looking suspiciously at one another. I'd wager they were each ready to claw the other to be the next in line to be told if their lover was true or what riches awaited them in the future. I did not want to wait for them to receive their fantasies before I learned what guidance Catherine was giving to the Comtesse de Soissons lately.

"You know, they say that La Vigoreaux is just as talented as La Voisin," I said lightly to the women. "I heard that last week, one of her clients celebrated a wedding to a Marquise, and two others are pregnant."

"Where is she?" the younger woman asked, breathless.

"She lives on the Rue des Tournelles," I told her. "And she's not as busy." The girl rushed off and the other woman followed quickly behind her. Moments later, Catherine emerged at the door, escorting a serious-looking woman out.

"What are you doing here? I didn't think I'd see you until tomorrow," Catherine said with no ceremony. The client walking down the street looking disappointed would not know that La Voisin was speaking to a fellow enchantress about a witch's sabbath the following night: a ceremony to mark the end of winter and return of the light, not so different from Candlemas in itself.

"What have you been telling the Comtesse de Soissons lately?" I demanded, and Catherine's face hardened. She pulled me inside with a sigh.

"Nothing you're going to like," she muttered as we entered her house, which improved in its furnishings and appointments every time I saw her. She had done well for herself and her family, like she had always wanted.

"Are you selling her poison?" I demanded, and at least Catherine had the decency to feign looking shocked.

"I would not give poison to someone who distrusts *you* so much," she replied to my surprise. "Or at least your mistress. I've been selling her curses."

"On Louise La Vallière?" I asked, both relieved and disturbed. Catherine nodded and gnawed her lip. There was more. "Who else?"

"Didn't she tell you? I thought that was why you'd come. She's moved on from me for now. She asked for curses against the Queen, and I refused as long as I could. But she's getting impatient with La Vallière's continued success. She wants something more. And she paid me quite a lot of money."

"Of course she does," I sighed. "Did you give her anything real?"

"What is real?" Catherine scoffed back. "I give her charms of plantain, bone, and dirt passed under the Eucharist by a drunk priest. I sell her spells with the names of saints and lie to her about her love lines."

"You give her poppycock, then?"

"She believes it's real though. She reports that it works, even when you and I know it's not right. Maybe she makes it real. She looks at the King's mistress and his Queen each day with hate and jealousy in her heart that is stronger than any will or intention I could put into a ritual or spell, and how is that any less foul than a hex? Magic is a force beyond us sometimes, I think: one we only pretend we can understand or control."

I stared at Catherine's face in wonder at her words, noting for the first time the redness in her cheeks and eyes and how she swayed. "Have you been drinking? At this hour?"

"You'd drink too if you had to cater to a line of pampered sows for hours, then cook for an oaf who will demand you bed him if you don't manage to drug his porridge."

"I thought you were happy with Antoine?" I asked in shock.

"If you bothered with your friends outside of when you need us for some scheme, you might know better." Catherine turned away from me and stumbled towards the table by the fire, where a bottle stood open next to a cup. "Adam would help me. He'd give me something to make Antoine complacent, but he's too busy with those *whores*."

"What?" I felt like a fool suddenly. How much had I missed in the last few months? Or was it more than a few?

"They're taking clients from me, and so is Marie Bosse," Catherine said and grabbed the wine to gulp it down. "Because that bitch the Comtesse says I'm working too slow! She tells her friends and they go to another witch! No one comes from you anymore."

"That's not true, I've sent you business!"

"So you can spy on them for your mistress and keep yourself in your comfort. So you never have to lower yourself to work for a living or submit to some man!" Catherine spat the insults like a curse and I fought the urge to slap her for the words.

"You know I've done my share of submitting, and I won't ever again," I hissed and grabbed the bottle from her. "Pull yourself together and I'll try to help. I can send more clients to you if you can keep Olympe under some semblance of control. Send a real curse on La Vallière if you like, but no poison. And keep your evil eyes off the King. And the Queen. Not that any spell could sway him."

"How can you be sure of that?" Catherine asked, defiant. "Maybe I can drive his mistress off or make her suffer. If I can do that, I can control the King, too."

I shook my head and laughed coldly. She was wrong. She had to be wrong. "No witch's hand can move the sun, no matter how she wants to."

M Y WORDS TO CATHERINE Monvoisin echoed in my head the next day when I followed the Queen and Athénaïs into the royal chapel on the Île de la Cité. It was a wondrous place, Sainte-Chapelle. Even on a winter's day, the stained glass that filled the walls glowed with color. The wondrous building had been built by Saint Louis himself, the personal chapel of kings when they had ruled Paris and France from this small island in the Seine, before the city had grown and grown, spreading ever farther into the horizons.

In the days when the Sainte-Chapelle was built, Paris had been safe behind thick walls, but my Louis had ordered those walls taken down so that Paris could never rise again in opposition to the King. He would never take up residence on the Île de la Cité, where he could be trapped by the river on both sides and where he'd be too close to Notre Dame – the beating heart of the people of Paris.

Maybe the island made him worried even now. In this place of light and color, he looked forlorn as he stood at the head of the congregation, waiting to partake in the Mass. Maybe he was missing Versailles, the retreat he had not been able to visit for many months as his builders did their work.

"He wanted Louise La Vallière to share his pew, next to the Queen," Athénaïs whispered to me when she noted me staring at our monarch. I suppressed a gasp as I turned to her.

"She's returned to court?" I asked.

"Yes, but she won't show her face today. The Queen won't allow it," Athénaïs explained softly. "I don't blame the woman. Louis wants her installed in rooms closer to his."

"He must have visited his mother recently," I muttered to myself. "Or she did. How can he be so blind when it comes to her?"

The beginning of Mass cut me off as the priest began to chant the Kyrie. The congregation bowed their heads, and I looked down at the intricate gown of green that I wore. It was a wondrous thing, this gown, lined in lace and billowing around my hips in the comeliest fashion. Athénaïs had bought it for me.

She said she liked how it made my skin glow, and it felt like a treasure. To wear it felt like I was in her embrace, safe in our bed. It was a talisman, this dress, a small bit of magic, protecting me as well as a spell.

My eyes rose to the altar, framed by stained glass illustrating stories of Scripture. Christ's crown of thorns was said to rest in the reliquary that crowned the sanctuary, kept as a prize since the Crusades. The alcoves of the chapel were decorated in fleur-de-lys and castle emblems, with painted stars on a blue ceiling. Even the carvings on the dozens of columns were intricate imitations of real plants: oak, acanthus, artemisia. Magical plants I knew well. All paled compared to the hundreds of glass panels that shone like jewels.

It was a sight as lovely and sacred as the woods where I walked to gather herbs that hurt and healed, or to conjure my desires with the sacred earth of Our Lady beneath my feet. It felt special and sacred here too, as the voices from the choir rose and the incense smoke wafted through shafts of light. This place was magic too.

What Catherine had said in her drunken melancholy echoed in my mind – that maybe it didn't matter if the spells she gave to Olympe de Soissons were real or right. She believed they were powerful, so they were. Maybe her curse had impacted the Queen. Or Louis. But maybe the prayers France said for him protected him in turn? It was a frustrating conundrum, but it made me wonder. I had never even considered what it would really take to alter the King's feelings; it was, as I had said to Catherine, as vain a prospect as trying to move the sun...

At that very moment, a cloud outside shifted, and the vibrant colors of the stained glass all dimmed. I craned my neck to look at

Louis's face and saw that it too had darkened with a frown. Did he see this sign as a warning from God against his sins with Louise? I took it as a sign that I had been looking at things all wrong. One could not move the sun, but we could change where its light went. We could even block it from reaching us, or someone else.

I felt a shiver up my spine, like a cold wind had touched me, and I looked up to see that the Queen's eyes were fixed upon Louis. I knew the look of a curse. I had felt the same hatred in my own heart that Marie Thérèse held for La Vallière at that moment. I knew exactly what she was praying for, but I could not tell if her evil eye was meant to fall on the King or the woman he had disgraced his wife with, but I felt the danger, nonetheless.

THAT NIGHT WE DINED and danced at the Palais-Royal, entertained by Philippe and Henrietta, who made sure that the hospitality and grandeur of the residence of Madame and Monsieur was dazzling, but not as glorious as the King's. It took all the efforts of Athénaïs to keep Henrietta from throwing a fit when Louise La Vallière dared to show her face in the gathering. She placated the Duchesse with gossip and encouraged her to snub the King's mistress, while the Comtesse de Soissons played the same role for the Queen, who left early.

I was left to wonder if the scandal would be talked of on the streets tomorrow; there were many guests there that would be excited to share the news. Louis was too happy to have his mistress at last at his side to notice, and La Vallière kept all her attention on the King. I could not tell if she was truly happy. She had great skill when it came to smiling in public when her heart was not in it. I wondered if she would smile for much longer if some curse reached her, or what it would mean for her if it did.

It took me half an hour of watching her with the King to notice that I was not the only one watching. Jean-Baptiste Colbert had his eyes on the King too. I made my way through the milling crowd, waiting for dinner to be served at midnight, as was the custom at court, and bowed to the minister.

"Mademoiselle La Vallière has made a quick recovery, I see," I said, taking my place next to Colbert, who stiffened. He knew better than anyone where Louise had been – his wife was the one looking after her child. The King's child.

"Yes, she is a resilient woman," Colbert muttered. "And a persistent one."

"You don't like her, do you? Or to be more precise, you've come to distrust her of late."

Colbert turned to me in surprise. "What makes you say such a thing? Why would I mistrust an esteemed member of our court?"

"Because you cannot influence her, even though her... patroness has lost her grip on her. I see it in your eyes." And I heard about his spies in La Vallière's household, but he didn't need to know that. All he needed to know was that I remained an ally.

"Why should I need to influence her? I have the ear of the King," Colbert replied with a thin smile.

"A King who cast off the mantle of his mother's control, then Mazarin's. Who threw Nicolas Fouquet in jail for encroaching on his glory. A King who wishes to guide France entirely on his own with no whispers in his ear. From you – or even her."

"What is your point, Mademoiselle?" Colbert asked, face darkening.

I smiled politely. "Nothing, Monsieur. Just an observation."

It was a web of influence and secrets, this court. I saw that better every day. Each of us sought stability or advancement, but men like Colbert were different. They wielded real power – or tried to, and they did it through Louis. He was the beginning and end of all things pertaining to the state. Colbert could not rule France as Mazarin had, and he could only influence the King so much. There was power to be had then by whispering to the one that shared his bed, if she was willing to wield it.

I turned away from Colbert, adding the knowledge that he too was tiring of La Vallière and her influence to my store of secrets. The unease I had felt since Olympe began boasting of her time with the King had not dissipated since my visit to Catherine.

My fears and hopes solidified into reality when I saw that Athénaïs was speaking to the King. I watched how they laughed as I walked towards them, stomach still knotting up with excitement to be so close to the sovereign, even after so many years at court. My jealousy was there too, for both of them. For the way Athénaïs smiled at him and let her pretty laugh ring out, and for the way he looked at her – like an equal worth knowing. Worth regarding. Yet they both smiled when they looked at me, and I felt weak with it.

"My King," I exhaled as I curtsied. "My lady."

"Just the woman we were discussing," Louis replied, and I felt like all the eyes of the world were upon me. "I did not know you had a history in the theater!"

I hoped that he could not see that the comment made me pale. I glanced to Athénaïs for assurance. What was I to say? Had I been found out for being an imposter?

"I was telling the King that you should be featured in more of the entertainments at court! There will be so many ballets and dramas at Versailles this spring," Athénaïs added.

"I have not acted for many years, but I would be honored," I heard myself say. The fantasy of such a role filled my mind. What would my mother or Thérèse du Parc say if they saw me performing for the King, or with him? Did they even know how far I had come from the dirty, simpering girl that had waited on them and been so easy to throw away? "My dancing cannot compare to my lady's. Or yours, my King."

"We shall both have to instruct you then," Louis said, and my mind spun. "Let us begin now, while there is music."

Was there music? I had no idea because I could hear nothing over the thunder of my heart when Louis took my hand and began to lead me in a dance. Athénaïs came behind me, guiding me like a puppet as we both laughed and the sun smiled upon me.

I would do anything to keep this. I had schemed and enchanted my way here, and I had lived in joy and debauchery for so many seasons, but this – to be in the presence of the King and know even a few of his secrets? I wanted only this: this glory that no one would believe had come to me, this thrill and joy. I would not let anyone else near it.

I WENT TO THE woods of Versailles, to the place where the King's hunting grounds and dormant gardens met, to do my work in the dark of the moon, days later. It had taken me that long to find something that Louis had touched that I could use. My prize was a kerchief he had bestowed upon the Queen to dry her tears, which would do well. I wanted to protect her too. Maybe even protect them from one another.

I buried the delicate square of lace in the roots of an oak, wrapped in rosemary and heavy with salt. I called on the earth and the wind and the drizzling rain and the fire of my lamp to empower the spell.

"Protect him from spells, let no witch harm or enchant him," I whispered. I knew better than any that Paris was full of dangerous conjurers, real and false, and that the court was populated with women and men who sought to influence our King – *My* King – any way they could. I would not let them. "Let no witch's power touch him but mine, oh my Lady of the Crossroads, Queen of the in-between places."

I shivered as thunder rolled in the distance and power pulsed up through me from the ground. An answer to my prayer.

"Protect the Queen too. Let her heart be healed."

The rain answered like a caress and I smiled to the sky.

Lightning flashed, and I heard the world whisper: *what of La Vallière?*

"Let the Queen and Olympe's vengeance fall only upon her," I replied, and thunder rolled.

It took me a long time to return home and make my way to Athénaïs's rooms in the house by the Tuileries, but she woke when I slipped into bed next to her. It was no strange thing for her maid and companion to sleep beside her and no other servant commented upon it. Of course, they did not see what we did after.

How she pulled me to her and kissed me, how she whispered that I smelled like the woods. We would be hauled into the streets and whipped for the affront to nature we indulged in, I thought, as I fucked her with my hands and mouth and made her come. I would be burned for the witch I was for the way I framed her cheeks with my thighs and cried out my climax with a spell and a prayer. But they would never know, because I would protect us.

M AGIC TAKES TIME, AND sometimes time makes us forget the magic we work. Or that others may be working. Time moves ever forward, and there is no protection from it, just as there is no running from death. The cards told me all through the spring that change was coming: some sort of disaster that would alter everything. But Olympe remained at bay, I thought, and the King and Louise remained entangled, even as every woman in court and beyond sought the monarch's favor and eye. And I grew comfortable with that. We all did. And I let my guard down.

But then, the sickness came. All through the city, baked by the summer sun and brackish waters, made worse by poor harvest and lack of rain. The people of Paris began to suffer, even as we left them behind again. The walls of Versailles that welcomed us with glory could not keep out death any more than my magic could. Disaster awaited, I knew it. I dreamed of Paris filling with hunters, not of game, but of witches.

CHAPTER 18

THE TOWER

FEAR AND SUSPICION GREW in me as the summer waxed on. I did my duty and enjoyed my hard-won position, but it was not the same as it had been the year prior. The debauchery of Henrietta's chambers was dimmed, the halls of the palaces stank of sweat and shit as the summer heat baked Paris, and plague was spoken of in the city.

Athénaïs's husband returned too often as well, pestering his wife to return home as much as possible to be with their growing children and give him more. I did all I could for her to keep him away, but I was distracted with worry over preachers that filled the Paris streets and the discontent of the people. Tensions were growing, and the people needed something to blame. Some said that France's suffering was a result of the King's sins in breaking his marital vows. Others blamed unseen forces of evil.

Every time I pulled cards, Death was there, and the Tower too, with her warning of doom. Louis took every chance to take the court away from the center of the city. We spent more and more time at the palace of Saint-Germain-en-Laye, which was distant from the Louvre to the South, across the Seine. The rooms were sumptuous and the building was old and intricate with perfect Italian gardens. We visited the châteaus at Fontainebleau or Vincennes, and even while it was still being built, to beautiful, peaceful Versailles. Where the world was still green.

The journey from those idyllic places back to Paris, especially when I would visit my friends, seemed longer each time I took it. Even Catherine Lapère's garden was wilting when I went at the dawn of August, summoned by a message from her to attend a full moon circle.

The front garden was dull now compared to the gardens that had become my home. The parlor, with its glowing coals and musty herbs, was cramped and stuffy compared to the high, frescoed ceilings of the Louvre, where painted Gods and angels looked down on Louis's court as we danced - especially now, as I waited to meet with women I distrusted as much as the vipers in the palace.

Even with my heart armored to be brave, to learn some morsel of truth, I was not prepared for the sight that met me at Lapère's door.

I should have known Veronique would be there. She came to Lapère's sabbats, and I always tried to be somewhere else at the times when she would be there. Maybe she was the reason I had not seen this circle in so long. There was no anger on her face when she saw me, just surprise that ebbed to something like pity. Of course, I was the fallen one to her. The damned.

"I've been staying to help Madame Lapère as she recovers," Veronique said flatly. "Yes. She's been ill. She worked hard this summer treating the illness. She had a fever for a while, but she's on the mend."

"I'm glad you were here," I replied, though internally I bristled at her judgment that I had not been there. That she was a superior sister in the craft because she used her skills to help and heal.

"I didn't believe it when she said you'd come tonight," Veronique said as she showed me into the dim parlor. "It's been so long since you've bothered with your old life."

"She knew I was coming," I muttered, laughing to myself.

"I always know, don't be so surprised," Lapère said to me as she entered the house from the garden in the back where once I had memorized the names and magic of herbs, learned of the stars and spells, and cast magic in a sacred circle. It looked small now too, as did Lapère, even though her eyes were still sharp and bright. She was bent and slow, and Veronique rushed to her side to help her. "You'd know more too if you stopped and listened."

"I know I've been remiss in my visits," I stammered.

"Everyone is coming tonight. It will be tedious," Lapère replied, her voice unsteady as she took a place in the seat by the fire.

"Everyone?" I didn't even know what that meant anymore. Did she have new students? Or was it our old circle, from days so long ago?

"Keep the door open: the stoat and the bull are here," Lapère said tiredly.

"Oh joy," Veronique sighed as Marie Vigoreaux entered from the street with a huff. Her dress was a confection of yellow, finer than I had ever seen on her (though not as fine as my gown of green), and she had, of all people, Marie Bosse beside her. Both looked shocked to see me.

"Life getting boring at the Louvre?" Marie smirked. "Madame Bosse, you remember Claude de Vin?"

"So the great Mademoiselle des Œillets deigns to visit her old friends at long last," the shorter, dark-haired woman said.

"You were never my friend, Marie," I hissed, confused as to why this woman seemed to hate me, but not surprised, given what I knew of her. "And I am sorry to have been away; I have a life of my own to live."

"In service to your fat Marquise, we all know," Vigoreaux replied, tossing her blonde curls so that the pearl-encrusted combs she wore sparkled in the light. "So little ambition."

"I am a member of the King's court," I snapped back. "How much higher could I rise?"

"You are a hanger-on to a woman with a husband of little consequence and a dwindling estate," Bosse said with a pitying sigh. "Or so the Comtesse de Soissons has said."

"So you're the ones she's turned to." I smiled but my anxiety grew. I didn't want the Comtesse where I couldn't keep my eyes on her.

"She needed someone with real skills," Bosse smirked. "We don't even need Le Sage anymore."

"Le Sage?" I had not heard of Adam Le Sage in months, since he'd spurned Catherine for these women. Hadn't he?

"Don't play coy. We heard about the riches *you* dangled in his direction on behalf of poor La Voisin," Vigoreaux said. Lapère sighed and sank further into her chair by the fire.

"What? I never—"

As if to answer me, Catherine arrived, her head held high, in her modest white cap and lace shawl. She looked like she was on her way to Mass, not a witches' circle.

"What is this about me and Le Sage?" I demanded, and Catherine's mouth fell open like a fish, all her bluster fading.

"You told me you'd send greater ladies to me! And to him," Catherine stammered. "Don't you remember? We've been waiting since Candlemas for you to fulfill that promise!"

"I made no such claim! I've sent you work – all of you," I cried, looking at the circle around me, even Lapère and Veronique by the fire. It was Lapère to whom I sent the most women, the ones who needed her most dangerous skills to relieve themselves of children. If she'd been sick, that meant Veronique had been the one acting as midwife to death. "Though I won't make that mistake any longer with such shows of gratitude."

"As if we need you with the Comtesse employing us," Bosse said with a scoff. "And we've found a priest of our own, so we don't need Le Sage's drunkard."

"You don't need a priest for anything," I muttered.

"Is that why you stink of curses?" Lapère asked over the growing commotion, and the room stilled. I focused my senses, the ones I had ignored too often, and realized she was right: the women carried a miasma about them I hadn't noticed.

"Don't speak as if you're above baneful work," Marie Vigoreaux scoffed.

"There's good money in it," Bosse smirked.

"What you're doing isn't worth money! Any of you!" She turned to Catherine with fresh accusation in her eyes. "I heard another one of her clients' husbands died last week!"

Catherine gave a scandalized gasp. "I don't know what on earth you mean," the great La Voisin said with a smile. "I mourn the death of Monsieur Béjart. He was a good man and had invested a good sum with our dear friend Adam Le Sage." That information was delivered like a dart intended for Marie and Bosse.

"How convenient," Veronique spat, then turned back to Marie and Bosse. "What about the other deaths at the Hôtel Dieu?"

"What do we have to do with that stinking hellhole?" Bosse sneered. I was confused too. The Hôtel Dieu was a public hospital for the poorest in Paris, a place where the lowest of society went as a last resort, tended by nuns and doctors who were unfit to be barbers.

"People go there to die," I interjected, and Veronique gave me a glare. I was not part of this, it seemed.

"Not the way I've been seeing them die," Veronique countered. Of course she went there to use her skills to help the poor and downtrodden. It fit her. "The way people are dying there, it's not natural. I know illness and what I have seen — it is your horrible magician's work. I know it! I saw you there, Marie, next to some noble lady who came to pretend to help the patients like some saint. And after that, people started getting sicker, not better."

"Why?" I asked before I could stop. "Why would anyone do that? It makes no sense."

"You're mad," Bosse laughed. "As the courtier says, people die there."

"And who are you to stand in judgement of us all?" Marie hissed. "You only minister to the poor to clear your conscience from the hundreds of babes you've seen to the angels."

Veronique sprang towards Marie, hand raised in readiness to slap her, but Catherine seized her, holding her back. "At least she's not a thieving whore," Catherine hissed at Bosse, and the room burst into a commotion of insults and accusations, words flying from all our mouths back and forth like a swarm of hornets.

"Stop. All of you." Lapère's voice cut through the noise like a sword, and we all stood to attention like errant children. Slowly, the old woman rose. "All of you must stop."

"She started it," Marie grumbled, sneering at me.

"I do not mean this childish bickering. I mean your abuse of your gifts and all I have taught you. It will lead to the end for all of us."

"What are you talking about?" Veronique asked, placating and concerned. It surprised me that this declaration was news to her.

"I called you all to me tonight, my errant children who have taken what I've taught you to pursue your riches and glory. You have forgotten that Our Lady lives in the dark places, the secret corners where she is sought when needed. I saw her many faces in the dark this summer, while I toiled and suffered. While you all forgot me."

"You could have called us then," Catherine said. Her face was stricken, as I knew mine was too. I was awash with guilt and shame.

"Your eyes have always been on the skies, all of you," Lapère went on. "Looking to greater and higher things. Using what I taught you as your ladders to the heavens. You have forgotten the earth that bore you. I summoned you here now to warn you that, if you continue down this path, I have seen what it will lead to. It will be your doom."

"What have you seen?" Marie asked breathlessly.

"Fire and torture. Suffering and death. I see it all when I look into your futures, but it can be avoided. I know it can." Lapère's voice grew thin, her breath quickening, and Veronique rushed to her side to help. "The crossroads has come to you, to all of us. Especially to you who think you can or should hold life in your hands."

"I have not hurt anyone," I whispered, and my mentor looked at me as I lied. "No one who didn't deserve it."

"The world is not in your control. Nor is it in mine. I've taught you this. No witch can move the sun or stop it from rising and setting," Lapère said with weary pity. "Thinking you can protect yourself makes you as deluded as the desperate women who believe these clucking chickens. Control is an illusion."

"How dare you question my skills," Catherine huffed.

"Those skills will get you killed," Lapère snapped back, her face growing red and drawn. "People are sick. The country is at peace and eyes are beginning to turn inward to find enemies. I dream of it, night after night: the witch hunters will come to Paris."

"I won't let that happen," I protested. Veronique rolled her eyes as the others chuckled. "Don't laugh. I can speak to the King."

"And I am the queen," Marie scoffed. "You overestimate your importance."

"You all do," Lapère countered, swaying in Veronique's arm. "I am begging you to stop. Stop selling spells and trying to enchant that which cannot be swayed! Stop trading in fortunes and charms like they are the newest fashion and meddling in innocent lives! And for the sake of us all, stop trusting that man Le Sage and his poisons! It will lead to—"

Lapère gasped and collapsed into Veronique's arms. "Madame!" Veronique cried, caressing her face. "She's feverish again. I had thought she was better…"

"I can send a physician," I stammered, but Veronique shook her head.

"I'll take care of her. I'm the only one who can," she declared. "All of you get out. She's said what she brought you here to say."

I met my old lover's eyes for a long moment as the other women shuffled out the door. I didn't want to leave. I didn't want to prove to her that I didn't care; that I had forgotten the secrets I had learned and the magic that had sustained me. But it had been many long years since Veronique had been willing to hear me. I followed my former friends and closed the door behind us.

"Are you going to listen to her? Are you going to stop?" I asked the broken circle of women in the street. Bosse huffed and shook her head, but Catherine and Marie looked more circumspect.

"Adam has been called away. We can't appeal to him anyway," Catherine muttered. "He says it is on a secret task, but I fear it is something nefarious."

"He's a charlatan; he's better off far away." Marie nodded. "And we are all better off being more careful, at least until the city is safer. Plague and drought and—" she sent a sidelong look at me and shook her head.

"And what?" I demanded.

"And a king more concerned with his palaces than his people being fed," Marie said firmly. As if it was my fault – and as if Louis could control the weather and sickness!

"She's right, I hate to say. If the winter is harsh like last year, it will be worse. It makes things dangerous for everyone," Catherine agreed. "Let us all agree to… be careful."

"You can agree to that. I'm going to live my life," Bosse snarled and stalked away, leaving the three of us alone. The road suddenly seemed darker. The windows where the light of candles flickered beyond the shutters became eyes watching us, spying upon the witches. This was one of those moments, the ones I tried too often now to ignore. When the world whispered. And now, it was a warning.

"We can live our lives too, in safety. We don't have to rely on our arts to advance: we are already far enough," I said. "I have all I want or need. So do you."

"Speak for yourself," Catherine muttered and turned away from me. Marie said nothing.

I made my way home alone into the night, still feeling the eyes of the sky and the earth upon me, listening to them whisper their warning. I hated this feeling, of some sword of Damocles still hanging over me and of guilt as well.

How was it I had done too much and yet not enough? I'd used magic and witchcraft to make my way to the court of the King, and yet I was merely a shadow there, an imposter. My skills had benefited and protected the ones I loved. Yet they still wanted more and still suffered. Was it a consolation to be so small and insignificant, or was it a curse?

I made my way into the Palais-Royal, sneaking like a spider through corridors and hallowed halls to Madame's chambers. Her husband was entertaining the Chevalier tonight, or some other debauched company, and Athénaïs was having a private audience with the frustrated princess.

It was not torture for me to wait beyond the door. On the contrary, it reassured me to hear how different the sounds Athénaïs made were, and how the honeyed words that spilled from her lips were from our own intimate moments. With me, she was only herself, and I was the closest thing possible to my true nature.

She didn't know all, of course. She did not know that I was a killer, but she knew I was a sinner in the eyes of the God we bowed to at Mass, and she loved me, even so. That was enough for both of us. There would be no need to enchant or interfere anymore if we could keep things like this.

I wondered in the waning summer of 1665 if spiders knew what happened beyond their webs. Could a spider foresee how some distracted girl traipsing through the woods might push through their home of silken thread and send them tumbling towards an abyss, with no choice but to start anew or die?

I kept to my promise. For months, I cast no spells and whispered no prophecies or secrets to ladies of the court. I sent no business to La Voisin and La Vigoreaux, and very few to Lapère. Luckily, the women in the palaces did not need her much at that time. A shadow had fallen over the court as Queen Anne's health worsened, and the ladies and lords spent more time praying and thinking on their sins than fornicating. Louise La Vallière was pregnant again, though she looked sicklier this time.

My cards told me that something was coming. The Tower. The King of Swords reversed. The Ten of Swords. Death.

They were right. The first disaster was the return of the Marquis de Montespan in earnest in the fall, and his incessant badgering of his wife. I hated it. I hated when he was in the house and forced her to return, using their children as leverage. I hated when he demanded his rights as a husband, hoping for another son. I hated that I had bound myself with a useless vow for the safety of women who cared little for me. There were nights when I watched him leave her room that I wanted to seek out Adam Le Sage and his white powder, or to pull some hellebore from the garden or belladonna from the woods. But Lapère's warnings and my promise kept me at bay. At least for a while.

My hate was stronger than my fear. Montespan became the first fly in a long while in my web, one that had to be dealt with. Potions and poisons to keep his cock at bay were not enough. Tonics for Athénaïs to keep his seed from taking hold were a comfort, but life was always better when he was gone. I began to wonder if it would not be better if he was not there at all.

And so I did what I had promised not to do, and I worked magic against him. I cast my spell on the new moon in the woods of Versailles where I had worked so many successful spells before.

The wind was cold and my lantern weak in the dark of the trees. Animals moved in the dark, but they did not scare me. If a wolf in the shadows scented the rabbit squirming in my bag, then so be it. I had never feared the wild nights as I had once feared the dark of my home on those nights when Giles Faviot had come for me. He was worse than any wolf, and I had done away with him. I would do away with the wolf that stalked my Athénaïs and send him further away than ever before.

The rabbit squealed as I pulled it from the bag, trying to wrestle from my grip. I could feel his poor heart racing under my hand, but he did not see my knife. The copper tang of blood filled my nostrils as the life drained from the creature. I imagined it as the life draining from the Marquis de Montespan's hateful cock and… No, not his body. Not yet. Athénaïs would have no status as a widow. I just wanted him gone once again. I wanted our freedom.

The price was death before, the night whispered as sure as if Our Lady was speaking to me from the veiled stars. I strew the rabbit with herbs – not poisons that would kill, only the sort that would make one ill – and I buried it all in a rotting stump, whispering the name of Louis Henri Grondin de Montespan.

Something moved in the shadows, and I jumped, then gasped. There was a face there, I could swear it. A face I had last seen swollen and sweating as I watched him die… The phantom of Giles Faviot was gone when I blinked, but another took his place. My father. The one who had wanted more for me than this. Who had given life to a witch. What a disgrace.

I rushed away from the woods as fast as I could, leaving the ghosts far behind.

THE GARDENS OF VERSAILLES were beautiful in September, if one looked at them in the right way: their symmetry and order and pleasing lines. I liked to walk there as often as I could, even when the court was huddled inside, waiting to return to Paris at the King's will. The court had come to the newly expanded residence to enjoy the gardens and new rooms added to the palace. It was because of Louis's love for this place that we had not returned to the Louvre or Saint-Germain-en-Laye, and I was grateful.

My feet were sore from walking for hours, contemplating the cards I had drawn this morning and the feeling of doom that still hung over me. I sat at the edge of a huge basin (a man-made pond, really) where swans made idle circles and took off my shoes, washing them in the frigid water to soothe their aches.

I closed my eyes and let the water comfort me, a bracing contrast to the weak sunlight upon my face. For a moment, I was at peace, the breeze blowing away my cares. I did not expect to hear quiet, polite laughter on the wind. I certainly did not expect to see the King himself when I opened my eyes.

"I did not consider that my fountains would be footbaths," Louis said. There was no malice to it, but even so, I had to grip the stone edge to keep myself from tumbling into the water in shock.

"Your Majesty, I am sorry," I gasped, struggling to extricate myself from my perch. To my horror, the King – my King – strode forward and offered me his hand.

"I do not begrudge you, Mademoiselle des Œillets. I am glad to see someone else enjoying my gardens," Louis declared. As always, his attention upon me made the world fade away around

me. My heart pounded as I took his hand and he helped me to
stand, supporting me as I forced my wet feet back into my silken
shoes.

"These gardens and the woods are where I find peace unlike
any other place I have known," I stammered, compelled to complete honesty by the King's piercing blue eyes. I was alone with
him as I never had been.

"You understand the magic of this place then," Louis replied
with a gentle smile. "Not all do. So many courtiers whine all the
while we are here about returning to Paris with their dull manors
and crumbling walls."

"Paris does have its excitement," I offered carefully as we began
to walk to nowhere in particular. "But it is so crowded and—"

"Chaotic. Impossible to control. Everyone is so close there. It
is so loud," Louis went on, and for the first time, I noticed that he
seemed melancholic.

When I had first seen Louis on the day of his wedding, years
before, he had appeared to me as joy and light personified. He
had been perfect, smiling, and handsome: the pinnacle of power
and happiness, for the former surely led to the latter. He had been
this distant, shining thing who offered me grace when his eyes
fell on me. Now that I served in his court, now that I had seen
him and his sorrows, I knew how often the sun passed behind
clouds that dimmed its light.

"There's more to your dislike of the city, isn't there?" I dared
to ask. Louis gave me a sly look.

"Dislike is too weak a word. I hate Paris. All my sorrows grow
and live there," Louis said with a surety that impressed me. "Yes,
there are theaters and shops and palaces. But the people of that

city are treacherous. Do you know what they did to my mother and me? When I was but a child?"

"During the Fronde?" I asked back, trying to remember my history. I had been nothing more than a poor child of an actress and a perfumer at the time of the first rebellion, and then daughter to a dead father, taking refuge in the convent for a few peaceful years, during the second uprising.

"They rioted and attacked the Louvre itself," Louis explained, eyes dark and distant. "We had to flee the city under cover of darkness. I was not allowed to return for years. My mother never liked the city after that either. Even when she took it back."

"She was a truly remarkable regent, your mother." That was the wrong thing to say, it seemed, for it provoked a fresh sigh from Louis. "I am so sorry. I know her health is failing."

"The doctors say a tumor has developed. They wish to cut it out and dress the wound with poultices. The poor woman is bled so often she cannot rise most days to go to Mass. Luckily, the priest will come to her.'

There was much I wanted to say about the brutal and useless 'cures' the doctors peddled. No witch or wise woman I had known would say someone was saved by bleeding or enemas, but that was all doctors knew how to do. "I distrust Paris's doctors, I must admit."

"And now, I must go to her with news that will weigh on her more. News that will weigh on us all..." The King's shoulders sagged in his blue embroidered coat, and I could truly imagine the weight of his office on him, as well as his duty to his ailing mother.

"May I be so bold as to ask what news, Your Majesty?"

Louis looked at me circumspectly, weighing if he could trust me, then nodded. "You will hear soon enough, though I hope you do not spread it yourself. Philip of Spain has died. My mother's brother – and my wife's father."

"I am so sorry for their loss," I murmured. "The poor Queens."

"The poor country," Louis corrected, and I wondered if he meant France or Spain. "This will mean great and terrible things for Europe. I have little choice in what I must do now, but it will upset my mother greatly, along with the loss."

I blinked, feeling a fool. "I do not understand."

"A gentlewoman and companion such as yourself would not, but in short, it will mean war," Louis explained as if it were the weather. "The Netherlands will be ours again. At least your mistress will be happy. I'll be sending her odious husband Montespan on the first campaign. It will have to wait for spring, alas."

The web I had made snapped.

"He will go to war?" I stammered.

"We all will, for the glory of France. To remind the people who their King is and what God put him on Earth to do. Ah, Monsieur Bontemps, have you summoned my ministers?"

I looked up to see that the King's loyal valet had arrived and we stood at the steps back up to the Palace. "Yes, My King," the tower of a man rumbled. "They await you in your chamber."

"If you will excuse me, Mademoiselle," the King said to me with a nod. I dropped into a curtsey, waiting to rise until his steps had faded. Only then did I rush towards the grand staircase and gallery where the court tended to mill about. I found Athénaïs in a knot of giggling ladies, the Vicomtesse de Polignac at their head.

"Ah, Claude, we were just discussing someone you might know – this actress, Thérèse du Parc, who continues to make a cuckold of Racine and Molière all at once," Athénaïs trilled, and at any other time I would have been ecstatic to hear such gossip. "Her latest conquest is said to be another actor who no one has heard of, much to all's dismay."

"May I speak with you alone, Madame?" I murmured with a curtsey. Athénaïs knew I would not make such a request without reason, so she smiled at the circle of women before following me back out into the gardens, to somewhere we could speak with only the trees watching.

"There is to be war," I burst out. "And your husband will be sent to it first." Her frown became a grin.

"What? How do you know this?" Athénaïs exclaimed.

"I was in the garden and the King came across me and – you must not tell anyone. He was melancholy because—" I paused. Would I so swiftly betray his confidence? But this was my Athénaïs, more than a lover or friend. She was my heart, and if my spellwork had played any part in this, it was all for her. "The King of Spain has died. Louis is discussing it with his ministers now."

"My God, he wants to start a campaign while Spain is weak. But he won't dare that while Anne lives," Athénaïs muttered, and I could see her mind racing.

"He said as much," I replied. "Her health is deteriorating. It will not be long."

"If only you could make it shorter," she muttered.

I stared at the woman in front of me. Who I shared my life with. I should have been insulted that she thought me capable of such a thing. But in truth, it meant she knew me and understood my devotion.

"To what end?" I asked back, swallowing. "There will be war, no matter what. No matter her objection."

"It is not the war. It is Louise La Vallière. When the old bat dies, Louis will declare her mistress *en-titre*. As soon as she's not a forbidden thing and as soon as Anne isn't pushing her into Louis's bed, she'll fall out of favor. I know it. This is my time at last," Athénaïs declared, eyes blazing with ambition.

"You wish to—"

"To finally make my move. Make our move. No more pleasing a spoiled princess. I will be with the King." And there it was, finally spoken aloud: her grandest ambition. "Don't look so shocked. You have always foreseen I was destined for greatness. This will be my greatness. And yours too. You'll still be with me, every step. I need you now more than ever."

I stared at her, the woman who had elevated me, who I had done so much to advance. The woman who held my heart in her hands. And she wanted the King's, only after breaking it.

"There are ways... But it would destroy him if it were to happen so soon," I fumbled. "I don't even know how I would deliver anything to Anne."

"Don't curses deliver themselves?" Athénaïs asked back, then blinked at me. "No. You meant something else. Oh God, Claude, no! I meant some charm not – not poison! Have you..."

"Oh, thank God," I sighed. Then lied. "No. Of course not. I never would. I promise you. We only need to wait and keep our conscience clear."

Days darkened and a harsh, bitter winter set in. Joy was gone from the court, especially the household of the Queen, with her father dead. Marie Thérèse was the seventh of seven children of King Philip and his first wife, Elizabeth of France. Philip had married his niece, Archduchess Maria Anna of Austria, after Elizabeth's death, and her children had not fared much better than her predecessor's. She'd borne a son, and because of that, Marie Thérèse had been allowed to marry the King of France *if* she forsook all claims to her father's throne.

But that little boy had died, and for a few days in November of 1661, Marie Thérèse had been the only living heir of Spain. That lasted until her new brother was born – the child who was now King Charles II of Spain. Whispers about the twisted, sickly Hapsburg heir had reached us even in France. The nobles of our court wondered aloud if the child's many rumored afflictions were a sign of God's displeasure with Spain, especially for denying the throne to pious Marie Thérèse. Never mind that such a succession would tip the balance of power in Europe irrevocably.

For my part, I listened to the masters of the King's horses, who knew something about breeding animals. You never wanted a stallion with too close a bloodline to the mare, for they always produced weaker children, sometimes malformed. I worried for the little Dauphin Louis, with cousins for parents, but he seemed to have been spared the curse of his inbred line and the ill health of his cousin. All the better for the young child's claim to the Spanish throne.

But Louis did not want Spain. Not yet. He knew it was too great a conquest; instead, he looked north, to the Spanish Netherlands, which he wished to claim as Marie Thérèse's inheritance, which had devolved to him. I did not understand the theory of how those lands were his; it was a concoction of Colbert's, along with input from Louvois, the minister of war, who had been urging Louis to increase his glory as a monarch by conquest, like a Caesar or Alexander.

Now, with Spain weak, it would be time to strike, or so Colbert and Louvois told anyone at court who would listen, hoping their words would echo back to Louis so incessantly that there would be no choice. It was only a matter of waiting, one sensed, for Anne to die. Alas, she hung on.

The Queen brought us to her aunt and mother-in-law's bedside at Advent to say prayers with the woman who had once saved France from the Fronde. She was a shadow of herself, and it felt like a tragedy. Though I had never loved Anne, I had admired her strength and her will to rule, even when I had not agreed with her choices. Now, she was pale and bloated, and no perfumes or flowers could stem the stench of her sickness. Athénaïs said sincere prayers for the Queen's recovery, to my relief. The Comtesse de Soissons's eyes sparkled with greed and ambition when she looked at the dying Anne.

The return to court that night at Saint-Germain was dour, and Marie Thérèse was filled with sorrow, and also anger. A boiling, helpless anger that I understood. She called on Louise La Vallière, heavy with child, to attend her that evening. Marie Thérèse made the woman stand, for she did not merit the honor of sitting in the presence of the Queen, and Marie Thérèse sent her to fetch and serve her well into the night. Louise bore her misery with dignity, but would not meet the Queen's eyes. Nor would Louis when he came for his nightly visit to his wife's rooms, then retired to his own chambers.

Many had seen Louis weeping in those days, along with his brother Philippe. They loved their mother dearly, despite everything. I wondered, as I watched the door Louis had shut behind him, how my mother was faring in the dark and the cold. Had she avoided the illness ravaging the city? Would she have enough to survive if she grew ill? Or would she end up in the *Hôtel Dieu* with the rest of the miserable poor, who rotted away like Queen Anne?

The way people are dying there, it's not natural. I know illness and what I have seen – it is your horrible magician's work.

Veronique's words echoed in my mind, as did my own dark thoughts and offer to Athénaïs when she had broached the subject. Yes, Anne was in her sixties, but she had always been strong until this year… when slow illness had begun to take her just in time for her brother to die. Was it possible? Had someone schemed to poison her? Or both of them? Who was mad or powerful enough to kill the King of Spain? Was I going mad? Was I seeing poison everywhere because it was all I knew of death and self-defense?

"Claude? Are you alright?" Athénaïs's voice cut through my rising paranoia. "Did you not see how kindly Louis spoke to me?"

"What?" I asked back, blinking. "I mean, yes. I saw. I was just thinking… foolish things."

"Your thoughts are never foolish, my dear," Athénaïs smiled back. "You will tell me later what made you go so pale. When we are alone."

I did mean to tell her that night, but we did not make it to bed until the small hours of the morning and fell into a fitful sleep immediately.

I meant to tell her in the morning too, but my dreams of her laughing at me and calling me a killer for knowing such arts kept me silent.

For days, I wanted to tell her, but the court was busy with celebrations of Christmas and New Year's. Then there was a scandal as Louise La Vallière, kept at court this time, began labor pains in front of Marie Thérèse and had to plead colic as the ladies of her household sniggered. By Epiphany, I had convinced myself I was being foolish. There was no plot here. No evil eye or machinations or poison.

It didn't matter in the end. Anne died on the 20th of January, and everything changed.

The tower fell.

CHAPTER 19

THE HIGH PRIESTESS

LA PAPESSE

1666

"WHEN WILL YOU TELL me?" Athénaïs asked as I removed the last ribbon that held her chemise in place.

She lay back on her bed – our bed that we shared so often now at the château of Saint-Germain-en-Laye – and smiled up at me. She was stunning, naked, and waiting for me, all curves and curls. She beckoned to me, knowing her allure and power, and I complied. I pressed my bare body against hers and kissed her, starved for her taste.

"That's not an answer," my lady chided as our lips parted. "We've waited long enough. I want to know how you shall do it. How we shall do it."

"Why do you need me to cast a spell?" I asked back, lips trailing down her neck. "You are incomparable. The most beautiful and witty woman at court. You need but direct your charms at Louis without holding back, and he will be yours."

"You flatter me," Athénaïs sighed as my mouth found her sumptuous breast. "I know I could have him, but I want to be *sure*. I want there to be no question of my triumph. I want *you* to give him to me."

I stopped kissing her, resting my forehead against her chest, my heart aching at the thought of them together.

"It is a hard thing, my love, to enchant a king. No normal spell or charm would do. Especially when he is so protected and already..." I shook my head and closed my eyes. "Already the subject of so many spells, if I'd hazard a guess."

"Then ours must be more powerful," Athénaïs protested, pressing her hands around my face and pulling me up to look at her. "I have seen you do incredible things, my Claude. My precious Arachne with your webs. You can do this. Don't you want to give me this?"

"I want to give you everything." I thought I was going to weep. For months now, I had delayed, but no longer could I keep her for myself. "I wish what I have given already would be enough."

"Claude, think what this will do for us – if I can not only seduce Louis, but take La Vallière's place as official mistress. He has showered her with lands and riches already. She has her own house and titles and freedom. Don't you want the same? Don't you want to be free and fearsome? We can rule this court," Athénaïs said, and kissed me sweetly. When she pulled back, she saw my tears.

"We?" I echoed weakly.

"Of course *we*. I will never cast you aside." The words made a dam inside me break, and I tried to hide my face. Athénaïs would not let me. "You silly girl, thinking I would not take you with me when this is done. This will be your glory too."

"I've been left behind for men too many times," I whispered. In my mind, I saw Thérèse's face. My mother's. Even Veronique had left me because of how I had dealt with a man. "But I will find a way to do this for you."

"Do you not know how?" Athénaïs asked, brow furrowed, and my fear surged.

"No! I do! I have ideas. This sort of magic is complicated and large. I'd have to consult others." Maybe I was afraid of telling her because I did not want her to proceed without me. Maybe I needed her to need me.

"Well, do that then. But now, tell me what you think we would need to do," Athénaïs said as she flipped me onto my back then straddled me. I was at her mercy all of a sudden, trapped and vulnerable as I rarely let myself be. She began to kiss me, ravenous and thorough, paying close attention to the places on my neck, ears, and nipples that she knew made me wild. "Please, Claude."

"It would have to be more than a simple spell," I gasped as she slipped her hand between us, pawing at my aching sex. "It would need to be a ritual."

"What kind?"

I cried out before I could answer, as her fingers filled me, stretching me taut. "It could be—" I tried to say, but I couldn't think with such sensation overcoming me. Not just the feelings in my body, but the intoxicating thrall of being hers at that moment.

"A witches' circle? A heathen sabbat?" she demanded fervently, voice joyful. "Would we dance naked under the moon? Or perform a Black Mass?"

She fucked harder into me and I shuddered, eyes rolling back into my head as lust sang through me. "A sacrifice of some kind! Or we could fuck."

"Is fucking magic?" Athénaïs asked, speeding up her hands and making me mewl beneath her, nodding blindly. "Are we doing magic now, my little spider?"

"I – yes." I could feel the tension rising in my body, the power of it coursing through me. "Make me come, please make me come, and it will be for you. It will be my spell. The first one—"

"But not the last?" Her voice was insistent, and when I dared to open my eyes, her face was wild with delight and ambition. I nodded frantically. "Not the last. Oh, Claude, come for me. Cast your spell."

I did as she commanded with a scream, sending all my power and pleasure towards one singular idea – that Louis would be hers. Ours. The climax shattered me into a hundred pieces that only my mistress could put back together. But she did. She stroked my damp face and held me as my pulse slowed. When I could see again, she was glowing.

"Now you," I managed to say. "Think of him. Think of what you want from him."

"Yes," she laughed, and I felt the vibrations of it in her belly against my cheek before I lost myself between her thighs. I licked and sucked and filled her and made her shudder and coo, but even there, I heard that she was speaking. Chanting a litany as she imagined what a true spell might win her.

"Louis. Louis… Louis."

I KNEW WHERE I needed to seek out help, and it was dangerous on many levels. The witches of Paris had made a promise to their mentor to be discreet and use their power responsibly, but now I had a higher purpose, and a strong sense that my friends had kept their promises to Lapère as poorly as I.

I had seen them, of course, in the months since Lapère had extracted that pledge, meeting in different places on full moons, to hold hands and pray to Our Lady. Catherine had joked at Candlemas how proper and demure we had become as witches – no more writhing together, slathered in flying ointment to get a glimpse of the divine.

The idea of those wild nights tickled at the back of my skull as I approached the tavern where we were to meet. What I wanted to ask was not proper or demure. Or safe.

I had sent Catherine a note that I required a sister's knowledge, and I had hoped she would know what I meant. The tavern was uncrowded this early in the night, but I still shivered when I felt people looking at me through the dim light. I had hoped to meet Catherine at her house, but her reply had been insistent about meeting here.

When I saw her, I understood why – she was with Adam Le Sage. She likely did not want her lover to run into her husband. The two sat by the fire, Catherine looking pleased and Le Sage looking as self-assured and bright-eyed as I had ever seen him.

"Mademoiselle de Vin, it has been too long," Le Sage said with a slick smile as he rose and pressed a vigorous kiss to my hand. I withdrew it quickly, shuddering. I hated the touch of men still. "You have become a great success in these years."

"I am flattered that you have kept track," I replied tightly, seating myself next to them. It would be harder now to explain why I needed another witch.

"And you hope to continue that rise, now that Anne is out of the way," Catherine purred in reply, and I frowned. "Don't pretend to be shocked. I have my gifts too. I see what is in store for the court and you."

"You've looked into my future?" I asked.

"I've seen into many futures." Catherine shrugged.

"You seeking out the help of the great La Voisin confirmed what we guessed: that now is the time for us to serve your esteemed mistress at last and place her..." Le Sage glanced sidelong around the room and lowered his voice. "In the center of the sun's light."

I held my tongue. It was not surprising that they should know, or more likely, guess, my aims. They knew who I served and how high Madame de Montespan had risen. It was a logical next step for her to ask of a witch what so many other ladies already had – a way into Louis's heart. These two knew and had worked for one such lady.

"Has not the Comtesse de Soissons already asked for such services?" I asked coolly, and a smile spread over Catherine's face.

"Indeed, but I have held back. We have waited so long for you to truly call on us. And as for Olympe, I would not want such a woman to gain so great an influence on the state," Catherine answered, equally calculating in her words. But not careful enough. I noted a twitch of Le Sage's lip and felt a whisper in the wind, like a ghost.

"I do not know if I would ever call upon your services for such a thing," I said with a shrug. "I could not trust that you would not pay the same duty to another. Perhaps I should speak to La Vigoreaux."

"Why would you bother with such an inferior worker?" Le Sage countered. "She cannot offer you what we can. *I* am willing to go to any lengths necessary – indeed, I will push you to go further than you could have dreamed to achieve your ends."

"I will decide what my methods are and my ends," I snapped back, but I sensed I had fallen into some trap.

"You wish to work with one you can trust in this endeavor, whatever it is," Le Sage went on, Catherine continuing to smile dangerously beside him. "And who can you trust but we who know of your many struggles… And tragedies. What happened to your poor father…"

My insides turned to ice as the trap sprang. It was a threat, clear and simple. Le Sage and La Voisin knew what I had done to save myself from my mother's husband. And if I did not use their services and pay them highly for it, they would expose me and my crimes. To risk such exposure themselves, they had to want this very much.

"Why do you care so much that I work with you?" I asked, my hands clenching under my cloak.

"Because we know that such a service would merit a substantial reward," Catherine replied with a smile. "At least 20,000 livres."

"That's insane!" I squawked so loudly that people looked at me across the room. I leaned closer to Catherine and shook my head. "I don't have that much, and neither does my mistress."

"She will find it when her time comes. We will be patient." Le Sage grinned. "In the meantime, let us prepare. We will meet on the Spring Equinox, when the energies of the sun begin to return."

I looked to Catherine, desperate for some help, but there was only triumph in her eyes. Not friendship or pity. This was what she had hoped for: her great victory and great riches. I hated being the one caught in another's web, but I saw no way out. Not yet.

"Send for me, and I will tell my mistress where to go," I replied with a sigh. Le Sage smiled and my fate was sealed.

I TRUDGED BACK TO the Montespan house, guilt and anger churning inside me. This was not how I had meant this to happen, and I did not know how I would save us. Save myself. There was no money to pay them; at least, not enough. I had no idea what sort of spell they would cast. Only that they wished my mistress herself to be part of it.

The house was quiet when I returned, but the Marquis's horse had been in the stable. Another ill omen. He had stayed in the country for much of the previous months, but now it was March and the talk of war had begun in earnest. Soon, he would be sent away for good, and none too soon for my tastes or Athénaïs's. The day was darkening outside and the halls were cold as I wandered through them.

I did not expect the door to Athénaïs's bedroom to be shut. Nor did I expect to hear Monsieur de Montespan's voice from within, ragged and strained.

"You will give me another son," the Marquis snarled, and my heart began to race as I heard Athénaïs's whimper. "You will bear that child for me."

"I'll hate it like the rest of your spawn," Athénaïs snarled back. I heard creaking. Rhythmic. It made me sick.

"I did not say you could speak," Montespan growled, and I heard the sound of flesh on flesh; whether it was a slap or something else, I could not say, but it was enough.

"Then I will speak for her," I declared as I burst into the room. The Marquis had her on her bed, his flat, pale ass bare in the air as he rutted into her. I was too late.

"How dare you come in here?" Montespan yelled, spinning on me and casting Athénaïs away to curl into herself on the bed. "You conniving, interfering whore," he sputtered, stumbling over the trousers around his ankles. I shoved him aside as I rushed to Athénaïs as he collapsed in a pathetic heap on the floor.

"I am doing my duty and protecting my mistress!" I snapped, taking her into my arms. I wondered what sort of fury was in my eyes when I looked at him, for he scrambled back in fear. "You have all you need of her – why do you torment her?"

"She is my wife! I will do with her as I please," Montespan spat back, but he looked pale and pathetic there on the floor. Powerless.

"You will get out of this room and leave her be!" I cried back, cradling Athénaïs's head against my shoulder. Montespan was livid, but I bared my teeth at him and he obeyed. It was not until the door slammed that Athénaïs relaxed in my arms and began to weep.

"I'm sorry he used you like that," I whispered. "Did he finish? I can make you a tonic to make sure—"

"It's useless. I hate him. He's ruined it all," Athénaïs muttered back, shaking her head. "I wanted Louis to save me from him, but now…"

"What do you mean?" I asked, pushing away so I could look into Athénaïs's face.

"Do you not think it strange that you find me weeping now for the same reason I wept all those years ago?"

"You're pregnant? Again?" My heart cracked in my chest as she nodded. This made everything worse. "But the tonic—"

"Your potions are not as strong as my damn fertile womb," Athénaïs groaned.

"Why did you let him touch you if you're already with child?"

"Because he does not know, and I don't want him to. I'll keep it secret until I can't anymore. But this delays everything! Louis is already growing bored with La Vallière, and if I can't entice him now, I will lose my chance when he's ensnared by some other."

"We could get rid of it," I said softly.

Athénaïs's eyes cleared as she looked at me. "You told me, all those years ago, that you knew people who could help women in need."

"Madame Lapère, the midwife. She can end the pregnancy for you," I replied with a nod. "I can arrange for you to visit her in secret. You won't be the first woman at court I've done the same thing for."

"Does it hurt?" Athénaïs's voice was small and distant.

"Yes. I've heard it's worse than a monthly cycle, but nothing compared to birth." I felt my nerves rising. Athénaïs had committed sins with me and knew of my godlessness and witchery, but this was different. Or it might be for her, a woman who still went to Mass often and listened to the priest's words...

"Make the arrangements. But start me a bath first: I want to be rid of his filth in all ways," she said at last.

"As you wish, my lady."

I could not tell her what I had heard from Le Sage now. I had to face those demons alone.

IN THE YEARS SINCE I had stumbled into Catherine Lapère's coven, I had met many dangers. I had supped with ghosts and taken the dirt from graves. I had learned the plants that could cure a fever or stop a heart. My soul had flown to visions and my hands had worked spells both baneful and blessed. But never before had I felt as wicked and dangerous as I did slipping through the alleys of Saint-Denis to where Le Sage and La Voisin had ordered me to meet them.

The night looked darker than I had ever seen it, thanks to the veil of lace I wore over my face to provide some concealment. Even half blind, I felt the eyes of the carved saints upon me as I waited by the great Cathédrale Saint-Denis. The kings of France going back 1,000 years rested there, and tonight, I sought to bewitch their son…

My heart pounding, I raced through the square. I could feel their judgement already, and I did not even know what impieties I was to perform tonight. The money in my pocket felt like Judas's silver.

Down the main street of the village, left through an alley and then another, to a quiet street of humble daub and timber houses. Hardly a place for devilry. Still, I jumped when a door creaked.

"Madame… Noire?" a quavering voice asked, and I spun to see a priest at the door of an empty shop. He knew the name I had told Le Sage my mistress would respond to. This had to be one of the accomplices. Perhaps it was the priest I had heard so much about, who had been working with Le Sage for years.

"Yes, it is I," I replied, lowering my voice to disguise it.

"Come with me. We must begin at midnight. The witching hour," the man said with a hiccough, and I smelled the strong scent of brandy on his breath. He gestured for me to enter the abandoned building he had come from. The front room was dark, save for a light from the stairway down to the cellar, and every sense in me told me to turn back and flee. There was danger here, and darkness.

The light from the cellar grew brighter, and a figure holding a candle appeared. Catherine Monvoisin was clad in a simple robe of black, her hair unbound, and she was smiling like a wolf that had sighted a wounded deer.

"I am glad you have come, Madame *Noire*," the divineress purred. "Did you bring our fee?"

"I brought your first payment," I replied, summoning every actor's trick and the magic of the charms of concealment in my pockets. Catherine did not flinch at the words. "We will see by your success if you deserve the rest."

I handed her the packet of notes: the savings I had accumulated, added to some funds from Athénaïs. It was only a thousand livres, but I could see from the naked triumph on Catherine's face that it was more than she had anticipated.

"Leave us, Father Guibourg," she told the priest, perhaps foolishly thinking it did not matter if I knew the man's name. "I shall prepare her and await your signal."

My stomach knotted at the thought of what these 'preparations' would be as Guibourg retreated down the stairs. I had to be strong.

"Undress. The ritual requires your naked body," Catherine ordered, and my head snapped up in shock. "Do not worry, there is no danger to your person, my dear lady. Your modesty is one small price for the power of the Black Mass."

A Black Mass.

I had heard whispers of such rituals and always dismissed them as fevered fictions conceived by hateful witch hunters to persecute us. Of course Le Sage – who called on demons and convinced fools he could turn lead into gold – conducted such blasphemous acts. It was the height of his theater to pervert the ceremonies of the church.

I threw back my cloak and did as I had been commanded, retreating to a corner for privacy from Catherine's eyes, for now. My hands shook as I unlaced my bodice and pushed off my skirts. The air that hit me as I finally removed my chemise was freezing, and gooseflesh covered my skin. I covered myself with my cloak, but I continued to shiver with cold and fear.

"Drink this. It will calm you," Catherine said sweetly from my shoulder. She was there, holding a cup of wine. I hesitated. Who knew what drugs were in it, and how they would dull my mind? But perhaps it was better to be intoxicated for this and to call on the power of whatever herbs she had mixed in the drink to help me. I took a careful sip and tasted the bitter, earthy scent of mugwort and wormwood in the brew. A mixture to bring visions and free the mind. With Catherine watching closely, I drank the cup down.

From the cellar, a bell rang.

"It is time, Madame," Catherine said, with a dark smile. "Follow me."

The stone steps to the cellar were cold beneath my feet as I descended, following my old friend who I barely recognized, hoping she would not recognize me.

The cellar was lit with a few candles, and they were all black, I could tell through my veil. They lined the bare walls, and more surrounded a low table set before Father Guibourg, who stood with Adam Le Sage beside him. Le Sage wore a black robe, as well, with a look of delight on his face as his accomplice approached, leading the woman he thought was Madame de Montespan. My Athénaïs.

I had braided a lock of her hair into my own. She had not begrudged it to me, and I had told her not to ask what it was I would do tonight with her funds. She was with me, in my heart and in that token, and I prayed to Our Lady that whatever I did tonight would bless her.

"Welcome, brothers and sisters, to the rite," Le Sage began, and I realized I had come to stand right in front of the table. And that I was no longer cold. The candles were warm, and the wine was already in my blood, as if by dark magic. "Let us prepare the altar," the magician ordered, and Catherine turned to me.

"I offer this sinful flesh as the altar for our sacrament," she declared with relish. My mind was slow to understand as she undid the clasp of my cloak and let it fall to the ground. The eyes of the two men before me widened in desire and delight at the sight of my nudity, but Catherine gave a small gasp.

"Come forth, my child, and present yourself for our working," Guibourg went on. My body did not resist as Catherine turned me and guided me backward so I was forced to sit on the table – no, not a table. An altar. Or a place for one.

I shuddered when Le Sage and Guibourg put their hands upon me and pushed me down so that I was prone and helpless before them.

"This altar of lustful flesh is laid before you, oh Lowest and Greatest One," Le Sage declared. Catherine was there again, and when I looked at her, she was nude too.

"I offer these candles, to consecrate the darkness," she said and handed the men two candles, exactly the shape that would be used on an altar in a real Mass, but black as tar. The priest and Le Sage each placed one in my hands as Catherine bent to whisper in my ear, "Hold them tight, my lady." I forced myself to be still as the men lit them, and I did not wince as wax spilled on my skin. I knew that pain. I'd known it so long ago...

"We offer this desecration to you, oh Lord of Midnight," Le Sage said as he took a place at my head. Catherine was at my feet. My head was spinning - or was I moving? The wine... the potion was working on me, whatever it had been. My breath was unsteady. I needed to hold on to something. Anything.

The flame of the candle in my left hand quavered, calling for my attention. *Just focus on the candle until it is done.*

Blackness from the bottom of my mind surged up like it had not done in years as Le Sage put his hands on my shoulder to hold me down... Like *he* had held me down.

"Eleison Kyrie, Elesion Christi, Eleison Kyrie," Guibourg chanted, desecrating the Mass by beginning it backward as he set a black cloth over my stomach. *"Patris Dei glória in—"* he went on, and the words became a drone. I couldn't hear over my racing heart. I couldn't scream when Catherine took my ankles in her grip.

"No! Not again..." I whispered, but no one could hear me over the distorted Latin chant from the faithless priest. No one could hear the girl I had been – the one Giles Faviot had bent over a table like this and defiled. I was going to scream, the memory was so vivid. I could feel him inside me still. Someone pushed my legs up so they bent, exposing the wound he had left in me...

"Oh yee of the dark places," Catherine's voice cut through my panic, murmuring against my thigh. "Oh yee of the graveyards. You who are growing green and black decay, you who are lust and destruction. We call on you to take this sacrifice."

I wanted to struggle, I wanted to shout, but I could not move with their hands upon me and panic gripping my heart! I was helpless and useless. I was a tool to be discarded. I was exposed. I was a sinner and a whore and an abomination. I was—

You are a witch.

The voice in my mind was like the baying of a hundred hounds and I gasped, my body arching upwards.

"Take her fear as sacrifice. Take her desecration and devour it," Catherine went on, and there was power in her words. Real power.

I felt mouths upon me, as if the shadows were alive and consuming me from all sides, upon my untouched cunt and bare skin and veiled face, they devoured me. I writhed against the hands that held me, my breath ragged, my muscles taut as I was torn apart like carrion. She would leave nothing left...

You are mine.

My eyes rolled back and my mind reeled. I was here and my fear was gone. There was only her, sated and fed on my terror. She had cleansed me...

Catherine was not praying to the empty devil these men called down. She was praying to Our Lady. She of the two torches. Of blade and key.

I felt her there beside me. In me.

Guibourg held them up – a rusted key like the seal of a pope and a small dagger – and placed them on my stomach.

We are the chalice of all life and death.

The chalice. He placed that on my womb. I groaned, my nipples tightening as visions began to dance before my waking eyes. Grain and sickle. Seed and rot. Root and leaf and bud.

"Blessed are you, oh Lord of Destruction," Guibourg went on, his voice ringing out in the cellar that suddenly resonated like a cathedral. "Through your wickedness, we have stolen this bread we offer you: it becomes the bread of life."

I half saw him hold aloft a communion wafer, then bring it down to rub it across one of my bare breasts, then the other, then to my cunt, grazing it. There was power in that little white circle too; power that I felt in every nerve.

"We consecrate this host in the service of Athénaïs de Montespan! That our great King will love her!" Guibourg intoned and placed a fragment of the host in my mouth. It tasted of a woman, and I swallowed it down. I could hear the rhythm of my heart through my whole body. The world was trembling with it.

"Blessed be, in the name of Astaroth!" Le Sage and Catherine said together, their voices rough. I could feel the heat through their hands and hear the ecstasy in their voices. Were they in the same place as me? A place beyond mere feeling and flesh, of darkness and subtle flame?

"Blessed are you, oh Lady of Demons! Through your debauchery, we have received this wine we offer to you! It becomes the blood of life!" Guibourg cried as he lifted the chalice. I was frantic with something beyond pleasure, my breasts heaving as the cold metal of the vessel pressed on my nipples. Catherine held down my hips and Le Sage pushed down on my chest, and I cried out in wanton feeling as the chalice touched my sex and wine sloshed over my cunt.

"We consecrate this host in the name of Athénaïs de Montespan, that her rivals may be cast aside, and her love for Louis returned!" Guibourg bellowed.

Wine poured over my lips and I lapped it up greedily before it was withdrawn.

"Blessed be in the name of Lilith," the others said, and my body was singing and tight now, invisible hands rending me, sending me into bliss and madness. My soul was above me, watching as Catherine and Le Sage picked up the key and dagger while Guibourg placed the chalice back on my belly.

"In the name of Asmodeus! We pray!" Guibourg cried, and the key and blade drove into the chalice as one.

I came with a long, animal cry, thrashing on the altar as they pierced me without touching me. As they undid me.

As She freed me.

I floated with her, in the dark. In peace, as the night held me to her breast.

Let him love her. Let me keep them. Amen, I whispered in my mind to whatever strange magic this was, culled from mocking the word of God and repeating the secrets of Our Lady. There was power in all rituals and prayers. *Let this power do my will. And Athénaïs's, too.*

One thing more, my child, and it is done, came the answer, and I nodded.

I drifted for an age, my mind peaceful and free, knowing the last thing I needed… The price.

When I came back to myself, the other three were fucking. Catherine had the priest's cock in her mouth and Le Sage's in her cunt and they all looked ecstatic. I laughed as they consecrated her with their seed and she gave her pleasure to the dark as sacrifice too.

But still, one more thing remained to be given.

MY KNEES WERE WEAK as I made my way back to the dark city. I could barely remember how I had dressed or if I had said any manner of farewell to the workers of dark arts I had left behind. It would have been easy for some brigand or thief to accost me, not that I had any money or coin left to take. But I was protected, and my feet knew the way to Lapère's house, even in the small hours of the morning.

I could feel power still vibrating within me, waiting for its final release. A flutter in my stomach and a whisper in my ear. It was almost the true witching hour, three past midnight. I could feel it.

I could feel her near still. Here at the crossroads.

"Where have you been!" the voice I cherished demanded from a shadowed door the moment I paused. I looked up to see Athénaïs's wan face framed by her hood and I rushed to embrace her. Holding her stilled my spirit, and brought it peace. She held me just as tightly in turn. "I was worried."

"I'm sorry, it took longer than I thought," I replied, surprised my tongue could make words.

"Is it done?" she demanded, pulling back to stare desperately into my eyes.

"For whatever it was worth. Yes," I replied, caressing her. "Do not ask what passed. It is not fit for your ears."

"Good. Now show me the way to your crone," Athénaïs sighed back. She held her hand over her belly as we walked the short distance to Lapère's house, where three candles burned in the window of the upper floor. A symbol for those who knew where to look.

I grabbed her hand before she knocked, doubt inching in on the peace I had found hours ago. "Athénaïs…"

"Is this not the house?"

"I have to ask once again – are you sure?" I held her gaze as her face hardened with resolve. "This is your blood. A child that could be. Is this truly a sacrifice you would make for a chance with Louis?"

"Absolutely," she replied with no hesitation. "This is my husband's blood too. And I would sacrifice it a hundred times to be free."

"It is resolved then."

Before we could speak more, Lapère opened the door. Whether she knew we were there by our voices or her powers, I can't say. But I suspected the latter. "Welcome, Madame. Come in."

Athénaïs did not hesitate, but she did take my hand, and we followed Lapère into the house and mounted the stairs. The room upstairs was as I remembered it – candles burning. A humble bed with a straw mattress, laid with clean sheets. To catch the blood.

"She's not here, so you know," my old mentor muttered to me as I passed her, and I let out a breath. Good. I didn't want Veronique to know of this.

"Do I just lay down?" Athénaïs asked, straining to keep the bravery in her voice.

"Yes, make yourself as comfortable as you can," Lapère replied kindly. Athénaïs nodded and crossed herself, whispering a prayer I could not hear before she did as she was told.

She kept my hand in hers. I sat by her head as Lapère laid another sheet over her legs then positioned them splayed open and pushed away her skirts. Her grip tightened and she looked into my eyes for a long, quiet moment as Lapère prepared and said her own quiet prayers.

"Our Lady of sighs, grant us mercy and safety. Guide us."

Those beautiful eyes closed with a wince when the midwife began her work. The hand gripping mine tightened as Athénaïs's face wrinkled in pain, but she did not cry out. Instead, she whispered something to herself.

For the second time that night, I felt a power coursing through me and filling the room. I felt the energy that had been in me since I came on that altar flowing out into Athénaïs as she muttered and Lapère pierced her womb with her ancient tools.

"Give him to me," I finally heard her say in place of a cry of pain. "Please. Let him be mine. Louis. Louis."

Louis.

The spell was cast.

CHAPTER 20

THE EMPRESS

L'IMPERATRICE

T HE WAY LOUIS LOOKED at Athénaïs changed that spring.
Slowly, as the days grew longer, his gaze upon his Queen's
favorite lady lingered like the growing light. It was not the same
as before; it was warmer. More curious. Perhaps even enticed.

Was it magic that had diverted the light of the sun? Lapère
always warned us not to attribute to evil spirits or a hex that
which human frailty can explain. The same was true of luck or
simple faith. I wondered, as I watched the King and my mistress
glance at one another across the galleries of the Louvre or the
blooming gardens of Saint-Germain, if it was Athénaïs who had
changed and thus begun to lure her prey. She moved through
the court with brazen confidence, the wittiest woman in every
room, a sparkling jewel in France's crown. Did that confidence

come from the magic she knew had worked for her? Was that the magic in itself – the simple act of believing in it?

Louis spoke to her more and more on his visits to the Queen's chambers – a place where Louise La Vallière was still excluded. He sought her out at grand suppers and danced with her in the court ballets. I benefitted too, attending Athénaïs as she walked with the King in the gardens, and we all spoke. Those walks together – when I could make both of them laugh or thrill them with some morsel of gossip they did not know – were my happiest moments. They filled me with hope, but also a kind of sweet regret, for they meant things were beginning to change.

Louise La Vallière was Louis's *maîtresse-en-titre* now that Anne had departed for heaven. Yes, as we all had expected, now that the pious lady was no longer forbidden, she drew the King's eye less and less. She was pregnant again, but carrying it badly. Louis shared her bed often, this I knew; for his lusts were great.

Louis shared his wife's chamber, as well, and oftentimes, there was talk of him taking a servant or some other lady for a night or an afternoon simply because she was there. His heart supposedly remained pledged to the woman who had risked her soul, reputation, and dignity for him on behalf of her god and a now-dead queen. Or it had been, before she became boring. Like the daffodils of March, La Vallière began to fade as the lilacs of May burst into bloom.

Now that Louis looked at Athénaïs, she wanted to make sure his attention stayed on her. That she was not just some quick conquest, but ruled his heart entirely. Her plot to plant a deeper seed of lust in Louis's mind was brilliant. Especially when it used one of the new, grandest features of the Château at Versailles when the court settled there in May: the baths.

As a child in Provence, our baths had been clear streams or fountains in the square. We washed like common folk, with a pitcher and basin in our home, when clean water could be found. It had not been until my time at the convent that I had seen a bathtub. Once a month, all the girls were lined up and scrubbed in the same wooden bath of scalding water, one at a time, whether we liked it or not. I had liked it, as long as I was one of the first to go in, before the water grew cold and clouded by dirt.

The baths at Versailles were nothing like that old barrel. They were more like fountains, or some Roman fantasy. Rooms of marble and tile, filled with clear, clean water that flowed from casks and shells held by delicate nymphs of marble. They said that when Louis was a child, his mother would talk to him about ruling in her bath, the only place they could be alone without valets and bodyguards lurking about.

Any member of court could enjoy these new baths provided by the King, upon request. Athénaïs and I began not just to frequent them, but to also make a regular circuit of the garden the hour before – a time when we would reliably be met by Louis, seeking out Athénaïs's company on our route, near enough to the baths to keep them in mind.

Until the day we did not. Or more accurately, Athénaïs did not. I still took our accustomed path alone, and, as planned, met the King along the way.

"My dear Mademoiselle des Œillets! Where is your esteemed mistress? Not ill, I hope?" Louis asked. I ignored the flutter in my heart when he called me dear and gave a demure curtsey before replying.

"No, Sire. She is in the baths. She had the opportunity to go alone and did not wish to waste it," I replied, exactly as planned.

I saw the interest spark in Louis's eyes before he tamped it down. "Alas, I was looking forward to her company," Louis said. "It is such a relief from these endless meetings over the Spanish inheritance to walk with such fine ladies in my gardens."

"She may be done soon, if you hope to catch her," I said, as rehearsed. There it was again: the spark.

"I shall consider it. Good day, Mademoiselle," Louis replied and turned away.

I followed him discreetly, keeping to the hedges and calling on my usual charms and the four thieves' vinegar on my wrists. The King did not see me as I watched him make for the baths, nor as I concealed myself in an alcove where I could peek in after him.

He did not know I watched as he came upon a view of Athénaïs, draped in a towel like a shroud, at the edge of the water. He drew back, of course (propriety and all), but he did not leave. Because Athénaïs had met his eye. She stared him down, my lady. She looked right at the King of France himself, a married man with a mistress who had given him three sons... and dropped her towel to reveal her gorgeous body to his eyes.

Perhaps he compared her to Louise La Vallière. Where Louise was skinny and pale and bent, Athénaïs was robust and curvaceous, her skin pink and glistening from the steam and heat. Or perhaps he saw her beauty all on its own, as I always had. From her round hips to her large, dark nipples, she was perfection. He had to see it.

Athénaïs plunged into the water, and when she emerged, the King was gone. But I was there to tell her of her triumph. Perhaps that was a spell too, what she did that day, for it assured her that the King was enchanted. What was love and lust, but its own sort of magic?

LESS WELCOME IN MAY was an invitation to a soirée at Marie Vigoreaux's house. I did not want to go, uninterested in her attempts to make her parlor a new meeting place for the fashionable of Paris to ensnare them as clients, but I had received a note from Catherine Monvoisin. An insistent one, at that, reminding me of 'unfinished business.' Then another, reminding me that our 'wise friend' was waiting and paying close attention to the goings on of the court.

I had to go, or they might try to find me when the court returned to Paris, and that would not do. Not at all. I still had no idea of how I was to outwit Le Sage and La Voisin when it came to their money, but there still was no success to pay for as far as they knew. Maybe I could delay them.

Marie Vigoreaux's house was new. It was in the Marais, like Catherine's, but nearer to the church of Saint Paul, a glorious monument started by Louis XIII that had been well-supported in the years of his son's reign. I arrived past sunset, fashionably late enough that there was quite a crowd inside, all drinking and mingling and trying to philosophize. It was not one of the salons of the elite where women like Athénaïs sharpened their wit, but it was a merry gathering, nonetheless.

I saw many whom I recognized as I surveyed the crowd, making my way to greet the hostess. Most notable was the infamous Marquise de Brinvilliers. I had forgotten that she had been a client of Marie's, and I wondered whether her travails had ended. Her lover, Sainte Croix, had been released from the Bastille last year, and everyone believed she would resume their affair. If she had, it had been discreet at least...

Or perhaps discreet for now, because I saw with whom she was speaking – Adam Le Sage. He caught me looking and a hungry, wolfish smile spread over his face before he excused himself from the Marquise and made his way to me.

"Searching for more clients at such a party?" I asked boldly before Le Sage could start flattering me. He shrugged and shook his head.

"Madame de Brinvilliers sought out my advice in the past, regarding some of my particular areas of expertise, but has declined it of late," Le Sage said with no hint of a lie. "She speaks of an Italian friend her paramour Sainte Croix met in the Bastille. You know how deadly those Italians can be. She has no need of me."

That was troubling. One often heard of the expert poisoners of Italy – among women who sought to rid themselves of troublesome men, the name Juliana Tofana was especially infamous – but perhaps it meant nothing. Another ruse to throw off Le Sage, maybe. The man was like a dog with a bone when he sensed an opportunity.

"Who has needed you of late, I wonder," I replied, not hiding the acid in my tone. It did not dampen Le Sage's mood.

"I would never tell, my dear Mademoiselle." Le Sage smiled. "Ah, here is our friend."

I did not have to turn to see who he saw over my shoulder. Soon enough, Catherine joined us, and her demeanor was far less jovial.

"We have heard nothing from you, Claude," Catherine began without ceremony. "Nor from your mistress."

"There is nothing to tell," I replied. "No seeds you have sewn have borne fruit yet. In fact, if the field remains barren, we may have to pursue *you* for reimbursement."

Catherine responded by guffawing so loudly she drew the attention of half the room. "You are in no position to say such a thing."

"Oh, really?" I hoped that projecting haughty confidence and derision might affect her, but it was going nowhere.

"Yes, my dear," Catherine hissed and shocked me by grabbing my arm tight. She pulled me down towards her and whispered viciously in my ears, "Do you know that you have a particular group of three moles upon your hip? I remember because the first time I saw them, I knew they were witch marks…"

My heart plunged into the floor. She knew it had been me upon that altar. Another piece of blackmail to destroy me.

"I will tell the world about you if you do not pay soon," Catherine promised.

"We do not have it yet," I whispered back in surrender, praying for release from this trap. "But I will soon, I swear." It was like hearing my own mother's voice coming from my mouth. She had fallen into debt that had destroyed trusting in her luck, and now, I had done the same, trusting false magic.

"No!" Marie Vigoreaux's voice boomed from a door opposite us and we spun to gape at her. "You are not welcome here, whore! Not you or your traitorous conjurer!"

"Traitorous?" Le Sage balked, glancing about the room at the now-silent crowd staring at him and La Voisin.

"You steal him back and steal business from me, then dare to brag of it!" Marie shrieked. "Then dare to come into my house to consort with *her* – confirming it!" My old friend's eyes shifted to me and the fury in them did not abate. "I should have known. You always favored her."

"Marie, I thought—" I stammered.

"You think I asked you here to entertain you? I invited you so I could berate you, you faithless dilettante! I knew a party where you could gossip was the only way I'd get you in my sights again. Since you've forgotten all of us. All but *her*." Marie slurred the word. She was drunk, as much so as I'd ever seen her.

"Because she knows I'm the only one in Paris capable of helping her," Catherine replied loudly, a carnival performer advertising herself to the assembled crowd.

"I think none of you are capable of anything other than chicanery and ridiculousness," I snapped back. I would not be a prop for this rivalry. "I need nothing from any of you!"

I turned to leave, keeping my spine straight and proud even as panic and fear swirled in me. I could escape this. I could keep everything in control.

"We will see. What *my* lady has in store—" Marie began before another woman – La Filastre – grabbed her and silenced her.

I didn't want to watch them fight or be pawed at by Catherine and her magician. I wanted to go home to Athénaïs, hold her, and be assured that she was still mine, for now. For a little while longer.

It had to happen soon. Louis's interest was growing, I knew it. Every day, he looked at Athénaïs more. He liked the hunt, the game of waiting and anticipation, yet that same game threatened to destroy us. I prayed that soon, he would send for her... Soon, he would be ours, and we would be safe in his light.

T HE BLOW WAS SLOW to fall: a curse that had been waiting for years, striking at last, when least expected. Or perhaps I did not see it falling before it was too late.

Children die, you see. It is a sad fact of our world that the young and weak often are the first to be lost in times of plague or even a cold winter. But it was bright spring when a small babe known to his neighbors as Louis de La Baume Le Blanc went to the angels. I heard about it first from the servants to the caretaker for the little boy and his siblings – the servants of Madame Colbert. The young Louis was the smallest and weakest of the King and La Vallière's three children. It was not a shock.

This was not the first child the King had lost. Two daughters by Marie Thérèse had passed when they were barely alive, but this was the first son to die, and that made a difference to a man like Louis. I saw how he mourned, the way his countenance darkened for many days, and the way he retreated to the embrace of his wife for comfort. Louise La Vallière could not show her grief at court, or perhaps she did not feel it. She had not had the chance to nurse or care for any of her children by Louis, but they were still hers, were they not?

One child lost is a sad thing, but not peculiar. A second, a month later... That troubled me. Especially when it was the child I had helped bring into the world. Charles de Lioncourt had been a strong little boy, so it shocked me to learn of his death at the age of two and a half. Shocked me – and terrified me. Was this what Marie had warned of? No, it could not be. She did not have that sort of power. Olympe de Soissons would not stoop to this. I told myself that over and over in those sad weeks.

I avoided my cards, afraid of the questions they would answer. I put all my energy into Athénaïs and her subtle pursuit of Louis. She had to be very careful, or it could be seen that she was preying on his grief. Grief which he could not even make public. She doted as well as she could on the Queen, who hoped that her own womb had quickened, thanks to her husband's recent attentions...

Finally, in June, on the solstice, I did a reading. It flummoxed me, for it warned of deceit – the Moon – and lonely heartbreak – the Nine of Swords and the Five of Coins. Death was there, as well. Suffering. But so too was the Two of Batons. A new beginning? And the Ace of Cups and the Lovers.

Soon, Louis would turn to Athénaïs, but other pain waited. I avoided the city and any notes from my old coven. I was a witch alone now, casting my charms for beauty and protection and luck for me and my mistress in hopes that our day would come soon and grant us some measure of safety.

The third son, Philippe, died in July.

Three children. All lost in a few months. Even Queen Marie Thérèse pitied Louise La Vallière for that. We all knew why she looked despondent for days. Even as her belly swelled with a fourth royal bastard.

The Queen was pregnant again too and took great pains to preserve her health and peace. Praying many times a day, often with her husband. When he visited her chambers in Versailles one hot August night, his face was still sad. After he spoke to his wife privately, a rarity, they returned to her chamber and her ladies, and his smile had returned. And he turned that smile to Athénaïs.

THE KING's MAN, BONTEMPS, spotted me out when I was alone in the gardens, seeking out shade from the oppressive August sun. The giant of a man spoke infrequently, so that when he did, his words carried great weight… for they were the King's words. He was silent at first when he saw me, but I could hear words on his lips. Words of doom and accusation that had echoed in my dreams for weeks. Three children were dead and who but a witch hiding in the court was to blame for it…

I froze when I saw him approaching. All my bravery left me as I leaned against an elm.

For weeks, I had been waiting and hoping for something – anything – to happen. But at the same time, I had fallen deep into paranoia and fear. Catherine and Le Sage were still out there, doing who knows what. Perhaps they had cursed Louise La Vallière's children – or poisoned them. What if their ire fell on me? Maybe *I* was cursed. What if she told someone I had been there at the first birth? What if they guessed? I was helpless, and my spells had not worked. I had done terrible things and nothing had come of it…

What would happen to me if I was found out? What would happen to this life I had built? Would I have to go back to my mother in the slums? Or would I be thrown into prison? Would I be burned? I could feel the fires licking at my thighs and sweat sprang to my brow. At the same time, I was cold. I was shaking. I could see only Bontemps walking to me with purpose. With ruin?

Do not forget who you are, Claude de Vin.

The words came from the earth beneath my feet. The strong, steady earth that supported me. That would not let me fall.

You are a witch and the world awaits you. Be strong.

I would be strong. I would not fall.

"Mademoiselle des Œillets," Bontemps said to me, his voice a soft rumble. "I hope this day finds you well."

"It finds me hot, and looking forward to fall," I answered, hoping to explain the sweat still upon my brow. Bontemps smiled gently.

"Indeed, the sun is vigorous today. Perhaps it is lonely, looking for a fair face to smile upon," he went on. This sort of poetry was not his way, but it was Louis's. "Did you know that the King keeps a small cottage at the edge of the park of Versailles? Where the village of Trianon was before it had to be relocated. He goes there after hunting. It is very small, but it is shaded well."

"I did not," I replied. I was lying. I'd seen that cottage and knew the village. I'd watched Louis come and go from there many times. Often with Louise La Vallière.

"I assume your mistress endures the heat too. She is welcome – nay, invited by the King, to visit that cottage. Tonight. If she wishes?" Bontemps placed the offer at my feet. The world... at our feet.

"Nothing would please her more," I replied, my mouth now dry. "She shall be there. Of course, we will attend the Queen first, but—"

"She will understand, I assure you." Bontemps seemed confident, and with no more words and a nod, he left me.

I could still feel the fear in my body, like echoes. It still told me that this was some sort of trap, but I had to rush to Athénaïs with this news.

I found her in the gallery leading to the Queen's chambers, deep in gossip with Madame de Sévigné (the only woman in court half as observant as me, and well-known for her vibrant house and salon in the Marais). Of all people, I did not want her to know the news I had for Athénaïs.

"There you are, my dear," Athénaïs said with a smile. She was particularly beautiful today. We had taken great pains to make it so, layering her in the finest dresses and demure jewels and styling her flaxen hair in delicate curls. She was a goddess to me. "I worry sometimes, that you spend so much time in those gardens, you will become a tree like Daphne."

"If only I was so lucky as to have Apollo pursue me," I jested in return, though the idea stung something in my heart.

"Mademoiselle des Œillets, I have some tragic gossip for you," Madame de Sévigné interjected. She was older, and not a beauty, but I enjoyed her forthright wit and poise. "Have you heard about poor Madame de Brinvilliers?"

"Why, no," I replied. New fear took me, but I kept it locked inside me, painting benign interest on my face. "Has she fallen ill?"

"Not her – her father. He has died! After she long attended him as he ailed," Madame de Sévigné said.

"What a turnaround for her," Athénaïs muttered. "I thought she had fallen out with him after he arranged for the lettre de cachet that put her lover in the Bastille."

"As did I..." My mind was working too quickly now, but it stopped as Athénaïs gently took my hand. "You came in looking flushed: are you alright?"

"I have news – of the friend we were speaking of the other day," I whispered discreetly, and Athénaïs's eyes lit up.

"Oh, let us walk together then, and speak," my mistress said and took my hand. We left Madame de Sévigné staring after us, to formulate her gossip.

We found our way into one of the new, sweeping staircases that had been added to the château in the recent renovation, and Athénaïs clutched my arm in hope.

"He wishes to see you. Tonight at his secret lodge in the Trianon," I said, still not believing it myself. "Alone. You are to tell Marie Thérèse that you are going home. Bontemps informed me."

"Oh God, truly? Is it finally happening?" Athénaïs gasped. "I cannot wait to have him alone—"

"Do you not need me there?" I stammered. "To dress you or – or attend you in some way?" I was shaking. I felt like I was losing her.

"You want to be there?" she echoed – as if it hadn't occurred to her. "Of course. Maybe it will help! You can cast some spell when he is with me to keep him, can't you?"

I gulped, my mouth dry, and nodded. "Yes. I can do… something. Of course, *you* will cast your own spell on him. You already have."

"We shall see. It is one thing to snare a man once, quite another to hold his interest," Athénaïs said with a smile. "My goodness, it has been so long since I've even been with a man I desired at all. I wonder what it shall be like?"

"I wouldn't know," I replied. "I've never been with a man I wanted at all."

"It's not so bad, truly," Athénaïs laughed. "Especially if he's powerful. Oh, Claude. What a night this will be."

I HAD NEVER BEEN inside the charming cottage in the village that had been claimed by the crown. It was a lovely new building, with wood-paneled walls hung with tapestries and comfortable, smart furniture. I went into the bedroom and placed a charm of roses beneath the bed while Athénaïs watched.

"Do you think it will make him like me?" she asked like a besotted girl, and I had to laugh, though it was thin and empty.

She had wanted Louis for as long as I could remember, the same way every woman in court did. She flirted with him and took his counsel; she had known him for years. Yet still, it was nerve-wracking for me to imagine him as a man and a lover. For how could I ever compare?

I kissed her in reply. As deeply and lovingly as I had ever kissed her before, reminding her what one person felt for her. I hoped it would ignite her and keep me in her mind when she gave her love to another.

"I know he will love you, as I do," I said softly, and Athénaïs smiled at me.

A knock came at the door of the cottage, shocking us.

"Hide!" Athénaïs ordered and rushed away to the parlor, leaving me alone in the bedroom.

I rushed about, looking for someplace to hide myself. There was no way out, but there was a long, heavy tapestry in the corner, and I hid myself behind it like a fool, only to find there was a concealed alcove with space enough there for me and a place to peek through, as if the spot had been designed for such voyeurism. Knowing some of the exploits of the court, I was not surprised.

I still held my breath when Athénaïs glided back into the room with Louis in tow. He was dressed in his royal finest, a short cloak lined in ermine and embroidered with fleur-de-lys. His long, dark hair was mussed as if he'd rushed here, and his lips were upturned in a smile lined by his perfect moustache.

"I barely believed it when I heard you wished to see me," Athénaïs said, her voice husky and warm.

"I have thought of you so often of late, my dear Madame de Montespan," Louis replied, equally as lusty. "Something has changed about you, as if a torch was lit within you. Always, you were a jewel of my court, but now you are—"

"Its crown?" she smirked back.

"Indeed," Louis replied, and placed a hand against her cheek, cradling her face. I held my breath, and so did Athénaïs as Louis leaned down, his eyes upon her lips. He was slow about it, approaching so carefully for the kiss that I was unable to tell at first when his lips touched hers. I knew how those lips tasted. I had held her like that as she melted into an embrace...

But she was forceful in her response. Hungry and vivacious, she seized the face of the King between her hands, and he reacted in pleasant surprise. I wondered how different this was from Louise La Vallière's kisses. I imagined her to be sweet and coy, always needing to be seduced. That was not my Athénaïs's way.

She stepped back from the King and began to remove her clothes. It was not so hard: she wore a simple overdress fastened by ribbons above her bodice and chemise. In a flourish, it was on the floor, and Louis made an un-kingly sound of amazement.

"Beautiful." He commanded as she undid her stays, "Let me see those beautiful breasts. A man could go mad thinking of them."

"Could he?" Athénaïs teased, holding her chemise closed over her chest and laughing. Slowly, dramatically, she spread the garment open and showed him. Her breasts were much larger than thin Louise La Vallière's, and Louis looked ravenous for them. I always had been.

I did not expect lust to stir in me at that moment, but it did. My sex tingled between my legs as Louis set upon her, ravishing her chest with his mouth and taking one of her taut nipples between his teeth. Athénaïs cooed at the sensation, then boldly pushed Louis back. Pushed the *King*.

"And what is there for my eyes to see to drive me mad?" she said, bold and brazen, and it made my heart quicken more. "I have imagined you, my King. My Apollo. I wish to see all of you to do my worship…"

Louis was not coy with his disrobing. He did it quickly, throwing clothes onto the ground that were worth more than I could earn in a lifetime. His coat and silk shirt, and then his breeches.

Rarely had I seen what a man aroused looked like. The cock I had always found to be an absurd thing, with its comical ups and downs. Louis, as far as I could tell, was nicely endowed, and hard for my mistress, and he gasped in awe as she fell on her knees before him and licked that organ from balls to tip.

"Madame," he moaned.

"*Athénaïs*," she chided. If I'd had a cock, it would have been hard too. My cunt was aching watching them, watching *her* utterly dominate him. This was her witchcraft. It always had been.

"Athénaïs," Louis repeated. "Your wicked mouth can wait. If I cannot have you right now, I will surely expire."

"Then have me," Athénaïs said with a grin, rising and manhandling the King once again so that he stumbled back onto the bed. He grabbed her hips as she bent over and kissed him, catching his cock between them with her hand. He was trying to turn them so that he could take her from above, as he had to be used to, but she would not have that. On that blessed bed, she was going to show him exactly how different from pious Louise La Vallière she was.

Athénaïs straddled him, guiding him into her sex, and they both threw back their heads in pleasure. Hidden behind the tapestry, I bit my lip and clawed at my skirts, hiking them up so I could find my own aching wetness.

I rubbed myself as Athénaïs began to ride him, moving her hips wildly. I had been where he was on more than one occasion, outfitted with a cock of ivory that we kept hidden away. I knew what it looked like from below to watch her breasts bounce and her neck extend. It was different to see her like this, to see them *together* in such hedonistic abandon. Louis was groaning, in clear awe and fits of lust as Athénaïs undid him. This was for his pleasure, I knew that – but she was enjoying it too.

Louis's hand went to her sex where they were joined, and to my amazement, he began to rub her most sensitive spot with his thumb, the same spot on myself that I was now furiously caressing. He knew how to please a woman, our King. Ours. He was truly *ours* because *I* was the author of this triumph as well. It was because of me that she was in his bed, that his cock was in her so deep I could almost feel it in *me*.

Athénaïs began to make noises I knew all too well, signaling she was close to her little death. I bit back moans of the same ilk, but Louis did not have to be quiet.

"Yes, my love, perfect. Tighter for me – yes!"

"Louis!" Athénaïs cried as she came, and the King's eyes rolled back as he convulsed and followed her. I did too. My legs barely held me up as the climax shook me, clouding my vision. When I looked again, they were splayed on the bed together, panting in ecstasy.

"You are incredible, Athénaïs," Louis sighed. "I should have known."

"There is much more of me to know and learn, my King," Athénaïs replied. "I hope I shall see you again soon."

"Very," Louis replied.

The spell was done, but that meant I had a debt to be paid.

Chapter 21

Judgement

T HE FALL OF 1666 was complicated for the court. Louis was juggling a pregnant wife, a pregnant old mistress, and a ravenous lust for his new love, Athénaïs. It fell to me and Bontemps to arrange their assignations without discovery. Sometimes in a carriage. Often at the cottage. Once in Athénaïs's rooms. Often under my watchful eye.

I told Athénaïs of what I had done that first night and it had… aroused her. She begged me to tell her the details of what it was like to watch the King fuck her as I touched myself. I was shocked, but happy with the result. She let me do it again and again, and once, drunk on the excitement of it, I tasted his seed from inside her.

But I could not hide from my debts. Letters began to arrive for me at the Montespan house: angry missives from Catherine seeking an audience. I could not avoid it for much longer, but I was beginning to suspect I was not the only one to whom Le Sage had provided such services.

So I did not go to visit La Voisin or Le Sage myself. I waited and watched the women of the court, and when I heard that Olympe de Soissons had been seen in the Marais on one of the less fashionable streets, I knew I had my mark. Soon, her servants were my informants, and I knew when she was set to leave again. I followed.

I followed her to the house of La Filastre, where I waited in the dark street. I saw Marie Vigoreaux go in, and then Étienne Guibourg. Then Le Sage. Whether it was a Black Mass or some other sort of gathering, I did not know, but it was high time to remove at least one card from this cursed deck. Perhaps two, if I could manage it.

FIRST THOUGH, I WAS called to unexpected service. Bontemps came to find me late on the first day of October. This time, he found me in one of the galleries of the Louvre, avoiding Mass with the Queen and her ladies as I looked upwards to examine the ornate engraved ceilings of the antechamber where I lingered. There were H's on it, encircled by moons. For Henri IV, who had built the room, I suppose. But it scratched some other distant idea in my brain.

"Mademoiselle des Œillets," Bontemps rumbled next to me. I smiled at him and shook my head.

"She is at Mass with the Queen. My lady, I mean," I explained, expecting her to be summoned to the King's chambers. The valet shook his head in the negative.

"The King is not in his chambers, he is with Mademoiselle La Vallière. She is on the woman's battlefield again. It is not going well."

"And you need my help *again*?" I asked, incredulous. "But I serve—"

"You serve the King, Mademoiselle," Bontemps reminded me firmly, and I blanched. "Please come with me."

I followed him out of the Louvre and to La Vallière's private residence at the Palais Brion. I knew the moment I stepped in that something was wrong. The place smelled of shit and blood and felt like death. Yet I would be damned if I let a fourth child belonging to this poor woman and my beloved King die. Madame Colbert was there, looking older and paler than before, and she rushed to me.

"The doctors believe it is a breech," the matron declared, grabbing my hands. "I don't know if they are right. They've bled her—"

"For what reason!?" I cried, rushing with Colbert into the birthing room. There was a familiar shadow in the corner, but I could not think of him now. "Bandage her up! Do you have any poultices at hand?" I demanded of the doctor standing uselessly by the chair where a pale Louise La Vallière was splayed out, shining with sweat from her labors.

"I have mustard and seaweed..." the doctor stammered.

"For heaven's sake," I sighed. There was a door right next to me out into the garden, and I ran out into the courtyard that was overgrown with what some would call weeds. To me, they were old, reliable friends. Plantain and doc and selfheal. Perfect. I gathered up handfuls of the green and purple leaves, praying to Our Lady to protect this woman who was her child, as all women were, and ran back in.

"Put this on where they bled her," I ordered Madame Colbert, handing her a few stems and leaves. "Mash it first."

I did the same with my handful of plants. These herbs would staunch bleeding and stave off infection. They could also break curses.

Let whatever evil eye or spell is upon this woman be gone, I whispered in my heart. *My Lady, my Queen of the Stars, even if it was my ill will that has hurt this woman. Let it pass. Let it be gone.*

I don't know what it was that made me pray in such a way. Maybe it was guilt for what I had helped take from Louise La Vallière; maybe it was the pity I always had felt for her. Maybe because she was a woman used by the world too.

"I-I want to push," Louise rasped, life beginning to return to her.

"Almost, dear, almost. I need to make sure she can come out quickly, alright?" I said, calm as I could manage it. "Give me that," I whispered to the doctor, glancing at the blade he still held. He stared in shock then complied.

I cut carefully, right below where the child's leg was bent, and immediately pressed the herbs on the wound. Louise screamed in pain, but she knew what she had to do. For the second time in our lives, I held out my hands to receive the babe of the King as it left Louise's womb.

The girl was purple and bloody, and it terrified me. I hit her back, begging any god that could hear that she would breathe. A thin cry pierced the room and from the back corner, I heard Louis let out an exclamation of thanks.

"You attend to her, I will see to the mother," I told Madame Colbert as I cut the cord from the afterbirth.

It took all my skill and copious bandages and prayers to keep Louise alive, but I did it.

An hour later, I emerged in the hall to find Louis holding his daughter close to his chest. I saw the same pride and tenderness in his eyes as when he showed off the Dauphin, for I had never seen him with the other children by Louise. Perhaps, since they were gone, it had changed him. It had changed me.

"I am in your debt once again, Claude," Louis whispered. "For many things now."

"I only but serve," I replied in earnest before I could think. I was covered in the blood of one of his mistresses, yet still dazzled by him. I had saved one of his children, and yet, even now, his presence was so powerful.

Power. It had always been what I was missing, despite all my spells and schemes.

"Though perhaps there is... something."

"Name a reward and it is yours," Louis replied without hesitation.

"There is a man – two men, actually – who have threatened me and Madame de Montespan with vicious, impious lies," I began, and that was all he needed to hear.

"I will have Colbert send a Musketeer to you tomorrow to arrange for their arrest," he said with no hesitation. "If they are men of name, a lettre de cachet will be needed. If they are lesser characters, they will be dealt with according to their rank."

"Neither is a man of consequence," I answered, amazed at how easy this was. The babe in Louis's arms cooed and he smiled down at her. "What will she be called?"

"Marie-Anne," Louis replied. A strange choice to name his child with his mistress after his legitimate wife and lost mother. "Marie-Anne *de Bourbon*. When the time is right, she will be acknowledged as a child of France. As mine. No more hiding."

"That is a great gift, your Majesty," I breathed. I wondered if, perhaps, it was meant as some sort of parting gift for Louise. I placed a hand on the little one's head and smiled at her. She was so small. She knew none of the travails of the world yet. "May you be blessed, Marie-Anne de Bourbon," I told her. Who knew what my blessing could do in the face of all she had before her, but it was something, nonetheless. A little bit of magic.

I DID NOT OFTEN deal with the Musketeers, the royal guards of the King. They were ever present at court in their blue tunics bearing the King's fleur-de-lys, and they were the only men allowed to wield weapons in the presence of the King. I knew a few of them by name, and as I wandered into the manicured garden of Saint-Germain-en-Laye where I was set to meet one, I wondered what sort of man it would be that I dealt with. What exactly would I say to him?

Of all the Musketeers to arrive, I did not expect it to be their captain. Charles de Batz de Castelmore was rarely referred to by his title and was better known as D'Artagnan. He was a tall, handsome man with a sterling reputation for honor. It had been he who arrested Nicolas Fouquet years ago, and he who had let the poor man see his wife when she threw herself before their carriage. *This* was the man to whom I was to entrust my future?

"Mademoiselle des Œillets," D'Artagnan greeted me with a small, stiff bow. "I confess, I am intrigued by an order directly from Colbert and the King to—"

"To root out evil that threatens the court, if you'd like to think of it like that," I said. The man had streaks of grey in his long black hair beneath his wide hat. His eyes were sharp and thoughtful as they considered me.

"You will need to be more specific."

"There is a man who lives in the Marais, or near it. He puts himself out as an alchemist and sorcerer. He goes by the name Adam Le Sage, but his real name is Adam de Couret."

"Alchemists are charlatans," D'Artagnan chuckled, "but not necessarily dangerous."

"He works with a priest named Étienne Guibourg, a terrible drunk, and they have committed great—" How to say this? What morsel of the truth to give a good Christian man like this? "Impieties."

"Both of them?"

"Guibourg is a disgrace to the priesthood, and Le Sage has used him to further manipulate those around him," I went on. "Those he tries to ensnare."

D'Artagnan looked at me closely, as if trying to see into my soul. "It is the will of the King that the men whose names you give me be dealt with. Do you understand what that means for them?"

In truth, I did not. I wanted Le Sage and his accomplice gone. Once he was away from Catherine and the others, with his poisons and Black Masses, things would be better and I would be free. Didn't he deserve what he would receive if he was a killer?

Did I deserve that too?

I looked at the shining hilt of the Musketeer's sword at his hip, embossed with a silver cross. Surely, he had used it to take men's lives. He had cut down those he knew were evil. I had done the same thing to the man who had tortured me for years, even if it had been with Le Sage's help. Le Sage had not cared about the guilt or innocence of any victim. He was worse than me by far.

My eyes met D'Artagnan's.

"He is an evil man," I said, my conviction firmer than ever. "He must be dealt with. For the safety of all."

"Then it shall be done," the Musketeer replied.

I wondered how long it would take. It had only been a few days after their first coupling that Louis had made the Marquis de Montespan disappear on a complicated assignment to do with wrangling the army the King might soon send north. I was not Athénaïs, no, but I had done something for the King even she did now know of.

I T HAD BEEN MONTHS since I had gone to visit Madame Lapère. The former Court of Miracles had continued to change rapidly, like a field that had lain fallow for years being replanted. Or in this case, the Marais – the marsh – was suddenly an orderly garden.

Parisians, greedy to live in the now-fashionable Marais, had bought up the old houses to tear down to build new, grand residences. The old houses of daub and timber were being replaced, one by one, with miniature palaces of white Paris limestone. An entire complex of aristocratic manors had been built up around a new 'Place Royale,' a miniature of Versailles, in its way, with beds of flowers and avenues of trees where ladies could walk without darkening their complexions in the cruel sun like a peasant. It even boasted the same distinct mix of pink and white stone that distinguished the Château at Versailles.

Yet, even after all these years, there were still remnants of the old. Lapère's house still stood out with her flowers and plants in the front, radiating life in the darkening autumn night. The full moon rising in the east made the final few leaves of her verbena and nasturtium shine like silver, a few little buds still blooming in the cold air.

Years ago, I had been told that I was always welcome to join a circle under the moon, and as I entered Lapère's house, I felt shame that I had turned away from this community too readily.

There were some women in the little room that I knew and some who I did not. La Filastre was there, looking suspicious of me, but not hostile. I held my head high when Veronique met my eyes from her place by the fire where she was stationed like a guard. Lapère was beside her, and she sent me a smile before approaching me, grasping my hands, and pressing a dry kiss to my cheek.

"I knew you'd be here tonight," the elder told me, and I could not help but smile back.

"Of course you did," I replied. "Are Catherine and Marie coming?"

"Like a thunderous storm, yes," Lapère sighed. "Something has made them very angry."

"Has it?" I smirked, growing hopeful.

"Here is one now," Lapère said and as always, she was right. Marie Vigoreaux burst in the door with Bosse beside her, the two of them arguing fiercely and forcing their way in.

"There is nothing she can do!" Bosse was saying. "She is the reason for our loss!"

"I won't believe that!" Marie snapped back as the whole room looked at them in shock. "Madame Lapère, you must tell me – did you curse Adam Le Sage?!"

My heart jumped again as Lapère's eyes narrowed. "Why no, my dear. Why would I waste my time on such a man?"

"That man was half my income!" Marie shouted.

"Have you not a husband to help you? Have you not a trade and skills of many sorts?" Veronique interjected. She was pleased by the news – whatever she had heard of it – and I met her eyes for a moment to share some pleasure.

"What has happened?" Lapère asked calmly. "Oh, let us wait for Catherine to tell the tale."

Steps crashed outside the door and Catherine Monvoisin rushed in, the distress on her face even greater than that of the two Maries. When Catherine saw they were there, to my shock, she let out a scream and launched herself at her old friends, hands bent into claws. She seemed determined to scratch Vigoreaux's eyes out.

"Hold her back!" La Filastre cried as Veronique and I both jumped into action, holding back both women from retribution.

"What did you do?!" Catherine screamed at Marie, struggling in Veronique's grip. "Did you curse him? Did you tell some inspector or guard?"

"Me? It is you who has always wanted to keep him for yourself!" Marie yelled back.

"You seduced him years ago when he was supposed to be mine!" Bosse added from behind me and I shoved her back.

"All of you, stop!" Lapère's voice rang out like a church bell and all the women in her parlor fell silent. "No more accusations until someone explains what has happened."

"She's the one who would know," Marie sneered at Catherine. She had stopped struggling and Veronique let go of her with a huff. "*She* was there and did nothing."

"You think I didn't want to?" Catherine replied and looked around the room at the expectant faces of her sister witches. "It was midday in the public square – right outside the church of Saint Paul! Adam and I were speaking to a friend in need of help, and then two soldiers and a Musketeer came and asked his name. When he told them, they took him away before he could struggle!"

"You've all lost your minds because *Adam Le Sage* has been arrested?" Veronique scoffed. "You should be on your knees in thanks that he is gone."

"The same thing happened to Father Guibourg yesterday," a woman I did not know muttered. "Taken by soldiers. Who is to say where he will go? Jail or torture."

"He will go to the galleys," La Filastre said distantly. "I heard it from a friend and I did not believe it. There was a quick proceeding at the Palace of Justice and they were both sentenced today. Oh, we are lost..."

"The galleys?" I echoed. I had not considered that possibility, and that made me a fool. Prison for life was a rare thing, except for the nobility. Hanging was for the violent and heretical. I had assured that Le Sage and Guibourg were not so doomed; instead, they would spend years working in fetid conditions, barely more than slaves, rowing the great ships of the Kingdom of France.

"He is already sentenced?" Catherine said with something like a sob. "That idiot."

"It's better if he's gone soon, so he will not speak of what he has done with all of you," Veronique said, reasonable as always. "This is a blessing."

"Is it?" Catherine hissed, turning on Veronique with cold eyes. "Were you behind this? Or you?" she asked Lapère.

"I warned you all a year ago that Le Sage was dangerous, and none of you listened," Lapère replied, her voice cool as steel and her gaze just as unquestionable. "You should never have let a man as useless as him tear you all apart. Yet, you continued to work with that man, to sell promises no one could fulfill."

"Oh, I did fulfill them," Catherine snapped back, and finally, her eyes alit on me. "I have yet to be compensated for how I did so," she added, and I could see her mind working. She saw me as a conspirator with her and Le Sage, but she realized now that he had made himself my enemy.

"I do not think that is true, Madame Monvoisin," I said slowly, and all the eyes of the room turned to me. "Did not your Le Sage claim that God works in mysterious ways? Was it not here that I learned how magic can take time and render rewards in unexpected forms? God and Our Lady have blessed you – and indeed all of us – by removing a dangerous man who wanted nothing but to use and swindle all around him. That is your payment."

I did not care what the other women made of my words or if they guessed at my or my mistress's dealings with La Voisin. What mattered was that Catherine – who had so often berated me for weakness and hesitancy – finally saw that I had power too.

"What did you do?" It was Veronique who asked the question, something like amazement in her voice as she looked at me. Had no one suspected? Had I been away so long that they had forgotten who I was and what I had achieved? Had she already forgotten that I had saved her from the witch hunters in Rouen, or had she never believed it? "How could you?"

"You have used your power and knowledge to raise others and cling to them in hopes they will pay you back," I said to Catherine. "I have used my power to raise myself. To the court and to have the very ear of the King. With that, I have protected myself."

"You are a *servant*," Marie whispered, and Bosse laughed. Catherine was silent. She knew what Athénaïs's aims were. She realized now she had made me the most powerful and dangerous woman she knew.

"She is a spider," Catherine said, like a curse.

"I am a witch, as much as you, and my magic is not in fortunes or frauds," I countered, baring my teeth. "I have done what was needed to survive and to protect myself. And women like me. Like us."

"You have sent a man to his doom," Marie said with a bitter tone, aghast and offended.

"He was not the first," I shrugged, meeting Veronique's eyes instead. Let her judge me now. "I hope he will be the last." The threat was there in my words for all of them, and a chill went through the room.

"It is done. The interloper is gone at last," Lapère declared with a sigh. "Now that he is gone, perhaps at last, we may all thrive."

"What do you mean?" Catherine scoffed. "Without him, we have no—"

Marie sent Catherine a silencing look. There were still things that could not be spoken of aloud, such as the poison powders only Le Sage had been able to procure for so long.

"You never needed that man," Lapère said. "No more than any witch has ever needed a man. The fools who seek to hunt us or destroy us think we seek power from outside ourselves. You made the mistake of proving them right, but they aren't. You have always known where to find your magic."

"His craft was not ours," Veronique added. "Working with him was never in service to Our Lady."

"It could have been," Catherine said softly. "She hides in the dark places."

No one else in the room but me could understand what she meant. She had brought Our Lady into her rituals with Le Sage, inserting old secrets and hidden names into the Black Masses meant to mock Christ and the Holy Spirit. Wasn't that what her daughters had done for centuries, finding an old goddess in the Holy Virgin? But men like Le Sage would not understand that. She was not for them.

"It was a mistake to think that you could make a tiger change his stripes and that he would not notice the paint," I muttered. Again, Catherine laughed.

"You are one to speak of futile causes, great lady of the court," Catherine spat. "One day – oh, I foresee it – one day, your web will strangle you."

The threat was there, once again. Of exposure and ruin. I would not let that endure either.

"If it does, I won't be alone," I stated, holding Catherine's gaze. She stared at me, anger boiling under the surface. Years ago, I would have shrunk to see such fury directed at me. It would have broken my heart for a friend to make such threats, but maybe Catherine Monvoisin had never been my friend.

"I will never forget this," Catherine seethed, and I felt a calm come over me.

"I should hope not," I softly replied.

Catherine turned on her heel and left with such fire in her face, I expected scorch marks behind her. It was done. My debt was gone and my life was safe. I had done it, and it had only cost me one friend. And two mens' imprisonments on my conscience, but that was not such a burden. To punish men like that was honestly an honor.

The women in the room were quiet now. Bosse and Vigoreaux and La Filastre all looked at me with fear and respect, which I had earned. Veronique, though, looked at me with wonder.

We moved to the garden and joined hands in a circle. It was not so different from the ritual of Mass, these gatherings. It was not a mockery, like the Black Mass; but as all the good Catholics came together in their great cathedrals beneath the towering pillars and stained glass that filled me with awe, now we witches came together in the chapel of the earth, a garden. No stained glass or gilded splendor for us except the sky.

Lapère reached out to me and I took her hand. Her papery skin was thin over her gnarled bones, but I could still feel the power in her grip. The power of these hands that had brought so many lives into the world and ended the potential of so many others. That was strength.

"We meet in the circle below the moon," Lapère began as I clasped hands with La Filastre on the other side of me, and we all looked up to the silver disk in the sky above. "When she is brightest, she reminds us of her power and light. She is Our Lady of the stars and the sky, but do not forget her other faces."

"She is the dark of the earth," I heard Marie say.

"She is the life in the bud," La Filastre added, and I began to feel something magic and numinous flow through our hands.

"And she is the poison in the same flower," I said, the words welling up from deep within me.

"She is the crossroads. She is the key and dagger," said Marie.

"She is the fire and the faces of the night," Veronique went on.

"She is all magic and all the unknown. We call her down to bless us," Lapère said, but her voice was somehow not her own. It was resonant and triumphant. It was Her.

"Diana," someone whispered.

"Venus and Pallas in one," said another.

"Saint Genevieve and Mary. Anne and Cécile."

"Demeter and Persephone…" one more voice whispered, and I felt a name dance upon my tongue: a name I had read of in myth years ago and remembered now, as the moon shone down.

"Hecate. Be with your daughters."

We lingered there, between worlds, for a wide, quiet expanse of time before we let go and the magic faded back up into the night. I stayed for a while with my eyes closed, savoring the power I felt. The triumph. Then, I felt Veronique's eyes on me in the garden.

The old disappointment was gone when I looked at her, replaced by something more fond than sad. "Are you here to admonish me for what I have done to Adam Le Sage?"

"I had a dream about you, in Rouen, years ago," Veronique replied.

I cocked my head. "When you were jailed?"

"I dreamed you were whispering into the ears of a golden man in a chariot, like Apollo. He drew an arrow and shot it towards me. It did not hit me. It loosed the bond that held me," Veronique went on, and I stifled a gasp. "I did not think of it then, but now… I wonder. Was it really you who set me free with your whispers?"

"Louis offered me a gift for attending the birth of his child," I explained. "I used my chance to save you. I attended another birth a few weeks ago, and with that debt, I saved myself."

"You truly have the ear of the king," Veronique sighed in sadness and awe. "I would never have believed it."

"Why? Because I am not worthy of it?"

"Because it could do so much good. Claude, don't you understand?" Veronique pressed with a bright smile. Even after all these years, that smile was so beautiful.

"You think I can influence Louis on matters of… what? Politics? Or would you rather I meddle with the affairs of the city?" I laughed. "Do you know how many people every day come to him with their needs and ideas for what is good for us all? I am but one voice, and a small one."

"One voice can still make a difference! When the people starve or suffer, you will know and you can—"

"You think the King does not know when his people suffer?"

"Not all of them. There are so many who could benefit from a better France… the Jews and the Huguenots and those held in bondage," Veronique went on. "*You* could help them."

I saw the illusion of myself that was reflected in her eyes. She wanted me, as always, to be like her. To feel as deeply for the lost and the righteous. But I was not good like her. It had been for that reason that she had left me. Yet still, she wanted me to change not just myself, but the world.

"I have done things you would not ever condone in these years, Veronique," I whispered. "I have grown my power and influence, and it has been to help those I love, not strangers. I have done it for myself."

"Don't you think of the future?" she asked, despair growing again. "You must want more than to be a servant to a King's mistress?"

That gave me pause. What did I want? What had this been for? What had been the dream? I had moved heaven and earth to find my peace and join the court, as ephemeral as it was. I had seen the laughing, joyous women of the court through the iron bars of the palace gates and decided I would share the same carefree joy as they. Finally, now that the threat of Le Sage was gone and Athénaïs was ascending... I would have it. Wouldn't I?

"I just want to be happy," I replied softly. "That's all."

"Then I hope you are," Veronique replied, sadness in her face now. It cut me to my core.

"I hope you find it too," I replied. I wondered if she had a new lover. I wondered if she would remember me if I never saw her again.

"Be careful, Claude. You walk the most dangerous path of us all. It comes with a price."

I felt a gaze upon me as she said the words and I looked up to see Lapère was watching us from across the garden. She knew all we had said, I was sure of it. She had a look on her face that bore a warning too. She was, after all, the one who had counseled me years ago that my path to glory would come with a price in blood.

"I know," I whispered back. "I have paid it."

CHAPTER 22

THE SUN

I THOUGHT THE DAYS after such a triumph would have been full of reveling. I felt more powerful than ever, but it was a lonely sort of power. I could not tell anyone what I had done. Not really. Athénaïs knew one part of it, my sisters another, and a final secret belonged to Louis and his Musketeer. Only I and Our Lady knew the power I wielded; power no one would believe belonged to pathetic little Claude who had simpered and served for so long.

There was one thing that would be clear to everyone, however. I was rich now. Louis was generous in his appreciation of his court, always quick to bestow gifts and baubles on his favorites. Though Athénaïs was not his official mistress yet, she had been honored with secret gifts of money and more, and so had I. I could walk the Marais in fine clothes: blue silks embroidered with pearls and lined with white lace, with pink ribbons in my hair.

I was entitled to a box at the theater at the Palais-Royal where Molière played. I had never gone before, but in November, I went at Athénaïs's side.

She knew the reason I had avoided the theater, given my previous profession. I told her I did not wish to dwell on my old life. I'd never told her that there were people at the theaters I did not wish to see. But tonight, I wanted to be seen.

Thérèse du Parc was Racine's mistress again, so she was not on the stage. But Alix Faviot was. She was older now, relegated to grotesque roles of crones and lecherous matrons, but she still had the presence on the stage that drew every eye. When she was up there, my mother was the woman I had always chased as a child. That elusive bright light full of joy that had somehow never shined on me.

Even then, when she looked out to the audience, to the box where the Duc d'Orléans sat with his wife, Princess Henrietta, and her friends, her smile faltered when she saw a face she knew among that shining company. Her smile was never for me.

Athénaïs laughed beside me, not noticing how the old actress's face fell when she saw me. My lady's focus was on Henrietta, at some joke she had made at the expense of the spectacle on stage. I wished she would look at me to reassure me that her heart was still mine. At least a part of it. I grasped her hand, laughing as well, and she granted my wish. The loveliest woman in court looked at me and grinned, her gold hair sparkling in the lights of the theater. *She* was mine.

When the play ended, it fell to Philippe and his wife to congratulate Molière for another amusing success, and the actors came to mingle among the audience. I drifted away from Athénaïs when I saw my mother rush towards me. I did not want her to see this.

My mother and I stood at the edge of the seats and she gaped at me: at my jewels and gown and clean face and pert shoes. At my glory.

"I kept hearing you'd done well," she muttered. "So many people told me that you were at court in the service of a Marquise. I never believed them. I told them you would not have left me to rot, if that were the case."

"I left you to lead my own life," I replied. Even now, I could feel her grasping at me, determining which way she might use me. "You never sought me out."

"You left me to die," she snapped. "Like you let him—"

"You survived," I snarled back. "I wanted you to know though. To see what I have achieved." I raised my chin high, once again the child who had wanted a speck of her pride. She gave me nothing. No expression of awe or love. I should have known better. The parent who would smile at me for what I had done was long dead, and his spirit rarely answered me when I dared to call.

"Don't you think my father would be proud of all I have done?" I asked, even so.

"Proud that you are a servant to greatness with no greatness of your own?" my mother scoffed. "Proud of a spinster who has such riches and does nothing for her mother? Claude, I thought you came because you heard about my debts. They are so large."

"So that is all you have to say to me? To ask for money?" I wanted to laugh. I didn't even know what kind of satisfaction I wanted from seeing her, but it was not this.

"What else would you like to hear?" the great actress asked, but did not even bother to put on a façade of caring.

"Nothing. I want nothing," I replied.

I turned away and went back to Athénaïs. She was radiant and she joked and flirted with the men and women around her, smiling at Henrietta, winking at Philippe, clasping my hand.

We were invited back to the private quarters of Monsieur and Madame afterward. Perhaps it was because she knew Louis was with La Vallière that night (seeing her out of some sad sense of obligation), but Athénaïs was as flirtatious and voracious as I had ever seen her in that company. She was utterly enthralling, a glowing flower at the center of the gathering drawing us all in.

It did not surprise me to find myself with her in Henrietta's chambers, tangled together with the spoiled, drunk princess. We made her come easily together, and then I set upon Athénaïs like a woman starving.

"What has gotten into you?" Athénaïs laughed as she kissed me back. Beside us, Henrietta made a soft noise as she fell unconscious.

"I missed you," I said softly. "You have been so taken up lately with everything."

"Not as much as I'd like," Athénaïs sighed. A shadow passed over her face, and I furrowed my brow.

"But Louis has called on you," I protested in the softest whisper. "He has been distracted with Louise's recovery, but his heart moves towards you."

Again, Athénaïs looked crestfallen. "But not me alone. I tolerate that because... Oh, Claude, I must confess something to you."

"You love him too," I finished for her, and she met my eyes with tears in hers.

"You know?"

"Of course. Athénaïs, I never thought to keep your heart entirely to myself. There is too much love in you," I laughed. "Perhaps there is too much love in Louis too, and that is why he still calls on Louise."

"I think you may be right," Athénaïs said with a soft laugh. Henrietta snorted a snore and I giggled. "Love is not so limited."

"For her too?" I giggled, but Athénaïs shook her head.

"No. With her, it was lust and duty, like with my husband. With Louis, it feels different." She bit her lip and looked at me expectantly. "It feels like when I'm with you. Do you truly not mind if I... love him?"

"Not as long as you do not mind that I do as well," I exhaled, one burden lifting from my soul. "I cannot begrudge a flower loving the sun. We all love him, in our way."

"You, my Claude..." Athénaïs sighed. "You are magic."

"I told you, love and magic are the same," I confessed, kissing her and tangling our bodies together. "It gives me joy each day to serve you. To love you. I know I cannot have you always, but sometimes... I need you. I need to feel you..." She filled me with her fingers and grinned.

"Feel me?" she teased.

"Yes," I sighed. "I would give you anything, you know that?"

"I know, my precious Claude," Athénaïs said, and I felt my heart would burst. "My love, together we will achieve every-thing."

"We will." I didn't have any more words. I let her make love to me, taking my pleasure in the halls of a palace. Held and seen.

T HE REVELS OF CHRISTMAS that year were exceptional. They were the first to be held entirely at Versailles, and Louis engaged all the artisans in Paris to fill the gardens with wonders. We rowed on the new grand canal at the end of the garden as lanterns floated on the water. We danced on the new terrace between the grand new chambers of the King and Queen. Every courtier had new clothes, procured at the greatest expense from the best shops in Paris. There had been rumors that the city was running short on lace and silk, but Louis had sworn to endow a new wing in the Louvre entirely for artisans and makers of the finest French textiles so that such a thing would never happen. So his France would be the beautiful wonder of the world.

The expense was worth it. On the longest night of the year, we all wore wintery silver, white, and gold as we danced to a new work conducted by Monsieur Lully. The château sparkled with candles, and Louis presented to us the new wonder of Versailles: an orangery filled with the finest trees in pots of pure silver. We ate of the delicious fruit fresh from the branches, all laughing.

All but Louise La Vallière. The King's official mistress had recovered from childbirth quickly, as usual, but remained a shadow. I wondered when she would be pregnant again as I looked at her in her gown of white. Louis tended to lose interest in her when she was with child; maybe I could work some spell to encourage such a thing. Though the situation did not seem to require such aid.

Louise was trying to get the King's attention tonight. I watched her from my place behind one of the new orange trees with interest. So much so that I did not see until it was too late that someone was observing me.

"She is back to her best, do you not think?" Jean-Baptiste Colbert, the court's chief financier and Louis's closest advisor asked me in my ear, and I jumped. "I'm sorry to surprise you, Mademoiselle des Œillets."

"It won't happen again," I grumbled, looking over him. He usually dressed in somber blacks and blues, not subject to the battles of fashion waged by men of the court, but tonight, he was in a coat of blue embroidered with silver. It suited his square, thoughtful face.

"My question still stands: do you think Louise La Vallière has recovered all her charms?" he asked me again. It was more than a question, I could tell. It was a test.

"No. She has not," I answered honestly. "She wants everyone to think she has, especially Louis. But she's trying too hard, and those that she wishes to enchant can see that."

"You're good," Colbert smiled. "Tell me, Mademoiselle, have you heard of the latest intrigues regarding the Grande Mademoiselle taking a new lover?"

Another test. But why? "She started a rumor about her and the Comte de Soissons so Louis would not interfere with her actual assignations with the Duc de Lauzun. We all know he's penniless and a cad, but the Grande Mademoiselle is still besotted." At this, Colbert's eyebrows went high.

"Oh, you're very good." Colbert looked as if he had received an unexpected gift. "My wife was right."

"About what, Monsieur?"

"Marie has been telling me to turn to you for years. She says you have insights into the court and more. I dismissed her because she made it sound like poppycock and alchemy that had something to do with midwifery and women's troubles," Colbert explained nonchalantly. I wondered if he'd say that if he knew about the curse that was placed on Nicolas Fouquet that put him in prison and Colbert at the right hand of the King. "But you do have a gift, Claude."

"I'm not sure what you mean." I straightened my spine and fiddled with a pearl on my dress. I was in gold, a near match to Athénaïs's resplendent gown so that we were twin stars in this firmament. I was not accustomed to being so gaudily outfitted.

"You know everything happening in this court," Colbert said. A declaration, not a question. "You know all the secrets. Perhaps the dearest secrets of the court, given that your mistress has the attention of the King."

I narrowed my eyes. "You tried to have a spy installed in Louise La Vallière's household to report back to you on her relationship with the King, years ago," I recalled aloud. "That was a stupid and transparent trick."

"It became easier to influence Mademoiselle La Vallière when her children came into my wife's care and the Dowager Queen, God rest her soul, loosened her grip," Colbert confessed. "But Louise has never been easy to deal with. She has no spine for sharing ideas with the King."

I had to laugh. It all made so much sense. Louis was a King like no other before, a King with no ministers to do his ruling for him – a King who was drawing more and more power to himself, involving himself in each office of governance. A King who could not be steered or controlled by regular means and typical political scheming like Colbert's. So he had tried to use La Vallière to whisper in the King's ear or keep apprised of his private thoughts, but now her star was about to fade.

"You wish me to be your spy *and* to influence what my mistress says to the King?" I asked in awe. In all my years weaving my webs, learning the secrets of servants and nobles alike, I had never thought it would mean anything but my own gain... But perhaps, Veronique had been right. Perhaps I could do more.

"I wish for us to continue to help each other," Colbert replied warmly.

"Continue?"

"I made no problems for you when you asked Louis to eliminate a known sorcerer and provider of... exotic remedies," Colbert said, and I felt the blood drain from my face. "Oh, do not worry, Mademoiselle. I was assured by my wife that many ladies seek out conjurers for charms and end up trapped in their schemes. I am sure that is all that happened to you, and no scandal need arise from it."

"So long as I assist you."

"War is coming next year. A war that Louis will undertake to expand his land and win himself glory, no matter the cost," Colbert said with much more seriousness.

"And you are martialing your own army," I sighed.

"It will be of great benefit to you, Claude," Colbert added, warm again. "And to your mistress. I have the ear of the King too, in my way. I can steer his attention to where it benefits us all."

"You cannot move the sun, only control where you reflect its light," I murmured, and Colbert nodded.

I stepped beside him and nodded. Together, we looked at the crowd milling through the exotic trees in their pots of silver. I pointed to one trio of courtiers: Olympe de Soissons, her husband, and a third man I knew they were attempting to build an alliance with. "That is Louvois, is it not? Minister of war. Be careful who you let get their claws into him before the war begins."

Colbert looked at me with a thoughtful and appreciative smile. "What is your retainer with Madame de Montespan? Is it paid out of the funds of the Queen's household or the Marquis's?"

"I receive 200 livres a year," I said, swallowing in embarrassment. "The Marquis is cheap and—"

"You'll receive 1,600 livres now," Colbert said, and my jaw dropped. The man smirked and gave me a bow. "Enjoy the festivities, Mademoiselle."

In a heartbeat, I was alone again. In another, I was racing to find Athénaïs. The court was going inside. There had been dinner at midnight already and we were done with the ritual of Louis tasting dozens of dishes before the court could eat. Now the meats and fish and vegetables were gone and replaced by tables laden with sweets and confections and huge bowls of elixir for the gods, but I had no time for it now. I had to find my own goddess.

My heart leapt into my throat when I saw her at last – deep in conversation with Louis himself. They were speaking to one another as if they were the only two people in the world. And in my world, right now, they were all. Had I just been convinced to manipulate or spy on them? I couldn't betray them like that, could I?

I had no time to decide: Athénaïs had seen me and waved for me to come to her. To her and the King.

"My sweet Claude!" Athénaïs exclaimed, as she clasped my hand and kissed my cheeks. "We have missed you."

"We?" I had to laugh as I looked at the King. He was radiant tonight, outfitted in gold that shone like the sun in the midst of winter.

"Of course, Mademoiselle des Œillets," Louis said and took my hand to kiss it. It made my head spin like a gallon of punch. "We are both bereft without you. How am I to present my gift to Madame de Montespan without you beside her?"

"Gift?" I echoed again. Athénaïs looked at me in a desperate request for me to be more articulate.

"Of course," Louis said and leaned down to whisper in my ear in a way that made my heart double in speed. "Though we must be careful to not let anyone else know. It is not ready for them yet. Come, let us make our escape while all are distracted by the pre-dawn feast."

I had no choice but to obey. This was the King, leading me and Athénaïs, laughing, from the hall, down the great north stairs, and out into the freezing night and the gardens. Before I could swear at the winter cold, Athénaïs pulled me to her and hissed into my ear.

"Claude, please – what I will ask of you will win him forever." I shivered at the words, even though I did not understand them.

"Here!" Louis cried with the excitement of a child as we reached a pavilion that I had thought was still under construction. He withdrew a great key from his belt, unlocked the door, and pulled Athénaïs in with her dragging me after her.

I could not understand what I saw. Torches and braziers lit the room, which was warm and welcoming, but it was not a room at all. It was a bath and a cave – a grotto. There was water cascading through fountains and pools, as well as benches and plush couches to lounge. At the center, the largest, most beautiful statues I had ever seen dominated the space. I recognized the chariot of Apollo, but his horses were not yoked. There at the center was the God himself, lyre at his feet, attended by nymphs.

"It is the grotto of Tethys, the daughter of Oceanus," Louis explained with delighted pride. "She and her nymphs soothe the God of the Sun as he rests in the ocean west after his long labors in the sky."

"It is incredible," Athénaïs gasped.

"I have never seen anything so fantastic," I added. Truly, it made me feel drunk on beauty and opulence itself to look at such a creation. "And this is a gift for—"

"For our Athénaïs," Louis confirmed. Athénaïs covered her mouth in delight. The King pulled her back to his chest, chuckling, then bent to kiss her neck, right there in front of me. "A grotto of a goddess, for a goddess."

"You must not make such a statement public," Athénaïs protested weakly as the King's mouth continued its work, and my tongue went dry to watch them entwine together. His hands swept over the exposed skin of her décolletage, and she sighed in lust.

"I shall not, but you will know. As will our Claude, who sees all." Louis's eyes flicked up to me, his dark hair falling about his flushed face. He smiled. "Who does not need to only watch."

I surely had died. This had to be the last fantasy of a fevered mind. No... I was still breathing, though it was ragged and panicked.

"Come here, dearest," Athénaïs whispered, extending a hand. "I have a gift for our King too, but I need you to help me give it."

My body moved without my will, floating towards her. Louis took my other hand and guided me – guided me to kiss the woman I loved and sighed in awe as I did. I was dizzy when I drew back, so dizzy that I did not realize that the King was close to me until his lips met mine.

Athénaïs held me tight so that I did not fall. Had I ever kissed a man before? Some actor, a hundred years ago, had tried to seduce me, and I had let him fumble until he touched me in the wrong way. These lips, though, they were as soft and expert as my lady's. The texture of his moustache was so different. And he was the King. He was as warm as the dawn.

I was speechless when he pulled back and smiled. "Yes, this will do. Now, help me undress your mistress, Mademoiselle," the King commanded.

I wasn't sure if my hands would work, but I had to obey. I kissed Athénaïs again to find solid ground as Louis and I groped at the complicated fastenings of her dress. She was ecstatic as we took turns kissing her lips, neck, and shoulders. Louis took one of her breasts in hand when it was freed and I took the other into my mouth. Then his hand was against my cheek in my hair. His hands – they were soft. Soon enough, Athénaïs was nude, and she spun me to be between the two of them.

"Now you," Athénaïs laughed. I feigned no resistance as the two who ruled me started to kiss me as thoroughly as we had done for Athénaïs. I had been with two before, but it had never been this passionate, this intoxicating. Louis's hands cupped my breasts as they were freed from my bodice and Athénaïs's found my hips. His lips kissed my mouth, hers my collar bones, and I was sure I was going to die. The man behind me pressed his groin against my bare ass and I felt that he had hardened.

I gasped and spun away, panic taking me. The darkness – the dark that my stepfather had cursed me with and put inside me with his horrible cock – was still there screaming inside me. It was going to drown me and burn me alive with shame. But Louis and Athénaïs did not let go of my hands. They were laughing and kissing, insensible to my panic.

How could Athénaïs ask this of me? Yet, how could she know the horrors within my memory when I never spoke of them? She had broken through my pain for years, teaching me to love pleasure again. I'd been penetrated by her and Henrietta in so many ways - was a man so different? Yes. It was. But this man was unlike any other.

"What is wrong, my dear?" Athénaïs asked as she looked up from undressing Louis. There was concern in her face. Was I as flushed and panicked as I looked? To my shock, she pulled me to her arms. To their arms.

"I haven't… I've never been with a man…" I blurted out, then I shook my head. "I mean willingly. There was—"

"Who was he? I will have him beheaded," Louis said and my heart jumped as I met his eyes. He was bare-chested, all his finery gone, but in that moment, he was the most powerful man in the world. In a few words, he had freed me. He had commuted my sins with an order of execution for one long gone.

"He is dead already," I said and I felt the fist around my heart loosen at long last.

"Claude, I didn't know." Athénaïs met my eyes as she spoke, and there was an entreaty there. I had told her I'd do anything for her. This – letting Louis have both of us, giving him a tangle of pleasure and sin no one else would even contemplate or could give him – was the thing that would win him to Athénaïs forever. No. Win him to us.

"I told a friend once," I began weakly with a thin laugh, "that the only man I would ever let touch me in all the world was the King himself. I never thought such a boast would be tested."

Athénaïs smiled as Louis laughed. "Claude has a way of speaking prophecy," my lover said. "You will learn."

"I hope I shall," Louis said and extended a hand to me. I clasped it in mine.

The King's hands were not Giles Faviot's. They were soft and kind, and I chose to feel them on my skin. I chose to walk the path I had spoken and enchanted into existence.

They laid me down on the floor of the grotto, in this temple to a goddess. Athénaïs embraced me tightly from behind while Louis kissed and caressed my body. The King I had seen from afar, who had looked up to a balcony where a poor girl watched him on his wedding day licked and nuzzled the bare skin of that same dreaming fool. Athénaïs touched me too; she delved into me with gentle fingers, testing that I was wet and assuring me pleasure. I fumbled for her cunt behind me, filling her too.

"She's wondrous, my love: feel her," Athénaïs sighed, and Louis did.

I did not scream or freeze or die. I chose. I lived.

The monarch whose name I had known all my life made me whimper that name as fingers I could not count filled and stretched me, and then... Then, he was between my legs, Athénaïs was kissing him and me, and writhing on my fingers. It was time.

"My King," I sighed as Louis filled me deep and warm with his manhood, and stretched me with his heat.

There were no more words. There were no more borders between our bodies. We were three hearts in one flesh and I was consumed by love. I was consumed by pride and joy and the ecstasy of being possessed by them. In that secret grotto, in their arms, I forgot who I had been before them. I became a creature of pure pleasure as my King and my love claimed me.

Or had I claimed them?

The thought made my pleasure spike, made my cunt tighten, as the ruler of all of France fucked into me. Me. Claude the curious. The naïve fool who had become a servant and a spider. Who had killed rather than live as a prisoner and a victim.

"Claude," the world spoke my name. The world that no longer awaited me. The world I had taken and woven and made mine.

I came, the earth beneath me, power rushing through me as a King made love to me. A King whose heart I had enchanted, in whose court I was now the most powerful spy. Athénaïs and Louis followed me as if I compelled them. I had. For I was magic.

I was not a servant. I was a daughter of the crossroads. Mistress of my fate at last, at the pinnacle of all my dreams. And yet, at the beginning of a new one.

Claude de Vin. Lover and confidante of the mistress of Louis the God-given. Paramour of the Sun King. Mademoiselle des Œillets. The lady of the carnations and the spider.

The Witch of Versailles.

Claude de Vin des Œillets' story will continue in 2026 in...

MISTRESS OF POISONS

Acknowledgements

Thank you to everyone who has had a hand in helping *The Witch of Versailles* come to life. First and foremost: thank you to Heidi, my wife and favorite reader. Thank you to Tamsin for always inspiring me. Thank you to Marlon and Dewey for being the best fuzzy writing assistants. Thank you to Jordan for your keen eyes and Ana for your open ear and encouragement. And thank you to all my readers and supporters who have stayed with me for this new adventure.

Merci beaucoup to the Château de Versailles for both their in-person and online resources, as well as staff and administrators of: the Louvre, the Château de Vincennes, Sainte-Chapelle, the Basilica of Saint-Denis, the Église de Saint-Eustache, the Église Saint-Paul, and especially the Musée Carnavalet.

The following list of resources is not exhaustive, but this book owes a great deal to the knowledge and scholarship of many.

- Anne Somerset. *The Affair of the Poisons: Murder, Infanticide, and Satanism in the Court of Louis XIV.* (St. Martin's Press, 2004)

- Antonia Fraser. *Love and Louis XIV: The Women in the Life of the Sun King.* (Knopf/Doubleday, 2006)

- Aurora von Goeth's incredible blog: Party Like 1660 at

partylike1660.com

- Scott Cunningham. *Cunningham's Encyclopedia of Magical Herbs.* (Llewelyn, 1985)

- Judika Illes. *The Encyclopedia of 5,000 Spells.* (HarperOne, 2009)

- Theresa Reed. *Tarot: No Questions Asked.* (Weiser Books, 2020)

- Courtney Weber. *Hekate: Goddess of Witches.* (Weiser Books, 2021)

About the Author

Jessica Mason lives near Portland, Oregon with her wife, daughter, and corgi. She has studied opera, practiced law, and worked as a fandom journalist and podcaster, among many varied careers. But first and foremost she has always been a storyteller. When she manages to stop writing, she enjoys gardening, travel, music, and witchcraft. She is passionate about stories of all kinds and loves to discuss and create them.

To learn more, please visit:

www.JessicaMasonAuthor.Com

Find her on social media: @ByJessicaMason

ALSO BY JESSICA MASON

The Phantom Saga:
Angel's Mask
Angel's Kiss
Angel's Fall
Erik's Tale
Coming 2025: Angel's Flight

The Binge Watcher's Guide to Supernatural: An Unofficial
Companion

The Binge Watcher's Guide to the Marvel Cinematic Universe:
An Unofficial Companion

Made in the USA
Monee, IL
03 July 2025